What Readers Are Saying About

THE LAST GUARDIAN

"Readers who love Frank Peretti will love this book. The message is there. The drama is there. The suspense is there. This is a book I most likely would never have picked up from the bookstore shelf. Yet once I did, the hooks kept me moving forward. I had to see what was going to happen!"

—Tricia
Montana

"[Through this book] I was given a renewed sense of God's love, grace, and forgiveness. Perhaps the type of Christian [most likely to] be drawn to and encouraged by this story would be one just like the author himself was at one time—a believer who had rejected Christianity for a time and needed some answers to his questions about God's plan for redeeming fallen man."

—Jeri
Colorado

"The Last Guardian defies categorization. It is an epic adventure on the grandest of scales, and yet it is a personal journey of faith. Through exquisitely descriptive narrative and snappy dialogue, Shane Johnson has crafted a tale that ignites the imagination, inspires every emotion, and points toward the power and sovereignty of God."

—Martin
Texas

"The Last Guardian is one of the best books I've ever read—definitely in the top five! Shane Johnson is an incredibly gifted writer. My family didn't get any attention from me all week because I couldn't put the book down. His descriptions were breathtaking and so completely believable that I felt like I was there."

—Cheryl
Washington

THE LAST
GUARDIAN

Called by God.
Targeted by Darkness.
Destined to Lead.

THE LAST GUARDIAN

SHANE JOHNSON

WaterBrook
PRESS

THE LAST GUARDIAN
PUBLISHED BY WATERBROOK PRESS
2375 Telstar Drive, Suite 160
Colorado Springs, Colorado 80920
A division of Random House, Inc.

The characters and events in this book are fictional, and any resemblance
to actual persons or events is coincidental.

All Scripture quotations, unless otherwise indicated, are taken from the *New American Standard
Bible*® (NASB). © Copyright The Lockman Foundation 1960, 1962, 1963, 1968, 1971, 1972,
1973, 1975, 1977. Used by permission. (www.Lockman.org) Scripture quotations marked
(NKJV) are taken from the *New King James Version.* Copyright © 1982 by Thomas Nelson, Inc.
Used by permission. All rights reserved. Scripture quotations marked (KJV) are taken from the
King James Version.

ISBN 1-57856-367-4

Library of Congress Cataloging-in-Publication Data
Johnson, Shane.
        The last guardian : a novel / by Shane Johnson.—1st ed.
        p. cm.
        ISBN 1-57856-367-4
           1. End of the world—Fiction. I. Title.
PS3560.O38638 L37 2001
813'.54—dc21   00-043867

Printed in the United States of America
2000—First Edition

10 9 8 7 6 5 4 3 2 1

FOR DAN

Publisher's Note

Dear Reader,

Thank you for considering this exciting new work by Shane Johnson. We are pleased to publish *The Last Guardian* and believe you will find it to be a unique contribution to the world of Christian fiction.

Shane has carefully woven scriptural truth into this creative exploration of God's plan to redeem humanity. We weighed the more graphic passages of *The Last Guardian* very carefully, not wanting to permit any gratuitous scenes. Although certain events in this novel are shocking, we hope you will see that Shane's purposeful inclusion of them is undeniable. By exposing mankind's utter depravity, God's love, mercy, and grace are revealed to be that much more clearly astounding, as they truly are.

We, along with Shane, wish to emphasize that the dominant themes of this story are life and salvation. I encourage you to step behind the scenes with Shane by reading both the Author's Note and the Afterword. These are in themselves captivating evidence of God's redemptive hand at work in our daily lives.

Sincerely,
Dan Rich
Publisher

Author's Note

This book has been a long time coming.

In late February 1975, I met a young man who had just recently moved to Texas from New York, where he had lived until that time. He was a fellow high-school student and, as I was then, a ravenous Star Trek fan.

We hit it off immediately.

His name was Daniel John Cheney. We instantly became inseparable, as close as brothers, sharing our thoughts and our lives as teenage friends will. We often shared private things—fears and beliefs and uncertainties—each of us finding encouragement in the support of the other. Dan, who now lived with an uncle and his household, had been a Christian just a short time—but his faith, though young, was rooted in a solid understanding of what he believed. Unlike him, I had strayed from the faith, doubting it all due to the simple fact that no one I knew had answers to my questions concerning the solidity of the faith.

How do I know it's for real? How do I even know there was a Jesus Christ? How do I know He was God? Why should I trust the Bible at all?

No one had answered me, and I wasn't going to buy into it all simply "because you're supposed to." I had attended church as a child, but the rebellion and questioning nature of the teenage years demanded solid answers. None were forthcoming, and secular science seemed to have plenty to offer.

So I quit. I considered myself an agnostic, and God had little if any place in my daily life.

Then came Dan. He was the first person I had ever known who was Christian and could tell me why. He knew how to share his faith with me, knew when to bring it up and when not to. If he did not know offhand the answer to a question, we would look for it within the Bible and/or the many apologetic books he had gathered. He had a remarkable sense for when to open up and when not to push—amazing for a kid in his late teens, and exactly what I needed. Having begun to get answers, I considered myself a "theist" at that point, believing there was a God but uncertain which form He took or which theology was the correct one. I know now that I was a Christian even then, that the salvation I had accepted earlier in my life was still in force, an eternal blessing from a Savior Who walked with me even when I did not walk with Him. Slowly, I came back to Christ, still with much to learn but with a well-founded measure of faith that would continue to grow.

Dan enjoyed writing fiction, generally stories that reflected both his enjoyment of adventure/science fiction/fantasy and his love for Christ. That is not usually an easy mix. He had a wonderful imagination and peopled his stories with colorful characters and vivid locales. Some of his stories dealt with existing film or television properties, while others were wholly original. I illustrated a few of them and had story input on others.

One tale entitled "The Open Door," a sixteen-page creative writing assignment written in 1974, dealt with a college student named T. G. Shass, who found himself inexplicably and involuntarily flashing back and forth between times and places. Though brief, some of the imagery contained in those pages was memorable, as was the main character.

That class assignment later grew into the incomplete, handwritten draft of a longer story, one that Dan asked me to read that summer. Renamed *The Noron Event,* it was only a few dozen pages long at that point and written in the first person. I read it, and at his request I also added notes and suggestions of my own. The project quickly became a collaboration.

In late 1975, my family left Texas and moved to Charleston, South Carolina, and the naval base there. Dan, in the meantime, went on to college in Sherman, Texas. We kept in touch by mail and by telephone, writing and sharing and trying our best to minimize the thousand or so miles between us. Slowly, work on the story continued, almost entirely in the form of telephone discussions. In late 1976, Dan took the still-incomplete manuscript to the school paper there in Sherman, offering it for serialization, hoping to see it in print. Unfortunately, it remained unpublished.

In early 1977, I returned to Texas and took an apartment there after graduating from high school. Dan, having moved back to New York, was attending Cornell University, something he had always wanted to do. Later, as the summer of 1978 approached, Dan called me and said he wanted us to get together and finish *Noron*. School was almost out for the semester, and he suggested we spend the summer months writing. I agreed at once. I looked forward to sitting down again in the same room as my collaborator, the two of us huddled over his well-worn manual typewriter—I really miss that old machine—pounding the great American novel into existence with our ever-present, one-pound bag of M&M's close at hand.

So, as I awaited his arrival, Dan arranged to carpool south with a few other students who were to be dropped off at homes along the way. They took turns driving on the several-day trip, traveling around the clock to save time and expenses.

On Tuesday, May 23, sometime between midnight and 4 A.M., on a two-lane stretch of Ohio highway, there was an accident. Only the driver survived, but with no memory of the wreck. Dan, mercifully, had been asleep in the backseat. Those who died, died instantly.

I was devastated. I even felt responsible, telling myself that he would not have died had he not chosen to come see me. In those first few days following the accident, I dreamed that he lived still, that the reports of his death had been mistaken—but upon awaking each morning I knew it was not so.

A few days after his death, on the day he was to have arrived, I received an insured parcel. It was wrapped in the brown paper of a grocery sack, a packaging that had become quite familiar to me over the past few years.

It was from Dan. Judging from the postmark, I knew he had mailed it just before leaving New York. Breathlessly, I opened it.

It was *The Noron Event.*

The entirety of the story (as it existed at that time)—the original and only copy of the story—was there, along with all of our notes and a brief, quickly handwritten cover letter. In the letter, Dan stated that there were many things he wanted rewritten or deleted. I would never know specifically what those things were. He also said he wanted to revise the tale—to take it in another direction while maintaining the same basic story concept—and told me to feel free to make any changes I thought would make it better.

There I sat, reading and rereading his unexpectedly final words to me, which had been written upon a plain sheet of notebook paper. The importance of the words was magnified simply because they were his last. I knew at that moment that the best and truest way to honor the memory of my dear friend was to finish the book we had started, since he had wished so greatly and for so long to see it completed and ultimately published. What I did not know was whether I could do it alone.

Yet I vowed that day that I would do so.

I learned later that his typewriter and the other stories he had written had been in the trunk of the car in which he had died. I never saw them again. Why he chose to risk mailing the manuscript instead of bringing it with him, along with his other things, I didn't understand.

I still don't.

But had he carried the story with him, rather than trusting the postal service to deliver it instead, it would have died with him on that dark Ohio highway that night so long ago. This novel would never have been written.

Years passed. I made several abortive attempts at finishing the book but kept stumbling over the many things in our original, unfinished version that simply did not work dramatically. I reluctantly came to realize—as had Dan, apparently—that most of the storyline would have to be replaced with new, more cohesive elements of plot and theme, with many added characters. I practically had to begin again. My writing skills were not yet what they needed to be in order to overcome these obstacles, nor had I gained the life experience and theological insight necessary for the telling of such a tale.

Yet I believed in my heart that *Noron* had survived for a reason. The story rested in a desk drawer off and on for many years, waiting patiently to be finished—waiting to become what it was meant to be when it alone, of all the work we had shared, was left in my hands.

As time went on, I married. My wife and I welcomed a son, whom we named Daniel. As my writing improved, I gained a literary agent, and doors were opened to me. In 1986 my work was first bought by a major publisher, and over the next decade I went on to write and illustrate several other books in other genres.

I knew the time had come for me to pick up the manuscript again.

It has taken more than two decades, but I hope I have finally forged *The Noron Event*—since retitled *The Last Guardian*—into what it was meant to be. Very little of the original story remains, but in writing this novel I have retained, I hope, the heart and essence of its innovator.

Maranatha, Dan. I hope you like what I've done with the story. I have missed you, and I've missed working with you—and the next time we meet, I look forward to sitting down and talking about the book. The M&M's are on me.

Shane Johnson
November 1999

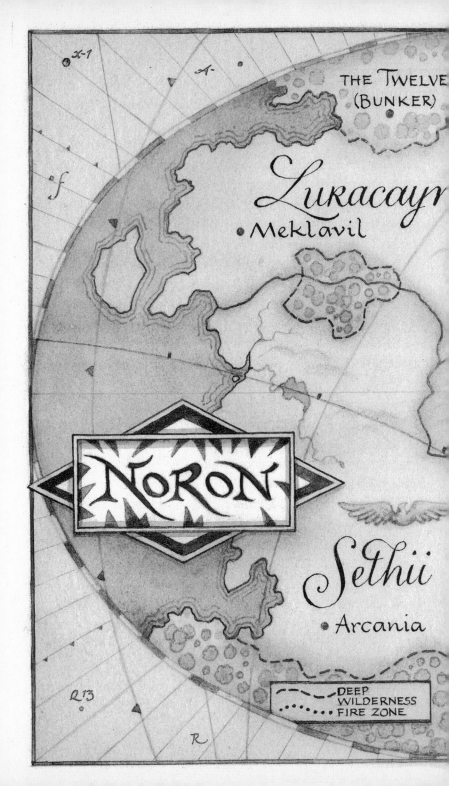

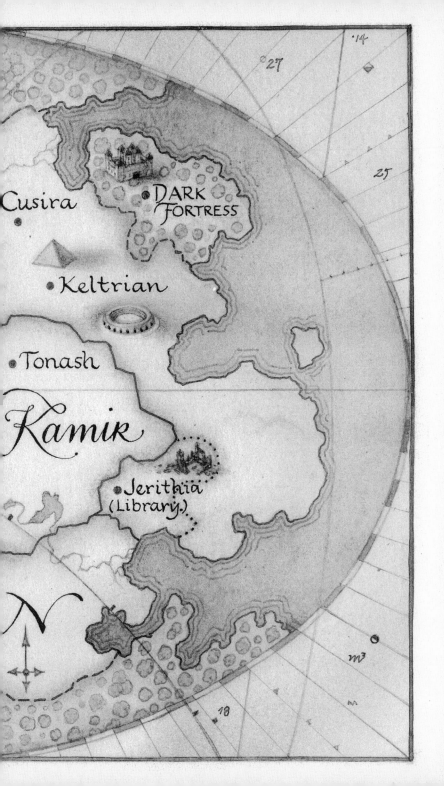

"Who are you, O man, who answers back to God?
The thing molded will not say to the molder,
'Why did you make me like this,' will it?
...Does not the potter have a right over the clay?
So then, it does not depend on the man who wills
or the man who runs, but on God who has mercy."

—PAUL (Romans 9:20-21,16)

Prologue

3496 B.C.

D *eath.*

It is an unseen, unfelt, unwanted companion, closer than arm's length throughout every hour of every day of a man's life. It is a silent, fathomless shadow, falling surely and inescapably within one's own, step for step, move for move. It is a numbing, irresistible, black abyss of a shroud, never sleeping, always watchful; its icy grip always coiled, always at the ready.

It waits.

The ancient man's heart raged against his ribs, forced beyond the limitations of aged flesh. Razored fingers of pain cut into his throbbing temples and aching, dusty lungs. His stringy hair, matted with sweat and dried blood, stung his eyes. He was beyond the point of collapse, his body now an enemy, but he knew he could not safely stop. Not to rest, nor to heal, nor even to die.

Again he fell against the floor of the forest. Again tiny angled pebbles carved cruel signatures into his face and hands. Again he rose and labored onward, dragging the weight of his tattered robes and coming down hard against bloodied soles with each step. The excruciating fatigue that had become his life was far beyond the tolerance of mere man; still, something unseen cradled him, carried him, gave him a strength not his own.

That something bore him onward even as he bore his precious burden, his world's last hope, cradled in both arms with its weight heavy on a leather sling that pulled constantly at his neck and shoulder. He was a Guardian, the last of they who were once many—and no mere Guardian, but a chosen Voice of Light, the last of eleven who had borne that same ponderous hope, one after the other, throughout the centuries. The others all had died.

Forcefully. Slowly. Painfully.

Memories of a kinder time flooded his mind. He and the other Guardians once had been revered, long before, and the precious Truth they told had been known throughout the world. For ages it had been so.

Then came the New Order. As new and more restrictive ideals took root within the government, the Guardians went from being beloved to being tolerated, then shunned, then hunted. For a time, people who still cherished that for which the Guardians stood provided them with scattered havens, where rest, food, and water were plentiful.

With the rise to power of the High Ones, a terrifyingly efficient program of government-sanctioned extermination wiped out those sympathetic to the Guardians, systematically and mercilessly. Overnight the once-venerated group had become pariahs, exiled from their world, sentenced to die because they lived.

The ancient man, like the others of his kind, had finally fled in the night, warned by precious friends in high places of the already bloodied ax that was about to fall. When he took flight, he abandoned what remained of his possessions, for their burdensome weight, like a millstone, would have dragged him into the icy depths of capture and execution.

He was alone and had been for more than six decades. He had lost everyone he had ever held dear, for his family and friends had all been put to death—without warning, without trial, without mercy.

Ahead in the deep twilight, beyond the last few timbers that separated him from a clearing, he caught sight of a small lamp resting beside the stone doorstep of a tiny, hewn-rock dwelling. He stopped at the edge of the deep wilderness that had protected him for weeks, fell against the jagged bark of a tree trunk, and stared with dry, fatigued eyes into the village clearing. From hard experience he knew that every shadow, every wall could conceal those from whom he fled, those who had stalked and hunted him for so long.

Those who wanted his singular load destroyed at any cost.

For years he had managed to elude them, across thousands of hard miles of raw nature and polished city. He had no destination, not now, and no goal but to preserve that which he clutched so tightly against his heaving ribs. His life was secondary in importance to him, and if his death would have ensured the safety of the cherished object, he would gladly have walked into an inferno long before.

He knew death was near. Every bone and sinew of his nearly skeletal form cried out for rest. The deeper forests provided fruit and the streams there gave him water, but for weeks he had not slept more than moments at a time, and the stresses within him were reaching lethal levels.

His pursuers were closing in with every beat of his heart, but he had to stop. He had no choice, not now, not if he wanted to live. Should he die, they would win.

They could not be allowed to win.

The Guardian looked toward the western horizon, toward the bright place where the sun had just relinquished its rule to the deepness of night, and he wondered if he had witnessed his last sunset.

His mind, still sharp, ran through his options as he surveyed the quiet village. It was so small, so isolated. He did not recognize it. How far north had he fled? How far south? Surely they would not find him resting there, not if he moved on quickly. There was no motion in the valley, no stirring in the streets, not even a breeze.

The obsolete man decided to risk seeking some modicum of rest in one of the outer residences. After only two, perhaps three hours here, he would have gathered the strength to press onward and away from those who strove to silence him. With a deep breath and a renewed grip upon his treasure, he burst into the clearing and moved as quickly as he could across the hundred or so feet of open land that surrounded the town. The cool grasses soothed his dry, cracking feet, thick clover cushioning his toes with each desperate step. His endurance faltered as he reached the nearest stone cottage, and as his battered legs failed him he stumbled and fell headlong into the dwelling's intricately carved wooden door. The oak was hard and cruel against his weathered face. He sank to his knees, a stinging sensation clawing at his cut lips. A familiar, metallic taste filled his mouth.

With great effort, his left arm came up and he slammed the flat of his palm against the hard, dense wood. The corner of his eye caught a blur of movement, and turning toward a window beside the door, he saw a drapery fall back into position. Again he struck the door face, his weight fully against it. Only silence answered him as he waited, each breath a struggle, each movement a labor.

One final time, he pounded on the unyielding door. It opened, dropping him onto the floor of the house. He was only vaguely aware of hands upon his body, straining to pull him inside. The door closed. He opened his weary eyes to see a dimly lit wood-beamed ceiling, with a man and his wife kneeling over him in the warm, amber light.

"He is hurt," the woman said. "Look at his face. We have to bring a healer."

"Get him some water," the man ordered. The woman rose and quickly returned with a porcelain cup of cool liquid. They helped the beaten man to sit up, and he greedily swallowed the life-giving drink.

As he emptied the cup, the Guardian's bedraggled robes opened just enough to reveal the object he carried. It glinted in the meager lamplight, betraying itself to the eyes of the husband, who immediately rose to his feet. Almost in a panic, his eyes wide, he lifted the old man by one arm and began dragging him to the doorway.

"Get out of here!" he yelled, terrified. "You will bring them here! They will kill us all…my wife…my children…get out!"

His wife did not understand. "Regon! Stop it! What is wrong? What are you doing?"

"Out!" he ordered forcefully, shoving the old man outside to fall against the cruel, sharp stone of the doorstep. Regon tried to slam the heavy door, but it was blocked and it cut into the old man's ankle. Kicking the bloodied, shoeless foot out of the way, Regon tried again and shut the door with a thud. "He is one of them!" the frightened husband whispered frantically to his confused wife. "To touch him means death!"

"You mean he was—I thought they were all dead!"

"So did I! But I saw it...under his robes."

"He had it with him?"

"Of course, he had it with him!"

"And it was in here? No!" She quickly dimmed the lights and fled the room, running to the rear of the house, where she knelt in the dark beside her sleeping children, shaking, weeping, stroking their hair, hoping that no one outside had seen what had happened.

Regon scanned the tree line discreetly from behind the curtained window. He saw no one approaching, no one who might have seen that the old man had been within his walls. Looking down at his doorstep, he saw the cursed figure struggling to stand, leaving bloodstains upon the cold stone. Regon knew he would have to wash the telltale splatters away as soon as possible. He could not risk otherwise.

On unsure legs the deathly figure finally rose, supporting himself for a moment against the heavy doorframe. The Guardian felt no anger and did not blame the man for what he had done, for he knew what faced anyone who helped him. He had grown accustomed to such treatment.

With short, wobbly strides he made his way along the side of the house and toward the village common, at the center of which stood a huge granite likeness of a great warrior of antiquity, the symbolic protector of the community. With an increasingly frail hold, the man embraced the priceless object beneath his robes, knowing that those willing to help him would be few—but he also knew that there would be those few. There always had been.

More dead than alive, the Guardian rounded a corner and took a single step into the central plaza. Abruptly he stopped.

His remaining strength flowed into his arms and his grip tightened, leaving the rest of his weary flesh unresponsive to his will. He dropped to his knees. He could not move. Could not run.

It did not matter.

There before him, surrounding the base of the towering stone sculpture and encircled by the low stone wall of the wide circular common, was a legion of government soldiers on horseback. Their dark metallic armor, like that of their horses, gleamed in the flickering light of the dozens of wall-mounted torches that encompassed them. They had been waiting patiently for him, there in the plaza, playing the game. They had been with him all along. Unseen, unheard, unfelt. They were his pursuers.

His death.

Two hundred eyes with their terrifying red glow looked upon him from within polished, angry helmets. They glared down from their mounts, encased in bronze, steel, and leather that was more befitting a prolonged military campaign than the pursuit of a single individual. Indeed, the extent of their armor and weaponry betrayed their level of determination in robbing the Guardian of that which had become his sole reason for living. The fact that they were on horseback told him something else as well: Those before him were elite troops, and their leader was a man he knew well.

Their long, polished ripsticks glistened in the torches' dancing light. The Guardian had seen firsthand what a ripstick, one of the most inhumane weapons ever devised, could do.

One ripstick could reduce a man to shreds in seconds. Ten times ten times that many were aimed at their aged target, primed and ready.

Fear filled him, though it was not a fear of death. That dread, he had conquered long ago. What he now felt was the despair of failure, for he had not succeeded in safeguarding his precious burden. His grip on it tightened yet again as a profound sorrow clutched his heart. In a moment, he would be but a torn remnant of a man and they would simply pry the treasure from what remained of his arms. Silently, never taking his eyes from those before him, he prayed.

A voice softly spoke within his mind, and his despair began to fade.

After decades, so many decades, he had reached his final destination, he suddenly knew. In this clearing, in this village, had come the end of his journey. Here he would stop running. Here a crucial event in the great battle would now take place.

One of the warriors, an enormous, black-armored man with shoulders seemingly as broad as he was tall, dismounted and approached the Guardian. His heavy steps crushed the ground beneath him. He was both beast and human, monster and man. The polished rankstones arrayed upon his breastplate showed that he had attained the rank of Deathlord Prime, a leader of hundreds of thousands and a man with the blood of tens of thousands upon his own hands.

The massive warrior walked closer with proud, arrogant strides and came to a stop some ten feet away. For a moment, the two foes stared into each other's eyes. Then the dark soldier reached up, released a leather strap from beneath his chin and slowly removed his scarred battle helmet.

The Guardian glared into the cold, chiseled face of his enemy, a face with which he was horrifyingly familiar, a face he had known for most of his life. It was a face utterly devoid of compassion or humanity, carved by too many blood-soaked years spent destroying those whose ideals lay outside those of the State. The man's hard, glistening eyes were radiant with the cold fire of final victory.

"Well, Parmenas," the Deathlord began with mock cordiality. "You have led us quite a chase. Did you really think you had eluded us? I could have taken you months ago, but I chose instead to shadow you, letting you lead us also to any who might choose to help you. And you did…I thank you for that. I was hoping, perhaps, that you might even lead us to number twelve, but alas, there is no number twelve…and now there cannot be. Such a pity. I hate odd numbers."

The Guardian stood mournfully silent, his eyes fixed upon the incarnate death before him. More had died. So many had died.

"So many times I could have killed you," the dire figure continued, stepping closer. "But I did not want you to die, not yet. You see, where there is life"—he leaned down into the deeply lined, leathery face, his hot breath searing weary but still bright eyes—"there is pain."

The Deathlord turned and took a few steps toward his men, then looked up at the heroically depicted statue looming above them. Allowing himself a moment of distraction, a deep, wry smirk crossed his face as he read the inscription on its pedestal.

MORDILARIS

Native Son

Who Fell in Battle at the Siege of Dolara

∞

The People of This Village Are Mine—
And in Safety Shall Mine Dwell

He then looked up into its face, at the noble jaw line, the piercing eyes. *Ah, Mordilaris—such a proud warrior they have made you out to be. Who would have thought they would one day dedicate the village of your birth to you? Good thing they did not know you as I did, eh?*

Renewing his focus, he whirled to face the Guardian once more. His attentions centered upon the object the man carried. It glittered in the firelight, its amber nodules aglow as if with inherent power. It was so close now, within the Deathlord's grasp at last, and this time there would be no losing it. "Your time is up," he stated flatly. "Face the fact. Give it to me."

The aged man remained stone, unmoving but for a trembling that shook his limbs.

"Give it to me, old friend, and I will let you live," the dark warrior lied.

Parmenas shut his eyes for a moment. Terrible, fleeting thoughts flared up in his weary mind.

If I just give it to them, perhaps they will let me go. Then I can rest at last. Do I really know I am right about this? Is it really worth dying for?

He squeezed his eyes more tightly shut and, with a strength not his own, buried the temptation. He had dedicated his life to this, had seen and felt and learned too much to begin doubting now. Even if it meant losing that life.

He looked up into the cold despotism of the Deathlord's stone face and uttered one simple, massive, terminal word.

"No."

The Guardian knew he had fought the fight, and well. Now he also knew it was time to leave the struggle in the hands of another.

"You cannot let me live," he calmly stated. "My heart is a threat to you, for you cannot own it. My allegiance lies—"

"Your misguided allegiance," the Deathlord sharply interrupted, "is of no importance. You cling to a rotting corpse, one that shall not rise again." The warrior gestured widely. "In doing so, you have also doomed the good people of this village. So many children. You know what we must do. Give it to me and I will spare them."

"Please…they know nothing."

"The law is the law. The contagion must be destroyed. You carry a plague, Parmenas. One that cannot be allowed to infect our happy populace. And now, only you can save them." The Deathlord leaned closer, and the ancient eyes peering up at him saw a stream of sweat coursing down the warrior's temple. Above, steam rose from his black hair. "I will say this one last time," the man ordered, his cavernous mouth betraying a glint of polished metal. "Give it to me."

The Guardian took a deep breath and spoke his own death sentence, knowing the word would be his last. "No."

The Deathlord shook his head in disgust, took a deep draw of cool air, then turned and walked back toward his men, donning his helmet once more. "Kill him," he ordered. "Then take it."

"Yes, Deathlord," the second-in-command nodded, dismounting.

"Then level the village and leave no one alive," he added with no regret. "Burn what will burn and use shock charges on whatever will not." The Deathlord impatiently reached over to the top of the stone wall and wrenched one of the huge torches from its embedded metal bracket. "The old ways are often the best…and one should always use the tools at hand," he said, handing the searing flame to one of his soldiers.

The Deathlord had been denied the pleasure of seeing the old man surrender. For years he had dreamed of hearing pleading words spill from a Guardian's mouth, but it was never to be. None of those who had fallen to him had begged for their lives, not one. And none had relinquished the treasured object he carried so long as life remained within his arms.

All had managed to pass it on to the next Voice chosen, and all had kept it safely from the clutches of the Dark.

Until now.

The Guardian found a measure of reassurance in the fact that, even then, his murderers had such a fearful respect for what he carried that they dared not try to take it from him, not while he lived.

Not that they could have.

He prayed for those of the village. Then, eyes still closed, he listened as dozens of soldiers dismounted and walked toward him, their leather-and-steel boots crunching against the rocky ground of the plaza. Silently readying himself, he waited.

A flowing warmth washed over his body and curled deep into him. *This cannot be their ripsticks,* he thought, *not this gentle, soothing embrace.* The feeling swelled into his dry, sinuous arms, then intensified into the space between his forearms and his aching chest, beneath his ragged robes.

Where his treasure was.

The heat there grew, yet never became uncomfortable or threatening. In fact, the greater it became, the more wondrous it felt. The joyous sensation cradled him for a moment, whispering words he heard in his mind, words of comfort to his heart. Then it vanished as quickly as it had come, leaving empty arms against his chest. The leather sling no longer dug into his neck and shoulders. The weight was gone. His burden had been lifted.

He heard a scream from the Deathlord, a cry of rage.

Jubilation welled up within Parmenas. The soldiers had been robbed of their prize, and the Dark had been denied the victory it had sought for so long.

The ripsticks dug in. Their fiery flameblades tore, seared, and unraveled his nervous and muscular systems, ravaging him, igniting and dismembering his flesh from within. But the momentary agony he felt as he was released from his broken body paled before the eternal joy in his heart.

The pain vanished. A white light shone. The weary old man embraced the tranquillity he found then, and as a lightness took him, he looked up into gentle eyes he had not seen for a very long time.

His first love had freed him.

⚭

Paradise.

A world of pure poetry, beyond the imaginings of man, beyond feeble utopian concepts. The simple perfection of a nature in total harmony with itself.

Diffused sunlight sparkled upon the dance of a crystal cool stream, throwing overlapping ribbons of light against the horsetail reeds on its bank. Jeweled fish of ruby and emerald darted among their roots. A distorted reflection rode the surface of the water, the mirrored image of a lush forest of towering timbers that spread to the horizon. The massive trees dwarfed even the mighty sequoias of modern Earth and threw mile-long shadows over flowering clearings of meadows.

Behemoth lifted her head into the dense foliage of a tree that hung over the lea where she stood. Eyeing her options, she chose, and her small trunk wrapped around an inviting, heavily laden branch. With chisel teeth she pulled free a clump of broad leaves and began to chew, her heavy lips drawing the juicy fronds into her wet mouth.

Behemoth and her world had never known clouds, nor wind, nor rain. Only the great light, as it traversed the pink sky in its course each day, and the lesser light that moved among the brilliant stars of the deep magenta night.

A commotion at her feet drew her attention downward. There upon the dense cushion of grass and blossoms her seven children played, squealing as they rolled and wrestled on the riverbank. One of them, rising to his feet too quickly, lost his balance and fell with a thud into his mother's foreleg. His eyes looked up, following the lines of that long, leathery green-gold neck, and came to rest upon the scowl he had come to know too well. A roar swelled deep in his mother's throat as she corrected him, and as the little one cowered he rubbed his cheek against her knee in apology.

Behemoth looked toward the horizon, toward the unnatural dwellings there. The Strange Ones lived there, in their odd, angular homes made of stone that they had dragged from elsewhere. Why they did not live among the welcoming forests and fields as she did was a mystery to her. With the towering wall they had built around themselves, they could not even enjoy the beauty of the timberlands around them. So small, so fragile were these beings—not even as tall as her knee was high.

From pole to pole it was a world of elegance and brilliant color. Its gentle atmosphere was filled with the perfume of billions of flowering plants and the rhythmic flapping of multicolored birds. Huge, graceful reptilian kites hung in the warm, still heights as their keen eyes scoured the seas below for food.

It was a world where life had reached its full genetic potential. Paradise.

Then came The Word.

For 120 years it had traveled, undiminished, across interstellar space. It was a word. A single word. A voice.

A judgment.

It entered the stellar system of Paradise along the planetary orbital plane. The immense outer planets, spared any contact with it, stood by in cold silence as it swept past. Faster than light it continued on, deeper into the system.

It was nearing its destination. Had they chosen differently at any time during its deadly journey, had they only heeded the pleading warnings, The Word would have turned away, would have spared them.

But they had not.

Entering the inner system, The Word grazed a small, rocky, lifeless world. Though its impact was only partial, the power of the passing voice was such that even a glancing blow was enough to initiate an irresistible and irreversible chain reaction within the little world. As its crystalline inner structure struggled to absorb the passing utterance, the planet began, with increasing intensity, to ring like a bell.

It took only moments. The tiny sacrifice began to come apart at the seams, its purpose fulfilled. Inner geothermal pressures, surpassing the world's ability to contain them, burst forth as crust and mantle yielded. The planet exploded into a vast cloud of rock and dust as it died, leaving behind only a postmortem river of cold, lonely debris.

The Word, now properly modulated, maintained the course it had begun more than a century earlier and continued toward Paradise. Millions of fragments of the pulverized planet were drawn into its wake, trailing behind, also headed into the core of the system.

If only there had been another way.

Behemoth moved her head toward the glittering stream and her body followed, as did her children. Massive yet gracefully flowing strides carried her closer to the cool water. Deer, unafraid of the approaching immensity, continued to drink on the opposite bank as she dipped her trunk into the refreshing current.

The thunder of the flapping of thousands of wings suddenly filled the air as every bird in every tree took flight. The dark, winged cloud repeatedly changed direction in panic, seeking a safety that was not there.

The deer bolted and dashed into the forest. Behemoth lifted her head and looked out across the meadow, then up at the fear-filled sky. Something was wrong. She felt it too, deep within her. Her children huddled beneath her in terror.

A deep rumble, more felt than heard, rapidly crescendoed around them. Trees began to sway. Screams arose from the place of the Strange Ones. The ground began to move like a rough sea.

On the other side of the world, The Word had hit with full force, driving deep into Paradise's very core. Those who had lived on that side of the planet lived no more. They were the lucky ones.

Thousands of vast subterranean reservoirs began to boil as two and one-half billion vibrations per second worked against them. As the underground oceans strained against their rocky boundaries, fissures began to open. Paradise fought valiantly to resist the unmerciful torture that built within it.

For a few precious moments, the planet held its own. Just a few.

The ground again rolled as if fluid, more violently now. Behemoth was thrown and fell hard against the unsure surface beneath her. Struggling to stand, the huge animal cried out and fell again against rocking trees. She bellowed for her children and could hear them clamor in the distance. A glare drew her attention to the horizon, and as she watched, the planet's crust just beyond her view succumbed.

There, past the edge of the world, immense plumes of white erupted skyward, ascending for miles, driven by forces thousands of times more powerful than volcanic upheaval.

Behemoth heard nothing at first—then the shock wave hit. A painful thunder drowned out the screams of her children just before a hammer of wind threw her full against the face of the forest. Immeasurable winds began to uproot even the largest, most ancient trees as they slammed into everything in their path, filled with deadly projectiles of stone, flora, and flesh.

More fissures tore open planetwide, throwing plumes of steam into the upper atmosphere with an intolerable roar. The once-solid crust of Paradise broke into thousands of tectonic plates as its single eggshell continent fractured into smaller, separate land masses. Still the pressure increased, and superheated waters exploded through the narrow openings forged by the preliminary fists of steam. A prolonged, deafening concussion shook the face of the world as the immense blades of boiling water screamed white into the turbulent sky.

At an altitude of eleven miles their forceful, upward rush came to a sudden stop.

Since the planet's birth, its intense magnetic field had held suspended around it a shell of water that, at that altitude and temperature, had become a thin stratum of metallic hydrogen encased between deep layers of ice. The shell had made possible the worldwide warmth Paradise had enjoyed, and it had protected the planet from the harmful radiation of its sun. The elevated atmospheric pressure exerted by the shell had made possible the massive size of beasts such as Behemoth, and its pink hue had stimulated both plant and animal growth. The canopy had even multiplied the brightness with which the stars had shone at night.

But no more.

The canopy shattered like fragile crystal as the boiling knives of water tore into it. Millions of icy shards fell into the turbulent maelstrom below, melting back into that which they had once been long before. The atmospheric upheaval was such that it would take nearly a month and a half for the splintered shell to fall completely to the dying world below.

And Paradise knew rain for the first time.

Temperatures dropped instantly at the poles as the atmosphere fought to equalize itself. Powerful sub-zero winds blasted the once tropical polar forests. Pounding, freezing rain shrouded terrified animals as they struggled through the rising mire, encasing them alive in tombs of thick, muddy ice. Hailstones more than a foot in diameter pelted anything that stood, breaking bone and splintering timber. Fiery projectiles of molten stone and volcanic ash rained down.

Mountain peaks ten thousand feet high arose violently and valleys sank down as the crust beneath them shifted along its new fault lines. Scalding mud and water exploded out onto the surface, destroying earth and nature along with any who struggled to evade the rising onslaught. The merciless slurry scraped the planet's face, unleashing the power of the planet's inner forces for the first time.

As the cataclysm progressed, tidal forces alternately hid then exposed fresh turbid plateaus of hot mud. The few worldwide who still survived, both human and animal, were forced to tread the violent waters until each twelve-hour cycle allowed these new alluvial layers to be revealed. Again and again the waters rose then receded, and with each cycle less land appeared until finally none rose at all. The tiniest and most simple creatures, unable to avoid the rising waters, were the first to be buried by settling, waterborne sediments. The largest or more mobile beasts, especially those with warm blood and the greatest ability to swim, were among the last.

The waters would inundate Paradise for more than a year before eventually receding, but it took only days for life worldwide to succumb. The last to leave their footprints upon Paradise dwindled rapidly in number as they drowned or starved or were crushed or boiled alive—until none remained.

Behemoth struggled through new mud, buried up to her breastbone in the hot, deadly muck. Corpses and carcasses, whole and torn, surrounded her, contorted by fear and hydrodynamic forces. The thickening mire burned her flesh. Its powerful suction finally held her immobile, unable to continue on. Her eyes found nothing but the stinging gray torrent of rain and hail that battered her.

A new thundering roar caught Behemoth's attention. Blindly, she turned her great neck for the last time and listened. And wearily waited.

A wall of boiling mud and water a mile high was moments away.

She was ready. A rebirth had begun, one that would result in a world in which she and her kind could find no place. Paradise was gone.

But something new would arise from its scarred remains.

Part 1

THE PROPHET

1

October 1975

A crystalline veil of stars stretched like a dewy web from horizon to horizon, each radiant pinpoint a gem set into the black velvet expanse beyond.

T. G. Shass lay on his back, his hands behind his head, peering wide-eyed into the inky depth of the cold Colorado night sky. As the warm glow of the campfire washed over his still form, he wished that the city sky at home could be even half as clear and wondrous as the panorama above him. He imagined himself looking not up but out, as if the ground beneath him were a wall to which he had been pinned and the sparkling display were spread head to toe before him. Meteorites cut momentary scars of brilliant light into the chilled autumn air, dramatically underscoring the eternal stillness of deep space.

T. G. listened to the trees all around him, their branches and leaves sounding a timeless serenade of wind against wood. The cold mountain air was cleansing and pure, causing his breath to fog. He would sleep well tonight.

He rolled onto his left side, adjusting the warm cocoon of his sleeping bag, and saw in the distance a brilliant orb of cold orange rust. The moon rose slowly over the mountain peaks, throwing an ocher sparkle upon the blankets of snow at their summits. He remembered the sights and sounds of the past vacations he and his parents had once taken there in the Snowmass Wilderness.

The beauty of his surroundings faded then. Gentle memory was replaced by the hard bitterness that had become T. G. Shass only two years before. Since that time he had struggled in vain to find an object that could sustain the blows of his blinding anger, but his rage and cruel words had only alienated his friends.

The unwelcome and hated image fell before his mind's eye as it had so often, a reflection through tears that had first registered three days after his twenty-second birthday. T. G. saw the glint of polished bronze as it was gently and conclusively lowered into the cold, hard November earth, a twofold farewell unwarmed by the bright hues of floral sympathies and the meager words of the peripheral few who had shared T. G.'s life. The emotional disfigurement had slashed deeply into his being, leaving him hollow and alone—little more than a shell of inconsolable, bitter misery.

He slammed his eyes shut as if to cut off the memory. His right hand clenched the thick, zippered edge of his down bag, his palm warming as his grip tightened. Anger burned within him, anger toward a God he could no longer believe existed. His parents had believed so, but they could not have been right—surely a God such as the One in Whom they had had faith would never orphan an only child and leave him so agonizingly alone, with no living family whatsoever.

Never.

He sat up, ran his fingers through his dark hair, and looked at the dusty chrome bumper of the white hatchback parked beyond the tent. He allowed himself a moment to simply sit and watch the firelight dance upon the polished metal of the car's trim. Such moments of respite had become few, for his guilt-racked mind had determined to torture itself, as if it deserved no better.

With difficulty he forced himself to think of tomorrow, when he and David, who slept inside the tent, would awaken for a day of serious hiking.

David Cernan was his best friend, one of the handful of friends who remained.

There was another, but tonight T. G. feared he had lost her forever. She had been more than just a good friend. He had wanted to marry her. He had loved her.

Her name was Jenni.

He had known her since elementary school, though their relationship had deepened only a few years before. She was the loveliest girl he had ever seen, and he had been stunned beyond words at her acceptance of his awkward, nervous request that she accompany him to their senior-year, high-school homecoming dance. T. G. could still smell her perfumed hair, could still see her wondrous, vibrant smile—

And he could still hear the irrational, cutting words he had hurled at her on another, more recent night, hurting her more than she ever deserved, forcing tears to stream from her dark, sparkling eyes. His pain had driven away all those around him, finally even the woman who might have been his wife.

How could I have been so stupid—?

The brightest remaining light in his life had been all but extinguished, and he knew he had been in the wrong that night, hammering away at her over an insignificance that now shamed him. But pride had prevailed in the moment, and the harsh words would not stop pouring from his bitter lips until she was gone. A part of him deep inside had wanted to cry out to her, to embrace her, to keep her from leaving—but his pain was too strong, too unyielding, too stubborn. In seconds, the damage had been done, and T. G. had since tried to relegate himself to a life lived in the dark.

When his parents died so cruelly and so unfairly, the T. G. that David and Jenni had known died with them.

He stood and stretched, drawing his six-foot frame to its full height. Momentary dizziness made him sway slightly. After it passed, he picked up his sleeping bag and walked toward the yellow nylon-and-canvas tent. A little dirt on the campfire and it was extinguished, leaving a frustrated, knotted finger of smoke to rise into the gentle, biting breeze.

The night sky and its cast of characters were familiar to him, thanks to a once-intense but since-neglected interest in astronomy. He paused to look again at the vigilant moon, which rose alongside its bright, reddish guardian that night, the warrior planet Mars. A few weeks from now, once T. G. had returned home to New York and had settled back into his daily routine, it would be a lonely moon, stripped of its ruddy escort, that would shine through his window each night as he lay in bed, alone in his apartment.

Alone.

He easily pinpointed the tiny spot on the lunar terminator where human footprints had first compressed the dusty surface of the dark Sea of Tranquillity. He knew all the Apollo landing sites, just as he knew the faces and names of the men who had so bravely walked there. He, too, had wanted to be an astronaut once, long ago.

Someday, somehow, I'll get into space, he had sworn. *I'll be up there, on the moon, looking down on this blue planet—someday.*

With great excitement he had followed each manned mission, building plastic models of the spacecraft and drawing pictures of the flights and their spacesuited astronauts. But that was when he was much younger, and much had changed since.

Too much, too quickly.

He opened the tent where his friend slept and hoped he would be able to endure the intermittent snoring that shook its nylon seams. The warm air of the small camp heater welcomed him, and he tossed his sleeping bag into the vacancy beside his friend.

T. G. paused to take one last look at the watchful moon. Once, as he and his father had shared their small, backyard telescope, the rugged, lifeless world above had seemed almost a friend. Now it was but a cold, distant outsider—uncaring, unknowing, and unreachable.

He turned to the west, toward the twin moonlit peaks of the Maroon Bells. Almost imperceptibly, each tiny, flickering star disappeared beneath the horizon, slipping inexorably away, just as his family had—leaving only a dark emptiness in its place.

He went inside.

∽∞∽

Click!

The shutter of the SLR camera snapped again, perhaps for the hundredth time that day. T. G. adjusted its zoom lens once more, focusing on a distant snowcap.

"You about through, Ansel?" David asked, watching the lengthening shadows around him. "I'm beat...and we need to be getting back."

"Just a couple more," T. G. replied, ignoring the playfully sarcastic reference to the great photographer. "Look at that...beautiful."

"Make it quick, T-square. October's running out on us." David had given T. G. the nickname in junior high, soon after they had first met, after he had taken note of T. G.'s love of classical music, Shakespeare, and time-honored literature—the longhaired stuff for which David had little use. T. G. was the only person his friend had ever known who had actually read *Wuthering Heights* on his own time, of his own free will. An act to be considered only at gunpoint, at least in David's mind, the deed had been a defining moment in his growing perception of his friend and had, once and forever, certified that T. G. was unlike anyone he had ever known.

Even in name. No living person knew what T. G.'s initials stood for, and he worked hard to keep it that way. Even his driver's license reflected this one privacy, a secret David doubted his friend would ever share with anyone.

They were on the northwestern bank of tiny Crater Lake, one of many small, glacial bodies of water that were fed by the snow runoff from the Maroon Bells. The water was pure and cold and clear, its surface like glass. The lake mirrored the densely surrounding trees and the distant mountains, reflecting them with an inverted image of almost equal clarity.

The young men's hiking expertise had been earned over time, first in the Boy Scouts and then in summer classes they had taken together during their stint in high school. David, however, had gained far more experience in the wilderness than T. G. had and often served as the guide. A self-admitted adrenaline junkie, he had always embraced the more adventurous and athletic aspects of the great outdoors, seeking any opportunity to stretch his limitations, while T. G.'s primary interests had been in sights, sounds, and smells. The thrill-seeking David had often talked his reluctant friend into attempting the riskier activities of climbing and rappelling, citing the photographic possibilities that existed at greater altitudes.

Peering through his viewfinder, T. G. was having trouble lining up the shot he wanted. Frustrated, he leaned out over the edge of the bank, trying for an angle that paralleled the grassy shoreline.

"Watch it," David called from a distance as his friend leaned dangerously out over the water. "Remember your knee. You could—"

Unstable ground gave way, sending T. G.'s left leg into the cold, shallow water just below. His foot sank deep into the muddy bottom as he rallied to keep his balance, and he fell hard against the shore. Only the strap around his neck saved his heavy camera from a watery grave. He felt a twinge in his left knee beneath the elastic brace he wore. He grimaced.

David laughed, seeing that his friend was more embarrassed than hurt. He walked up and extended a hand, providing the leverage T. G. needed to pull his boot free of the viscous ooze. "You okay? If you wanted to swim, you should have brought your trunks."

"Yeah, yeah…laugh it up," T. G. complained with all seriousness, wiping his bemired hiking boot against the grass and cursing under his breath. "These boots are brand new…thirty lousy dollars…" He slammed his mud-caked sole into the ground, shaking loose as much of the brown sediment as would let go. "I don't know why I came on this stupid trip in the first place."

"Lighten up, T-square. Getting a little wet never killed anybody."

"I guess you never saw *The Wizard of Oz,*" T. G. moaned, shifting the weight of his daypack. As they walked on he continued to complain, the incident opening a floodgate of negative comments about dozens of ridiculously trivial things that had irritated him in recent days.

"Look, I wasn't going to say anything," David interrupted, "but you've been in a sorry mood ever since we got here. I know you've been through a lot the last couple of years…but, you know, you're not as nice to be around as you used to be."

David continued to scold him as they walked uphill, away from the shoreline, as T. G. paused every few steps to shake more water from his wet pant leg. "Sure, life's dealt you a lousy hand, but, man…the attitude's gotta stop."

"Is that all?"

"I guess I should thank you for the fact that you stopped whistling 'Rhinestone Cowboy' a little while ago. Don't get me wrong…the first couple of hundred times weren't so bad."

"Sorry."

David shook his head. "Listen…it's not just today, but going back a good while. I mean, haven't you noticed how the guys at the university have been going out of their way *not* to be around you? It isn't coincidence. And I know it may not be any of my business, but you were way out of line with Jenni last week. You know that. You need her…she's the best thing that ever happened to you. You've been close since *grade school,* man. Don't blow it, if you haven't already. It's time to get on with life."

"Lay off, Dave," T. G. snapped, his head down. "I'm coping with things in my own way."

David stopped and wheeled around, his face in his friend's. After an awkward silence of a few seconds, he spoke slowly and distinctly. "Because I'm your friend—one of the few you have left, I might add—you can believe me when I tell you that *your way ain't workin'.*" He turned and walked on, up the hill and into the dense forest, leaving T. G. to weigh the words alone.

T. G. hated what he had become, yet his anger would not be appeased. The world had taken from him that which was most precious, and he would make it pay. Somehow it would pay.

They did not speak again for half an hour, and only then because T. G. stopped to rest on a downed tree trunk. "Wait up…"

David paused and turned back to face him. "Tired already?"

"It's my knee. It's starting to act up. I guess I strained it a little when I got wet. I should have known better than to try such a long hike."

"It's been, what, since you hurt it...four years? They say a knee injury like yours never really heals. It'll force Namath to retire...you watch."

"I wish my knee had been as hard as my head," T. G. monotoned in an effort to smooth things over. "Listen, about what happened back there—"

"It's forgotten." David winked at him, nodding.

T. G. pulled up his pant leg and adjusted the tight elastic brace on his left knee. "I hate this thing. How far have we gone anyway?"

A dead branch snapped beneath David's heavy boot as he stretched to step over the trunk of a fallen pine, and as he leaned to catch his balance, the bark of a standing one made a deep impression in the palm of his hand. "Well," he began, calculating aloud, "we left camp at nine, and it's about five-thirty now. We've kept up a pretty good pace..."

"All uphill, seems like," T. G. said.

"We stopped for lunch and rest stops, and so you could get your exciting action shots of the lake. Figure about...eight miles."

"You *could* check the pedometer," T. G. suggested.

"Anyone could do that," David smiled. "This is pioneer instinct talking..."

"Check the pedometer."

He grudgingly looked down at the small aluminum gauge. "It says six and eight tenths. Happy?"

"Thank you." T. G. looked toward the dropping sun. Its rays filtered through the glorious autumn foliage above, leaving thin, brilliant pencils of light to scatter below.

David looked around, enjoying the splendor of the magnificent terrain. "The colors are great, aren't they? I love this time of year..."

"You know, considering the point where we began to loop back, we might not be more than a couple of hours from camp."

"Good thing," David said, adjusting the visor of his baseball cap. "I'd say that's about how much light we've got left." They continued on, encountering no one along the way. Not that they expected to, since they were well away from the marked trails, blazing their own and enjoying the adventure.

The sun disappeared from sight, though it was not yet sunset; the warm, brilliant orb had hidden itself behind the mountains, throwing a cool shadow upon the surrounding timberlands. The rims of advancing cumulus clouds glowed a golden, incandescent orange in the falling light, and the temperature began to drop as the still of the early evening blanketed the mountains.

T. G. and David moved quickly along the wooded mountainside, their pace hurried, their conversation minimal. Should dark fall before they reached their camp, the inky blackness of the night woods would rob them of both landmarks and stars, making their return extremely difficult. Even their flashlights would be of little help, they knew, without a solid fix on their destination.

"I'd say we're still at least forty-five minutes away," T. G. noted, pausing to check his pocket map and his watch. "I don't think we'll make it. It's already almost sunset."

"That's what I like. A good, positive attitude."

"Must be a shortcut here someplace," T. G. hoped aloud, examining the map more closely. David stepped up to take a look.

"Well..."

"Tough call. We're just east of West Maroon Creek. Could be that's Len Shoemaker Ridge just there," he said, indicating the high forest terrain to their right. "As for a shortcut..."

"See one?"

"Not right off, nothing definite. But if we cut across the northwest shoulder of Pyramid Peak, and if we really hustle, that could put us back at the car just before dark. Then we just unload, pitch the tent again and we're in like Flynn."

"Okay...it has to be double-time from here on," David said, adjusting the straps of his daypack. "Maybe triple-time. Can your knee take it?"

"I'll be fine. Let's go." As T. G. folded the map he noticed a new and sudden drop in temperature. It was sharp and worrisome. "Feel that?"

"Yeah. Not good. Conditions don't seem right for a storm, though."

"No…but when they hit out here, they hit fast."

They began again, their pace more rapid. "If we get caught in a downpour, it'll be trouble," T. G. said. "Night's bad enough as it is…"

They watched the light trickle away as a boiling mass rapidly built in the sky overhead. "Sure there isn't a real shortcut on there somewhere?" David hoped.

T. G. opened the map back up, studying it as closely as he could while walking. He spotted an indefinite area near their position that was not clearly characterized by any of the markings in the map's legend. "Might be something right here," he called out. "Could be a narrow valley or something, well away from the marked trails. Hard to tell with the scale of this map." He checked his compass. "North-northeast."

"I say we go for it. Don't think we've got much choice."

Forcing their aching legs onward, they changed direction, moving quickly. Dark, menacing clouds swirled as they formed in the sky overhead, giving every indication that an intense and violent storm was minutes away. The thunderhead grew, fueled by a complex vortex of winds, churning within itself as it became increasingly brutal. T. G. looked up as he ran, catching glimpses of the threat through gaps in the dense foliage. He feared the angry mass.

"The cloud base is dropping lower," he said. "Look at that. Bad news…real bad."

The wind picked up dramatically, numbing their ears with the clatter of shaking branches and rustling leaves. A wail rose among the towering pines, sprinkling needles onto the hikers, and the temperature drop increased, throwing sheets of cold air against their sweat-coated skin.

Adrenaline kicked in, and T. G. and David ran faster. The dense forest grew even more crowded, making it difficult to find a sure path. The carpet of fallen leaves deepened, and the thick underbrush made their hurried footing less certain. Tangles of dead branches clutched at their legs as they ran past, like pleading skeletal hands. David leaped over a fallen trunk, almost twisting his ankle as he came down on a second, smaller one he had not seen beneath its brittle, leafy covering. T. G. leaped wide, avoiding it, but paid the price when he lost his balance and fell sideways into a pine trunk. Its stabbing bark drew blood as it dug into his left forearm, just above the wrist.

"Aaahhhh!" he shouted, momentarily pausing to put pressure on the jagged, bleeding, L-shaped scrape. The sweat of his palm stung against it. David turned to check on his friend, knowing they could not stop.

"No time!" he warned, examining the injury. "Bleed later…come on!"

They began again. The heavy rasp of their breathing grew, as did the ache in their lungs. A flash flared around them, displacing the gloom for an instant, followed moments later by a dull, rolling roar that came from no discernible direction. A new twinge of pain began to flare within T. G.'s knee.

"We're not going to make it," he feared.

Suddenly, a lightness appeared ahead, beyond the towering trunks. A clearing promised to open before them at the end of another hundred feet of forest. They picked up their pace, their aching legs cramping.

"Finally," David managed, his breath coming in sharp gulps.

But T. G. got there first, and as he passed the last tree before hitting the open expanse he suddenly cried out, clutched madly for a low-hanging branch to his right, then slid to a sitting position as the slender limb held and his feet shot out from beneath him. David, not understanding, ran headlong into T. G., who reached up and managed to grab hold of his friend's fluttering shirttail.

It was barely enough to stop David's momentum, but it was

enough. He fell onto T. G., coming to rest less than three feet from the edge of a sheer drop of nearly a hundred feet.

His heart pounding, David carefully peered over the precipice, unbelieving. Their limbs weak from fear and exhaustion, the hikers lay there for a moment, gathering themselves.

"Man…," David managed, breathing heavily, "you saved…my life."

"We must have…missed something…," T. G. replied, also breathing heavily. "I misread the map…I guess…"

"You guess?" David laughed in relief, his hands shaking, still pumped on adrenaline. "One more step…and we'd have been…customers for Dad."

"At least we'd have gotten…the family discount."

"Now what?" David asked, greedily gulping the cool air. The wind increased, and as the weary pair looked up into the dark turmoil above they saw rotation and dark fingers of enraged air that seemed to reach down toward them.

"We'll never make it around this drop-off…not before the storm hits. It goes on around the bend for as far as I can see."

"Okay…forget the car…where's the public campground from here?"

T. G. pointed out beyond the cliff. "About half a mile that way, as the crow flies."

"Then we take the direct route," David said. "No choice." He looked over the cliff once again and saw what appeared to be a dense carpet of knee-deep brush covering the valley floor below. Inconvenient to wade through, but much quicker than the alternative.

T. G. watched as his friend dropped his pack and unhooked the bungee cords that held his colorful blue-green kernmantle rope to its base. "Really bad idea," he said, indicating the swirling mass above. "Sure we even have enough rope?" A flash of lightning in the distance punctuated his warning.

"No more than a hundred feet to the bottom, at most," David

assured him as thunder rumbled around them. "We'll be down in less than two minutes. Thick as those clouds are, it'll be dark in ten minutes, and we can be at the campground by then. The storm will be here sooner than that. No choice, buddy." He tied his rope to a tree trunk, then, satisfied with its solidity, slipped into his leather harness. "We lose the ropes at the bottom and come back for them tomorrow. Look there…" He pointed down and across the way to a small, distant light, which flickered like a single bulb among the trees on the other side of the rough clearing. "Gotta be a public rest room, at the very least. Maybe even the campground itself. Shelter, at any rate. You coming?"

T. G., seeing no other option, reluctantly began to unpack his equipment. The sky was growing darker by the second, and the building wind was heavy with the dampness of coming rain. Another flash struck out as David began down the face of the cliff, carefully easing the rope through his carabiners. "Come on!"

T. G. fastened his harness and checked the buckles one last time as he watched his friend rappel out of sight, below the cliff's edge. Tossing his 165 feet of rainbow rope over the edge, he took one final look up into the dark sky, dreading the violence above him. For a moment he thought he saw a face amidst the throbbing, black whirlpool churning overhead. A face of primordial malignancy. A face of death, skull-like and angry.

A new sound echoed against the walls of the cliff. A solid curtain of cold rain advanced upon them, only a few hundred feet away and moving rapidly. David was already halfway down, but T. G. was only just beginning his rappel. Thunder roared closer. "Move it!" T. G. heard Dave shouting at him. He knew that time had run out. The glittering wall swept closer, reflecting the ever-increasing lightning flashes like a distorted, living mirror.

It got dark. Too dark, too fast.

A sudden, violent gust threw David against the cliff face, twisting him on his rope like a puppet on tangled strings. As the first icy drops stung his face he regained proper attitude and quickly dropped the final twenty feet into the bed of lush growth below. The rain became hard and painful as huge drops swept cruelly into him. Then, as he began to free himself from his harness, David's face and hands were stung repeatedly by something else, something solid. An incessant clicking sound all around him became louder and more intense, and he realized that a torrent of small hailstones was pelting the rockface, T. G., and himself.

"T-square!" he yelled, unable to look upward into the driving rain for more than an instant at a time. In the darkness he saw no sign of his friend, but the cold glare of lightning against the cliff wall revealed T. G.'s rope still hanging there. The rope was moving, but as if tossed by wind, not as if it were being shaken by a rappeller above. "T-square! You okay?" David shouted, straining his voice as he shielded his face from the storm. Struggling to look up again, he saw that darkness and rain some thirty feet above swallowed their ropes. There was no sign of his friend, so David fearfully and quickly searched the brushy ground around him for any sign that T. G. had fallen. There was none.

No one who began a rappel could climb back up so quickly, David knew. T. G. could have reached the ground in a tenth the time it would have taken him to make his way back to the top. David feared that his friend had become entangled or injured and was hanging, beyond the darkness, at the storm's mercy. Dropping his daypack, he quickly reached for his ascenders and attached them to the thin rope that had taken him safely to the base of the cliff. "Really good idea, idiot," he chastised himself, knowing that rappelling in the face of an oncoming storm, under any circumstances, had been less than wise.

The rope had become wet and slippery in the fierce downpour, but the ratchet system in each ascender would hold fast nonetheless. David began a tedious, painful climb, pelted by frigid rain and marble-sized hail, bucking winds that were gusting harder than any he could remember. He angled his head so the bill of his cap might protect his face, but a sudden gust caught the hat and knocked it away. It disappeared into the darkness below.

He managed to swing over and grab hold of T. G.'s rope, using it to guide him to that spot just above where he knew his friend had to be. Slowly, one leg at a time, he inched upward. A too-close, white-hot lightning strike momentarily blinded him, its instantaneous and deafening crack shaking him and turning adrenaline loose in his bloodstream. Fear filled him, pushing his already beaten limbs to move faster and more surely upward.

"I'm coming," he shouted, barely able to hear himself. The hail ceased, but the rain became more intense as if to compensate. David passed the fifty-foot mark, but still could not see his friend. "T. G.? Can you hear me?" he yelled, his voice breaking. "Answer me…"

At sixty feet, a cold, drenched David found something that his mind labored to accept, something that met his hand as he glided it upward along T. G.'s wet, slippery rope. It was an impossibility that caused David to hang there, staring in disbelief, pressing against the wet, raw stone with his fingertips. The storm, the darkness, the danger all paled as the lightning revealed for an instant at a time a sight that could not be, yet was. Again and again he ran his numbing fingers up T. G.'s rope.

Right up to the point where it disappeared into the rock face.

At a point some six feet higher the rope reemerged, taut and headed upward, where it quickly disappeared into the dark rain above. A steady torrent of chilled water coursed down the rope, streaming onto the cliff face at the point where rope and rock became one. David frantically tugged, throwing himself off balance again and again as he fought to free the line, but it held fast as if embedded in concrete. His knuckles became battered and bloodied as, with each desperate pull, they banged into the stone. His shoulders slammed repeatedly into the wet rock as his motions and the wind threw him about, yet he felt no pain.

"T. G.!" he screamed again and again. His cries bounced uselessly off the rock and were swallowed up by the hungry, raging storm.

2

J enni Parklin sat side-legged on the floor of her family's home, watching the gentle snowfall outside. As she leaned on the sill of the tall, multipaned living room window, her eyes drank in the white stillness of Ithaca, New York, and even through the glass she could feel the cold against her face. Her mind was far away, wrapped up in the heart of another, someone she had loved for a very long time.

But now he was gone.

Her breath spilled into a splash of fog as it hit the frost-rimmed pane just inches from her nose. The scene beyond should have been so beautiful, so lovely. Covered by a chaste white blanket, the world had always seemed so much kinder, so much cleaner, so much more fragile somehow. Yet the absence of that special someone, who had once held out the promise of many shared winters to come, diminished its loveliness.

Now it seemed merely cold outside—cold and harsh and so lonely.

"Jenni?" a voice called from behind her.

"Here, Mama," she replied quietly, remaining in place.

Janice Parklin looked down and saw a foot protruding from behind the plush Queen Anne chair near the window. Canting her head slightly to peek around it, she smiled.

"You've been doing that your whole life," she said. "Sitting there, looking out that window like that"—she walked up to her daughter, knowing the girl was troubled—"but only when you were upset."

"It helps somehow," Jenni said.

Her mother reached down and stroked the girl's back. "Sweetheart, it wasn't your fault. You did nothing wrong…you were just doing a favor for a friend."

"That doesn't matter. He's still gone."

"Maybe not, honey…maybe he'll come around. The poor boy's tied up in knots. You know how close he and his parents were…he's just been through so much. It does things to people."

"What if he doesn't come around?" Jenni said, looking up into her mother's eyes. They sparkled with the generosity, the kindness of her nature. "He's like another person now."

"I know."

"I miss *my* T. G., Mama," she said.

"I do too, honey," her mother said, stroking the girl's shoulder-length, honey blond hair. "He'll come back. You just watch."

Jenni took her mother's gentle hand and held it close, then rose and hugged the woman.

"Thanks, Mama," she smiled.

"Come on," Janice said. "Dinner's ready, and your father's hungry."

❧

Schoolwork was not much of a comfort, but Jenni managed to push her concerns for T. G. aside just long enough to undertake the assignments before her. The nightshirt-clad student, sitting up in bed, struggled against fatigue and preoccupation to focus upon page after meticulous page of distribution maps depicting the regional habitats of several South American bird and animal species. Her career plans pointed toward a future position with one of the major American zoos, and that long-held dream now seemed but a couple of years from realization. Zoology was her love and also the major in which, one day soon, she would acquire her postgraduate degree.

Jenni tried to focus on the academic task at hand, but more than once, as she read in the warm light of a single bedside lamp, she caught herself staring at the floral wallpaper of her room, seeing his face before her. As she had told her mother, she missed *her* T. G., the one she grew up with, the one she loved—the boy who had taken a place in her heart she knew could never belong to anyone else. He had earned that place through his own long-expressed love for her, a gentleness and pure kindness she had never seen in the eyes of any other boy she had ever known.

But that had been before. Now she could only hope he would come back to her.

She thought about her young life, about the decisions she had made. Already most of her friends either had moved away, gotten their own apartments, or had married, but the twenty-three-year-old Jenni had chosen to remain at home and put every dollar she could toward her career goal. Living at home while working a part-time job in an exotic pet store had saved her thousands of dollars, which could now be used for travel and a place to live once she had joined the staff of whatever zoo facility would bring her aboard. Her mother was delighted to have her daughter still under her roof, for whatever reason, and her father greatly enjoyed the fact that the two ladies in his life enjoyed such a strong relationship.

The hour had grown late, and sleep was closing in. Bed was the wrong place to sit and study at such a late hour, for the comfortable mattress beneath her and the soft pillow behind called to her. Surrendering, she set the textbook, notebook, and pen on the bedside table, then fluffed her pillow and slid her bare legs under the cool covers. The remainder of the cherished weekend stretched out ahead of her, so she did not set her alarm clock. As her head nestled into the soft down cradle beneath it, she clicked off the green-shaded reading lamp beside her.

She lay on her back, looking up into the darkness, listening to her own breathing and the sound of the flowing, gentle heat of the floor vent. Sleep descended like a soft comforter, and its subtle embrace quickly enveloped her.

And then she was sitting on the peaceful grassy hillside of a woodland clearing, bathed in gentle rosy sunlight. A blanket was spread beneath the skirt of her flowing cotton dress, and T. G. sat beside her.

"Great lunch, Jen," he said, finishing a piece of fried chicken.

"Thanks," she smiled. He leaned over and kissed her, the scent of eleven herbs and spices still on his lips. "Mama made the pie."

"Pumpkin…my favorite," he said. When she looked down, however, the half-eaten pie was suddenly not pumpkin, but coconut cream.

And that was just fine.

Life and motion encircled them. Towering trees blocked much of the reddish sky, their copious branches densely laden with rustling foliage. Birds sang, darting across the sky and from tree to tree, swooping amid the leaves. Deer gathered at a nearby river. Herds of antelope darted through the clearing a short distance away. It was nature multiplied by ten, a song of color and music that seemed more a single, all-encompassing entity and less a gathering of singular creatures.

"Marry me," T. G. asked, taking her hand.

Her smile was reply enough. A happy tear rolled down her cheek as she leaned forward and kissed him. She held him tight, savoring him, then slowly pulled away as something remarkable drew her attention.

Jenni's eyes fixed upon a huge dark shape moving among the vast trunks nearby. She saw it only in part, but it seemed a massive, elephant-like beast, a colorful Goliath of purples and oranges that lumbered slowly amid the shadows of the forest.

"It was Uncle," T. G. said.

"What?" Jenni asked, before nodding as if she understood. Somehow, though she did not know what he meant, the statement seemed to make sense. "Oh…okay."

A rope as thick as her arm snaked its way toward them, reaching out from the trees. As Jenni watched, the end of the heavy cordage wrapped itself around T. G.'s waist like a boa constrictor. He seemed to take no notice of it.

"What is that?" she asked him.

"Don't be afraid," he said, reaching out to caress her cheek.

The rope grew taut and pulled him quickly toward the edge of the grassy clearing. Jenni rose and ran to follow but could not catch up. Something unseen slowed her, forcing her to strain with each stride as if she were running through a sea of thick gelatin. She saw the great mysterious beast moving deeper into the dark forest, the rope tied to a harness it wore, and she heard it crashing through the dense under-growth even after the darkness there had made it invisible to her.

She could not understand why T. G. did not resist the force that was taking him away from her, drawing him into the woods and its tangle of vegetation. Following as closely as her hampered speed would allow, Jenni finally reached the tree line and paused, exhausted, to catch her breath, leaning against a massive trunk as she peered into the dense timber. Her eye could barely discern him as he was swal-lowed again and again by dark curtains of ground foliage. After a moment, she began to move after him.

"Jenni," a deep, resonant voice sounded from behind her. "You cannot follow."

She stopped. And then T. G. was completely gone, dragged away into the deep woods.

"I can't lose him again," she cried out. "I can't…"

"He is mine," the voice said. "He always was. Do not be afraid."

"Who are you? I don't know you."

"You will."

She realized she could no longer hear any sign of the huge animal that had taken T. G. from her. The sky went dark and the woods even darker. Then, though she had been alone, she suddenly felt eyes upon her as if she were standing in a crowded room.

Jenni spun to find thousands of people surrounding her, dressed in hooded robes of dark umber. They gazed at her, their eyes filled with both pain and hope.

"Who are you?" she asked.

"We who hear the Voice."

And then darkness swelled around Jenni, and she became aware of her bedroom again. She awoke only partially and rolled over in bed, her mind struggling to retain its tenuous grip upon the ebbing scene.

In moments the dream faded quickly and completely away.

3

W*hy me?*

The story was no more believable than it had been the first ten times the detective had heard it. "I told you," Dave repeated, "we were rappelling on Saturday. Low on a mountainside near Crater Lake. Pyramid Peak, I think he said it was. All of a sudden, this storm blows in faster than I've ever seen and—"

"I know, I know." Police Lieutenant Robert Sebastian frowned, cutting him off. "Your friend just disappeared into the rock." The Aspen police detective was less than satisfied with David's story, for obvious reasons. But one thing seemed sure—the kid was not going to crack. "You're still stickin' with that? Really?"

"That's what happened," David insisted, looking down at his bandaged knuckles, avoiding the disbelief on the faces around him. "Look…don't you think I know this sounds nuts? This kind of thing just doesn't happen! But it did…and T. G. is gone!"

The graying mustached man seated across the desk from him was hard-nosed and impatient, and his steel eyes darted accusingly between David, another officer, and the dark single eye of a sleeping television in the corner of the room. He had looked David over pretty closely, studying the torn and disheveled clothing, the matted hair, the bandaged hands, the reddened eyes. Was the kid on drugs, maybe?

For days David had practically camped out in the police station, napping on a bench in the lobby. Again and again he was asked to speak to this officer or that, yet he knew that no one in the place took his frantic claims seriously.

"You know," Sebastian went on, "I missed the game on Sunday because of you. One of the biggest of the year. I was going to Kansas City, kid. I had tickets. The Broncos and the Chiefs, right on the forty-yard line. You know how hard it is to get seats like that, especially for an away game? But because you walked in here and brightened up our lives, things got complicated and I couldn't even watch the game on TV."

"The Broncos lost," the other officer, Detective Conner, commented.

Sebastian's nostrils flared. "That's beside the point!" He glared at David. "I'm still in a lousy mood, kid, so don't try to con me. Cut the comic-book stories."

"Here," the second officer offered, handing David a cup of cocoa. He had noticed the boy's nervousness and thought it might help calm him. But instead, David lost patience and slammed the cup to the desktop in front of him, splashing the hot liquid onto a stack of papers next to it.

"Get out there again and find him!" David demanded.

Sebastian rolled his eyes and with a loud sigh tried to save his paperwork from the rapidly expanding brown puddle. "Geezamanetti!" he shouted, his patience all but gone. "Conner, get some paper towels in here, will ya?" The second officer rushed out.

"Look…something happened that I can't explain…but it *did* happen. I came here for help. And now you grill me and look at me like I killed him or something."

"I never said you killed him…but maybe *you* just did."

"I did not! Don't twist my words around…he's missing! It's been three days now! He could be out there dying…"

"Look, kid. By the book, I shouldn't have even talked to you until last night. But like I said, on your word, we went out Sunday afternoon and looked at the spot on the cliff you told us about. All we found were two ropes…one long enough to reach the base of the cliff—"

"That was mine."

"—and another length hanging halfway down with more in a pile at the bottom. Looked like a clean cut, too."

Conner returned and handed a roll of paper towels to the detective, who immediately mopped up the spilled cocoa.

"I can't explain that," David struggled. "Like I said, when I saw it, the rope was embedded in the rock."

"During the storm."

"Yes."

"In the dark."

"Not at first—"

"And you waited out the storm by sleeping in a park rest room."

"I didn't sleep…well, maybe a little…I was so tired."

Sebastian flipped through a file folder. "Listen—"

"No, you listen. We're sitting here while T. G.'s out there somewhere—"

"Somewhere? I thought he was in the cliff side—"

"He is! I mean—"

"Look, son, we're not totally convinced that this 'T. G.' of yours even exists. No one we talked to remembers seeing him. A clerk saw *only you* when you went into his store on Forest Route 125."

"I needed a few things. T. G. waited in the car."

"Well, maybe and maybe not. But nobody just vanishes into solid rock…"

"I know!" David trembled, his head in his hands. After a moment he stood and leaned over the desk, tears welling up, his arms desperately flailing. "Look! What do I have to do?! I know it sounds impossible, but it happened! Get out there with jackhammers or something and find him! Now!"

Something had shaken the kid, Sebastian knew that much. Any thoughts he had entertained of this being a prank were fading. But why would the kid make up such a ridiculous story? What was he hiding? Was this just an elaborate hazing? The officer paused, motioning David back into the chair. His voice took on a more soothing tone.

"We get reports on all kinds of weird things in here, kid, most of 'em related to some first-time city hotshot getting out on the snow without a clue what he's doing. Too many showoffs don't stick to the marked slopes. They want to impress the girls, so they head out into the sticks…and some guys don't turn up 'til spring when the thaw hits."

"This wasn't like that…"

"So you said. Look, in your case the only evidence we have is a cut rope. Could be this friend of yours took off with someone else, and you're just wasting our time, and I missed the biggest game of the year for nothing. Isn't that it?"

"No! I told you…" Despair took hold. He dropped his head and finished quietly, weakly. "I told you what happened."

A woman entered the room and handed a large envelope to the detective, then left without saying a word. He opened it and pulled out a couple of fresh reports, along with photos of T. G.'s rope.

"Well," he began, skimming the words, "the lab says preliminary findings give us a standard eleven-millimeter kernmantle rope, or rather two pieces of one. And the ends of the two lengths don't match up, like they would with a single cut. Which means there's a piece of rope missing."

"I told you I didn't cut it. I don't know anything about a missing piece."

Conner leaned toward David. "Maybe it's wrapped around a body. As in…maybe we should dredge Crater Lake."

"You look like you're in pretty rough shape," Sebastian added, indicating the torn shirt and battered knuckles he saw before him. "A struggle, maybe?"

"No! Call my dad. George Cernan in Ithaca, New York. I told you he'll vouch for me. I already told him everything I told you."

"Look. We're all tired. Wouldn't a shower and a soft bed be great about now? The truth, kid…come on. It's getting awful late. My shift's about over. Do us all a favor. Tell me this is a prank and just go home."

As David began to protest anew, the phone rang. Sebastian answered it, then after a few seconds threw a fiery, irritated glare at the university student before him. David went silent, trembling slightly, trying to figure out what the detective was being told.

"Uh-huh. You're sure about that…I thought as much. Okay, thanks for your trouble, Lieutenant. Put him on. Line four, was it…?" He punched a flashing button on the phone, and looked accusingly at David. "We made a call and had the Ithaca police check on the whereabouts of this friend of yours. Here…" He hit a button on the speakerphone. "It's for you. Long distance. New York."

David slowly leaned close and spoke hesitatingly, not knowing what to expect. "Hello?"

"Dave? Are you okay?" The voice filled the room.

"Who is this?"

"It's T. G., Dave. Where are you?"

"T. G.?!" His thought processes froze, struggling. He stared into Sebastian's angry eyes, unsure of anything any more. "Uh… uh…where are *you?* I mean, are you okay? What happened? I saw the rope…"

"I'm *at home.* Where are you—?" He was cut off as Sebastian disconnected the call with the slam of a button. David's face was a tangled map of confusion.

"Get this kid out of here before I lock him up." Conner shook his head as he escorted the weary and bewildered hiker from the room. David struggled to explain but failed, his words echoing a jumble of nonsense down the hallway.

Sebastian stared in mourning at the cold, gray television screen.

H e was exhausted, sore, and confused.

T. G. sat sprawled on his couch, still in his climbing gear. His head back, he struggled to recall the events of the last few days—the images, the sounds, the feelings—but he kept hitting the same dead end. He remembered first the campsite, then the hike, then the storm, then—*nothing*. There was a tender place on the back of his head, a decent-sized lump that felt as if it might earlier have been even more painful and swollen. Earlier—when?

T. G. looked again upon the leathery stranger resting before him, atop the coffee table. Only its solid presence kept him from believing himself totally mad, yet at the same time it made him doubt his sanity.

He rolled his head to one side and just breathed, resting, not moving a muscle, letting gravity have its way with him. It was night, and the room was lit only by the dim, golden light of a table lamp in one corner, the one he always left on when he was going to be away. He absently and vacantly stared at its yellowed lampshade for several minutes, wanting to drink in the sight of something very ordinary, very everyday, very earthbound.

He was home, in his apartment in the old four-story Brookfelder Building. It had a largely undeserved reputation at the university for being "Nerd Central" and was occupied by more than a dozen Cornell students, but also among its residents were older folks who had lived there for twenty years or more. Although he largely kept to himself, T. G. knew many of them and, with his quiet lifestyle and taste in music, had been welcomed into the "family" of the building's elderly occupants.

He rolled his head toward the dining-room ceiling, toward the toppled dinette set and no-longer-hanging light fixture that lay in a shattered tangle on the carpet beneath. He had broken them, had crushed them less than an hour before.

When he had *landed* on them.

He sat there looking at the splintered table, his memory a blank. In the quiet of his apartment he fought to drag images up from the murky depths, before they vanished into an abyss of things cold and damp and forgotten.

At least in part, he began to remember—

∽◦∾

He was in a free fall within a hungry darkness, tumbling through a rush of acceleration and dizziness as his equilibrium was tossed and scrambled. He feared that he had fallen from that high point on the cliff face, that his rope was no longer tied at the top. For nearly ten seconds he plummeted until finally, with a loud, echoing, faraway crash, he collided with something solid and came to an abrupt, jarring stop. Lying on his back in the sudden stillness, gathering his wits as he opened his eyes, he found shapes beginning to form in the darkness, angular shapes that began to define structure and form around him. His ears heard the familiar comforting sound of a dog barking in the distance somewhere. He then noticed something soft against the back of his hand and knew it to be carpet. And familiarity finally crept in, comforting him.

T. G., groaning, rolled slowly onto his knees. Hard wood was beneath them. He stood up on wobbly legs, bracing himself against a solid form he knew, a wall. Something threw off his center of gravity. A weight of some kind.

He stumbled for a few steps, then reached out into the darkness and found a lamp switch exactly where he hoped it would be. Daggers of light flared outward as the bulb ignited, forcing T. G. to squint as his weary eyes adjusted to a scene that was one he needed to see.

His apartment. In Ithaca, New York. Two thousand miles from the cliff down which he had been rappelling.

He saw that his dining table, two of its chairs, and the overhead light fixture lay broken on the floor, and realized that he had been lying upon the tabletop since coming to rest there. He looked up at the ceiling and found not a gaping, man-shaped hole, but the same intact plaster that had always been there.

Yet I fell through it!

Looking down, he saw a segment of rope looped through his carabiners, its cleanly cut ends lying loosely a few feet away. He banged on the wall, wanting proof of the solidity of the room around him. It was quite real.

So was something else. A heavy, leathery object dangled from a wide, tooled strap slung over his shoulder, a cylindrical thing some twenty-four inches long and nine in diameter. He had no clue as to where he had gotten it, yet it seemed to belong to *him*. T. G. looked at the odd animal hide from which it was constructed, a purplish leather unlike any he had ever seen. Small bony nodules protruded here and there, glistening like pearl. Transparent yellow jewels, oval in shape, were embedded among tooled characters of a language he did not recognize. The object's entire presence seemed to speak of antiquity, of a time thousands of years past.

He lifted the strap over his head and laid the thing on the coffee table, studying its engraved symbols and jeweled inlays in the hope that some flicker of memory would come to him.

Nothing.

Running a hand along its gently pebbled surface, he was startled by a sudden pounding on his front door. "Police Department," came a deep voice from outside. T. G., still in full gear, walked over to the door and answered it as casually as was possible.

"Yes...can I help you, officer?"

"Are you T. G. Shass?" the tall, uniformed patrolman asked. He looked with some surprise at the sit harness and daypack the young man wore, noting the strands of rope trailing behind him. *Odd way to dress—*

"Yes sir," T. G. replied, knowing his appearance was unusual, if not suspicious.

"We were instructed to check on your whereabouts, Mr. Shass. May I see some identification?" T. G. fished into his pocket and produced his wallet, then handed his driver's license to the man. "Okay, son, may I come in and use your phone to call the station?"

"Sure," he answered. Closing the door behind the man, T. G. absentmindedly reached up to rub his normally clean-shaven chin. His fingers found there more beard stubble than he had ever allowed himself to have. Puzzled, a question leaped from his lips. "What day is this?"

"Tuesday."

"No, I mean the date."

"It's the twenty-eighth...for about another hour."

"October?"

The middle-aged policeman studied him, having noted the smashed dinette. There was no sign, no scent of alcohol in the room. "You sure you're okay, son? Did you fall?"

"Uh, yeah...sorry," he said, having no real idea what to say and hoping the man would not question him too heavily. "Lost my balance."

The officer eyed him a bit suspiciously, but determined nothing untoward had taken place. "Yes," the man concluded. "It's October."

After a moment, T. G.'s addled mind finally remembered the wristwatch he wore. He glanced down at its familiar round face and wide leather band. Silver metal gleamed in the dim light. Its hands read six forty-five. Its calendar read October 25. Its second hand was moving.

Assuming it was correct, he had lost three days somewhere.

T. G. shook his head slightly and muttered quietly to himself, his jarred mind struggling to make sense of the facts. "We were hiking...it was Saturday...and that was the twenty-fifth...but that was *just now...*"

And T. G. suddenly realized just how intensely he really, really had to use the bathroom.

When he reemerged, he found the policeman still on the phone, looking at the mysterious object on the coffee table.

"What is this?" the uniformed man asked.

"Just an, uh, art project. For the school."

The officer turned his attention back to the phone. "Okay, Mr. Shass, your ID checks out. I'm being hooked into long distance, here…seems someone wants to talk to you." The officer handed the receiver to T. G., and the call was patched into another one to Aspen.

It was a short conversation. As T. G. set the phone back on its cradle, the officer headed back toward the door. "You're *sure* you're okay?"

"Yeah. I'm fine…I just…fell. Clumsy…lost my balance." He glanced at the phone. "The guy I was just talking to…David…where was he?"

"I don't know, son. They didn't tell me."

T. G. nodded. Wherever David was, T. G. assumed, at least he had the car and could get home.

"You're *sure?*" the officer asked, leaving.

"I'm fine…thanks."

The officer took one final glance at the smashed table. "Well, from now on, Mr. Shass, you might want to do your mountain climbing on a mountain. Good night."

∽∾∾

T. G. looked at the collapsed furniture. He was grateful that his pack had at least partially cushioned his fall from—no, *through* the still-intact ceiling. For some reason, it occurred to him that the crushed dinette was a rental. He smiled when he caught himself wondering about the damages he would have to pay.

Like that matters now…

He knew that something transcendent had happened to him, something larger than he was ready to comprehend. He hoped that all would be explained to him somehow—and soon—for he was dying to understand. His factual, normal, explainable existence had melded with the supernatural, the paranormal, the unreal. He did not know what had happened to him, but he did know that his life had changed forever. He was not ready for that.

He was too wound up now to sleep. His body was physically weary, but he was mentally alert and pumped on adrenaline. What to do? There was no immediate way to reach David—he would just have to wait for him to call again. What had *he* seen? Had he been with T. G. those three lost days? Did he know where this artifact had come from? Was he as sound as he had seemed on the phone?

Running down a mental checklist, T. G. leaned over, reached for the phone, and dialed a number he had dialed many times over. After a few anxious rings, a sleepy, feminine voice answered with the unmistakable seasoning of an upbringing in Hertfordshire, England.

"Hello?"

"Dr. Abelwhite, this is T. G."

"T. G.? It's…" She checked her alarm clock. "It's after midnight. Are you calling from Colorado?"

"No…but I *was* there, until just now…I mean…something's happened. I need to see you up at the lab."

"Now?"

"Yes."

"Can it wait 'til morning? I'll be up there first thing."

He looked down at the tooled leather object. "No…I don't think so. I have something here…and I need to talk to someone. Someone I can trust. Things have happened…and I found something."

"What is it? What did you find?"

"I don't know, but I'm pretty sure it's an artifact of some kind. It's in great shape, but I get the feeling that it could be older than, well…it could be older than *everything*."

"Is it Shoshone, do you think?"

As T.G looked at the intricate artifact and its odd tooling, a slight smile snuck into the corner of his mouth. "I really don't think so. This isn't exactly a pine-needle basket."

There was a pause, then the professor continued. "Okay. Can you give me about forty-five minutes?"

"Sure. Thank you. I'll see you then." T. G. hung up the phone and stood, hefting the object by its carry strap before setting it on the couch. "What *are* you?" he asked it, half expecting an answer. He shivered and noticed for the first time how cold his apartment had become.

The thermometer on the thermostat read in the low sixties. He adjusted it up and heard warm air streaming from the vents. The room only got colder.

After pausing to shower and shave, T. G. dressed in fresh clothes, treated his scraped-up forearm, and began to gather those things he would be taking with him. He found the exposed rolls of film in his day-pack pocket, but did not remember taking them all. *Perhaps there's an answer there!* He put them into a paper bag and left the apartment, the artifact once again slung over his shoulder. As he made his way down the dimly lit hallway, looking back every few steps, he had an intense, very uncomfortable feeling of being watched. Of being followed.

Of being hunted.

He finally reached the front door of the building. Swinging it open, he was hit by a wall of frozen air. It had snowed, transforming Ithaca into a wonderland of white and crystal. His breath fogged, the phantom cloud vanishing as it glowed in the yellowish glare of the parking lot lights. There was a heavy silence hanging all around him, one so intense that he could almost feel its pressure against his eardrums. No wind, no sirens, nothing, as if he were indoors within a huge domed enclosure of some kind. He had always been amazed at the way snow muffled sound.

He quickened his pace, almost running, and found his car safely in the parking lot outside. He never saw anyone else, except for an elderly man in the distance who routinely walked his cocker spaniel each night at midnight. But the feeling persisted, and even as he tried the ignition he continued to check his rearview mirror. The old blue Chrysler started after only a couple of attempts, but not soon enough for T. G. He felt an intangible panic that screamed at him—*hurry!*

It had been an early snow. The white blanket shrouded everything except the streets themselves, which were dark and wet, reflecting street lights, stoplights, and even a smattering of Christmas lights put up by a family who could not wait for Halloween and Thanksgiving to pass first. He drove quickly down the slick road, checking his mirror one more time as he turned onto a wide well-lit street. A measure of relief set in, which increased with every mile he put between himself and his apartment.

"What's the matter with you?" he asked himself aloud, banging the steering wheel as he tried to talk himself out of the feeling. He glanced down at the artifact on the passenger's seat, watching as the cold light from the passing street lamps played upon it again and again. It looked like something alive, somehow.

As a comfort he turned on the radio, but found himself still checking his back every so often. The heater in his car blew warm air against his sneakered feet, which felt colder than they should have, despite his thick cotton socks. T. G. cranked the fan up all the way, but even with his heavy coat he remained uncomfortable and could not get warm.

The feeling that he was being followed finally disappeared as he neared the school and saw, above the trees, the familiar lines of the bell tower, bathed in floodlight against the dark gray night sky. *One hundred sixty-one steps to the top*, he smiled, remembering a time the previous spring when, with an hour to kill, he had counted them.

He arrived at a parking lot near one of the science buildings. T. G. had seen but a handful of other cars on the lots around Cornell, for there were few night classes and none that ran so late. He allowed himself a slight smile as he pulled into a space, for he recognized one of the few vehicles nearby as belonging to Dr. Abelwhite. *Good, she's already arrived.*

∽◦∾

"Amazing," she uttered quietly, using a magnifying lamp to examine the surface of the puzzle upon her lab table. "I've never seen hide like this. And this style of tooling is unknown to the archaeological world, as far as I know. Where did this come from? There in Colorado, you said?"

"I…think so," T. G. cautiously answered, excitement building within him. "To be honest, I can't quite remember. I know I wasn't *looking* for anything. I must have found it…accidentally." He leaned over the table for a closer look.

"How can you not remember? Are you all right? Did you hit your head?"

He rubbed the knot. "I do have a bit of a bump back there, but—"

"Here, let me see." She looked at his head, gently feeling the lump. "Quite a goose egg," she said, motherly concern in her voice. "Have you seen a doctor?"

"No. But I'm okay. Really."

"Possible amnesia doesn't sound okay. You may have sustained a concussion. Do you have a headache?"

"No. None. Honest…I'm okay. But I'll see someone tomorrow, anyway."

"See that you do," she smiled.

The lab was well equipped, with every conceivable analysis tool placed at the disposal of Dr. Abelwhite, her staff, and her students. A tray of stainless steel instruments sat to one side of the leather-bound mystery.

"Well, I'm sorry to say this, T. G., but whatever this is, it can't be very old. The leather's like new. Still full of natural oils and very flexible. No dryness or cracking at all." The hint of British upbringing that lived within each word she spoke seemed to lend added authority and finality to her prognosis. "I'd say maybe forty years, at the outside, but that's just a guess." T. G.'s hopes fell at that, for he very badly wanted the artifact to be ancient.

"Are you sure? I mean, it *has* to be older than that."

"Why?"

"I don't know. It just…*does*."

Carlene Abelwhite knew her stuff. The woman had mastered archaeology at Cambridge University at the youthful age of twenty-one, attaining not only her degree but the deep and abiding respect of those who instructed her as well. She had led three expeditions to the Valley of the Kings in Egypt, uncovering two previously unknown tombs belonging to the family of Ramses, and was largely responsible for the discovery and partial excavation of a subterranean tunnel network beneath the Incan city of Machu Picchu in Peru. Her work near the Temple Mount in Jerusalem, leading to definitive proof of the reign of Pilate, had won worldwide acclaim from her peers. Museums around the world, including those in Cairo, London, and New York, prized the ancient treasures she had unearthed during her many travels, and her reputation had caused Cornell to bend over backward in bringing her to the university. T. G., who had accompanied her as a grad student on two recent expeditions, had grown quite close to her following the death of his parents, and he looked upon her as both friend and mentor—with a tiny bit of grandmother thrown in.

She had been a primary factor in T. G.'s fourth-year decision to switch his major from political science to archaeology, the course in which he had then decided to pursue his master's degree. Her passion for the uncovering of the past had been infectious, and his time spent with her in the field had given him a personal satisfaction he had never found in any other calling. Dr. Abelwhite recognized his gift for antiquities and had taken him under her wing, sharing with him the intricacies of her chosen field and giving him encouragement in every way possible.

"It's simply in too fine a condition to be any older, I'm afraid," she concluded.

T. G. looked at it for a moment, a memory surfacing. "What if…what if it had been preserved somehow, so it wouldn't dry out and would stay looking new?"

"No one in the ancient world had a method for doing that, T. G."

"What if someone *did?*"

She looked at him suspiciously, thinking he was holding something back. "Preserved...*how?*"

"Well," he began, a fleeting image flashing in his mind. He turned away, struggling to keep a grip on it. "What if this was sealed or something, in the dark, inside a"—his hands made motions as if to define the size of an object—"inside a...*something?*" He shook his head, frustrated. "I don't know. It's as if I can almost remember...as if there's something there that just won't..." He sighed.

The professor ran a cotton-gloved hand along the supple surface of the artifact, considering the possibility. "Then, I'd say, it could be much, much older...but a simple vacuum would still draw the moisture out of it." She waited a moment, looking at him, hoping to jar a memory. "What kind of container are we talking about?"

"I can't remember..." He tried again to approximate a size and shape with his hands. "I'm not sure...I think..." His face fell. "Oh, it's completely gone now. I'm sorry. I just can't seem to grab hold of it." He reached into his coat pocket and pulled out the small sack of film. "But I took these slides while I was in Colorado. Maybe something's in one of them that will give us some answers." Handing the bag to her, he looked down at the relic and pointed to an embedded amber crystal on the surface of the hide. "What are these things on here, anyway? Jewels?"

Dr. Abelwhite looked closely at the deep yellow substance, tapping it with a steel probe. "I don't know. It looks a lot like amber, but it seems flawless." She tapped it again. "And it doesn't sound organic. Doesn't seem quite crystalline, either. I'd have to take a sample."

"I don't want to damage it."

"Well, maybe the lab could run a spectral analysis without harming it. But I'd probably have to take samples to pin it down. Same goes for the other 'stones' and whatever's inside this. Have you opened it?"

T. G. moved closer in order to look through the magnifying lens. "No. I didn't see any way in, and I sure didn't want to mess it up before I knew what I was doing. Look at it. Do you see any seams? I didn't. It almost looks like it *grew* that way."

She examined it again, rotating the artifact with T. G.'s help so as to look at it from every angle. "No. I don't see anything either. But it must open in some way."

There came a knock, and T. G. turned to see Dr. Al Virdon of radiology leaning through the doorway. "We're ready, Carlene. Anytime you are."

"Thank you, Al," she smiled. "And thank you for coming in at this hour." One of her standing rules had always been for unpretentiousness among those with whom she worked, meaning that titles were out. She liked to keep those around her on a first-name basis, for it had been her experience that she and her peers had always functioned more as a unit when the walls of formality had been removed. For the sake of proper respect, that rule had never extended to her students, save those few with whom she had grown particularly close. T. G., however, had never felt comfortable calling the fifty-nine-year-old scholar by her first name, despite her repeated requests that he do so.

"If you will bring this along, T. G.," she began, rising from the lab table, "we'll see what the x-rays will tell us."

It did not take long. Side views, end views, exposures from every angle were shot. Then standard detail photos were taken of the artifact's exterior, which would provide close-up views of every square inch of its surface, further aiding their attempt at analysis.

T. G. paced like an expectant father as he waited for the results. After twenty minutes had passed, a call summoned the professor and him back into radiology.

"Doesn't look like these are going to be of much help," Dr. Virdon said, handing the x-ray transparencies to Dr. Abelwhite. She slid them into clamps over the wall-mounted light table, then studied them for any sign of revelation. As they examined the film, it became apparent very quickly that the artifact was not going to give up its secrets easily.

"Look at that," the learned woman sighed, pointing to a dark mass that filled the artifact to a point just within its outer edges. "It's opaque to x-rays for the most part. It must have an inner lining of some kind. Leaded cloth, maybe. The artifact *is* heavy, but I don't think it's heavy enough to have a solid metal core." She looked closer, focusing her attention at the dark patches along its outer contours. "This is odd. Those amber gems along the periphery, here...and here...don't look like they should. Stones wouldn't have this signature. Whatever these are, they x-ray like...well, like metal."

"What could cause that?"

"I don't know, T. G. It would seem that your prize is going to be a tougher nut to crack than I originally thought. Can you leave it with me for a few days?"

"Well," he began, thinking carefully, "you know I'd trust you with my life. But this thing...something keeps nagging at me that, well, that isn't like anything I've ever felt on any dig I've been on. I mean, I've found all kinds of pottery shards and fossils, and even that jeweled urn, remember? But this...I just can't let it out of my sight. Not yet, anyway. I feel a *responsibility* connected with this somehow. You know? Does that make any sense?"

She smiled. "It's all right, T. G. I know how you feel...I felt the same way about *my* first major find." She glanced at a wall clock. "I'll tell you what...could you meet me back in the lab in about twelve hours, say this afternoon around three-thirty?"

"Sure. What's up?"

"First thing in the morning, I'll show the detail shots we just took to Professor Kerrod in zoology and see if he can help in determining what kind of hide this is. That'll help pin down its area of origin. No need for you to be here for that. Besides, by this afternoon the photo lab will have finished developing the slides you took."

"Sure, Doctor," T. G. smiled, wearily lifting the relic from the x-ray table. "I'll be here. I need answers. Right now, though, what I need most is some sleep in my own bed."

5

T. G. slowly opened his eyes to find himself on his back, staring up into utter blackness. He sat up, then stood, hoisting the arti-fact into place over his shoulder. He was dressed in his pajamas. His mind fought to grasp his surroundings, to understand how he had come to be in their midst, but failed.

He stood on a vast featureless plain, one that was utterly flat, totally smooth, devoid of either color or life. He looked off into every direction, seeing only the extreme monotony of the terrain as it extended into infinite distance. There was no curvature, as one would expect of a planetary surface, no actual horizon—only the haze of dis-tance unimpeded by any obstacle—and without landmarks, he could not begin to determine how far he could see before the failing clarity fogged his perception. He realized that blinking did not interrupt his vision—whether his eyes were closed or open, his hand held up before them or not, he saw just the same. He began to realize that there was no real illumination, no light that he could see, yet somehow still he *could* see, with his mind as if with his eyes.

A wind whipped up, tossing his hair. He felt a palpable isolation more intense than any he had known in his life. He felt even more lonely than when his mother and father had died.

It was a deep aloneness, one that permeated his being down to its most basic and primal foundation. As he looked from side to side, straining to make out anything that might have stood in the distance, he realized that he was the sole occupant of whatever place this was. Insecurity built within him, drawing its strength from all of the fears and confusion of his childhood.

"Hello, T. G.," a voice suddenly said, coming from right behind him.

Startled, he spun, expecting to come face to face with whoever had spoken. Instead, he found himself still alone, shaking slightly from the adrenaline rush. Disorientation tried to gain a foothold and he began to lose his balance, but T. G. fought it back, focusing his reason upon the impossible situation at hand. Then his eyes detected a tiny, dark shape emerging from the uncertainty some miles away, a human shape. "Hello," T. G. tried, speaking quietly, experimenting.

"Remember this place," the voice continued. T. G. realized that sound carried most oddly here, that distance and volume and clarity had no quarrel with one another. He stared intently at the tiny far-away shape, knowing that it was the source of the words, watching as it steadily and patiently walked closer.

"Where am I?" he asked it.

"Nowhere."

"Why am I nowhere?"

"This is all there is."

T. G. blinked. Suddenly, the figure stood right before him, barely more than an arm's length away. The stark white of his hair and the blue of his robe contrasted harshly with the warm bronze of his skin. His eyes were kind yet intensely powerful, his expression tranquil yet determined.

"How long have I been here?" T. G. asked.

"No time, T. G."

He glanced around. "I…I don't want to be here," he said.

"You're not. Nothing…*is*."

"I don't understand."

"You will." The cold wind increased, but silently. No whistling in the trees, no roar in the distance. The man's hair and robes danced and billowed as he spoke. "All that must be, will be. The dawn declares the end, from eternity to eternity."

"Who are you?"

"I'm someone who is here to keep you safe."

"I feel so…alone."

"You're never alone." There was a pause. The man gestured toward the horizon. "Look. It is *time*."

As T. G. watched, the vast flat plain began to drop from sight in the distance, curving away from him, sloping down in all directions as if it were melting over something immense and spherical. It then fell away beneath his feet, and he found himself floating free, hanging like a feather on air. Suddenly, from nowhere, rose a silent and engulfing deluge of duration and motion and substance, a newborn current of actuality, sweeping him along violently as it sought its limits. A brilliant light flared to life directly above, a light of warmth and brilliance like none T. G. had ever known, rolling back upon itself the blackness that had been overhead. Vertigo overtook his senses and he began to black out. He heard the roar of waters, already intense and growing louder. Closer.

The phone rang.

T. G.'s eyes flashed open and were immediately filled with the textured white ceiling of his bedroom. Gray daylight flooded through the curtained window. He was utterly awake, alert and ready, his heart pounding in his chest as if he had just run up a flight of stairs. Cold sweat chilled his forehead. He rolled to one side and reached for the bedside table as the phone once again sounded.

"Hello?"

"T. G.? It's almost four o'clock. We're waiting for you. Are you coming?"

He sat up, rubbing his eyes. "Oh…yes, Doctor. I am…I'm sorry…"

"Listen. We've come up with something. Something incredible. Please get down here right away, and bring the artifact with you."

"What? What did you—"

"It would be better if you just got here as quickly as you can. Hurry."

"Okay. I'll be right there. Fifteen minutes." Hanging up, he clicked the hook and dialed a number that long had been precious to him. There was a ring.

"Hello?" a welcome voice asked.

"Jenni?"

"T. G.? Are you okay? I tried to call you last night, late. David called, looking for you. He said something about you vanishing in Colorado and suddenly being back here—"

"Is he okay?"

"I think so. He wasn't on the phone for long. What's going on? Why are you back and he's not?"

"Long story. Look, will you be home tonight? I really need to talk. Something's happened and…well, it's just a long story."

There was a note of hesitation in her voice. "I'll be here."

"Listen. Call David's mom and tell her I said everything's okay, so she can tell him if he calls…" His words fell away. "Never mind. I'll call her later."

"Well, okay."

"I have to go, but I'll call you in a little bit."

"There's a lot I want to talk about too," the girl said.

After a quick good-bye, he hung up, seeing her face before him. Perhaps it was not too late, after all.

T. G. realized that the apartment was even colder than when he had gone to bed. Wrapping in his bedspread, he walked to the thermostat. It was set for eighty, yet the room had dropped all the way to the high forties. He held his hand up into the register airflow and found the stream to be quite warm.

"I don't get it," he said. He glanced at the windows and saw no movement of the thick, white drapes. They were shut, just as they were supposed to be. *So why is it so cold in here?* A nervous chill coursed down his spine, forcing a shiver from his shoulder blades. The whole place suddenly gave him the creeps.

He hurriedly dressed, grabbed the artifact and his long coat, and left, pausing in the hallway as he locked the door. He was glad to be out of the apartment. The hall was cold as well, but then it always was. He ran down the three flights of stairs, as he had so many times, into the building's ornate, aged entry hall. Walking past the mailboxes, he paused to check his own and found it empty.

"T. G.?" a voice asked. "I *thought* that was you." He turned to see the smiling, elderly Mrs. Lucreia, dressed in a floral robe, leaning out of her apartment door and into the hall. She was the oldest of the building's residents, having lived there since a year after her marriage in 1921. Her husband had passed away during the war years, and she had never remarried. For her the world had changed little since then—the crooning of Bing Crosby usually filled her apartment, she still listened to an old 1930s-model Philco radio, and she even left her door unlocked most of the time. She was one of the friendliest people T. G. had ever met, and he had developed quite an affection for her. "I thought you were going to be gone until next weekend."

"Well, I thought so too. But it didn't turn out that way."

"How is that pretty girlfriend of yours?" As she spoke, T. G. noticed the slight fog of her breath as it danced fleetingly before her.

"We had a fight…and, well, I think that might have been it as far as anything serious goes. I don't know. I *did* call her, just now, actually…"

"Oh no, dear," she frowned. "Please…you two make such a sweet couple. Work things out, okay?"

He smiled, looking into the bright eyes of the kind woman. "Yes ma'am…I'll see what I can do."

"Oh…I almost forgot the reason I came out here in the first place. Is your apartment cold?"

"Yes, very."

"I tried calling the super, but he can't get out here until tonight. It's never been this cold in here…not even when the old coal boiler had to be taken out, back in '56. I thought once we went to gas this kind of thing wasn't supposed to happen. At least that's what they said…"

He cut her off gently, knowing from past experience that she would keep him there in conversation all day if he let her. "Boy," he said, looking at his watch, "you know, I'm late for an appointment at the school, Mrs. Lucreia. Let me know what the super says once he gets here…tell him my apartment's cold too."

"I will, dear."

"I'll talk to you later. Stay inside and try to keep warm." He hurried away, down the stairs and out the front entrance, into the snow.

∞∞

"Sorry I'm so late," T. G. apologized, walking into the professor's office. He loved the feel of the place—hundreds of books lined the walls, along with statuettes and curios from Dr. Abelwhite's many travels. It was a busy room, assembled by a busy woman who was seated at her desk, speaking with another professor who sat across from her.

"Ah, T. G. Excellent. I think you know Professor Eugene Kerrod," she said, indicating the white-headed, white-bearded, heavyset man. They shook hands.

"Yes," T. G. remembered. "We met once."

"So this is the artifact?" the man asked, indicating the object hanging from T. G.'s shoulder. "Forgive me for being so abrupt, but this is rather extraordinary."

"Yes, this is it," T. G. answered, swinging the object outward so that the man could get a better look. "I brought it here last night and—"

The man interrupted, speaking excitedly to Professor Abelwhite. "May we get this right to Dr. Leighton? Now that I see it in person, I'm more certain than ever."

"Of course," she said, picking up the phone.

"What...what is it?" T. G. asked, puzzled. Professor Kerrod motioned for him to remain quiet and wait.

She dialed an extension then spoke. "We have it with us now. We're on our way up." She hung up then began toward the door. "Come along, gentlemen."

"Dr. Abelwhite," T. G. began as they made their way down the largely empty corridor, "what's the big deal? What did you figure out?"

"We're not sure yet," she said. "Professor Kerrod suggested I send some of the detail photos I took last night up to Dr. Leighton's office, and he got back to me about fifteen minutes later. He seems to have at least a partial answer to our little puzzle, but he hasn't fully shared it with us as yet. He said he didn't want to sound foolish, so first he wants to examine your find personally."

"But he's a paleontologist."

"Wait just a few more minutes. Perhaps you'll have an answer."

T. G. nodded, hating to wait. Patience had never been a virtue of his.

They entered the faculty conference room. Dr. Corbridge Leighton was seated at the head of the table, looking over some notes. He was an intriguing figure, his well-lined leathery face and pale hair betraying decades spent under the Montana sun. He stood as the others entered, holding a pipe in his teeth, his right arm outstretched.

"Come in, come in," he said. "So…you must be Mr. Shass."

"Yes sir," T. G. replied, extending a hand and shaking Leighton's.

Dr. Abelwhite, wanting to cut to the chase for T. G.'s sake, indicated the artifact. "This is the object, Corey. I certainly hope we aren't wasting your time."

After Kerrod swept a few papers aside, T. G. set the heavy object on the large, polished walnut table that took up most of the room. Leighton leaned closer, adjusting his glasses, intently studying the twenty-four-inch leather-bound mystery. The others took seats at the table and sat quietly, watching him.

He puffed on his pipe a few times, never taking his eyes from the artifact. T. G. barely breathed as he watched the man, wondering what was firing in his mind as sharply analytical wheels went into motion. The man ran his fingers along the object, turning it over now and again, studying its every detail.

"Incredible," Leighton finally said, taking his seat. He opened a textbook he had brought with him, then sorted through a few notes in an adjacent file folder. After looking at an entry in the textbook, his ancient, brilliant eyes pivoted upward toward the others. He took a deep breath then sat silently, undecided whether to speak.

"What is it, Corbridge?" Kerrod implored him. "Was I right?"

"Yes, my friend." He looked at T. G. "Son, you have made the scientific and archeological find of the century." The young man's eyes widened.

"Say it, Corey," Abelwhite prodded.

He removed his glasses, then puffed on his pipe yet again. T. G. looked at the others, then at Leighton once more.

"The hide that covers this artifact," the man began, "is ceratopsian. There is no mistake."

"Inconceivable," Abelwhite said, her voice low and incredulous.

"Yes," Leighton continued. "I thought so too, after seeing your pictures. But a find in southern Wyoming just last year gave us an almost perfect impression of the ventral skin of a juvenile *Torosaurus gladius,* the first we've found. Much like triceratops, but a bit larger. Until then, in fact, the genus itself was known only from a pair of skulls that had been found, and one of those was incomplete." He stood. "Not only was the new skeleton complete…but beneath it, preserved in the rock, was an impression of much of the skin of the neck and forward abdomen. It matches this precisely," he concluded, indicating the artifact.

T. G. was stunned. "Dinosaur skin? How can that—"

"When I saw it," Kerrod began, "I knew it was unlike the dermis of any known living species. Those bony nodules and that pebbled scale pattern don't exist in nature. Not anymore."

Dr. Abelwhite looked to Leighton, hoping for an answer. "So what does it mean, Corey? Is this artifact millions of years old? Were there men alive back then to make it, if it is? Why isn't it dust by now? Or were there a few dinosaurs around until recently, waiting to be made into luggage?"

He smiled. "I doubt that. In a part of Siberia, so many woolly mammoths are frozen in the tundra that their remains make up more than half the soil. Hunters have long fed their sled dogs on the mammoths' frozen meat, although it isn't fit for human consumption. I suppose it's possible that this hide was recovered in the same way, but the evidence we have makes that seem unlikely. So far as we know, the genus represented here existed nowhere other than Wyoming, and frozen tundra has been a bit scarce there for a very, very long time."

Kerrod spoke up. "Not to mention that those mammoths lived only a few tens of thousands of years ago. Millions are another matter…"

"And this hide," Leighton added, once more leaning over the object, "gives the appearance of having been taken from a living animal. For it to have been tooled this way, with the flexibility it had to possess then, and still possesses now…this could only have been done if the creature had been freshly slaughtered and the hide tanned immediately."

"But the apparent age of the artifact…," Abelwhite began. "It seems no more than a few decades old, if that. T. G. believes that it was somehow preserved…sealed in a protective container of some kind."

"Aliens?" Kerrod threw out, only half kidding.

Leighton smiled. "Oh, now don't let our friend Carl hear you say that."

"My pictures," T. G. questioned, looking to her. "Did you develop them?"

Abelwhite shook her head. "They were all overexposed, T. G. No images at all. Something ruined the film. Whatever photographic evidence you may have had of the artifact's place of origin is gone."

His eyes fell. "What about the characters inscribed in the leather? What does it say? Anything?"

She shook her head. "As far as I've been able to determine, it isn't even close to any language ever known to have been written on Earth. I'm not a linguist, but I've seen a lot of writing in my day. I've found no root language to compare it to. Nothing."

Kerrod made a warbled whistle under his breath, imitating the sound of a flying saucer in an old science-fiction movie. Leighton and Abelwhite both smiled. Both wondered if he was not so far from the truth.

"Quite a mystery we have on our hands, my friends," Leighton went on, puffing on his pipe. "A jeweled relic, apparently no more than half a century old, covered in a seamless dinosaur hide with no apparent access to the interior and tooled with words in a language never recorded by man."

"The jewels," T. G. asked. "The amber things all over it. What are they?"

"There we have an answer," Abelwhite said. "But even so, that holds another puzzle, I'm afraid. We ran a spectral analysis this morning. As I suspected, they're not amber."

"What are they?" T. G. asked, on the edge of his seat.

"Gold."

"Gold? But they're clear…you can see right through them. I mean, gold isn't—"

"These must be *atomically pure*…so absolutely pure they're transparent. There's no known way to produce gold like this from any ore ever found on the planet. There are always some impurities, if only on the molecular level. In thicknesses like these, no. We cannot produce gold like this."

"How can gold be transparent? Just because it's pure—"

"You've seen it, T. G.," Kerrod chimed in. "Remember the visors on the helmets of the astronauts who walked on the moon? They were coated with a protective layer of gold, one only microns thick so as to allow light to pass through. It served as a radiation filter and heat reflector. It was an awfully thin layer, I'll grant you, but transparent it was." He looked at the relic. "But she's right. Transparent 'nuggets' as thick as those just can't be. Not by any process known to man, now or ever."

T. G. stared at the artifact, excited and fearful. "So now what?"

"I announce my retirement and go fishing," Leighton smiled.

"We open it up," Abelwhite said. "We see what's inside."

❦

It had not gone well.

Kerrod and Leighton, with pressing appointments to keep, momentarily left the artifact in the very capable hands of their esteemed fellow educator and promised to return as soon as they were able. Alone in the controlled stillness of the sciences lab, T. G. and Abelwhite huddled over the object with a battery of swing-arm lamps, macro-focus cameras, and magnifying lenses arranged in place around them.

"This doesn't make any sense," the woman said to T. G., who sat next to her at the worktable. Leaning back, she slammed the handle of her scalpel to the hard tabletop and sighed loudly.

"It won't cut," she said in frustration. "The blade won't even make an impression in the hide, despite the fact that it's pliable to the touch. It's as if the more pressure one applies, the firmer the material resists. Going the other way, I even tried a very light touch…but whatever I do, it just dulls the blade."

"What could cause that?" T. G. asked.

"Nothing," she said in disbelief, turning to him. "Nothing can. It's impossible…which seems more and more a common trait with this thing. A few minutes ago, while you were in the other room, I put a drop of sulfuric acid onto it, near the end, here," she indicated. "It rolled off like water on a duck's back, then proceeded to eat a decent pit into my table."

"Well, what's Plan B? How else do we open it?"

She directed T. G. to carry the relic over to an oil-cooled band saw normally used to section geodes and other mineral specimens. He hesitated, eyeing the toothy blade.

"Must we?" he asked. "I hate the thought of just ripping into it like that."

"So do I, but—"

"Maybe there isn't *anything* inside it. Maybe it's just a solid, purely decorative thing used in some sort of ritual."

"Possibly," she agreed. "But the gold, the hide it's covered with, and the fact that it won't yield so much as a scratch to a scalpel all seem to indicate that a technology beyond our own fashioned it. I can't believe something so sophisticated could be but a talisman. But it's your decision, T. G. If you want to leave well enough alone, we will."

He ran a hand along the cool surface of the artifact, hoping to stumble upon some way into it that their microscopic examination had missed. It continued its silence, its secrets held within.

"Okay," he agreed. "Go ahead." He helped to position the object on the saw table as she adjusted the guide plate and blade height. Handing T. G. a pair of safety goggles, she placed her own over her eyes and flipped the switch on the saw. It roared to life, its thin blade becoming a blur as it reached full speed.

"I'm going to try to slice into it near the end of the object, here," she pointed, shouting over the roar of the saw. "I'll take the very end off. That should do the least damage to whatever's inside." She pressed the artifact forward, rolling it slightly until it came into contact with the flashing teeth of the saw blade.

The blade screamed as pressure was applied. T. G. put his hands over his ears as the piercing sound bored through his eardrums and into his skull. She pressed harder and the metal of the saw blade whined louder in protest, making a sound T. G. did not know metal could make. After a few seconds, she pulled back to examine the point at which the hide had contacted the cutting edge. There was not a mark on it, nothing to show that they had even tried to penetrate it.

"Well, I'll be a—" she said, tossing her goggles aside in defeat.

T. G. moved over to take a closer look at the still-pristine object. "I don't get it. You've been all over the world. There has to be something you can think of that explains this. I mean—"

"We're in uncharted territory now, T. G. I can't begin to explain this. All my years of experience and research put together mean *nothing* right now, not when something like this happens."

He noticed the saw blade. "Look," he whispered, reaching out to run a fingertip along its edge. At once he jerked his hand away and put the burned finger into his mouth. "Aaahhhh…it's hot!"

Abelwhite looked closer. The blade was discolored, with odd blues splotched along its length. The little detail T. G. had been trying to point out was that its teeth were gone.

"That was a tempered carbon blade," she said slowly, shaking her head in bewilderment. "I've cut everything from granite to titanium to spacecraft-grade steel on that saw. If I weren't so fascinated, I think I'd be scared to death."

"Maybe we should just leave well enough alone," T. G. suggested, shaking his head in stunned amazement. "I guess we can just let some museum display it as it is. I mean, I'd love to see what's inside it as much as you would, but—"

"T. G., I don't think you understand," Abelwhite began, gripping him by the upper arm, her tone intense. "This thing shouldn't have stood against that blade for a millisecond. What we just saw was a violation of physical law. *Something* got in the way, keeping the blade from touching the leather…something harder than any material we know of. Something invisible—"

"But I can feel the grain of the leather with my fingers," he said, rubbing it.

"Whatever is there is there only when it needs to be, to protect the object. That carbon blade never touched the dinosaur skin. It couldn't have. It would have gone through it like butter." She walked over to a table and took a seat, then momentarily removed her glasses and rubbed her tired eyes with one hand.

"And so much for pulling a genetic sample of the hide," she continued, making a few notes on a yellow pad. "Poor Eugene was positively drooling at the prospect." She almost smiled. "I'm getting too old for this. Everything I've ever unearthed…everything *anybody's* ever unearthed…has always been made of known materials, has always obeyed the laws of action/reaction, and has always aged as one would expect according to the second law of thermodynamics. This thing looks as new as the day it was made. And at this point, since all the rules have been thrown out the window, I'd be willing to concede that that day could have been millions of years ago."

"Millions?" T. G. whispered under his breath.

"Maybe billions. One thing's for sure. This object, whatever it is, is utterly priceless. Not only to the archeological community, but to all of science. It holds a mystery for practically every field of study. It's covered with tanned dinosaur hide. It's studded with a form of gold that is impossible for our technology to produce, even in the laboratory. It's inscribed with a language that as far as I can tell is totally unknown to man. It has some kind of protective layer about it that kicks in only when it needs to. And given all that, it could contain anything from a compact thermonuclear device to a weapon that's millions of years ahead of anything we know. For all we know it may even contain the original blueprints for Earth, or God's home address and telephone number."

"Maybe it's a specimen container," T. G. offered. "Think of what it might hold. Wouldn't that be something…maybe a living dinosaur egg in suspended animation or something."

"Or what if it contains a disease organism or virus…maybe even one that *wiped out* the dinosaurs. That'd answer that little puzzle, wouldn't it?" She threw down her pencil and hung her head, rubbing her eyes. "I've been so foolish. Just goes to prove that you're never too old to do stupid things. If this thing really is that old, we dare not open it, not even if we find a way to. Not unless it's done under strictly controlled conditions." She rubbed her eyes again, then the back of her neck. "I've been thinking like an archaeologist, not like a pure scientist. A virus that was commonplace so long ago would have disappeared by now or at the very least would have mutated. We'd have no defense whatsoever against its original form. This object needs to go into a quarantine facility before we even think of trying to open it again."

"Do you think Professor Kerrod's right?"

"About what, T. G.?"

"Aliens. Maybe this thing comes from somewhere else. Sure would explain a lot, wouldn't it? I mean, I've read about 'lost time' and all. It's a UFO phenomenon, and I've got three days to account for."

She smiled. "I'm not ready to give up on an earthbound explanation, not just yet. But ask me again tomorrow."

T. G. paused to wash his hands in the table's sink. "So what do we do with it?" he wondered, running cold water over his burned finger.

"I've been thinking about that," Abelwhite said, nodding. "For now, I'd suggest we lock it in the specimen vault downstairs. The room's got high security and very limited access. Then I'll make a few calls and get it into a proper quarantine lab. I think we need to bring others in on this…the combined experience of some of the leading minds in science may help to unlock some of the mysteries shrouding your discovery."

"Yeah," he agreed. "I don't guess it can stay our little secret forever. How long do you think it'll take for news of this to get out?"

They both smiled, looking at the silent enigma on the table. T. G. had the disquieting feeling that it was looking back.

6

T. G. drove home, glad not to be lugging the artifact around any more. Its size and weight made it an uncomfortable companion, and the fact that such an apparently valuable prize was locked safely away helped to put his mind at rest. One less thing to worry about, one less thing to keep him awake.

It had grown late and dark once again, and he knew he still had a bit of sleep left to catch up on. He shivered inside his long, heavy coat, for his car's heater was still not working. Despite the warmth that seemed to pour from the vents, the inside of the car would not warm up.

It was Wednesday night, and as usual, the roads were deserted. This part of Ithaca always seemed to retire early, readying itself for another busy day of work and classes. Most students were huddled over their books this late at night, most likely, not out for pizza, studying like Jenni was and—

"Jenni!" he remembered. He banged himself in the forehead, angry with himself for forgetting to call her. "Stupid!" he muttered, cursing himself. *It's late...but I'll call her as soon as I get home!*

As T. G. pulled into the small lot next to the Brookfelder Building he was struck by the absence of other cars. Many of those that were there when he had left were gone now. Usually, he had a hard time finding a space, but the lot looked more like it might on a Thanksgiving weekend, when most of the students living there would be gone for the holidays. The building above was dark, more so than usual, towering into the icy night air like a brick-and-cinder-block memorial to days past and times forgotten.

He pulled into a parking space close to the main entrance. Snow had begun to fall again, and for a moment before getting out of the car he watched the large, wet flakes glittering in the beams of his headlights. He loved snow, and as he listened to the rhythmic beat of his wipers he thought back to other winters, absent friends, and family.

He thought again of David. Where was he? How long would it take him to get back to New York? Would he be angry? Only the winter before, during a heavy snow, T. G. and Jenni had inadvertently given her family and Dave a scare by taking a spur-of-the-moment road trip to Syracuse, where a weekend-long student film festival was taking place. It had been irresponsible to tell no one where they had gone, they had come to realize, but the hurt was unintentional. That did little to soothe the angered worries of Jenni's mother and father, who had been ready to drag the river looking for the two. David had chewed T. G. out for disappearing like that.

"I'll never smooth *this* over with him. Thanks loads," he sarcastically commented to the absent artifact as he shut off the ignition. The car's dome light came on as he opened the door, and for the first time since leaving the college its yellowed glare filled the car's interior.

Just as T. G. turned to climb out, something caught the corner of his right eye. Startled, his body jerked and he dropped back into the driver's seat, his gaze fixed upon the passenger's seat next to him. His hands shook. His hair stood on end.

There, as if it had never left, rested the artifact.

He could only stare. He had seen it placed gently into the specimen vault. He had seen the lid lowered, the lock closed. He had seen the drawer slid shut and the steel mesh gate outside securely sealed. He had walked away, trusting it to the care of others. Then, after all that, it had silently and surely followed him home.

It had had the last word, apparently. *Not so fast, pal. I'm all yours.*

T. G. reached over and lightly touched it, as if to check its materiality. It was real enough. He fell limp in his seat, head back, eyes closed, and heart pounding, trying to sort things out. A fear swelled within him, but he told himself that if the thing meant to harm him it surely would have done so already. Time passed without his notice.

The insides of the car's windows fogged over then froze, obscuring his vision of the wintry world outside.

That settled it in his mind. There was definitely something other than human technology behind the thing, however advanced, whether it was earthly or not. There was something going on that could not be explained by scientific convention or physics or any rational theory anyone could come up with. He had a metaphysical tiger by the tail, he knew, and he was not going to be allowed to let go until the ride was over.

And he feared that it would be a very, very dark ride.

With renewed determination, T. G. grabbed the artifact by the strap and hoisted it up, stepping up out of the car in the same motion. Momentarily slipping out of his knee-length coat, he draped the object across his left side then put the coat back on, concealing the prize as much as possible. There was gold on it, after all, like none other, and there was no sense in taking unnecessary risks. He slammed the car door behind him, forgetting to lock it, and stepped heavily through the slush that had built along the curb. The biting wind had ceased, leaving behind a gentle snowfall and a cold silence.

T. G. tried to imagine the conversation he would have with Dr. Abelwhite once he got inside and phoned her. How could he explain to her that he still had the object and that logic had been cast into the wind? What would she believe? Possibly *anything* at that point, he hoped.

He made his way carefully along the snow-spotted sidewalk, avoiding the icy patches in his way. As he approached the old building, an indefinable apprehension began to fill him, one that intensified as the edifice loomed closer. It was so still, so quiet. He glanced up, thinking it odd that so few lights were on inside. Those that glowed were obscured by the glaze of ice and frost on all the windows, diffusing what light there was like the glass of a shower door. But he gave it little thought as he pulled the high collar of his coat closed with one hand and hurried toward the door. He failed to notice something that might have served as a warning, had he only looked closer.

The translucent layer of ice that had built up on the building's windows had done so on the *inside* of each pane.

Climbing the last couple of steps, he chose his footing carefully. Ice remained upon them despite the fact that they had been sprinkled with rock salt, leaving white splotches upon the dry areas. He reached out to push on the worn brass door handle, but looked up to discover the door standing wide open. *Just great,* he thought, irritated that the cold had been allowed into the building. *It's been hard enough to keep it warm in here as it is.*

Puzzled, he slowly entered the darkened structure. In the entry hall his feet found not polished tile, but a thick coating of ice.

What the...!

As he tried to push the door shut behind him he realized that ice had built up under and behind the door, along both floor and wall, pinning it open.

It was so horribly quiet.

No sounds of televisions playing behind closed doors. No Bing Crosby music. No voices. No rattle of the air ducts as they carried warm air into the hallway. T. G. took a few steps down the hall, toward the stairway, gazing in awe at the polar scene around him. Icicles hung from doorknobs, light fixtures, heater pipes, and anything else that protruded into the hall. Each of the yellowed fixtures that dangled from the hallway ceiling glowed dimly from within layers of ice and frost, which gave their light an unreal, dreamlike quality. A glistening layer of clear ice half an inch thick in places coated the floor, walls, and doors, leaving no surface bare. *Did the pipes burst?* Atop that, much of the bizarre, arctic corridor looked like a freezer that had not been defrosted for years. The air was still and frigid. His breath hung white before him. The place smelled like a slaughterhouse.

The cold burned his face and stung his eyes. *It's so much colder in here than outside!*

T. G. paused at one familiar door and began to pound on it. "Mrs. Lucreia?" he shouted, knocking a shower of brittle ice flakes to the floor as his fist struck the old, hard wood again and again. "It's T. G., Mrs. Lucreia…what happened in here? The front door's stuck open…are you okay?" There was no answer, just the same, awful silence. Turning the knob, he forced his weight against the door and heard the crack of breaking ice as the antique oak gave way in its frame. With another push it yielded a little more, and T. G. peered through the narrow opening.

He saw nothing. The room was dark, save the meager glow from the street lamp outside, which managed to penetrate the hazy frost on the windows. "Mrs. Lucreia?" he repeated into the near blackness. Listening more closely, he could just make out a subtle noise from inside, a muffled buzzing of some kind that sounded over and over. He again put his weight into the door and it gave another foot, allowing some of the light of the hallway to spill into the room.

It fell upon a sight that made T. G. blink in shock.

The woman was seated in her rocking chair, still holding the phone to her ear, eyes open, lips parted as if in midword. She was glazed with an inch-thick coating of ice, a semitransparent cocoon that covered her completely, flowing over the chair and phone in a continuous, glistening blanket that melded into the glacial shroud that covered everything else in the room. The buzzing he had heard, muffled through the ice, came from the phone, which was crying out in the loud warning tone of a receiver left off the hook.

T. G. backed away from the sight, eyes wide, his breathing sharp and uneven. As he looked along the hallway, imagining the horrors that might await behind any one of the doors there, an odd wind began to build in the hallway, an icy airflow that carried back toward the door through which he had first entered. He had no explanation for it but was no longer interested in mysteries. His first instinct was to flee the building, fearing that the cause of the white, impossible death all around him might still lurk somewhere within.

He was right.

Before T. G. could take a step toward the entry something appeared there, blocking his view of the door. He held his breath as that something moved, swaying from side to side as if staring back, planning its next move. It was as black as the depths of any pit T. G. had ever seen, a shape of absolute pitch that absorbed all light and heat, its outer contours obscured by the haze of a form-hugging event horizon. A shadow without a source, roughly man-shaped but much larger, horned, and grotesquely misshapen, filling the end of the hallway.

It took a step toward him.

T. G. struggled down the corridor and into the icy gale, away from the shadowthing, trying for his only exit—the stairway. Fighting the increasing wind on the glazed floor was arduous, forcing him to pull himself along by doorframes, pipes, or whatever else he could grab hold of. He bloodied his knuckles on the hard, jagged ice, but his quickly numbing hands did not feel the pain. He would have to go up, to try to make it to the relative safety of his apartment and the fire escape outside, where he could run for help.

The wind roared in his nearly frostbitten ears. Too terrified to look back, he bounded up the stairs two at a time, slipping on the ice as he reached the landing. His body twisted in a manner it was not meant to know, and his already injured knee came down hard against the edge of the step, the hard marble rim slamming like a blade against the bottom of his kneecap. He cried out in pain, sheer terror alone lifting him back to his feet. The third floor seemed miles away, and the pain in his leg begged him to stop, collapse, and rest.

Deep laughter reverberated from below. Supporting his weight on the handrail, T. G. felt the vibration of something grabbing it downstairs. He climbed again, forcing his way upward, his center of gravity thrown off by the heavy artifact.

He finally reached his floor and no longer had the rail for support. Almost at once, he fell hard against the ice as his feet again splayed at cruel angles. He came down in an awkward tangle, his left leg caught under him. His closed eyes filled with sparkles, his face contorted in pain, and he cried out. His original knee injury had occurred in the same manner, wrenched sideways and backward as muscles strained and ligaments tore. Lifting himself just enough to put his weight fully on the other knee, he managed to crawl, dragging his useless leg across the sea of white rust, toward his apartment door.

He looked back. The shadowthing had not yet appeared, but its depraved laughter still filled the rushing air, blending with the whistling roar. T. G. pushed himself up to a shaky standing position by leaning on the artifact and the door, and he fished in his coat pocket. With a welcome jingle, he pulled his key chain free and quickly found the one small piece of precisely cut metal that was his salvation. Reaching down, he focused on the keyhole.

It was covered with ice. He could not get the key in.

In sheer terror, he glanced back at the stairs. A deformed hand-like thing was sliding along, coming up the icy rail. The laugh grew louder, echoing from the walls of the frozen corridor.

T. G. began to panic. There was no other way out.

Staring, frozen in fear, words suddenly sounded in his mind. *Something harder than any material we know of. Something that is there only when it needs to be...*

He looked down at the artifact, then braced himself and drove it into the face of the doorknob again and again, like an ancient, priceless battering ram. The thick coat of ice that covered the keyhole fractured with each impact, falling away like glass dust. T. G. forced the key into the freed lock and turned it, and rejoiced in hearing the familiar click. He pushed the heavy door open, then turned to take one last look over his shoulder and down the hall.

It was almost atop him, scant feet away. T. G. felt a burning cold he had never imagined possible and a hunger in that cold that was beyond mere imagination.

He fell into his darkened apartment and slammed the solid oak door behind him, putting all his weight against it as he frantically slid the trio of deadbolts home. Listening intently over the pounding of his own heart, he heard nothing beyond the door, no sound in the hallway. He hobbled backward and into the opposite wall, his fearful eyes trained upon the doorknob. His unsure legs finally gave way and he collapsed, sliding down the icy wall—his entire apartment, like the hallway outside, was covered with frost. Its sterile whiteness sparkled in the dim light of the street lamp beyond his window. He sat, riveted with fear, his eyes fixed upon the door. Waiting.

It was common knowledge among the residents of the Brook-felder that the old building had been built sturdily of hardwood, concrete, and brick. Back in the early 1950s, T. G. had learned, its basement had even been designated a neighborhood bomb shelter. *If that door will just hold, the walls will, too!*

He tried to move, but his left knee, wracked with the same tormenting pain as on that rain-slicked football field six years before, would take no weight at all. Even the adrenaline filling his limbs could not dampen the agony he felt. Raising his bloodied knuckles to his mouth, T. G. looked across the room and toward the glowing, ice-sealed window where the fire escape was.

Someone…help…!

Knowing no deliverance would come, he tried to move toward the window. After getting one leg under him, his bad leg collapsed and he fell heavily against his icy glass-topped coffee table. The scream of brittle, violated glass filled his ears and shards filled the air as he slammed into the hard floor and rolled onto his back. He felt warmth coursing from the back of his right hand and looked over to find a jagged thorn of glass embedded there, a rivulet of blood flowing from the wound. Gritting his teeth and inhaling sharply, he pulled the small, sparkling dagger from his flesh and tossed it away.

Almost blind with pain, he sat up, pushing with his hands, and backed himself against the wall opposite the door. Still he waited, but there was only silence from the hallway. He began to breathe again.

Maybe it went away…

Reaching far to his left, he managed to wrest his phone from its icy cradle atop a lamp table. *Who do you call for something like this?!* He tried to dial, only to find the buttons were held fast by the ice encasing them.

No!

An explosion of noise came from the other side of the door, a roar of flailing claws and teeth and bone against the dense, hardwood barrier that was T. G.'s only protection. The merciless noise of the renewed attack shook him, knocking the frozen phone from his grasp. He covered his ears as the tumult increased, a horrible din like a thousand lions fighting to get in. T. G. screamed. All the while the deep, menacing laughter continued, building in intensity, becoming more and more maniacal as, outside, more and more of the door was ripped away. He saw a tiny hole appear near the center of the door, a hole that grew larger by chunks, a hole filled with the flurry of chaotic darkness beyond.

Then, as suddenly as it had begun, the assault on his door ceased. The silence was heavy and far too sudden, as if the plug had been pulled on an earsplitting stereo system.

In the dim stillness, T. G. stared in terror at the hole in the door. Something new was filling it now, an odd blue point of light that moved slightly before locking upon him—

An eye.

For a moment, he could not tear his gaze from the horror. Finally, he closed his eyes and covered his head, hugging the artifact tightly. He waited to die, knowing now that the door could not stop the thing outside. Then, after several moments of oppressive quiet, T. G. fearfully peered between his fingers and saw only the faint light of the hallway streaming through the hole.

He allowed himself a breath, closing his eyes once more in relief. In the intense silence, the pulse of blood rushing through his ears whined loudly and rhythmically, making him feel alone, isolated, somehow sheltered. He felt safer.

He should not have.

A sound of breathing not his own filled the room. Heavy and wet and very near. T. G. trembled and refused to open his eyes. The temperature of the already-frozen room plunged.

"Give…it…to…me," a voice thundered from just above him, a foot or so away. T. G. jumped at the booming, raspy voice, but kept his eyes shut. The stench of rotted flesh filled the air all around him, nauseating him. Cold, dank breath splashed upon his face. Finally, trembling with cold and fear, he forced himself to look upward, an inch at a time.

It towered over him, filling the entire room, it seemed, an abomination eight feet tall and six wide, a cadaverous Goliath. T. G. looked up into a skull-cut face beyond words, beyond belief, beyond terror. It was the shadowthing given form and substance, absolute horror made flesh.

A deformed, inhuman beast of hair and talons and fangs and glowing blue eyes in deep black sockets, a thing of corrupted flesh, its tissue rotting from its huge frame as it stood there filling T. G.'s world with excruciating fright. Its clawed hands stretched toward him, only inches from his face. Wanting.

"Give…it…to…me," the monstrosity repeated.

T. G. was petrified, unable to move.

It reached over to the shattered table and picked up a long, heavy shard of glass, then swung around and pressed it to T. G.'s throat. *Always use the tools at hand!*

T. G. felt the crystalline blade begin to dig into his flesh. He closed his eyes again, hard, his body trembling.

"Give me the Gift you carry, or I will take it *and* your head," the thing said. T. G. opened his eyes and saw it smile. Its tone became one of mock concern. "We wouldn't want that now, would we?"

"This?" T. G. managed to ask the monstrous thing towering over him, shifting the relic slightly. "You want *this?*"

T. G. wanted to throw the artifact at the creature, but he could not will his arms to do so. The cursed, haunted relic was the cause of it all—it had to be. It had brought death upon his neighbors and then had brought the ghastly thing at his throat down upon him. Yet somehow, instinctively overriding his hatred and all else, he felt an inexplicable need to protect the artifact at all costs. It was as if it had become an extension of himself, as much a part of him as his arms or head and as precious as a child.

"Now!" the shadowthing ordered. It was not merely a voice but a cold, deep sea of anguished voices, all wailing and echoing, the sound swelling as if it were rising from some cavernous, stone tunnel leading up from a moldy and ancient torture chamber.

Trembling, T. G. waited to die. The shard pressed deeper. T. G. felt something warm—which quickly became as cold as ice water in the frigid room—coursing down his neck and onto his chest.

Then T. G. felt something else. In the midst of his terror, a warmth began to well up within him, an energy that somehow restored his wits. It was not a power from within, but one that was using him as a conduit, empowering him to act. A power that had been made manifest time and again in the face of impossible odds, in foxholes and burning buildings and dark alleyways, a strength that stood tall in the face of death and stared it down.

T. G.'s mind began to work again. He glanced down at the treasure held tightly to his chest, then back up into the unspeakable face above. "Forget it!" he shouted, clutching the artifact as a drowning man would cling to a life preserver.

"Give it to me…and I will let you live!" it lied. "Otherwise, you'll die like all the others! I will devour you…I will suck the meat and marrow from your bones, here and now!" Its voice shook the walls. It leaned down, almost nose to nose with him, then finished slowly and deliberately. "And you will not die until I let you. You will watch as I consume you, swallowing your flesh, bit by bit…"

"I said no!" T. G. yelled into the grotesque face, his mind racing, a boldness flowing within him that he had never before known. He was suddenly filled with true anger toward the abomination, remembering the sight of the woman in the rocker downstairs. The shadowthing reached out and ran the threatening tine of a six-inch black talon down the defiant face, from forehead to chin and down his nose. T. G.'s heart pounded, threatening to burst his rib cage.

The increasing cold had grown painful. T. G.'s breath clouded into a sparkling snowfall of ice crystals before him. He was losing feeling in his face and hands.

"I can hear your heart," the shadowthing gloated. "You are dying even now. Ish cannot help you. You are mine...finally!"

Then T. G. nervously smiled and spoke, staring into the luminescent, inhuman eyes so near his own. Eyes that, impossibly, he no longer feared.

"What's wrong?" he demanded, the cold soaking into his jaw, slowing his speech. "I've got...a bad leg...and you outweigh me by a ton." He dared it, his body shivering. "You can't, can you? You can't...*take* it from me. I have to *give* it to you." Had he been standing, he might have poked the thing in its chest with a defiant finger. "You're not laughing now. What part of Hell...are you from, anyway? I mean really—don't they have Listerine down there?"

The shadowthing, taken by surprise, reared back and roared, fists clenched. It saw that T. G.'s fear had vanished. Its primary advantage was gone. Blind terror had been its greatest weapon against the young man, but no more.

"Give it to me!"

"No!" T. G. shouted, his shaky voice firm despite the horrible death he was certain would follow. "Never!"

"Then die!" the shadowthing thundered, raising the huge glass blade high into the air. As its infernal limb arced downward in a razor blow that surely would decapitate him, the icy floor beneath T. G. swallowed him, and he dropped safely out of reach. He found himself falling through the same viscous, smothering, icy blackness that he had endured before as he had passed through the ceiling of his apartment.

He never heard the deafening, guttural bellow of frustration that shook his frozen apartment, a cry of rage powerful enough to echo across millennia.

T. G. quickly passed beyond the initial thickness and was able to breathe freely, still blind but feeling the increasing acceleration of his body. His equilibrium had again been thrown askew, and he found that there was no longer up or down, forward or backward, left or right—just escalating velocity. Then, without warning, the gelid thickness surrounded him again, and he held his breath for the final passage he knew must follow.

He landed hard on a lush hillside covered with thick, spongy growth that fairly absorbed his impact. He bounced once and rolled downhill a short distance before coming to a stop, face up. Disoriented, his sense of balance still scrambled, he could only lie still, the wind knocked out of him, his eyes closed, his thoughts random. His injured knee screamed, for it was twisted awkwardly beneath him. Biting his lip, he managed to pull it free.

His hands and face were nearly frostbitten. His fingers were sluggish, his cheeks numb. Slowly, as he lay there, they began to warm.

Despite a sharp soreness in his rib cage, he again caught his breath and found it increasingly easy to breathe. He moaned in pain, feeling as if he had just run a fifty-mile marathon while being pelted with stones. There was an uncomfortable pressure in his ears and T. G. opened his jaw wide. His ears popped, relieving the discomfort, and as he lay still, his panicked heart gradually slowed to normal.

He listened and heard no sign of the shadowthing. It had not followed him.

He slowly became aware of the cylindrical mass of the artifact beneath his coat, still clutched tightly against his bloodied chest, and he relaxed his clenched arms. Once more, the relic had made the trip with him. If only he could remember how their journey, their partnership, had begun.

Again and again he took the cleansing air into his lungs, as deeply as they would allow, until a slight lightheadedness set in. The ordeal had drained him, and all he wanted was to lie still and sleep. But curiosity overruled his physical needs. He reluctantly opened his eyes, stretching his arms to the sides. The backs of his hands found the luxurious softness of thick grasses and cool clover, and as T. G.'s blurred vision cleared he saw a sea of sparkling jewels suspended before his eyes, gems of every color and intensity. Brilliant blues, reds, whites, and yellows glittered like city lights in the crystal cold of winter. *Look, David...the stars are so beautiful...but there's no moon...where's the moon?*

Off in the distance, a bellow sounded, the call of a great beast. A deep, resonant cry, it drew immediate responses in kind from many different directions. T. G. could not imagine what creature had made the mournful call, but he knew he had never heard the sound before. Night birds sang high in the lush, distant trees, which glistened a brilliant green even in the subdued light of night.

Just before sleep engulfed him, T. G. realized that he had been looking into a night sky like none he had ever known. Instead of velvet blackness, a dark span of the deepest, purest magenta stretched above him. The shimmering rainbow of stars was set against it, glowing in more colors than he knew stars could have, and so much more brightly. Other lights moved quickly across the sky, swelling in brightness then dimming again, crisscrossing high above him. Aircraft of some type, perhaps? Or were they angels, coming to greet him...?

The sight took his breath away. *I died,* he concluded, his mind too weary to consider anything else. The last thought he had before passing out was that he was gazing into the sky that shone above Heaven.

He could not have been more wrong.

7

A mountain of a man looked down upon the sleeping figure and marveled at the color of his skin and the unusual dimensions of his small body. Taking a bite from a huge apple, he held his lampstick out over the man to get a better look. Even without it, in the diminished light of night, he could see that the man's skin was oddly pale, a hue unlike any he had ever seen. And his size—he was no larger than a child, but this man was no child. True, there were a few who were of similar stature, but they all had misshapen bodies, not the proper proportions of the stranger before him. And those clothes. *What kind of fashion is that? Where could such a person have come from?* The little man's appearance gave no clues. The smoothness of his face and darkness of his hair, however, betrayed his age—he was ninety, perhaps one hundred years old. And he was hurt. The stranger's right hand, throat, and chest were covered with the brown grit of dried blood. Bright crimson mixed in where the wounds still seeped.

The giant stood over the stranger, finishing his apple, watching quietly as the exotic little man in the eccentric clothing stirred slightly in the dense clover of the hillside. He was uncertain whether to wake him or leave him where he lay. He looked into the distance, at the floodlight-drenched city wall, considering.

Feeling adventurous, the man chose the former. Reaching out with a right toe, he gently tapped the stranger's leg. The sleeper stirred, a wince spreading across his face. "Julota crees," the giant apologized to the waking figure. "Vetdrova keltrian, cusoona fes myhaal."

T. G. opened his eyes at the odd sound and discovered the unusual figure towering over him. He stiffly sat up, gingerly bracing himself as he put his weight on the hip opposite his injured leg. The figure stepped back another couple of feet, carefully watching T. G.'s every move.

"English?" T. G. hoped, doubting that such would be the case. The figure only stared at him, his expression unsure, apparently waiting for a word or two he recognized.

Tossing his gnawed apple core aside, the giant looked upon the little man in puzzlement. *Why does he make such odd sounds?* The enormous man had known only one language all his life. The whole world spoke but one.

In its entire history, it had known only two.

T. G. became fearful as more of the strange language flowed from the giant's lips, knowing that any chance for communication with the people here was unlikely. It was bad enough being dropped into the middle of nowhere, but it terrified him to realize that he was unable to speak the native language.

"So, where is this?" T. G. asked. "The Middle East, somewhere? No? Somewhere on Earth though, right?" There was a blank look on the giant's face. "Please?"

"Vaya kesta," came the reply, puzzlement in his tone.

T. G. spoke slower, as if it would help. "I just found myself here. I'm not *from* here. I hurt my leg, see?" he said, indicating his knee.

The giant looked down at the injured leg, understanding, and spoke again. More gibberish, this time with feeling.

T. G. studied the man holding the torchlike object, his eyes studying a figure like none he had ever seen. He was gigantic. His hands were twice as large as an average man's. Beneath a wide, brilliant blue cloak his bright clothes were wrapped about him tightly, revealing that his frame was muscular and sharply defined. Even from a seated position, T. G. could judge that the man soared to well over seven and a half feet tall and maintained normal body proportions overall. His shoulders were tremendously wide and would have been the envy of Charles Atlas. His hair was quite short and golden brown. He appeared to be in his midthirties, as best T. G. could ascertain.

The most striking thing about the huge man was his coloring. His skin was an odd, almost metallic bronze, darker than T. G.'s. His deep black pupils stood out in harsh contrast against the ghostly pearlescence that surrounded them. Despite their unusual appearance they were intelligent, bright eyes, and behind them T. G. could see that the man's mind was working. At the same time, the piercing eyes seemed to stare right through him, making T. G. a bit uncomfortable as he looked up into them.

The giant smiled, disarming T. G. Reaching up with a massive frying-pan hand, he patted himself on the chest and introduced himself. "Pretsal."

"T. G.," he replied, making the same gesture. He then pointed at the man towering over him. "Pretzel?"

"Pretsal," he nodded. "Teejee," he pointed.

"Nice to meet you, Pretzel," T. G. said uneasily. Without warning, the imposing figure bent down and easily lifted him, cradling him like a man carrying his bride delicately over the threshold. "Hey! Hold it…what are you doing?"

The giant moved toward the city in the distance, careful not to hurt T. G.'s injured leg. He spoke again, in a tone of voice his unwilling passenger had most often heard used in addressing dogs.

"I'm sure that's all well and good, pal, but I'd just as soon as not…come on…put me down!"

Pretsal uttered a few short syllables in a reassuring tone as he continued downhill through the clover. T. G. talked himself into remaining calm.

He tried a few more times to get the huge man to put him down. Giving up with a loud sigh, T. G. looked ahead and for the first time saw the immense, glowing city that spread as wide and far as he could see. The powerful man was obviously bent on taking him there, and T. G.'s attentions turned from his leg to the priceless artifact hidden beneath his long coat.

"If I get mugged in there," he began, looking up at the smiling Pretsal, "I'll *sue* you for everything you've got."

As if he understood, Pretsal reached up with one hand and

unfastened the clasp of his cloak. Pulling it free, he placed it over and around T. G., hiding his unusual skin color and small proportions completely from any who might see.

"Revo pocuatos," Pretsal said, nodding.

"Swell," T. G. replied, his voice muffled beneath the wrap.

∽∾

T. G. heard the sounds of thousands of people around him, though he could not see. A monotone of strange voices, all uttering the same, unfamiliar language. He heard voices only—no cars, no horses, nothing that one might expect when entering a city of this age or any other. Just voices.

After several minutes, T. G. felt Pretsal climb some steps. The sounds changed, becoming closer and quieter, and he knew they had entered some sort of structure. Music was playing, sounding a bit like the awful, easy listening–type stuff he had heard in every department store and elevator back home. *Muzak rules the universe.* He smiled. But this music had a different quality to it, one rife with disjointed percussion and woodwinds and reflecting a culture that T. G. already knew had little or nothing in common with his own.

More voices. Then Pretsal came to a stop. T. G. heard him insistently speaking to a woman, whose deep tone in return resonated with irritation if not anger. Then, almost at once, Pretsal began walking again. A turn to the left, more steps, then one to the right. T. G. was laid upon a table of some kind, and the cloak was pulled away.

The light momentarily stung his eyes, but as they adjusted he found Pretsal standing beside him, smiling. T. G. looked around and was amazed at the sophistication of the room.

Overhead, a faceted, inverted crystal bowl some thirty feet in diameter glowed with the purest pink light he had ever seen. Hanging down from within the bowl was a huge, complex device of intertwined colored glass and metal, comprising dozens of component units linked by polished metal rods. T. G. could only guess at their functions—assuming they had functions—for they looked more like a work of art than anything else. The room was nine-sided, its walls each seemingly cut from a single piece of a rosy, highly veined wood with which T. G. was not familiar. Metal instruments of incredible variety and complexity hung upon the walls, their polished surfaces gleaming. He lay on a cold, metal table that was much larger and longer than he was tall, putting him almost five feet off the ground. He felt like a child at a—

"Doctor's office," he realized aloud. "It's a—"

Pretsal quickly motioned for him to remain silent by patting his sealed lips with a flattened hand, a motion similar to that of a child making a "woo-woo" sound while playing Cowboys and Indians. T. G. looked at him and shook his head, not understanding.

On the wall to his immediate right was a huge rack holding dozens of colored vials. Each was pearlescent and filled with a different, brilliantly colored liquid. On a tablelike protrusion beneath, three chromed spheres floated in the air, motionless, wholly unsupported so far as T. G. could determine. Another wall featured a holographic chart of the human body, or rather of the huge, gargantuan version of man he had seen reflected in Pretsal. There was no apparent door into the room.

Again Pretsal motioned that he wanted T. G. to remain silent. T. G. nodded, not really understanding, holding up a hand reassuringly. At that moment, one of the walls pulled soundlessly away from the others and another immense man, even larger than Pretsal, walked in. There was a bit of chatter between them, as T. G. looked on in fascination. Pretsal pointed to T. G.'s injured knee as the other man looked at the diminutive stranger with a scowl.

The man scolded Pretsal, it seemed, and he replied, apparently reassuring him of something. As T. G. watched, the man walked closer and leaned over his leg, looking down at the knee. *So, you're the doctor!* He then grabbed T. G.'s chin and pushed his head back to examine the cut on his throat. Shaking his head, he muttered a few syllables, then lifted the lapel of T. G.'s coat and made an apparently derogatory comment about his clothing. The man obviously did not like having to examine him and was in a hurry to be done with it. He took a cursory look at T. G.'s many minor wounds, and a few moments later, following the application of a bluish fluid that stung where it touched him, his cuts and scrapes had been cleaned and sterilized.

T. G. watched as the medical man reached up into the apparatus in the ceiling and pulled down a device, a metal rod with small spheres at either end, like a tiny dumbbell. It remained connected to the unit above by a flexible crystalline filament, which glowed faintly as the instrument neared his knee.

He looked worriedly at Pretsal, who smiled, trying to assuage his fears. The doctor held one end of the device against the injury, and T. G. instantly felt a warmth there. Just as instantly, an image sprang to life, filling one entire wall, floor-to-ceiling, with a three-dimensional magnified image of the knee along with all of its cartilage, tendons, and ligaments. The physician repeated the procedure on T. G.'s throat wound, then released the small device, which retracted back into its spot above. The image on the wall faded away.

T. G. almost spoke, but then he thought better of it and watched in quiet fascination as the doctor reached over and plucked one of the floating spheres from its place above the table. Holding it in one enormous hand, he placed the palm of the other against T. G.'s knee, spoke an unintelligible phrase to him, then looked down at the back of his hand. A warmth built anew beneath it, and T. G. felt a pleasant tingle in the knee. It lasted only a moment, after which the doctor pressed his fingers against the throat wound. More tingles, and T. G. had to bite his tongue to keep from laughing at the sensation. Then the huge man pulled his hand away and the sphere was returned to its hovering position.

The doctor again scolded Pretsal, shaking a finger at him. His tone seemed to be one of warning. Pretsal nodded and answered in apparent gratitude for the errand of mercy. The doctor spoke again, asking T. G. something. For several uncomfortable moments he scowled at the diminutive stranger, waiting for an answer. The giant man finally looked away, shook his head once more, then departed through the same passageway by which he had entered.

T. G. swung his legs off the edge of the table. His knee was no longer painful, no longer stiff. More than that, the constant ache he had known for years was gone. He tested it repeatedly, smiling at Pretsal. "That's incredible...I mean, it hasn't felt like this since..." He dropped the considerable distance to the floor, his long coat still concealing the artifact he had almost forgotten he was carrying. "Thanks. It feels great."

Pretsal again wrapped the cloak around T. G., this time letting him walk under his own power. They left the medical building and stepped out into the busy streets of the city, and T. G., the cloak draped over and around his head like a hood, looked out upon a world carved from the stuff of legend.

Statues were everywhere, from the terrifying, gargoyle-like carvings that adorned most of the buildings around them, to the towering, two-hundred-foot-tall rock-hewn warrior figures that stood nearby. The sky overhead was largely obscured by ornate, monumental spires of stone and steel that soared thousands of feet into the air, their lines dramatically emphasized by dazzling rows of lights that gave an impression of highways ascending into the heavens. Forged human faces and highly complex geometric structures adorned their sides. Towering buildings of cut glass and brilliantly tooled granite— along with smaller structures that gave the appearance of shops and restaurants—seemed to extend forever in all directions, as if the streets below them were a hopeless maze.

Swarming like fireflies at and above the building tops were thousands of tiny blinking lights of red and white, swooping into graceful paths as they sought their destinations. If not for their motion, they would have been utterly lost in the dense celestial display overhead. The closer man-made stars were flying vehicles of some sort, but their size was impossible to determine without a readily identifiable sense of scale.

A more brilliant light ahead drew T. G.'s gaze, and he looked up at the huge city's central structure, some five to ten miles distant, at the end of the wide street. It was an immense pyramid of mirror-polished stone and steel towering a mile into the night sky, dazzlingly brilliant in the red wash of the burning lights splashed upon it. At its summit a purple strobe flashed, possibly a warning to low-flying aircraft. What looked like immense open hangars with flat, oblong bases protruded from its sides at a point halfway up—landing bays, T. G. suspected. The pyramid's surfaces gleamed with hundreds of thousands of brightly lit windows, shining like stars in a tightly packed, random pattern. Most of the other buildings immediately around him were just as beautiful, though more conventionally shaped.

Playing upon the still, cool air in front of the pyramid was an immense moving image, a speaking head. Its impressive face was stern and heavy with authority as it uttered word after word. Not elaborate sentences, not statements. Just single words, as if it were reading out of some bizarre foreign dictionary. T. G. watched it for a moment, and as the holographic projection continued its strange liturgy, he felt strongly that somehow, some way, it was speaking directly to him. For a few moments, he could not look away from it. Pretsal's hand on his shoulder pulled his attentions back to ground level, and T. G. turned to see his companion smiling as he pointed down the way. They began to walk.

The city air was heavy—not with exhaust fumes, but with the scents of flowering plants and delicious foods. T. G.'s stomach flip-flopped in response to the delightful smell of something that had to be related to barbecued brisket, and only then did he realize how hungry he was. The wonderful aroma grew stronger as the pair walked along, and soon they passed in front of what appeared to be an open-air restaurant. T. G. saw dozens of people sitting and eating in a pleasantly lit dining area, with several reddish items that he did not recognize rotating on a cluster of rotisserie spits. As he watched, a chef basted the mysterious food with a rich, glossy brown sauce. Looking closer, he realized that the unusual delicacy was giant locusts, each nearly a foot long, eaten like chicken by the patrons.

Momentarily repulsed, his stomach continued to growl nonetheless. He began to think longingly of a thick, juicy rib-eye grilled to perfection and smothered in sautéed mushrooms. As his mind drifted to a small steakhouse he had frequented near the Cornell campus, he heard a deep, loud woman's scream and looked upward, toward its source. Several stories up, in a window across the street, he saw a frantic woman obviously pleading to the streets below for help as she was attacked by several men, who finally dragged her away from the window to whatever fate they had in store for her. T. G. looked toward Pretsal, who kept his gaze forward. *Why isn't anyone doing anything to help her?* T. G. wondered.

The deeper into the city they got, the more surreal and frightening it became for T. G. There were people everywhere, all brightly clothed, their conversations rising then fading as they passed by. There was no pattern to their motion, no direction as would be expected were they traveling along sidewalks. The tall bronze people moved in confused crosscurrents back and forth between the towering sculpted buildings, mindless, programmed, coursing like fish through the water of a cold lake.

Not all of those around T. G. were of flesh. Moving among the living—outnumbering them ten to one and apparently accepted as commonplace—were figures that could only be described as *ghosts.* The spectral, almost translucent beings gave an appearance of solidity yet at the same time were vaporous and incorporeal. They radiated a dim gray light and appeared to be young and old, male and female, wealthy and poor. Most were involved in conversations with their living companions, showing all the normal emotions one might have expected from anyone. On occasion, one of them would look up at T. G. in a passing glance, then stop suddenly to fixate upon him as if in recognition, its eyes igniting into flames of dull red. T. G. looked away each time, trying to avoid the piercing, nonliving stares. They gave him the creeps, causing the hair on the nape of his neck to stand on end.

Also among the throng, crowded into corners and begging for handouts, were persons in tattered clothing who were more disheveled in appearance than the others. They were smaller, about T. G.'s size, and their deformed bodies were bent and twisted, with oversized heads and feet. Males, females, and children, they appeared to have been victims of birth defects, genetic miscues whose lives had been made miserable through no fault of their own. Those who passed them largely ignored what must have been pleas for food or money. Apparently second-class citizens, they seemed fearful and wary, their dull gray eyes continuously darting from side to side.

T. G. watched as thefts and assaults occurred all around him, ending as startlingly as they had begun and leaving shaken victims in their wake. Disbelieving, he tightened his grip on the artifact hidden beneath both coat and cloak, growing paranoid that he had "victim" written all over him. *Where are the police?*

Many of those in the crowd topped nine feet, T. G. estimated, but the average height seemed to hover near seven and a half feet for men and seven for women. Several times T. G. became so fascinated by the enormity of the beings that he almost became separated from his guide, to be swallowed up into the sea of giants. But Pretsal was watchful and quite careful to maintain a fix on the stranger, never letting him stray out of arm's reach.

The doorways were filled with women who again and again tried to lure passing men closer. Their profession was obvious to T. G., and he was startled by their aggression. One reached out and grabbed Pretsal by the sleeve, jarring him off balance as a second leaped up and put her arms around his neck. The big man uttered a few words and threw an arm up, knocking the woman back into her associate. As the harlots cursed Pretsal, he led T. G. onward, moving more quickly now. The shouts and whistles of the women went on behind them as they continued toward their destination.

Drug use of some kind was rampant. All along the way, T. G. noticed most of the men and women putting odd crystalline objects of differing colors and shapes to their faces as they walked, inhaling a bluish smoke that emanated from them. Each user's expression became immediately unfocused, reflecting a mindless euphoria that lasted several minutes. How they could continue to walk, much less get where they were going, was beyond him. As soon as each dose wore off, the users took another, keeping them in a continuous, trancelike state.

Suddenly, only a few feet away, a loud crackle and flash sent a painful tingle across T. G.'s body. He spun to see a huge dark-haired man fall to the ground next to him with pavement-buckling force, viciously burned and obviously dead. A man with a strange metal device in his hand then hovered over the body, stripping it of valuables. T. G. was horrified and astonished at the nonchalance with which the others all around continued on, never even taking notice of the crime.

"Somebody stop him!" T. G. cried out, pointing at the murderer and thief. Pretsal yanked him violently backward and put a huge warm hand over his mouth, covering most of his face in the process. Those same people who had not so much as turned to look upon a murder taking place snapped their attentions toward T. G. and the strange words he had uttered, murmuring among themselves as they pointed at the odd-looking stranger. Pretsal hurried away, practically dragging T. G. with him.

They rushed down a side street and entered a moving walkway that sped along so quickly that T. G. had to grip the handrail to keep from falling. Pretsal looked down at T. G. with a concerned scowl and spoke in low tones. "Nosta ludana jeo, Teejee…kuda! Kuda!" T. G. could only stare back, totally confused and having no clue what the man had said.

"What *was* all that?" T. G. replied in vain. "A guy gets murdered, and there's rape, and who knows what else out there, and you guys don't even notice?! Where are the cops? What kind of place is—?" Pretsal's hand once more shot up and covered T. G.'s mouth, silencing him.

"Nosta…*kuda*, Teejee…," he slowly and deliberately whispered, his tone that of a man trying to save their lives. "Kuda…" After a moment, he slowly pulled the hand away, watching T. G.'s eyes. Then he relaxed, satisfied that no other words would be forthcoming.

T. G. had learned his first word.

Kuda—quiet.

The walkway ended almost a mile away in an area dedicated to vehicular traffic, and T. G. learned why he had not heard the usual sounds of scurrying automobiles. There were cars all right, at least their equivalent, but the hundreds that darted past did so in near silence. They had no wheels, no apparent engines, no exhaust. They hovered a foot or so above the smooth glassy streets, their sparkling windshields and metal bodies glistening in the light. Their general configurations approximated those of conventional cars, and all but a very few were open with no canopy of any kind.

Pretsal led T. G. onto a small platform next to the busy street. Almost at once, a rounded, oblong vehicle stopped and opened its door. It had no driver. The huge man took a seat on its leather-upholstered cushions, gesturing for T. G. to join him. T. G. reluctantly stepped into the car and sat opposite Pretsal, facing him, then watched as the door slid silently shut beside him. With an almost violent acceleration, the cab shot away from the platform and merged at a hundred miles per hour with the flow of traffic.

The wind filled the cloak over T. G.'s head and pulled it back, almost throwing it from the car. Even as he caught it and pulled it more tightly around him, T. G. studied the interior of the cab. The bench seat wrapped all the way around, covered with bluish leather. There was no instrumentation, no steering wheel, nothing that one might expect. Pretsal sat comfortably, obviously unconcerned by their great speed and lack of a driver.

"Amazing," T. G. said, speaking quietly since there was no engine roar or sound of tires against pavement to overcome. Watching other vehicles, T. G. saw that many of them had drivers at some form of control console, and he surmised that those were personally owned cars, unlike the public transit unit in which he and Pretsal rode.

After a short minute and a half, the car pulled off of the main thoroughfare and traveled at a greatly reduced speed along a more narrow street. It came to rest at another platform identical to the first, and as soon as it stopped, Pretsal sprang to his feet and led T. G. off. The empty car shot back onto the concourse once again, apparently seeking its next passenger.

T. G. looked around, making certain that no one was close enough to overhear, and spoke, more for his own benefit than anything else. "How...how did it know where you wanted to go? You never said a word." Pretsal simply motioned once again for T. G. to remain quiet.

They soon entered another crowd of pedestrians like the first. Again, though the living did not give T. G. a passing glance, the eyes of the ghostly figures ignited with light as they glared accusingly at him. Like an ocean wave they turned toward him, one after another, for as far through the sea of huge citizens as he could see.

T. G. defiantly stared back at what appeared to be the ghost of an elderly man and saw the dull red glow in its eyes intensify as if to threaten him. Reaching his creep threshold, T. G. finally averted his eyes and pulled the cloak farther around his face. As he did, Pretsal turned left into the arched doorway of a tall building of veined green stone, and none too soon for T. G. He wanted to get as far from the phantasms as he could, but he was dying to know what they were and why no one else gave them a second glance. Their dreadful eyes haunted him.

"Please tell me this is the Earth Embassy," T. G. sarcastically whispered. They entered an open-air hallway lined with dozens of huge doors, each with an engraved metal plate upon it. An apartment building, T. G. guessed, only one far more exquisitely fashioned than any in which he had ever lived. The people of this world had refined masonry to an art, and as he followed his guide along the softly lit corridor, he studied the exquisitely carved murals in the marble of the walls and ceiling. Portrayed in vivid, full relief were heroic figures fighting huge monsters and gargantuan soldiers, their weapons drawn and ready—a vast, encompassing glorification of war surely rooted in mythology rather than history. Burnished wooden detail subtly melded into the stone, adding a clever and refreshing organic feel to the work. One character struck T. G. as being similar to the shadow-thing, whose clutches he had narrowly escaped.

They reached a huge door fashioned from the same knotted pinkish wood T. G. had seen in the doctor's office. Into it, like the walls, were carved complex and elegant patterns that played as if alive in the light of the hall. There were no hinges holding the door that T. G. could see, yet it smoothly and silently swung open at the slightest touch as Pretsal manipulated a jeweled plate next to it. Pretsal motioned for his guest to enter first, and T. G. reluctantly walked into the darkness that lay beyond the high, wide doorframe.

As Pretsal closed the door behind them a few dim lights came on, revealing three huge men standing to one side of the door. All three were clad in dark gray and dressed alike, wearing straight-cut robes with broad shoulders, and seemed shrouded in governmental authority. The apparent leader looked a lot like Ed Asner, T. G. thought, only much, much larger.

Before Pretsal or T. G. could react, the men pinned them to the wall and thrust weapons, such as the one T. G. had seen used in the street, into their ribs.

"IRS trouble?" T. G. asked Pretsal, under his breath. At that, he was slammed anew into the polished wood-and-plaster wall, bloodying his nose.

"Kuda!" the man ordered.

I know, T. G. almost said aloud.

"Hyra dou!" one of the men shouted at Pretsal, who to T. G.'s surprise seemed to be the primary focus of their attentions. "Kera fionica desla, te doco kir *Shass!*"

T. G. reacted to the sound of his name, turning to look up at the enormous man who had uttered it. *How can he know my name?*

Pretsal remained utterly silent as the men, one after another, continued to pummel him with questions. For several minutes the interrogation went on, questions mingled with blows, but Pretsal bit his lower lip and remained silent. The huge hand pressing T. G.'s head at an awkward angle into the hard wall was like iron, and he could do nothing but watch as the apparent leader reached into a shoulder pouch and withdrew a small gleaming sphere. He pressed it against the back of Pretsal's neck, where it issued a soft hissing sound. Pretsal slumped, his unconscious form kept upright only by the grip of the third man. From the corner of his eye, T. G. saw the Asner-like Goliath with the sphere turning his way, reaching toward him. Something cold pressed against his neck, just below the base of his skull. Darkness came, and he felt himself falling. Then he felt nothing at all.

⮂〇⮀

T. G. awoke with a tremendous headache. He sat up, reaching back to caress the tender spot on his neck where the device had been applied. He was centered on a hard, enormous leather cot, larger than a twin bed, and had to make a concerted effort to get his legs over the side. As he looked around, he immediately realized that he was in a cell, one not altogether different from holding cells he had seen on television back home. Adamantine bars of polished metal sealed off one end of the room, with stone walls making up the rest of the secured enclosure. He was in a sunken pit, and a few steps led up to the cell door. The corridor floor outside cut across the other side of the bars at waist level, forcing prisoners to have to look up at their jailers. He could hear others muttering, some loudly complaining it seemed, in nearby cells. Looking toward the other bed in his cell, he saw Pretsal sprawled there, still unconscious.

T. G. stumbled over to a basin mounted low against one wall. A mirror above it showed him that dried blood covered his upper lip, and he looked down at the sink, needing water. There were no faucet handles, but twin green-glass spigots extended up from the metal bottom of the basin. He dipped his hands beneath them and water immediately poured forth. He splashed his face and washed away the brown stain beneath his still-tender nose, then dried off on an odd leathery sheet of reddish fabric that hung to one side. *I hope that was a towel...*

He heard new, distinct voices outside, a few cells away across the corridor. Another prisoner had visitors.

T. G. went back toward his cot, momentarily swaying as his drugged body fought to find its center of balance. The stuff had nearly worn off, enough for him to realize he felt unusually light on his feet. A few seconds later, he understood why.

His long coat was gone. So was the artifact.

He cursed aloud, striking out against the air in frustration as he sat down hard on his cot. The yell pierced Pretsal's sleep just enough to start him toward consciousness, and T. G. watched angrily as his companion began to stir.

"Nice planet you've got here," he complained. Pretsal groggily opened his eyes and looked over at T. G., then tried to sit up himself. "And don't give me that 'kuda' lecture of yours. What can they do, arrest me?"

Pretsal was fully awake now, having come around much faster than T. G. He stood and went to the bars, where he took a quick look up and down the corridor. "Cedri tycla, Teejee," he said in a quiet tone as he sat back down.

"Save it," T. G. moaned in frustration. The pressure and fear of being a stranger in a very strange land was getting to him. "I know one lousy word of your language. Come back in a year or so...by then I may be able to ask where the bathroom is."

Pretsal looked away, obviously recognizing T. G.'s anger.

"They took my artifact," he continued. "By now they've stripped all of the gold off it. They even took my coat…" He reached to his back pocket. "And my wallet. Great. If you were afraid of what would happen if anybody heard me talk, wait until they get a load of my driver's license."

The voices in the corridor grew louder. T. G. and Pretsal both looked up to see a family slowly walking past, their visit over. T. G. saw spectral figures, an elderly woman and two children, among them. A uniformed and armed guard whose expression indicated dissatisfaction with his career escorted the group. As the gathering shuffled past, the ghostly forms stopped and approached the bars of T. G.'s cell, their eyes igniting into the same hideous red glow he had witnessed earlier. The faces of all three flared into expressions of hatred, glaring intensely into his eyes as they stared him down. T. G. was grateful for the bars separating him from the ghastly things, though he had no doubt that the wicked apparitions could pass through them if they so desired.

T. G. became aware of something at his side, heavy against the leather of his cot as it slid up next to him. Startled and certain that it was one of the ghosts, he leaped to his feet with a cry and spun to look upon his assailant.

There was indeed something on the bed, but not an attacker.

The artifact had returned to him.

A sudden bloodcurdling screech came from the corridor. T. G. looked up to see the ghosts react to the artifact in terror and anger as their eyes burst into brilliant flames, hundreds of times brighter than they had been before. They backed away, their chilling shrieks ringing out as if they had reverberated all the way up from the basement of Hell. T. G. followed their gaze back to the artifact and quickly picked it up, holding it like a shield before the horrid phantoms.

His hands shaking, he took a step toward them. They backed away again, then screamed in unbridled fury and vanished as if they never were. Their final cries echoed down the corridor as the living members of their group, still present, peered into the cell in confusion. One of the women, upset by the abrupt disappearance of her spectral loved ones, cried out and wept hysterically, then was comforted and led away by the others with her. The guard outside walked closer to the cell and saw T. G. holding the object, then glanced at Pretsal. Without a word, he shook his head and walked away.

T. G. looked down at the relic, breathing a sigh of relief that it appeared undamaged. The transparent gold stones embedded into it were all still there, and the hide was as flawless as ever. Fortunately, it seemed the people of this world had no more clue about how to open it than he had.

Pretsal stood and slowly approached, then stopped and reached out with his huge hands. Gently, lightly, almost reverently, he touched the odd leather of the artifact and turned his head slightly to peer at the alien words tooled into its surface. He stroked the hide gently, almost dreamily, then held his hand up and gazed upon his subtly trembling fingertips. His eyes then found T. G.'s, an unspoken question playing upon his face.

"This is…uh…kind of hard to explain," T. G. began, momentarily forgetting the language barrier between them as he saw the expression on the giant's face. "Why are you looking at me like that? Pretzel?"

"Dovo Kosi," Pretsal stammered under his breath, his breathing becoming erratic as he stared at the stranger before him. "D… Dovo…Kosi…"

"Dovo…what? What does that…?"

Pretsal extended a hand and touched T. G.'s cheek, then backed away a few steps and continued to repeat the phrase, amazement and disbelief in his voice. "Dovo Kosi…keil ta Dovo Kosi…" T. G. watched the huge man, seeing that he had been shaken by something very deep and very important.

"This?" T. G. hoped, holding the artifact a little higher. Pretsal reacted, and T. G. suddenly realized that for the first time an answer—*the* answer—was within reach. "You know what this is, don't you? Speak English! Please speak English! Tell me what this is!"

"Dovo Kosi!" the gentle giant stammered, near tears.

"Pretzel!" T. G. demanded, indicating the artifact. "What is this? You have to make me understand! What is this? Where did I get it? Why do I feel like I've owned it all my life? Why is it following me around?" He walked closer to the man, holding the artifact higher. Pretsal backed into his cot and fell hard against it as T. G. stopped right before him. "This is Dovo Kosi?" T. G. asked, shaking the artifact slightly, then pointing to it. "Dovo Kosi, right?"

Pretsal's brow knotted in puzzlement. That surprised T. G., who had expected a nod. The man reached out and gripped T. G.'s pointing hand, turning it gently until the extended index finger pointed at T. G. himself.

"Dovo Kosi," he gently said, pressing the fingertip into T. G.'s chest. "Dovo Kosi ta Teejee!" Pretsal smiled, a little shakily, a hint of triumph in his voice.

Confusion reigned. "Me?" he asked, losing the handle on things he thought he was gaining. "What does *that* mean?"

Before the huge man could utter another syllable, the stone floor of the cell opened up for the barest fraction of an instant and, as Pretsal watched, T. G. and his artifact were swallowed into the icy nothingness between places, between worlds. Then, as fast as it had opened, the portal was gone and the gentle giant reached out with a cautious foot only to find solid stone.

Pretsal was alone. *What* had happened, he did not know. *Who* he had found lying on the hillside outside the city walls, he now did. He sat back onto his cot, his hands to his face, his mind and heart racing.

He pulled his hands back, hands that had crossed the ages, and gazed at them in stunned silence.

They had touched God.

∽∾

As T. G. fell, the sense of shotgun acceleration once more swept him deeper into blackness. That meant, he knew, that he was about to come crashing down somewhere else, probably somewhere far from the jail cell.

Anger filled him. *I almost had the answer!*

As he clutched the artifact more tightly his acceleration slowed, and he sensed that the trip was nearly over. *Does holding this thing the right way control my fall?* With a sudden deceleration he had not experienced before, he almost came to a full stop before seeing daylight once again. He fell gently the last few feet, into a lush grass that caught him with soft arms. He lay there, his heart pounding, his breathing heavy. A warm breeze washed over him as he rested.

In the distance, he heard the sweet bells of the campus tower.

Home!

He opened his eyes to find himself back in Ithaca, where it was no longer cold and white. Once again, the fully adorned trees had embraced their springtime rebirth. The sun was just breaking through the cloud cover, its warmth welcome against his face. Time flowed differently where he had been, he realized. *It wasn't just days this time. Months passed here while I was away.* T. G. looked up and saw the old rusty street sign that marked the intersection where the Brookfelder Building had stood sentinel since the First World War. He smiled, knowing that once again he had made it safely home.

He rose to his feet and picked up the artifact. He remembered the shadowthing and the unspeakable things it had done to his neighbors, his friends. Was it still up there, waiting? He turned and looked toward his apartment.

Rather, toward where his apartment was supposed to be.

Toward where the *building* was supposed to be.

8

T. G. stood frozen, staring at the vacant lot. He looked back to the street sign, toward its cruel confirmation, then spun around, seeking further proof. Buildings he recognized were everywhere—all but the Brookfelder—with a few subtle changes that confirmed a season had passed. The parking lot was still there, empty and slightly overgrown, its faded white lines still inviting cars to come and rest, its patches of unkempt grass showing that they had not done so for quite some time.

"So, where's my car?" he cried out in frustration. "And my stuff?"

He glanced down at his watch before remembering that the hour was not important. Months. It had been months. T. G. realized that David must be worried sick about him, especially given the bizarre circumstances surrounding their last parting. He had never had a chance to call David's mom, to explain as best he could what had happened so she could pass the story along to her son. Knowing David, he might even be frantic. In fact, both David and—

Jenni!

He hefted the artifact and began the half-mile trip to her house, breaking into a dead run, his rhythmic breathing loud in his ears. He was almost grateful to those who had taken his coat, for he certainly did not need it anymore and its added weight would only have made his run more difficult. As he ran, feeling the warm breeze against his skin, he focused on his destination as if with tunnel vision. He took the familiar short cut down back alleys, between houses, and through hedges, only occasionally meeting repaired fences or other obstacles that had not been there before. It was an old neighborhood, one that had not changed noticeably for as long as he had lived there. Had he been paying closer attention, however, he would have noticed that the trees all around him were not merely full of foliage now—they were larger.

Much larger.

T. G. ran on, holding the bouncing artifact against him to minimize its incessant tug against his tiring shoulder. At last, he cut across one final lawn and reached the white-trimmed wood-and-stone house that had been his goal. He bounded up the familiar trio of pebbled steps and onto the wide covered porch then rang the bell, winded. Impatient, he waited but a few seconds before pounding on the door. "Jenni!" he cried, his voice and volume cut short by his lack of breath. "Jenni, it's T. G.!" He moved to one side and peered into a window, cupping his hands beside his eyes, and saw a china hutch that he remembered. *They still live here...*

There was a sound and the doorknob turned. As he moved back in front of the door, it opened. Slowly at first, pausing, then wider. T. G. looked into the face of a woman whose auburn hair had gained a hint of gray since he had last seen her. Had she stopped coloring her hair? She looked terrible—ill. Lines cut into her face, making it seem more harsh than the last time he had seen it. He almost didn't recognize the woman.

Years before, his aunt's appearance had changed as drastically when she underwent cancer treatments. *Could Jenni's mom have suffered the same fate?*

But Janice Parklin had endured a pain far greater than any disease could create. The woman looked into T. G.'s eyes for a moment, as if in disbelieving shock.

"Mrs. Parklin?" he asked gently, trying to see her as the woman he had known. "I need to see—"

"Where's Jenni?" the woman interrupted, her voice rising in intensity. "Where is she?"

He was surprised by the question. It was the one *he* was supposed to be asking. "I don't know...I've been away. I came to see her. She isn't here?"

"She's with *you!*" the woman suddenly exploded, startling him. She looked beyond him, toward the street, her eyes frantically searching. *"Where's Jenni?"*

"Mrs. Parklin, listen. I don't—"

She was frantic. "No, *you* listen! How could you have done this to us? You were like my own son...and then you took her away and...*where is she?*"

He was totally bewildered. What could he say? What was she talking about?

"Tell me where she is, T. G.! Now!" She seemed no more than an instant away from grabbing him and shaking an answer free. In the years he had known the Parklins, he had never seen her like this. He saw an intensity and sadness in her eyes he had never seen in anyone before.

"Jenni's missing?" he stammered, suddenly fearful for the girl and trying to piece it all together. "Look, I promise she isn't with me...I wish she was! Why do you think *I* would know where she is?"

"What did you do to my baby?"

"If I'd done anything to her, why would I come here now? I last saw her a few weeks ago...no, that's last year, now...I mean..." The woman's eyes went wide.

"Last *year?* Where? Where did you take her?"

"No, I didn't...wait, you're confusing me."

"Get in this house...right now!" she demanded, grabbing his arm and pulling him inside. Janice slammed the door behind him, spun around and ran to a phone. Puzzled, T. G. took a few steps farther in. Despite the woman's obvious anxiety, the familiar house was a comfort to him. Little if anything seemed to have changed. The same potpourri and hardwood scent he remembered filled his nostrils, sparking memories of happy times spent there with Jenni. The furniture was in the same positions he had known, and the air danced to the same loud ticking he had heard every time he had come to see the girl. He had to remind himself that the antique clock atop the mantle had measured hundreds of days since the last time he had seen it. *Could it really be?*

"In here, T. G.!"

He found the woman in the adjoining kitchen, standing at the phone. He paused next to the kitchen table, waiting. A couple of newspapers were there, with a cup of coffee, half-empty, sitting to one side. An open checkbook and several bills were laid out as well—obviously, he had interrupted her monthly banking.

The room had been remodeled and repainted more brightly, with new cabinetry. The hardwood floor was highly polished, although worn areas of discoloration here and there betrayed its age. Something that looked a bit like a television set sat to one side of the stovetop.

"Hello, Police? I...no, don't put me on hold!" She slumped a bit in frustration and spun to see him standing next to the kitchen table. "You stay right there!" she ordered, a frantic warning in her voice. T. G. was puzzled by her demeanor toward him—why the anger? He nodded.

"Don't move," Janice repeated firmly, still on hold. "I have the police on the phone. I want them to get a statement from you—they'll need it to find her." She watched the young man intently, as if trying to put her finger on something about him that was *wrong*, something that kept nagging at her.

"Yes ma'am," he nodded. "I'm right here. I'm not going anywhere."

He casually looked down at one of the newspapers, his eye caught by all the color on its pages. His amusement became something else as he looked closer.

"*USA Today*? What's *USA Today*?" he puzzled.

He looked up at the woman again to see her growing increasingly impatient. Not really thinking, his eyes drifted to the wall right next to her, to a brilliant photo of autumn leaves surrounding the base of a majestic, snow-topped mountain peak. A smile curled into the corner of his mouth—he had taken just such a photo during his trip with David, but his film had been ruined. After a moment, he realized that the glossy print was the upper half of a large photo calendar. His gaze shifted to the date printed beneath—

His heart tightened within his chest. His breathing became that of a dying man. His mind tried to shut down altogether.

T. G.'s eyes snapped back down to the table, to the odd, multi-colored newspaper. Next to it he saw the more familiar banner of the good old black-and-white *Ithaca Journal*. The headline grabbed his eye—

U.S. SPACE SHUTTLE DOCKS WITH RUSSIAN MIR

What the—

His eyes skittered across the page, seeking the date. He found it—then dropped into one of the dinette chairs, his mind numb. After a moment, he looked again—

THURSDAY, JUNE 29, 1995

His eyes bored into the date as if to alter it by a mere act of will. He grabbed the woman's checkbook, then her monthly statements, rifling through them all, searching in vain for something—*anything*—that would tell him it was not true.

But it was.

"What are you doing?" the woman asked as he dropped her papers.

Stunned, he looked out of the kitchen window, at the wind in the trees, the birds in the sky, watching a world that had gone on without him.

Twenty years. *Twenty years*. Almost the length of his lifetime had passed while he had been away. He glanced at his hands and felt his face and knew that he himself had not aged a day beyond 1975. He was still the same twenty-four-year-old he had been before, finding a new world like an awakening Rip Van Winkle. The life he knew had vanished.

"No!" he yelled, gripping the artifact as if strangling the throat of a sworn enemy. "It isn't true!" His grip tightened in vain until his fingers went white, trying to crush the uncrushable. Janice moved away slightly, unsure of him. In utter helplessness, he pulled the artifact from his shoulder and flung it to the floor. It slid heavily into the base of a cabinet, near the woman's feet. "I'm sick of being bounced around…you put me back! Now! I have a life!" Only then did he notice that the woman was staring at him, fearful now.

"That…when I threw that…it wasn't aimed at you," T. G. managed to mumble to her, his breathing settling down, his head now in his hands. "I'm…sorry."

I have a life. He realized that it had been quite some time since he had really believed that or had acted as if it were true. And now it was as if squandering his life had caused it to be yanked away, to be given to someone who would make better use of it.

Lost, he looked into Janice's eyes and, with a shaky voice, pleaded with her. "Mrs. Parklin…please. Sit down, talk to me…I'll tell you what I know." He spoke further, though not necessarily to her. "I've lost it all. Jenni…my friends…my home…everything I ever knew…"

She looked at him for several moments and slowly hung up the phone. With cautious steps, she walked over to the table. "Start talking," she said. "You said you've 'lost everything'?"

"Well," he began, still in shock, "this is…so hard to explain. I don't understand it myself."

She sat down, staring into his face. *How could this boy have done this to me? Look at him…sitting there like always, as if he's done nothing wrong…*

And then, she realized what that nagging "something" had been.

"Like always," she muttered aloud.

"What?" T. G. asked.

"You haven't changed. You don't look any different," she stated flatly. "You look exactly as I remember you. Exactly as I remember. How is that possible, T. G.? How?"

He thought about the question. What could he say? The truth was as believable as any false explanation he might come up with—

"I don't expect you to believe this, but I swear it's true. I look twenty-four years old…," he sighed, almost in resignation. *No way she'll buy this.* "…because I *am* twenty-four."

"What do you mean, you *are* twenty-four?"

"Listen…look at me. I…" He went to reach for his wallet, to show her his driver's license, his photos of Jenni, everything that 1975 had put there. His hand found only an empty back pocket.

"Oh, I forgot. They took it."

"What? Who took what?"

"My wallet…but that probably wouldn't have helped anyway. See, I don't know how all this has…I mean…" He paused, knowing he sounded like a nut. "Time must have skipped me ahead, somehow. When I woke up yesterday, it was October 1975. Now suddenly it's 1995 and I've missed so much…"

Janice began to get angry. She was in no mood for another mystery after dealing with her daughter's disappearance. "T. G. Shass, don't you dare—"

"Mrs. Parklin, look at me! Am I laughing? Am I acting like this is a joke, or am I about to come unglued?" His voice quivered. "Look at yourself! Look at the world! Then look at me! I haven't changed at all! I'm even…" His voice trailed off for a moment, then started anew. "Look. Things have been happening to me, strange things." Furious, he pointed at the relic. "And they all center around *that*. It's some kind of ancient artifact. I seem to have found it a couple of days ago…no, I mean, in 1975. While I was in Colorado with David. But I can't remember how…" He rubbed his face with both hands.

That sparked something in her. "David…David Cernan? He told the police you disappeared in Colorado and then just turned up back here without him. Before he could get home, you were gone again…with Jenni, we just knew. He said he didn't know where you were. We thought it was just a story, that he was covering for you. It's been so long, but I remember he was just frantic that you had vanished a second time. The police talked to him, and he passed a lie detector test, so we finally came to the conclusion that he didn't know any more about Jenni's and your disappearance than we did."

"He didn't. Look, Mrs. Parklin, you know me. I've never lied to you. You're like my own mom. I know I've done some stupid things, but I promise you…I don't understand what happened to me. I don't know where Jenni is. I wish to Heaven I did, but I don't. Please, tell me what *you* know. What happened? When did she disappear?"

"October 29, 1975. That date is burned into my memory."

His mind raced. "Yesterday…"

"What?"

"For me, it *was* yesterday."

"When you two vanished at the same time, we all assumed that you'd run off together. Jenni's father and I were so angry, so worried. I could have throttled you. But now you're here and she isn't, and I don't know what to think anymore. She had been talking about that fight you had…about making up with you. She was so upset she barely touched her dinner…" The woman was living the day again.

"I'm so sorry to put you through this."

"When she left the house—the last time we saw her—she said that she was going over to see you. She had been waiting for you to call, I think."

"What about her car? Did you ever find *it?*"

"She didn't take it. Even though it was getting dark, she walked. I remember snow…it was so cold outside. But she said she had a lot to think about, and walking would give her time to do that."

He ached for Jenni, for her embrace, her smile. He wanted to cry out, to trash the room in frustration. Attempting to suppress his emotions, he fought to change the focus of their conversation. "Tell me what happened to my building. When did they tear it down?"

"Years ago. Back in, oh, 1982, '83. After the police went in and found all those poor people dead, no one ever wanted to live there again."

"How many people?"

"More than twenty, I think."

No…please, no…

That would have been everyone inside. T. G. closed his eyes and hung his head, seeing their faces. He had known them all.

She went on. "At first, we were scared that you and Jenni would be found in there. But you weren't. The police wouldn't disclose everything they found, but at least we knew you two weren't in the building. We had hope then. That's why we thought Jenni was off somewhere with you. As close as you and she had been, before that one big fight, we assumed you had made up and run away together. I always thought you'd wind up married...I know Jenni thought so. And after the way you and she had gone to Syracuse that time, we figured you'd done something like that again, that you'd eloped."

"No. I wish we had. I wish it were that simple."

The woman, much calmer now, picked up her warm coffee and took a sip. "The Brookfelder case made national headlines. Anyway, the place just stood there empty for years afterward, bringing down property values all around it. No one wanted to live in a neighborhood where such horrific deaths had taken place.

"There was talk of hauntings in the building and such...strange lights...you know. All the tabloid kind of stuff. The owners said the building was historical and tried to get a landmark designation for it, but there was a huge petition drive by the homeowners in the area and they finally tore it down. No one wants to rebuild on the site. Can't say I blame them."

"Where's Mr. Parklin?" T. G. asked.

"Jonathan died six years ago." She paused and took another sip. "You know, he hired one private detective after another, trying to find you two. He knew you couldn't just have fallen off the face of the Earth."

"You'd be surprised."

"They never turned up anything. Not a clue. We finally gave up, but we always held out hope that the two of you were together out there and...happy. But now, if you don't know where she is...oh, T. G...." She began to tremble and weep, her shoulders shaking. Old and very painful wounds had been reopened. T. G. tried his best to comfort her, but knew that the only thing he could do to accomplish that was to leave. He felt that he was nothing to the woman now but a reminder of her lost daughter, and that was something she did not need.

He stared blankly at the wood plank floor, thinking. Could the shadowthing have gotten Jenni? Had she even made it to his apartment building? Perhaps she had fallen victim to some other crime, some other fate, a common, earthly one. Kidnapping? Assault? The thought of what might have befallen her horrified him.

Twenty years ago. His mind fought to accept that the same girl he had held, had laughed with, had loved just weeks before, by his memory, had likely died a young lifetime ago in the eyes of the world. He glanced up at the refrigerator door and saw there a red-tinted, faded photo he had taken of Jenni at the family's cabin on an isolated and beautiful lake in Canada. *That picture…it's been there all this time!*

He remembered that day. For him, it had been only the summer before. T. G. had accompanied the Parklins on their annual fishing vacation, deep into the Canadian pine forests several hundred miles north of International Falls. The cabin Jenni's father owned there was large and comfortable, though well hidden and, for all practical purposes, accessible only by a longtime friend's floatplane. While not too much of a fisherman, T. G. had always enjoyed the majestic beauty of nature and was anxious for any opportunity to capture Jenni, the cabin, and its surroundings on film.

At the moment he had snapped the photo, Jenni had just caught her first fish of the summer. But an instant after the shutter clicked, the walleye slipped from her grip, flopped across the boat dock, and plopped back into the cold water. T. G. had laughed then, and she had playfully splashed at him in retaliation, just before he went to her and held her, enjoying her—

Tears swelled in his eyes, as they had in Janice's. He loved Jenni, and their last fight had been such a stupid one. Trying still to keep a lid on his emotions, he rose. "I'd better be going. I've got to find David. I'm really sorry…I never meant to hurt you."

"No, T. G.," she began, drying her tears with tissue. "I know you didn't mean…that is, I didn't mean to be so angry before. It's just that I'd accepted things as being one way, and now…come to find out they're not."

He walked around and hugged her, then retrieved the patiently waiting artifact from across the floor. "I'm sorry," he said, hefting the leather strap onto his shoulder. "I'll try to find her. I love her. You know that."

Janice forced a smile. "Yes. We all knew. So did she."

He started toward the door. She rose and followed him, still wiping her eyes. "Where is David living now?" T. G. asked.

"He's still in the house that his mother lived in, before she moved to Vermont. Over on Mitchell. I run into his wife at the supermarket every so often. This time of day, you'd probably be able to catch him at work. He took over the funeral home after his father passed away."

"Okay, I'll try there." T. G. stopped at the open door, leaned and kissed the woman lightly on the cheek, then glanced at the clock on the mantle. It was three-thirty.

"I don't know what else to say."

"I know, T. G. I know. Just stay in touch. Please."

"I'm not planning on going anywhere. I have a lot of catching up to do."

As T. G. headed down the street, Janice watched him until he could be seen no more. A flicker of hope burned anew within her for the first time in many years. However it had happened, she had been given a link to her daughter—tenuous though it might be.

And if T. G. could knock on her door, so could her Jenni.

∽○∽

He walked down the street, noticing now a thousand little things that spoke of two lost decades. Street signs had been replaced and new stoplights hung. New trees had been planted. New buildings of glass and metal had sprung from the earth, filling lots where he used to fly kites and toss footballs. He mourned for a few very old houses, once ripe with character and class, that had been torn down and replaced by small business parks. The high school pizza hangout was gone, replaced by a Chinese buffet that wanted a fortune for its food. *Must be a really good buffet for five bucks.*

As he passed a park, he saw children, watched closely by their parents, riding the swings and climbing upon a colorful thing made up of giant plastic tubes and dark wood. *They look like hamsters in a runaround,* he thought, amused by the thought. *What a great idea.* All that was missing was a big, squeaky mill wheel.

His thoughts grew more serious as he watched the families more closely. *None of those kids were even born the last time I was here. For that matter, neither were some of those parents.*

Twenty years. Despite his youthful body, T. G. suddenly felt very, very old.

As he neared the funeral home, now mere blocks away, he stopped. The last time he had been there was for his parents' funeral, and that wound had not yet healed. He had not allowed it to. He looked to one side, up a street that led eventually to Mitchell Drive, where David lived, and began to rationalize. *He'll be busy at work this time of day, and besides, I have way too much to tell him. Better I see him at home.*

He turned and walked down the shady side street, toward David's neighborhood. All along, he had been appalled at the apparent disregard for traffic law he repeatedly encountered—over and again, drivers all around him, impatiently, kept turning right at red lights. *And a dollar-thirty for gas? Are you nuts?* He marveled at the futuristic cars that zoomed past, with their sleek, rounded lines and bright paint jobs. He also saw a few for which he had, just scant weeks before, seen television commercials—the new '76 models, now in a worn, decaying, and sometimes neglected state.

The world of 1995 was nothing like he had hoped it would be. Twenty years should have brought rocket belts and picture phones and space planes to the moon and all the things he had seen in the movies. All he saw instead was a world of high prices, careless drivers, and no Jenni.

For a fleeting instant, he considered clicking his heels three times.

At about four-thirty he reached the Cernan house on Mitchell Drive, almost missing it, for the huge, stately maple that had stood in its front yard was gone. He rang the bell, then knocked, and waited for some response from within. There was none. He took a seat on the front step, hoping he would not have too long a wait. He was thirsty, and a tall glass of ice water would do nicely.

So much was the same, yet so much was different. It was as if someone had dropped him onto a false Earth, trying to fool him, but had gotten the details wrong here and there. He almost felt as if, any moment, George Cernan would pull into the driveway, step out of the car, walk over, and hug him with his big, reassuring arms. T. G. had always loved to hear David's father's hearty laugh, which had endeared the gentle man to the entire community. He had been so loved—he was not the dreary, morbid mortician of stereotype. He was a friend.

T. G. remembered, against his will. What comfort he had found the day of the double closed-casket funeral had come from Mr. Cernan, from his strong hand upon T. G.'s shoulder, from his gentle, reassuring voice, and from his just being there, taking care of everything.

His parents' deaths had come so suddenly, so unfairly.

John Shass and his family were returning from a vacation to Vermont, where the family had rented a small lakeside cabin. It was almost midnight, and his dad was at the wheel, allowing his mom to get some much-needed sleep in the passenger's seat. T. G. had been in the backseat, asleep after a long day. What had happened then he only knew from police reports, for he had no direct memory of the event and little memory of that entire day. He was grateful for that.

They had been traveling down a two-lane highway. A semitruck loaded with twenty-five-foot lengths of steel pipe had passed the

Shasses' two-door, trying to beat another truck coming on fast in the other lane. According to witnesses, the truck had plenty of time for the maneuver, but the intoxicated driver cut back too sharply into his lane, into the forward left side of the Shasses' car. T. G.'s father tried to stop, to pull free of the tangle of chains and metal that instantly ensnared his comparatively tiny vehicle, but it was too late. In less than a second, it was over.

Death claimed a good man and his wife.

The entire load of steel pipe shifted as the truck began to turn over, spilling onto T. G.'s car and crushing his family. His parents were killed instantly, and he was pinned to the rear floorboard for four hours as fire crews and highway patrolmen fought valiantly to free him. Repeatedly he called his parents' names. Apart from the scream of straining metal and a cacophony of blowtorches, chainsaws, and sirens, all he heard was silence. The voices he prayed to hear did not come.

He spent the next three days in the hospital, his only injury a broken arm. It was a miracle, they said. He was lucky, they said.

The intolerable silence of the empty house as he packed his things did not speak to T. G. of luck. It spoke only of death and pain and loss. He had been a Christian, yet in his pain he had angrily demanded comfort from the God he blamed for his parents' deaths. The emptiness continued—no comfort, no angelic messengers, no sudden release from his agony.

No deliverance from the bitterness of the guilt he felt.

His prayers seemingly unanswered, he had decided that God did not exist. Nothing held any meaning for him anymore. He never grieved for his parents—to do so was to admit to himself that they were gone.

And now, the only girl he had ever loved was also gone. She had been for two decades. *Oh, Jenni, if only...*

A nearby noise brought T. G. out of his reverie. As a four-door, midnight blue sedan pulled into the driveway, he realized that a single tear had coursed down his cheek. He wiped it away, then stood to face the slowing car.

It stopped, and the sound of the motor went silent. T. G. waited, gazing at the darkened glass of the driver's door, but no one emerged. Metallic clicks sounded as the hot engine began to cool. Finally, the door of the car cracked open and a foot stepped out. The driver, an impressive figure in an expensive business suit, emerged and stared at T. G. through mirrored sunglasses. After a few moments, the man closed the door behind him and continued to stand next to the vehicle, taking off the dark lenses, still staring.

"Hello, David," T. G. responded to the forty-four-year-old man before him. He stepped down from the porch and approached his friend, who suddenly burst into a smile and rushed toward him. They embraced, and David patted T. G.'s back repeatedly before grabbing his shoulders and pushing him back to arm's length.

"Where have you been?" he asked, tears flooding his eyes.

"Around."

David laughed, the flood of emotion and relief almost over-whelming him. " 'Around'? That's it? That's all I get? 'Around'?"

"There's more. Lots more."

"There'd better be," he said, needing answers.

"Man, you look like your father," T. G. said. "For a minute, I wondered…"

"I hear that a lot." He motioned toward the house. "Come in, stay awhile. Twenty years will do nicely."

They walked toward the house. Only as he unlocked the front door did David, like Jenni's mother, begin to realize that his best friend looked exactly as he remembered him. The person he saw was not T. G. the middle-aged man he should have been, but T. G. the Cornell student, T. G. the rappeller who had vanished into that Colorado rockface only to turn up in New York without explanation. David looked hard at the enigma before him.

"What happened?"

"Long story," T. G. responded.

"I've got nothing but time."

They settled into the den. David picked up a few toys and tossed them into another room, then stripped off his suitcoat and tie. "Sorry, the boys do their best to keep it messy in here." He managed to remember his hosting skills as he walked from the room, leaving T. G. behind but raising his voice to maintain conversation. "Thirsty?"

"Very. And I'm starving."

"Got it covered."

"Jenni's mom told me you were married," T. G. said loudly.

"Going on twelve years now. Angela Chandler. I don't think you knew her. And we've got two sons, T. G. and Rick."

"T. G.?" he asked, smiling. "Really?"

"Timothy Gerald," David smiled. "Did I get close?"

"Not even," T. G. laughed. "But thanks. I'm honored."

"So how's Jenni? Where is she?"

"I don't know, David. She was never with me."

"She wasn't?" he asked with mild surprise. "Oh, man…I wondered about that. We all did."

"So her mom told me," T. G. said, deep concern in his voice.

"I wish I knew what happened to her," David sympathized. "That was so long ago now. I'm sorry. I know what she meant to you."

"Yeah," T. G. replied. "Long time ago." For several moments the air hung heavy with worry and regret as neither spoke, each remembering the playful, energetic girl they had known. *That thing must have gotten her…I don't know.* His eyes grew very wet.

"Well," David said, mercifully changing the subject, "two cold ones, coming right up."

T. G. gathered himself, then leaned over and picked up a newspaper that rested on the coffee table. Too few of the names there were familiar, and neither were most of the places. *O. J. Simpson? No kidding?* He read the space shuttle story and was crushed to learn that the promised moon bases and flights to Mars had never materialized. *Did you guys take the rest of the century off or something? And where did the Soviet Union go?*

David reemerged with a Coke for himself. He handed T. G. a ham sandwich and an ice-cold Dr Pepper, remembering that the drink had become a favorite of his during a prolonged vacation down south.

"Hey," T. G. said, taking the frosty can with a smile, "this stuff used to be kinda hard to come by up here."

"Not anymore."

T. G. took a greedy bite of the sandwich and nodded approvingly. He looked down at the soft-drink can, and David watched the momentary, puzzled expression that washed across his friend's face as he considered the pull tab atop it.

"What's the matter?" David asked.

"Uh, nothing…"

T. G. popped open the top, then tried to lift the tab completely from the can before realizing it was not meant to come off. Having sorted that out, he sampled the soda, playing it upon his palate as would a wine connoisseur. "It isn't as sweet as before, but it's still good. Hmmm…the can feels funny."

"How? Funny how?" David asked, amused.

"I don't know…lighter. Really thin. Look how easy it dents."

"You haven't aged," David said suddenly, almost accusingly. "And you've never seen a can like that before, have you? Talk to me, T. G. *You haven't aged.* And what about the cliff? I mean, your rope just disappeared right into it! Where were you? What happened? Twenty years, man…*twenty years!*"

"You already know more than I do, Dave," he replied, downing the last of the sandwich. "I don't know what happened to me in Colorado or how I wound up with this." He indicated the artifact at his shoulder. "Whatever the blessed thing is, it's a mystery to me."

"Not good enough, T-square. I've waited forever for this story. You have to know *something.*"

T. G. paused. "Okay. I can't promise it'll make any sense, but…"

For the next few hours the weary T. G. told as much of the story as he knew, leaving nothing out. The tale was astonishing and unbelievable. David sat very little during the discourse, instead pacing or walking around the room as he listened, pausing every so often to consider the apparent evidences presented by T. G.'s youthful form and the artifact on the couch beside him. The story was intricate. Still, he doubted. It was all too incredible. It was fantasy.

It grew dark outside.

"And then I headed over here," T. G. went on. "At first I was going to go to the funeral home, but—"

He was interrupted and startled by a sudden lunge by David, who roughly grabbed T. G.'s left forearm and pulled it outward, palm up. Without a word he pushed the shirtsleeve back, then stared wide-eyed at the large, still-healing L-shaped gash above T. G.'s wrist.

"Ow!" T. G. protested. "Careful…it's still sore."

David went pale. He sat heavily into a chair just opposite T. G. and looked at his friend as if seeing him anew.

" 'Bleed later,' " David quoted under his breath, forced to believe.

"Oh yeah. You said that," T. G. casually remembered, looking at the wound for a moment before pulling his sleeve back down. "It's not too bad though…it's healing okay. That doctor cleaned it up." Then a light came on for him. "You're thinking that this should have healed twenty years ago."

"Yeah," David nodded. "It's true, isn't it. It's all true…"

"I can't stay here, David," T. G. concluded. "I can't stay anywhere. Not where there're people. That thing killed everyone in my building, and I have no reason to doubt that it will come here."

"Look. It might not. It didn't go to the school. Besides, that was back in '75. It must have given up on you by now. Angie and the kids are at her mom's for a few weeks for summer vacation. We do it every year. I was going to go with them, but business came up and the plan is for me to meet them up there this Sunday. I'll call and tell her that I'm going to be a little later getting there than I thought."

"No, David. I need to leave."

"You disappeared on me twenty years ago, and I'll be hanged if I'm going to let it happen again. I've played that day over in my mind a thousand times, every second, every detail. Whatever happened to you back then, it was my fault."

"It was *not* your fault. You know that. You didn't make the rock open up."

"It was my bright idea to rappel with a storm blowing up. And the whole Colorado trip was my idea to begin with, remember?"

"Like it was yesterday. But you didn't exactly have to drag me out there."

He knew David was unconvinced. "That aside, you didn't see this thing. Right out of Hell, David, I swear. I know what it's capable of. You have a family. I don't want it to endanger you or them."

David knew T. G. was right. He walked over to a family portrait that sat on one end table, considering his family. "You're right, I know. Listen, we'll take it slow. Stay the night, okay? Couple of days, maybe. Long enough to get you back on your feet, at least. Let's see what happens. But I won't have you facing this whole thing alone. Not any more." He placed a strong, reassuring hand on his friend's shoulder. "Anything you need, T-square. From here on out. Money, clothes, a car, you name it. I'll get you a place. And a job. At least let me do that much."

"Look, Dave…"

"T. G., I have to get past all the worry and lost sleep I've been through for the last twenty years." He was insistent, his voice soaked with emotion. "I see that rope and the rain and the lightning in nightmares, and I wake up in a cold sweat, wondering what I did to you."

T. G. looked hard into David's eyes. They were filled with pain. After a moment's hesitation, he smiled and nodded quietly in agreement, touched by the dedication of his friend. "Okay, Dave. Okay."

David walked over and turned on a couple of table lamps, filling the room with warm, comforting light.

"Come on. I'll fix us some dinner and give you the nickel tour."

As microwave entrées cooked—much to T. G.'s amazement—David showed him through the house, acquainting him with all of the wondrous appliances and electronic gadgets that had emerged during the prior two decades. David watched with glee as T. G. was introduced to such miracles as the CD player, the VCR, the wireless remote, the cellular phone, and the home computer.

Amazed though he was by his tour of the future, T. G. soon reached the end of his endurance. It took only moments for him to fall asleep in the soft bed his host provided, for it was the first comfortable rest he had had in days. Alone, David walked back out into the living room and stood over the artifact where it still rested, there on the couch. It was indeed a marvelous thing to behold, filled with so much mystery.

"How did you do it?" he asked the artifact, half expecting an answer. "Twenty years is a long time. And all the other stuff…" He paused, looking toward the hall before returning his gaze to the relic. "Find someone else to pick on. He's been through enough. Leave him alone."

David turned out the lights in the den and went to bed, leaving the artifact alone in the dark.

∽∾∾∾

Birds sang. Morning light poured in through the windows as David walked, barefooted and robed, into the den. The smell of freshly brewed coffee filled the air. "Good morning," he said, running a hand through his sleep-tangled hair. "Glad you're still with us."

T. G. sat on the coffee table, looking down at the artifact on the couch. "Morning." He took a sip from his cup. "I took the liberty of brewing a pot. Never saw a percolator like that…good thing there were instructions on the coffee package."

"No visitors last night, I take it?"

"No. Not a one."

David walked into the kitchen and poured himself a cup as well, then took a chair near the couch. Glancing up at an antique-faced electric clock on the wall, he saw that he had slept a little later than usual. "Hmmm. Nine-thirty…I guess I slept through the alarm."

"What time does the funeral home open?"

"Ten…but no one's booked for today. Willie—he's my assistant—he'll open up and get on some ordering he needs to do, but that's about it. I already called and told him I wasn't coming in."

T. G. looked hard at the leathery albatross. "I've been thinking about all this, Dave. I don't know what this artifact is or how I got it, but I'm tired of being yanked around. I'm not going to be a victim to this thing anymore."

"What are you thinking?"

"I'm going to destroy it."

"But you said it's invulnerable, that nothing can touch it."

"I haven't tried everything yet. There must be *something* that it can't stand up to. And once it's gone, that monster or demon or whatever it was will have no more reason to come after me. It killed everyone in my building, Dave. No one else dies, not on account of me." He glared at the artifact. "And not on account of *that*."

"So what are you thinking? What can we try?"

"How hot does your crematory get?" he asked, still looking at the relic.

"That should do it," David nodded subtly. "Thousands of degrees. Twenty-four hundred, depending. It's an older model. My grandfather had it put in back in the early '50s. Hotter than most they make now. It's like a kiln. Hotter."

"Hot enough to melt metal?"

"Bridgework and such. Gold, silver. What's left of most other metals comes out brittle and ruined." He indicated the artifact. "Seems mostly organic. It should reduce to ash pretty quickly."

T. G. looked over at David. "Let's go."

"Think carefully about this, T. G. Sure, you lost twenty years, but you're here *now*. And unlike the rest of us, you're still young. You'll live a lot farther into the next century than you would have. And if you incinerate that thing, you'll never get any answers. You'll never know what it is or where that place was."

T. G. was determined. "I lost my parents. I wasn't there for them when they needed me. I knew my dad was tired. If I'd been the one driving, instead of being asleep, maybe…" David saw tears welling up in T. G.'s eyes. That was something he had never seen, even at the funeral. "And now, I've lost Jenni. Because of this thing, I wasn't here when *she* needed me."

"You can't take the blame for that. You couldn't have helped your parents, and you don't know that you could have helped Jenni, even if you *had* been here."

"No," T. G. corrected him, determination edging his voice. "I don't know that I *couldn't* have."

∽∾∾

The reinforced door to the crematory room swung open with a metallic creak. David entered first then motioned for T. G. to follow. Wheeled stainless-steel tables like hospital gurneys lined one wall, but they had never carried anyone who could be saved. The room was quiet and dimly lit, and T. G.'s footsteps echoed as he walked in.

The furnace lay behind an ominous, fifteen-foot-wide, brick-and-steel structure built into the opposite end of the large, square room. From its arching roof a metal chimney pipe some two feet wide rose, continuing through the ceiling. Intense, flickering light streamed from a small window in its heavy, rectangular door, throwing a hellish dance upon the ceiling.

"Here we are," David said. He glanced at a thermometer gauge on the side of the old furnace. "It's ready. It takes an hour to come up to temperature, so I called ahead and had Willie fire it up."

T. G. slipped out of the shoulder strap and walked up to the furnace. "Let's get it done."

"Last chance. You're sure about this?"

T. G. nodded grimly, staring through the little window, into the flames. David lifted a gleaming silver handle and released the latch bar that held the door shut. As the mortician pulled, the clamshell door split at its center and one half rose as the other dropped down, filling the room with light and noise. Three feet above the ground, the floor of the chamber met the bottom of the door, creating a flush aperture through which to insert whatever would be cremated.

The roar of the intense diesel-fed furnace hammered T. G.'s ears as he lifted the artifact onto the sill of the doorway. As the blinding heat splashed against his face, stinging his eyes and singeing his eyebrows, he shoved the artifact forward, through the door and into the inferno. It slid a few feet into the firebrick-lined chamber and came to rest with solid finality at the center of the conflagration. T. G. then backed away, watching as the flames licked against the relic's ornate tooling, its amber gems glittering in the white-hot light. David slammed the massive brick-and-steel barrier shut, and before the thunder of the impact died away the locking bar had clanked back into place.

They stood there for a moment, silent. T. G. half expected to hear a scream from beyond the steel-faced door.

"That's it," David said.

"I hope so," T. G. replied.

"A normal cremation takes a couple of hours. This won't take that long."

"Don't count on that."

"We'll come back tonight and check on it. Don't expect more than ashes."

They drove home, stopping for lunch at T. G.'s favorite steakhouse, which still stood in the strange, new Ithaca. But he only partially enjoyed his medium-well rib-eye—he *always* had the rib-eye —because he kept jumping at every sudden noise, glancing out the window and peering around, as if he expected to be found by someone. He was obviously on edge and preoccupied.

"I feel like I'm eating with Richard Kimble," David said, watching his friend. "Settle down, will you?"

"It was too easy," T. G. stated, his voice burdened with worry.

"What was?"

"Burning the relic. It was too easy, tossing it into the crematory." He looked away, his eyes fixed upon nothing. "When that monstrosity in my apartment demanded I hand the thing over, I couldn't. I don't know why, and it was really weird, but at that moment I would have done *anything* to protect it. For some reason, all of a sudden it was more important to me than my own life. But not an hour ago I threw it into the fire without so much as a second thought and was glad to be rid of it."

"Well, a lot's happened between then and now. Like you said, look at all you lost. You want your life to be the way it was, for everything to get back to normal...so it's only natural to want the artifact out of your life."

"I suppose. But what if it's something else?"

"Like what?"

"Like maybe there was a real threat to it then but not now. What if something else is at work here? Something that led me to protect it against that shadowthing but not against the crematory fire...because the flames can't touch it."

"That's crazy," David insisted. "Look. Don't borrow trouble. It's ash by now."

"Maybe," he said, with a slight shake of his head. "Maybe." He poked at his mashed potatoes, watching absently as the dark gravy flowed in the wake of his fork. The momentary silence was ponderous and uncomfortable, its weight draped over the two men's shoulders like a tattered shroud.

A waitress approached and refilled their water glasses then left. David, looking upon his friend, sensed the knotted anguish in T. G.'s mind and heart. The pain he saw reflected a grave despair, one centered less upon T. G.'s own circumstances than upon those of someone else.

"That isn't all that's bothering you," he knew. "Ever since yesterday, this cloud's been hanging over you. It's Jenni."

"What happened to her, Dave?" T. G. asked under his breath, wishing for an answer. "I've gone over it again and again. I just don't see how it could have been a simple abduction. Something else happened. I don't know what, but I'm sure of it. I mean, what are the odds? How could she and I both go missing on the same day, from the same place, but for *different* reasons?"

"Same place?"

"Her mom said Jenni was walking to my apartment the last time she saw her."

David nodded. "So you think that shadowthing got her."

"It had to have."

"But she wasn't found there like the others were."

"I know…"

David saw a wetness pooling in his friend's eyes as they turned away. The two men finished their meal quietly.

Upon returning to the car, a toothpick in his mouth, T. G. cautiously peered through the car windows, checking the back seat for an unwanted visitor. The artifact was not there.

He began to breathe a little easier on the drive back to David's house. He tried to accept the idea that the artifact would no longer haunt him, that hellish creatures would no longer stalk him, that never again would he find himself in a strange, new world. Again and again he looked over his shoulder into the backseat, unable to believe that the nightmare was over.

"Don't worry," David assured him. "I think we got it."

"I want to believe that," T. G. answered, smiling a little nervously. "More than anything. I just want to get back to normal life again, where the worst thing I have to worry about is making rent."

"Speaking of which, I want you to come work for me. I'll pay you pretty well. Office stuff…filing, typing, that sort of thing. You'll never have to deal with the customers."

"You know, I might do that. For now, anyway. I wonder if I can pick up my hours at Cornell after such an extended 'vacation.' I still want my degree."

"I don't see why not. You know, Dr. Abelwhite's still around... she's just not teaching anymore. She retired back in the late seventies, and from what I heard I'm not so sure it didn't have something to do with you. Maybe you should go see her."

"She retired because of me? Why do you say that?"

"Well, Pete Burke—you may remember him—he said he had her class along with you. He told me she was never the same after you turned up missing. She took it kinda hard."

"Yes," he nodded. "I want to see her. I have a lot to tell her about."

They pulled into David's driveway and he killed the engine. As T. G. rose from the car, he once more looked into the backseat, scanning the floorboards as well. There was no sign of the relic. He smiled.

"I think you may be right," he said, breathing a little easier.

"Piece of cake," David grinned.

With a jingle of keys, David unlocked the door and entered the house. T. G. remained behind on the porch, his eyes closed, leaning against the stonework beside the doorframe, wanting to believe. Seconds later, he heard footsteps. They stopped.

T. G. turned and looked. David stood in the doorway, his eyes hard, his face pale.

The artifact, unharmed, was in his trembling hands.

9

The house had stood since the Civil War, a massive, glorious symphony of stone and wood and stained glass. Ulysses Grant had slept there once, they said, high in the third-floor bedroom of its eastern tower. Its cut stone had been imported from a French quarry, carried in the holds of the great sailing ships that once filled New York Harbor with tall, polished masts adorned with billowing linen. Now the house stood quietly, an imposing yet silent structure with a history that had been all but forgotten.

One woman knew of its wondrous past, for such things were her life. She was its sole occupant.

It was a breezy, overcast afternoon, filled with the sound of branches touched by wind. A deep blue car slowly pulled up to the curb, and two men got out and walked toward the house, awed by its very existence. T. G. had always been a bit intimidated by the monstrous structure and had never had a reason to visit before. Now, as he walked up the stone steps he looked down at the antiquity he carried, knowing that the old house was an infant by comparison. Reaching the heavy, carved front door, he paused for a moment to enjoy the light-play of the surrounding cut-glass windows before ringing the bell. He looked at David, who shrugged.

The door creaked open. An elderly woman, bent and grayed by time, peered out with eyes that still shone with the fire of curiosity. T. G. immediately broke into a huge smile at the sight of her, as did she.

"Oh, T. G....it *is* you!" she exclaimed, stepping out toward him. Tears of joy filled her eyes. She raised her weakened arms and embraced him. "Oh, I'm so happy to see you...when I got your call I couldn't believe it."

"It's really good to see you again, Doctor," he smiled, gently returning the hug. He noticed that she still wore the same perfume.

"You know David Cernan…he wasn't a student of yours, but he came up to the lab with me a few times."

"Yes, of course," she smiled. "Hello, David."

"Doctor," he smiled back.

T. G. went on. "So much has happened…things you won't believe." The woman invited them inside, and as he turned to enter she saw the artifact hanging from his shoulder.

"You still have it," she said, her eyes wide. "I'll believe, T. G. Whatever you have to tell me. I saw what that thing did to my saw blade, remember?"

"But…there's so much more. Like, it's been twenty years, but I haven't—"

"I can see. You haven't aged."

He smiled. She closed the door behind them. All the drapes were drawn, preserving a gloom that suited such a place. T. G. and David followed her into the depths of the house, into a sitting room walled with shelves cluttered with books and curiosities. The house smelled old, like brittle, yellowed pages and hardened leather. It was the scent of the wisdom of the ages.

"Corey Leighton raked Campus Security over the coals after the artifact disappeared from the specimen room," she said, chuckling. "For weeks he had them search, just for spite, I think. The whole campus, again and again. I tried to call you the morning after you left it with us, as soon as I realized it was missing, but I couldn't get through. I hoped that somehow you had come back for it." She indicated the artifact at his shoulder. "I guess you did. How did you sneak it out?"

"I didn't. It…well, it followed me home. It suddenly appeared in my car as I was driving, not twenty minutes after I'd left."

"Indeed?" she asked, not nearly as surprised as T. G. might have expected. "And here we are, all together again."

At Abelwhite's suggestion, David sat in a large leather chair that was every bit as comfortable as it looked. The woman sat on the sofa and motioned for T. G. to do the same. Even as he sat, words poured from his lips.

"Something tried to get it from me, that same night. Demonic. Horrible. Fangs. Claws. A huge thing. It killed everyone in my apartment building…"

"I remember. It was terrible. I tried to come see you after I couldn't get you on the phone, but the police had the whole building cordoned off. I lost another former student that day—Bob Holt, a good boy. A talented artist."

"I remember him. I didn't really know him other than sometimes running into him at the mailboxes, though."

"At first, I feared for your life, too."

"It *would* have killed me, for sure…but this hole opened up. No, not a hole, a portal or something. In the floor. I fell through it. It saved me."

"A portal," she repeated, thinking.

"Yes. And I know this sounds nuts, believe me…but I dropped onto what had to be another planet. With lush vegetation everywhere, and a dark pink sky with the brightest stars you ever saw. And the people…they were huge. Not misshapen or grotesque, just huge, but still normally proportioned. Their skin was a bronzish color, and the whites of their eyes caught the light…like pearl. Hard to describe, really. When I got there, I was hurt. My leg. One of the people there took me to one of their doctors, somewhere in this enormous city. I was healed instantly by some gadget he pulled down from the ceiling."

Dr. Abelwhite looked away at nothing, sightlessly staring as her mind worked. Her expression became one of deep concentration, of one working to solve a puzzle. Quiet filled the heavy air of the room.

T. G. paused. "Doctor?"

"Yes, T. G. I was just thinking. Bright stars, you said? Like…jewels, maybe?"

"Yeah, that's a good description for them. They weren't just white, but red and blue and orange and yellow. Brilliant color. A hundred colors. And so bright. I've never seen anything like it...like sparkling jewels set in the sky."

"And the people...huge people, you said? With eyes like pearl?"

"Seven feet, easy. Eight, maybe even nine sometimes. Even the women."

She stood and started to walk slowly around the room. "What was this world called, T. G.?"

"I don't know. I didn't speak their language. If Pretzel ever told me, I didn't realize it."

"Pretzel?"

"He's the one who carried me to the doctor. Some kind of police, I think, were waiting in his apartment. We were arrested. They knocked us out with this little hand-held gadget, and we woke up in a dungeonlike cell."

The woman was utterly open to his story. She drank in every word, no matter how incredible. He told her of the crime in the streets, of the advanced technology. Of the walking ghosts that had reacted so violently to his presence.

"And suddenly, I was back here. I was there only a day, but when I got back here it was twenty years later."

She looked upon him with a rare and gentle wisdom. "Come with me," she said, walking toward a downward-leading flight of stairs. "I need to show you something. David, will you excuse us for a moment?"

"Yes ma'am," the middle-aged man nodded, respecting her wish. "I'll be right here."

"Feel free to look through any of the books on these shelves. This shouldn't take too long."

T. G. followed her down the stairs and through a heavy, reinforced door at its bottom. Beyond lay an impressive basement laboratory and archive that would have made many a museum envious. The center of the room was dominated by a large and well-lit worktable, covered with small and obviously ancient pieces of jewelry, pottery, and statuary all carefully numbered and undergoing study. Next to the table on a rolling stand was a dream selection of analysis tools. Shelves of unearthed and painstakingly catalogued artifacts lined one wall, mostly clay figurines, tablets, and reassembled pottery shards. There were thousands of items from past civilizations, most awaiting future homes in museums. A floor-to-ceiling rack of long, plastic storage tubes was mounted nearby.

"Wow," T. G. said. "This is incredible. I could spend the rest of my life in here."

"I likely will."

She smiled, drew one tube from the rack and brought it over to the table. "I found this in 1953," she began, "during my third Valley of the Kings excavation. It was sealed in an alabaster jar among the burial treasures of a tomb I found near the site of the 1898 Royal Cache. They were completely undisturbed...the existence of the chamber had eluded robbers."

"You found another tomb? I never heard about that."

"Yes. Not adjacent, but nearby. At first I assumed it belonged to a member of Amenhotep's family, just as the others had. I thought so for months. Until I began to decipher this." She unscrewed the lid of the short, wide storage cylinder and gently withdrew a set of photographs. "These aren't the originals, of course...those have been hermetically preserved. The papyri they were written on were in relatively good shape, but I wanted to make sure they stayed that way."

He watched as she placed a series of old, large black-and-white photos onto the table before him and pointed to a line of hieroglyphics on one of them. "Read this."

T. G. cocked his head slightly, studying the symbols as she watched his face. " 'The...court...of...' "—momentarily stumped, he shook his head and renewed his concentration—" 'he of the gods...who is...no, *walks*...among us.' I know that's the cartouche of Amenhotep, there ...but this other name, though...I don't recognize it."

"Very good," she smiled. "That name is 'Astanapha.' You and I are the only ones to look upon these words since they were written by him around 1400 B.C. I doubt he ever let anyone else read them. And he probably ordered them to be buried with him so no one ever would. In a moment, you'll understand why. I never disclosed their discovery."

"You didn't? Why not?"

"T. G.," she began, "this is the diary of Astanapha, chief sorcerer of the Pharaoh's court during the reign of Amenhotep II. It took me three years of diligent effort to decipher it in its entirety. There are symbols here that I've never seen anywhere else, but eventually I was able to unlock them by cross-comparing different parts of the diary. Once I did, well…"

"What does it say?"

"A great portion of the text is comprised of his account of Moses' dealings with Amenhotep II. This is the first direct, extrabiblical con- firmation of the book of Exodus ever discovered."

"Ever?"

"Well, there was once a tablet unearthed in the Nile delta region that consisted of orders to the Egyptian soldiers in the area. They were instructed to allow the departing Hebrews to pass through unha- rassed, but *this*…" She looked down at the photographs. "This is a personal account of the *entire* event. Moses' flight from Egypt. The plagues. The departure of the Hebrews. Everything…everything."

T. G. was stunned by the import of what the diary represented. "Incredible," he managed to whisper.

She continued. "Archaeologists the world over have used the Bible as an excavation guide for as long as they've been digging. In all of recorded history, it *alone* told of the Hittites and of the cities of Sodom and Gomorrah long before evidence for them was actually discovered. You know that, I'm sure."

"Sure," he nodded.

"Astanapha was the most powerful sorcerer of Pharaoh's court. He was the teacher of Jannes and Jambres, the magicians who turned their wooden staffs into snakes after Aaron had done the same, during Moses' first confrontation with Amenhotep. That wasn't fiction; he lays it *all* out in here. The Nile turning to blood. *Real blood*, T. G., not just some reddish sediment in the water like some have suggested. The Egyptians knew blood when they saw it. He talks of the stench. Even in sealed water jars...*blood*. And the frogs. The hail. All ten plagues, in biblical order. This was his personal record of it all."

"It really happened? All of it?"

"Yes. All of it. Astanapha even lost his own firstborn son in the tenth plague! The pain of that event changed him, made him question everything. He goes on to express his doubt in the 'godhood' of the Pharaoh, and that is absolutely unheard of. Such doubts, if discovered, constituted a treason worthy of death. A horrible death... often by being buried alive."

"So why did you hide this?"

"Because of what comes later." She took a deep breath. "This entire account is obviously historical, not fictional. From the first word. And once I got beyond the destruction of Pharaoh's army, I realized that Astanapha was trying to convince himself, despite all evidence to the contrary, that the entire religious system of Egypt was true. He began recounting evidences he had seen with his own eyes. He and Amenhotep had both had face-to-face encounters with the 'gods,' well before the events of Exodus. Not spiritually, but *physically*. These 'gods' had appeared to the Pharaohs from time to time down through the centuries, it says, claiming to enter our world only when absolutely necessary. On one occasion, they came to give Amenhotep and Astanapha great power with which to defeat the Hebrews and their 'false god.' "

"I guess it didn't work."

"Apparently not, despite repeated 'visitations.' " Her eyes sparkled with fascination, and she held nothing back, pointing to another row of symbols. "T. G....he says here that the gods were 'like men, *but of great stature, with skin of bronze and eyes of pearl*.' And the afterlife domain from which they came was 'a place of wondrous music and *jewel-studded skies.*' How could it be mere coincidence?"

He was speechless. As he stared at the photos before him, she went on.

"Only the chief sorcerer and the Pharaoh were instructed how to summon the gods when necessary. The two of them had on occasion caught glimpses of another world through an open portal, but mere men were forbidden from passing through it and into the realm of the gods. That privilege, they were told, was reserved exclusively for the dead. It's just possible that, at one time, the *false* doors built into the walls of many Egyptian tombs, well, *weren't.*"

"But they're solid rock."

"So was your cliff face."

He looked blankly at the floor, remembering flashes of images recorded in a fleeting span of seconds. Lightning, rain, then swinging against the sheer wall—then, nothing. Looking back into her eyes, he considered her words.

"Maybe those 'gods' were just lying…maybe they didn't want anyone going through for some other reason. Maybe they were hiding something and didn't want to be found out. I mean, if this 'afterlife' was the place *I* was, those weren't gods. That place was physical. It was solid."

She nodded. "Perhaps. But Astanapha and his king were warned repeatedly of a *curse*…that if it ever happened, if any living man ever went through the gateway, it would mean the fall of utter devastation upon our world."

"How?"

"I don't know. He's unclear. But he's emphatic that the gods of the afterlife would unleash a terrible wrath upon Earth that would leave it desolate. I'm no theologian, but I'd say we may be talking about Armageddon here."

"But I was there already."

"Not by way of this gateway," she insisted. "Perhaps you snuck in somehow, through an accidental tear in space-time. What if activating Astanapha's gateway sounds an alarm on the other side?"

"You believe that?"

"I don't know. Let's just say I think it prudent not to risk it. When the blade of Armageddon falls, I'd prefer not to be the person responsible."

"You're telling me that you think the gods of Egypt were real?"

"Real, yes. 'Gods,' no. But something...*someone*...that Amenhotep and Astanapha spoke with had the power to pass from world to world. Whether these worlds are exclusively physical or spiritual as well, I don't know. Your experience certainly suggests the former. But these beings represent an immense power in any case."

"But what about science? I mean, how can a rational mind like yours think that a curse could—?"

"I'm talking about rationality. You're confusing it with the natural. This universe is not bound exclusively to the natural realm, T. G. If I've learned anything over my lifetime, I've learned that there is more out there than that which we can touch or measure or study. Logic...order...it's an integral part of *everything*. Chaos is an illusion. But the truth is that we simply cannot comprehend the incredible level at which that logic operates. It is utterly perfect and infinitely intelligent. *Logos,* T. G."

T. G. swallowed hard. "You're talking about God."

"Yes."

"The God of the Bible."

She paused a moment, removing her glasses. "Yes. This diary confirms the story of Exodus almost word for word, which confirms the *miracles* of Exodus, which confirms the God Who performed them. A flawless chain of progressive logic, T. G....one that, based upon the proven veracity of the Bible, could ultimately be carried all the way to the Cross."

He thought about that. After a prolonged silence, she turned back to the subject of the diary. "The rest of Astanapha's account is absolutely factual, an eyewitness report of his personal experiences with these beings. He obviously felt an enormous responsibility to record everything he knew, leaving out nothing, regardless of the possible consequences. At first, I wanted to take the whole thing as mere imagination, or as part of some religious allegory, but I couldn't. The context just won't allow it. He reports clearly and deliberately that he met and conversed with beings from another existence...and he tells *everything* he knew."

"I still don't see. What's the harm in anyone knowing about all this?"

"Because, my dear," she stated slowly and deliberately, in an ominous tone T. G. had never heard from her before, "he then tells how *to open* the gateway."

T. G. sat down on a nearby stool, letting it all soak in. He looked up into her eyes and saw the woman trembling with the deadly seriousness of her words. He began slowly, unsure what words would come. "How...uh...how have you kept this a secret for so long?"

"By keeping my mouth closed," she said. "I hid these papyri and my work on them from the rest of the archaeological community, and even from my dear, late husband. They have never left this room. At first, it was simply that I didn't want to show them until I had a complete translation, but once I understood the possible consequences of this becoming known to someone who might actually try to use it, I locked it away and pretended it never existed."

T. G. stood and paced a few times, thinking aloud, his face brightening as gears turned. "That's it...that *has* to be the answer. A gateway...and that thing wanted the artifact..."

"What?"

"The artifact! That thing in my apartment wanted it, and I'm sure that guy on that other world knew what it was! It must have come from there."

"The monster or the relic?"

"Both!" T. G. said. "She's there! It got her. It went back there, and it took her back with it!"

"Got who?"

"Jenni!" Hope filled him for the first time. "I have to go back there. I can save her! If I can open a gateway—"

"Absolutely not! It's too great a risk."

"Doctor, listen. On the day I vanished in 1975, Jenni Parklin did too. If some guy just grabbed her off the street, then she's gone forever, and I can't accept that. I can't. The only chance I have of seeing her again is if she's in that other place. She's got to be there. She's just got to. And if she is, I'm her only chance of getting home."

"No," the woman said, but T. G. thought he saw a sign of weakening in her eyes.

"Please, I'm the only one who can bring her back. But I can't do it by myself. I need your help."

"There's an old Roman saying, T. G. 'The only thing more dangerous than a locked room full of ravenous tigers is an unwitting child with the key.' "

He considered her words but was undaunted. "Please."

The woman looked at him long and hard, then turned and walked away. She stopped, her mind in conflict with itself, considering the proper action to take. "T. G.," she began, facing away from him and running her hand through her hair, "this artifact of yours bounced you there once already; it may do it again. Perhaps you should just wait and—"

"I can't just sit here," he insisted. "I have to get control of my life back. I have to go back there on my terms and find her. What if time's running out? What if she needs me *now*?"

"If you go back you may lose *more* time. Suppose you return home to find a century gone? Or two? Or what if time between the two worlds is utterly nonconcurrent, and you wind up back on Earth in the 1920s…or the Middle Ages? What kind of life will that leave you?"

"Suppose I *don't*. But even if I do, I have to take the chance. It's taken losing her for me to realize that without Jenni, I have no life at all."

"You'd risk Armageddon on such a wildly improbable chance of finding one girl again? T. G., you're only twenty-four years old. You're not thinking this through."

"I can't say how I know this, but I do...I need to go back there. I *have* to go back there. I'm *supposed* to go back there."

She turned and stared into his young, pain-filled eyes.

"Please," he whispered.

The woman stood for several long moments, unsure. T. G. saw the struggle in her glistening eyes.

"No," she said, turning away. "I'm sorry."

The student stood in silence, frustrated, yet understanding her position. Dr. Abelwhite, her face in her hands, walked slowly across the room and away from him, the turmoil within her still evident.

All things happen as they are meant to happen, she believed. *If God wants you to go back there, T. G., He will see to it that you go.*

"What is *this* thing?"

She spun to see him holding and unwrapping a softball-sized sphere of polished black stone, which had been covered in soft red cloth and resting on a shelf just behind him. Into its otherwise flawless surface were carved a dozen tiny characters, symbols barely an eighth of an inch high.

"Some sort of talisman," she replied. "I found it alongside Astanapha's writings, in fact. Odd that you should notice it among so many other objects on the same shelf."

"It just kinda stood out. Sure is heavy."

"It's solid stone as far as I can tell. According to that," she indicated the diary, "it serves as the final key to the gateway summons." Her discomfort was apparent in her voice. "I've said too much. Please don't ask me to tell you any more about the process than I already have."

He examined it more closely. "What does this say on here?"

"Where?" She walked up to him and took a close look at the mysterious carving. "I...I don't know," she said, very puzzled. "I never saw that before."

"It almost looks..." He stopped, the unfinished statement hanging heavily in the air. Turning away from her, he set the stone sphere on a table and hoisted the artifact a little higher on his shoulder, holding it out. He studied it for a moment, then spun and gazed triumphantly into her eyes.

"*Now* tell me I'm not meant to go," he said, holding the artifact up for her to see. She left his gaze and focused once more upon the purplish leather surface, where she found a surprise—several of the tooled symbols there exactly matched those cut into the ebony sphere.

"Whoever made this, made *that*," T. G. declared. "It's the same language!"

Dr. Abelwhite was still shaking her head in astonishment. "I examined that sphere thoroughly, many times, but I never noticed that writing. How could I have missed it?"

He could see a new fear etched into the face of the old woman, a face he had never known to be anything but confident. She was clearly torn by his discovery, and the solid decision she had made only moments before was now supported by legs of yielding clay.

"It'll be okay," he reassured her. "Please, help me."

Several tense moments passed. T. G. remained quiet, watching Dr. Abelwhite as she continued to struggle with the quandary, allowing the weight of the evidence before them to speak to her. Finally, the woman sighed loudly and walked over to a locked filing cabinet. Reluctantly, she dialed a combination and pulled the door open. With some effort, she withdrew a large, red, leather-bound volume, then stood looking upon the ruddy texture of its cover. Coming to a decision, she slowly returned and handed it to him, obviously unsure she was doing the right thing. "The complete translation. I never thought I'd be showing it to another living soul."

He ran a gentle hand across the tooled hide of the book, aware of the unbridled power of the dark secrets contained within it. He had been given the control he wanted. He hoped he was right in taking it.

"You'll need the canopic jars I found in Astanapha's tomb, and a few other things," Abelwhite said. "The book will tell you how to use them."

T. G. mentally inventoried the objects as the woman set them on the table before him. With her help, he then placed the varied items carefully into an adventure-worn bag of heavy canvas she had used on her many expeditions.

"That should do it," he smiled, feeling like a kid leaving for camp. "I guess I'm ready for the bus."

"I still think this is a bad idea," Abelwhite said. "I wish you'd reconsider."

"Don't worry," he smiled. "I'll send you a postcard."

"Be careful, T. G.," the woman said, her words heavy. "The world has been here for an awfully long time."

"I'll bring these things back to you."

"No," she said, placing a warm hand gently on his cheek. "They're yours now. I guess, perhaps, they always were."

10

T. G. pulled the dark blue sedan off of the old rural highway, veering onto a deserted dirt-and-gravel road that disappeared into the murky darkness beyond the glare of his headlights. A mind-gripping quiet swelled within the vehicle as he shut off the engine, its pressure magnifying the sound of the blood rushing in his ears. He was well outside of Ithaca, far from anything that could be called a town.

And, more importantly, far from anyone who might be endangered by such as the shadowthing again.

A few ominous lines of verse he had once heard flickered into his mind—

Like one who on a lonesome road doth walk in fear and dread
and having once turned 'round, walks on and turns no more
his head
For he knows a frightful fiend doth close behind him tread

A small shudder ran up his spine, then was gone. A flashlight blazed, and T. G. lifted the book from the canvas bag. He would have given anything to have been reading it in the comfort of the professor's home or in a crowded shopping mall or while surrounded by a platoon of well-armed marines. But he dared not risk other lives—from three days and a lifetime before, the ice-glazed stare of Mrs. Lucreia still burned in his memory.

Adjusting the seat back, he settled comfortably into the plush upholstery of the car. He pressed a button, and the power door locks all around him sealed with a loud and definite *clunk*, a meaningless yet soothing illusion of security. As he leafed through the pages, scanning in preview the true and ancient horror story that was about to fill his mind's eye, he was grateful for the professor's refined penmanship.

Monsters might soon be a problem, yes. Eyestrain, no. He reached out and readjusted the rearview mirror so he could see behind the car from his slumped position. Just in case.

He began to read.

∽◦∾

David rolled to the side, his clouded eyes seeking the blurry, red glow of the readout on his clock radio. It was two-thirty in the morning. The white sound of the fan running in the corner of the room was a comfort, one he had never been able to sleep without as an adult. But as its droning lulled him back toward sleep, he resisted and threw back the sheets.

Nature called. He rose in the dark and stumbled with awkward feet into the bathroom, finding cold tile and the light switch right where they always had been. Grateful for the commonplace after hearing T. G.'s monster stories, he certainly hoped that there would be no repeat performances within the walls of his home. His long-missing friend had been unusually pensive following their visit to the professor's house, which had David a bit worried.

A few minutes later, he was more awake. He walked out into the silence of his darkened house, making a security check. It was not something he normally did, but something nagged at him and the house did not feel quite right.

He found T. G.'s bedroom door open, his bed unslept in. Seeing a dim light at the end of the hall, he walked toward the den and called out for his friend, but his words found no ear there. A table lamp burned in one corner, a note taped to its base. David reached out and pulled the paper free, knowing intuitively what message awaited him.

Dave—

I'm going back to that place—I have to. I found a way, and I'm Jenni's only chance. She's got to be there. Please don't worry. Nothing that has happened is your fault. You've always been the best friend I ever had. I'm sorry I wasn't a better one to you. I swear I'll come back, and I'll bring Jenni with me.

T. G.

P.S. I had to borrow the car. You can pick it up at the funeral home.

He breathed a heavy sigh and fell into his plush recliner. T. G. was gone again, after a mere two days. Had he ever been there at all? *Was it real? Did I dream it?* He crumpled the note, clutching it tightly as proof of his visitation.

Go get 'em, T-square—show 'em how we do things on Planet Earth. I'll be waiting for you, both of you, right here.

Staring up at the ceiling, he did some quick math in his head.

"Twenty-fifteen," he whispered. "I'll be sixty-four."

∽∾∽

He did not know the man's name. He did not want to.

T. G.'s hands were shaky, his breath coming in quick gulps. *Am I really going through with this?* He looked over at the ancient herb jars spread at arm's length to his right on a stainless-steel cart. Beside them was the black stone sphere. Dr. Abelwhite had given him those things the spell demanded—they were all items that had belonged to Astanapha, and T. G. had the eerie feeling they still did. The book was spread there, as well, propped up and open to the relevant passages. She had told him that the precise words he spoke were crucial—a single misspoken syllable would render the entire attempt ineffective. He had read and reread the words, memorizing them. They were so simple, so unimpressive—how could they possibly bridge the infinite gap between worlds?

He considered the artifact hanging from his shoulder, as it had been for, it seemed, his entire life. He then looked down at the pale corpse spread before him, lying on its back atop one of the funeral home's gurneys. His intellect fought back the bile that swelled again and again into his throat—he had never seen a dead body before, let alone touched one. He felt unclean, wondering if he was any better than the grave robbers that populated so many of the old late-night horror movies he had seen on television. He wanted to run from the room, but the incantation demanded a human corpse and a large, hot fire, and he was in the only place he could find both.

A voice deep within him screamed that what he was doing was wrong, a voice beyond mere conscience. He turned a deaf ear, shutting out the warning, forcing back the rising apprehension that begged him to stop. Almost as a litany, he told himself over and over that he had to reach Jenni, had to bring her home again—and by any means necessary.

He kept imagining his own father spread before him on the gurney. He had refused to see either of his parents' bodies at their funeral—it had been a closed-casket service at T. G.'s insistence—but still his mind fought him, as if to drive him from the room and away from what he was attempting. Shutting out the image, he draped a sheet across the midsection of the lifeless form, preserving the man's dignity as best he could.

Cruel, crudely stitched autopsy scars coursed like ugly rivers upon the man's naked, grayish flesh. There were so many wounds that T. G. was unsure which had been postmortem and which might have served as the cause of death. It did not matter.

The forty-six-year-old car crash victim had been brought to the home only the day before and had already been embalmed. T. G. had found him in the preparations room after using David's keys to gain entry. The body would not be harmed—T. G. was thankful that the gateway invocation did not call for the use of daggers or internal organs, for he doubted he could have brought himself to mutilate a corpse in any way. But the spell did demand that the corpse be fresh, and this was the only one for miles. The man's makeup and clothing would be prepared in the morning, once a puzzled mortician's assistant retrieved the body from the crematory room, but for now the dead man had one last favor to perform on Earth.

T. G. looked up at the huge crematory before him, just beyond the corpse. The small, round window in its massive door told him that the fire had reached its peak, and a glance at the temperature gauge confirmed it.

But it was not a *dead* body that would be going into the fire. Not this time.

The flames once again threw their dancing patterns against the ceiling. The overhead fixtures were all off, leaving the crematory pyre as the room's only source of light. That was what the book called for.

Fire.

T. G. reached over and picked up one of the alabaster jars, a rounded one. Only six inches tall, it was still very heavy, and mounting nervousness made him doubt the steadiness of his grip. As his hands shook slightly he focused upon the jar, opened it, and peered inside. Then he extended his arm and sprinkled its contents onto the torso of the corpse.

Sand from the western bank of the Nile, mixed with natron.

Earth.

He returned the jar to the table, took a deep breath, and began to read from the book.

"O Osiris, Foremost of the Westerners, the planets are stilled for they have seen your power. You shall not perish, and your *ka* shall not perish, for you are a *ka*."

He steadied his quivering hands as best he could and placed the flat of his palm against the body's sand-coated chest. *This is ridiculous!* "O Horus, hear me. Light the pathway into the netherworld. Show me the door, which opens unto the land of the dead."

He reached for another jar. Onto the sands he poured—

Water.

"You are the strongest of the gods, Osiris…do not let Shu prevent the opening of the door, nor slow any worthy *akh*, nor devour it. For they will cross over into the realm of the dead, like those who are in your following."

The fire within the crematory grew brighter. T. G. swallowed hard, afraid to continue. Part of him had not believed he could open the gateway. That part was no longer so sure.

A voice within him cried out.

Stop!

He placed a carved, fist-sized object onto the corpse's chest, over its heart. It was a heart scarab of polished jade, the underside of which had been inscribed with hieroglyphics. T. G. then placed his hand upon the stone insect and spoke again.

"Do not allow my heart to be my enemy in the presence of Anubis, the guardian of the balance. Speak well. Draw forth the gate. Worlds must touch. We must know your wisdom and counsel."

A breeze swelled in the closed room. He sprinkled a precise mixture of juniper oil and rare spices onto the body. "Open now the passage…bring forth the ancient bridge." The breeze became a cold, biting wind that sliced right through his clothes. He reached to the table one last time, lifted the enigmatic stone ball and held it up before him. "Servants of Horus and Osiris, hear me…open the gateway!" His hair stood on end and a tingle raced over his flesh, an odd sensation that rapidly grew until the air against him crackled with static.

With a glass-shattering crack, a bolt of lightning lanced out from the still-sealed crematory door, destroying its window. T. G. reflexively yanked his empty hands away as the stroke arced into the black sphere he held.

The ball did not fall. It hung there, at eye level, with the dancing, white-hot bolt fixed upon it in a continuous flow of raw energy. The crackling hum of the electric appendage hurt his ears and the intensity of the bolt burned his eyes, but he could not look away. Like an unearthly arm and hand, the lightning held the stone ball suspended.

Something in him sensed that he needed to move away—and fast. He took several steps back, watching with dread.

The ball suddenly flared into a whiteness, a light that threatened to scorch his eyes and skin with its intensity. The brilliance was accompanied by great heat and a piercing scream—an intolerable, high-pitched whine that existed at the very edge of human hearing. The arc of lightning then ceased, but the blinding orb continued to hang there before him, forcing him to cover his face with his shielding arms.

Sun.

The power of the cosmos—unleashed yet contained. A circuit had been completed. A doorway had been opened, an infinite passage of a million dimensions, connecting two worlds that were never meant to touch.

The heavy door of the crematory flew open and intense heat poured forth, singeing T. G.'s face and hands. Cruel winds drove hard through the room, knocking over anything that was not anchored down. The ground heaved again and again as the floor rolled with shock waves. T. G. rushed forward and leaned over the body, trying to keep his feet.

The firelight spilling from the door fell away, shifting from a glaring white to a deep blue, deeper than any T. G. had ever seen. The flames within the oven changed, their essence altering as they thickened into an almost gelatinous substance. The dark fire flowed thickly like undulating molten metal, out of the crematory door and down its side, spilling onto the floor and into a rapidly widening blue-black pool of living viscous flame.

And it was cold. Very cold. The stone ball, its work done, went dark and fell to the floor with a loud thud. It was carried a few feet by the flow from the oven door before finally coming to rest.

A new roar sounded.

T. G. watched as the walls of the room faded from sight, giving way to a dark whirlpool that fully encompassed the chamber. It was as if he were in the eye of a megatornado, and as he squinted into the deafening cyclone walls he saw shapes form there, carried within the black winds. They were vaporous and indefinite, but T. G. got the distinct impression of ghostly victims caught in the insane, violent rush, their mouths open in screams of perpetual agony.

T. G., still leaning over the body, peered into the door of the oven. A swirl of darkness had formed there and was growing faster and deeper. In seconds, it had become a narrow tunnel that stretched until it vanished with distance. The winds instantly reversed themselves and rushed back toward the open oven door, drawn by the vortex. T. G. reached out and grabbed the book, and with the same motion shoved the table of Egyptian antiquities clear of the main winds. The artifact, slung over his shoulder, slammed again and again against his side, caught in the airflow. He pushed the corpse and its gurney to the other side, rolling it out of harm's way. Staggering back, he tried to maintain his balance against the gale.

The winds rushing through the oven door died down. The undulating floor stilled. The whirlpool surrounding the room continued, suddenly soundless. Pressures had equalized. The fully realized gateway lay before him, waiting.

A minute passed as T. G. stared into the incredible maelstrom within the crematory. The only sound he heard was that of his own breathing.

Not believing it possible, he found the already chilly room growing colder. His breath became white.

It was at this point in the incantation, with the portal open, that Astanapha had once summoned the gods to come forth through the tunnel. But T. G. had other plans, and they did not include a confrontation on his home soil. He hoped he would not come face to face with Egyptian deities along the way—it looked like a one-lane passage, and either he or someone else would have a long way to back up.

No one had been summoned. The gateway began to close. The slippery dark matter that flowed around his feet was gathering itself back toward the oven, flowing back up its side. Clutching the book, T. G. took a deep breath and bravely climbed through the oven door. The heavy black orb and the other elements of the incantation were useless without the book, so leaving them behind, he hoped, would not matter.

It was difficult getting through the door with both the artifact and the book. Before T. G. could squirm all the way in, his lower legs still protruding from the door, he felt something. Strong hands grabbed hold of him, trying to keep him from crawling any farther into the oven. *Don't stop me, David!* his thoughts cried out. Even as he turned his head to look upon his friend, he tried to shout over the renewed roar of the oven. "Let go! I have to do this!" But the words died away as his gaze fell upon the owner of the vise-like hands that pinned him.

It was not David. Something had indeed come through the portal, something unsummoned, something that had been waiting for this very opportunity.

Icy blue eyes—familiar eyes—glowed as they stared insanely at him, unblinking and inhuman. The corpse, clumps of wet sand still falling from its chest, held him immobile just short of the vortex. It did not try to pull him out of the oven—it wanted only to keep him short of the gateway but still *in* the oven. T. G. had heard its laugh before. He had seen its expression of depraved cruelty.

"You should have listened," it gloated.

T. G. began to kick, or tried to. The lifeless hands held fast, the laughter building. In just seconds, it would be too late. The vortex would be gone. The blistering heat of the crematory would return in full.

T. G. flailed wildly, struggling to free himself. The last of the blue-black matter, now inside the crematory once more and clear of the oven door, was flowing past him and into the receding gateway, leaving behind no trace of its passage. He screamed, pushing back with all his strength, and freed one leg.

The roar of flames and maniacal laughter filled his ears. He kicked as hard as he could against the chest of the corpse, again and again. The hard sole of his boot began to rend the autopsy stitches, opening the corpse's flesh wider and deeper with each impact.

Bloodless bone and muscle glinted wetly in the returning light of the crematory fire. He kicked back into the dead man's face, over and over, breaking teeth and tearing flesh.

With one final, massive kick, the undead enemy was thrown off balance for just long enough. T. G. managed to plant his free boot against the inside edge of the oven door and pushed as hard as he could, propelling himself completely into the crematory, out of the corpse's reach. The brick-and-steel door then fell closed and locked behind him. It could not be reopened from the inside.

If he failed to make it through, they would find his ashes in the morning.

He struggled forward, lugging the book and the artifact. The swirling tunnel still retreated from him, keeping him on its outer fringes as it withdrew across the wide oven floor. The chamber was already unbearably hot—in seconds it would be too late. He could no longer breathe the scorching air. He dropped the book, leaving it to burn. Time and again he reached out as if to take hold of the edge of the vortex, his fingers falling just short of their mark. He crawled faster. In final desperation, he kicked back against a raised ridge in the flooring and launched himself forward.

T. G. came down on the vanishing lip of the gateway just as it closed. Unsure that he had made it, he shut his eyes, bracing for the hellish flames of the crematory. Instead, the heat faded as he began to slide through the tight, dark tunnel, accelerating. His speed quickly approached that of sound, the air tearing brutally past him. He could not breathe, could not draw the rushing air into his aching lungs. In seconds disguised as hours, everything went completely dark. He passed out.

∽o∾

Carlene Abelwhite, holding a lace sheer out of the way, looked out of an upstairs window and into the overcast night sky. Winds had kicked up outside, tossing tree branches again and again against the walls of a home that had known blizzard, hail, and hurricane. Beneath a lamppost below, she watched as a newspaper page skittered along the street, accompanied by scattering leaves of maple and oak that then took flight.

Her hands shook. She looked upon them, gripping one with the other. How strong they had been, how sure. Where had the years gone? She had always been so busy, constantly surrounded by those who shared her passion for the past. Together they had toiled beneath the blinding desert sun. Together they had celebrated their finds. Carlene had outlived more of those companions than not. She was alone, now, in a house filled with the unearthed trinkets of peoples who had vanished dozens of centuries before. The treasures suddenly seemed so cold to her, so lifeless. So dead.

Letting the sheer fall, she again picked up the beige-tinged photos she had finally located and puzzled over the story they told. Their once simple black-and-white images had suddenly become a mystery she could not fathom, one more enigma in the supernatural mire that had ensnared T. G. She had taken the pictures herself, decades earlier, documenting her discovery of the black stone sphere he had taken with him.

As with all her finds, she had photographed the object from all angles, carefully making sure that no part of the sphere's surface went unrecorded.

None of the photos held the feature she so very much wanted to see. The cryptic writing T. G. had found upon its polished surface that afternoon simply was not there. It never had been.

Until today.

A sudden roll of thunder that slammed from house to house brought her out of her reverie and rattled the antique glass in her window as it swept past. She knew this was no mere storm. It couldn't be. It had swelled from nothing, centering itself upon Ithaca, stationary and rotating and growing more intense with each passing moment. As she watched, lightning again and again cut jagged scars across the darkness, arcing high above from east to west.

He did it, she knew. And she prayed.

T. G. became aware of something cold and smooth against his cheek. As his mind began to right itself, he opened his eyes and saw that he was lying on a flat, dark surface. Forcing his arms into action, he pushed against it and sat up awkwardly. His mind cleared.

He was in a chamber of black marble. As his eyes traced the dark gray veins that ran through the stone, he realized that the hexagonal, fifteen-foot-wide room was cut from a single piece. Walls, floor, and ceiling were one, as if fashioned from some hollowed, immense rock. There was no door, no window, no apparent means of entry or exit.

That's impossible, his sharpening mind knew. Yet as incredible as the situation was, it somehow seemed extremely familiar to him. He began to feel claustrophobic, despite the fact that on archeological digs he had often spent long hours in tight places without discomfort.

He fought the feeling. T. G. stood up, steadying himself against one wall as his legs found their strength beneath him. He traced every line of the room with his eyes, inspecting every seam where wall met wall or floor or ceiling. His fingers ran along the cool stone, searching for any sign of a hidden door or passage.

There was none. And then, he realized that there was no light source in the room. He threw no shadow. Yet he could see.

The artifact, he remembered. It still hung upon its sling.

He began to worry about air and looked down at the object he carried. "Is this *your* place?" he asked. "Sure could use a window…"

"Hello, T. G."

Startled, he spun toward the source of the voice. There, dressed in a flowing robe of shimmering white, a warmly glowing figure stood. It looked like every painting of an angel T. G. had ever seen, its kind face and blond hair a visage of tranquil beneficence.

T. G. fell back, overwhelmed by the heavenly personage. It stood its ground, not moving toward him, smiling but doing nothing else.

"Hello," T. G. slowly replied. "Where am I?"

"You are safe. You are welcome."

"Where are we?"

"A place along the way."

"It feels strange…like I've been here before. Like déjà vu or something."

"You have not been here before. But your burden has." He indicated the artifact. "It belongs to us. It was stolen very, very long ago. We had given up on ever finding it again, and feared it destroyed. You have now returned it to us, and we are indebted to you."

He looked down at it. "You wouldn't believe what this thing has put me through," he began, smiling. "On second thought, I guess you would."

"You have kept it safe, and we cannot sufficiently express our gratitude for that. Had this fallen into the wrong hands, many would have suffered."

"What is it?" T. G. asked, his heart racing. *An answer, at last!*

"What you hold is the power of life and death, the power to create worlds and to destroy them. It is a container for that which cannot be contained, yet is. It is older than your world, and must now be returned to its proper place before it can do the harm we have, for centuries, feared it would do. Those things that befell you are but the barest hint of its capabilities." The angel held his hands out, wordlessly asking T. G. to turn the artifact over to him.

T. G. took a step forward, then stopped. "I don't understand. Please…I need an answer, not a riddle. What is this?"

"It is ours. It is too dangerous for mortal hands."

"I gathered that much. I want to know what's inside."

"It is best you not know."

"But this thing robbed me of twenty years! All my friends aged and my world changed while I was off in another place. I was trying to get back there when I wound up here. There's a girl—"

"She is safe."

His heart leaped. He took another step toward the angel. "She is? Where is she? How can I reach her?"

"She awaits. Return the artifact to us, and you will be reunited …and those twenty years will be returned to you. It will be as if nothing ever happened."

T. G. couldn't get the strap off his shoulder fast enough. Pure joy overrode all else—all reason, all judgment, all caution. As he stepped toward the angel and held the artifact outward, something tore through his emotion and an inner voice screamed, frantically needing to be heard, a voice his own yet not his own—

No!

He hesitated. The smile on his face lessened. He looked into the kind, smiling face of the angel and studied the patient eyes, the gentle expression.

"I…I, uh…" T. G. stalled.

"She awaits you, T. G. Your world awaits. This object must be returned to its proper place."

"Why did it follow me around? If it's so dangerous, why did it save me from that thing in my apartment? Why is it sticking to me like glue…what's so special about me? Why did those ghost things go nuts when they saw it?"

The angel smiled anew. "It is time for it and you to return to your proper places."

T. G. felt increasingly uneasy. He tightened his grip on the leather strap and leaned heavier against his back foot. "Before I hand this to you, tell me how I got it. Where was I? Where did those three days go?" He paused, watching the angel closely. No response came. "If you're what you appear to be, how could this have been hidden from you? How could you not know where it was?"

The angel only smiled. "Give it to me," he insisted.

The hair on the back of T. G.'s neck stood up. Ice water flowed down his spine.

He backed away quickly, retreating from the angel until he hit the cold stone wall and could move no farther. He pulled the strap back over his shoulder and clung to it tightly, his knuckles white.

The angel stopped smiling. The temperature in the room plunged. Frost began to form on the walls, the ceiling, the floor.

A sound like thousands of tiny, screaming voices filled the room. Against the dark stone all around him, T. G. became aware of movement. At first, it looked like dark snow falling along the walls. It was not.

Millions of black, spiderlike things skittered down the smooth, whitening stone, spilling onto the floor as they reached it. They appeared from nowhere, flowing down the walls in dense waves. T. G. leaped from the wall behind him and dove into the center of the room, whirling to see that he had almost been engulfed where he stood. The chitinous clatter of rushing, exoskeletal legs against icy stone and against each other filled the air, blending with the combined voices of the hellish multitude. The tiny creatures had blazing blue eyes, and as they rushed toward him in a maniacal attack, drawing his fearful attention, he heard the angel's voice again.

But it was different, now.

"Kill him," it said.

He heard the breathing again. He felt the putrid, icy breath again. He heard the laughter again.

They swarmed him from all directions, wave after terrifying wave flooding up his legs as he fought to knock them off. Their millions of accusing voices filled his ears as they screamed things in a language T. G. did not know. As he kicked and jumped, trying to dislodge them, he saw that their distorted, misshapen faces were almost human.

The room went dark. All he could see were their eyes, pinpricks of blue light like densely packed stars, swirling, surrounding him.

They clawed into his jeans, their tiny, needle-sharp talons digging into his legs right through the denim as they climbed over each other, higher and higher, engulfing him, trying to devour him. Excruciating pain filled him as thousands of tiny fangs found his flesh. The laughter of the shadowthing was lost in T. G.'s own screams.

There was an explosion.

Blinding white light filled the room with a deafening roar. A shock wave slammed T. G. into the chamber wall, into the spider things that covered it. His head bounced from the hard stone, and his shoulder crumpled under the impact. He slid to the floor, senseless. His mind fogged by concussion, he lay there, nothing but smooth stone beneath him. He passed out again.

T. G. slowly came back to awareness, sensing a warm hand upon his forehead. The pain in his shoulder disappeared. After a few moments he opened his eyes and saw that the room, once again, was pure, clean stone and was no longer cold. There was a slight film of cool moisture where frost had been. There were no spider things, no horrible ocean of screaming voices, no hellish angel.

There was however, another person there with him, sitting quietly against the opposite wall. T. G. shrank against a corner, his eyes fixed upon the being.

Round two, he feared. "Stay back," T. G. finally warned, the threat hollow.

The figure just sat there, quite casually. "Don't be afraid."

"What happened to that other guy?" T. G. asked, indicating the place where the angel had stood. "What happened to those things? Where did they go?"

"One fled. The others I sent away." The man surveyed the chamber. "This place is usually very, very dark. And very, very crowded."

He looked different from the previous angel. He appeared to be quite tall, even though he was sitting. His hair was white, his shoulders broad. His brow was noble, his well-chiseled jaw set firmly. He wore a simple robe of brilliant blue that hung to the tops of his bare feet. T. G. looked past mistrust just long enough to realize that the man had the same bronze skin tone he had seen on the giants of that other world.

But the most striking things about the man were his eyes. They flickered like flame, golden and sparkling and warm, and they were gentle yet more piercing than any T. G. had ever seen. They looked right through him, he felt, seeing into his mind, his soul.

T. G. had seen the man before.

"You," he began. "It was you I saw in that dream. A gray place… no one there but you and me…"

"Yes, it was." Despite himself, T. G. was swept up in the man's voice. It was a voice as deep and broad as the sea, clear and authoritative and as soothing as the sound of waves breaking against warm sand. He gripped the artifact tightly, deciding never to be fooled again. "You can't have this," he almost shouted.

The man smiled. "I don't want it."

T. G. glared at him harshly, not trusting. "Well, you're the first." He stood slowly on shaky legs. He noticed small tears in the fabric of the legs of his jeans, evidence of the horrid things he had just faced. Oddly, he could detect no sign of wounds beneath them where he knew he had been repeatedly bitten. His loud breathing echoed in the chamber.

"Who are you?" he demanded. "What are you?"

"I have many names. You may call me Ish."

"Ish," T. G. repeated quietly.

"You're safe now. Don't be afraid."

T. G. had no instinct to run or to doubt the man—he felt just the opposite, in fact. Yet he kept a wall up, speaking without respect, showing no weakness. "Why shouldn't I be afraid?" He hugged the artifact. "Ever since I got stuck with this thing, I've been through the wringer. It's dragged me around like a puppet."

"You should *never* have used that incantation," the man scolded him.

"Why not? I had to do *something*."

"Those who were here before me are of those who have been seeking you out to destroy you. Their kind placed those markings on the sphere to entrap you. Not all signs are good ones, T. G., and feelings are dangerous and cannot be trusted. Carlene knew it was wrong to do what you attempted. So did *you,* as the moment of the summons grew close…yet you turned a deaf ear to the warnings you received. In trying to force things the way you did by coming here, you acted on *their* terms, using *their* methods. They've set up an intricate strategy in dealing with man, one that is so clever that it has rarely been suspected as existing at all. By walking out from under our protection, you almost got yourself killed."

"Your protection? What protection? Do you have any idea what I've been through since this thing took over my life? I've been tossed around, cut up, arrested, jailed, dragged from one planet to another and back again, thrown through time and almost eaten…*twice!*"

"Without our protection you'd have been killed long ago. The Gift we gave you would have been destroyed by now, and as a result untold millions would die who otherwise would not."

"What gift?" He looked at the artifact. "This? *You* gave me this? *You* destroyed my life? Why?" he demanded. T. G. swallowed hard, staring into the sparkling eyes before him, waiting for a response.

"Because we chose you. Before your world was born, we chose you."

"For what?"

"For ourselves. You must decide whether or not to fulfill the destiny that's been prepared for you."

"Well, I can tell you *that* right now," he said defiantly. "Forget it. What did I ever do to be chosen for anything? I want my life back. I want Jenni back. I want my world back. I want my twenty years back, and I want all this to be just a bad dream I'll finally forget someday."

"Those we choose, we choose not for what they are or have been. No merit speaks for men, making one more worthy of favor than another. We chose you for what you would become through us."

"And what would that be?" he asked, still doubtful.

"A long-awaited voice in the dark."

Great. Just great. Can't a guy get a straight answer anymore?

T. G. paused, still wary. "How do I know you're not just playing 'good cop, bad cop' with that thing that was just here?"

"I'm not."

T. G. was not satisfied with his answer but could see that no other was forthcoming. "Well…I guess I should thank you for saving me. They would have killed me."

"Yes. They would have." Ish looked upward, indicating the stone above. "You don't yet realize where you are. This is a place made not for you, or those like you, but for those like you encountered a moment ago. There are millions of chambers such as this, each of them isolated, each of them occupied by beings such as you saw."

"Those…spiders?" T. G. could still feel them upon him. A chill ran down his back. He shuddered.

"They're not spiders. What they are will be made known to you."

"Terrific." T. G. glanced around. "Why does this place feel familiar?"

He indicated the artifact. "Because, in appearance, it isn't too unlike the place where you came upon the Gift."

T. G. wanted it all. "Why can't I remember that? What happened? Do you know what it's like for a guy to have a three-day hole in his life?"

"In fact, I do."

"Why can't I remember?"

"For your protection." Ish gestured for T. G. to join him in sitting, and he did so, legs crossed, the artifact cradled atop them. "We're involved in a great war, T. G. Its soldiers don't dwell in the physical realm, although most of their battles take place there. Those of your world have participated in this conflict since your history began, and the battle lines are clearly drawn. There are no gray areas. One's allegiance lies with one side or the other, with our forces, or those of the Dark, and the stakes are life or death on a planetary scale.

"The Gift you hold is a powerful weapon, upon which billions of lives depend. You are now its Guardian."

"Guardian? Against what?"

"That object has been the target of a frenzied search that has continued for more than five thousand years. Those like Beltesha—the being who was here before me—have turned entire planets upside down seeking it, day and night, without ceasing. They desire to destroy the Gift before it can be used."

"Why couldn't they find it?"

"They're powerful, but they're not omniscient; they don't know all things. And they're not omnipresent; they occupy a single location in space at a time, just as you do. They operate within limits, but their great numbers allow them to cover entire worlds."

"Who exactly is this Beltesha?" T. G. asked.

"He's a prince of the Dark. He walks worlds, leaving destruction in his wake. Those beneath him fear him and cower in his presence, for he will as quickly devour any of them as he will men. The Gift is a thorn in his side…knowing it is out there somewhere, waiting to be used, is intolerable for him. He has made the destruction of it, and now you, his own special priority.

"Once you'd received the Gift, had you walked back out into the world with full knowledge of what it was, where it had come from, and how you had received it, the agents of the Dark would have found you in a second. The thoughts of man are theirs to share. You have no secrets from them. They did not yet know that the Gift had been given, that once again it had a Guardian. Until that happened and they were alerted, you were safe."

"Why does this Beltesha look different every time I see him? Except for the eyes, I guess. I mean, that was *him* every time, right? First that horrible thing in my apartment, and then that body at the mortuary, and now…"

"He is a user. They all are. They take that which they need and corrupt it to accommodate their purposes. To them, human beings, as well as every other part of the universe, are but things to be used…and then disposed of."

"Why not just show themselves?"

"They hide within shells, disguising themselves with whatever appearance suits their needs. But this takes great amounts of energy, which they draw from any available source so as not to deplete their own inherent power."

"Energy…like heat? Is that why my apartment building was so cold?"

"Yes. They were there, unseen, thousands of them…watching you, fearing you, waiting for Beltesha to arrive. The form he took during the attack in your apartment was meant to frighten you into giving up the Gift. The body at the mortuary, which he directly possessed after crossing over the bridge you created during your invocation, was meant to kill you so the Gift would have no owner."

"It almost worked," T. G. nodded.

"Then, following you back into the vortex, he diverted your course and dropped you into this place, where he took on the angelic form you saw. That form was meant to win your trust. He intended to leave you here, to perish horribly. But all of those approaches failed." He smiled. "We chose well."

T. G. had no response to that. Thinking, he ran a fingertip along the tooled leather of the artifact. "Why must I *give* it to him? Why can't he just knock me down and take it?"

"The Gift is yours. Legally. There are rules they must obey, even in this."

"So why did this 'gift' bounce me around all over creation? Why did it rob me of twenty years?"

"It didn't. *We* did."

"What? Why? And who is 'we'?"

"Again, it was for your protection. But before I continue…it is time."

Ish's eyes flared more brightly. T. G., transfixed, felt a warmth washing over his memory. A dark veil was lifted from his mind's eye.

He remembered.

∽∾

A throbbing ache owned his skull.

T. G. lifted his hand to the back of his head and found swelling, the signature of something hard against flesh. The pain of his own touch drove his eyes shut, and only after a few moments could he force them open again. He realized that something was wrong, blinked a few times, and began to panic.

Putting his hands before his face, he pulled them in until they tickled his lashes. He looked from side to side and felt his eyes roll in their sockets as he tried to discern something, anything, around him. He sat for a moment, fearing he had gone blind, listening to the deepest quiet that had ever surrounded him.

He tried to stand but was abruptly yanked to the ground by something he could not see. Startled, he spun to one side, fearing whatever had grabbed him. Off balance and unable to catch himself, T. G.'s shoulder hit something cold, dry, and smooth—a wall. Sliding down, he came to rest on his side and dared not move again.

His clouded thinking began to clear as he lay still, his heart pounding. As his mind sharpened, T. G. groped to find out what had grabbed him. His hand found his rope, taut against his harness, held fast at the other end by something unseen. Its familiar texture was a comfort. *My gear,* he recalled. *I'm still in my harness. I was rappelling...*

Going by feel, T. G. freed himself from the grip of the harness. It was an awkward process, for his center of gravity was thrown off by the heavy pack he still wore. Trying then to stand, he felt a last tug and paused in a strenuous crouch as he unhooked the safety loop from the back of his wide, leather belt. Finally free, T. G. leaned against the wall beside him and stood up.

"Dave!" he shouted, hearing his voice reverberate again and again into the distance. The acoustics sounded like—

"A mine shaft!" he said, those words also ringing far away. But there was no heaviness in the air, no musty smell, no dust he could detect—in fact, the air was as cool, pure, and refreshing as any he had ever experienced.

His thoughts returned to his eyes.

He dropped his backpack to the floor. Feeling for its side pocket, he reached in and found the ribbed metal handle of the flashlight he carried there.

What if I hear the click of the switch and still see nothing?

T. G. took a deep breath and closed his eyes. Sliding his thumb forward, he felt a positive connection as the switch locked into the "on" position. He slowly opened his eyes.

Before him spread the shine of polished stone.

He leaned back and breathed a sigh of great relief, thanking no one in particular that his eyesight was intact. Swinging the beam around, he discovered he was in a straight, triangular tunnel some twelve feet wide and almost as high that swallowed even his flashlight beam in the distance. The sloping walls were polished and seamless— as far as he could ascertain—as if bored out of a single, immense mountain of flawless, reddish stone. It was an odd-looking stone, like red marble mixed with pearl, glistening like the eye of a panther in the white of his flashlight beam.

He turned back and shone the light against the wall behind him. It was rough and of a different, more earthy type of rock. He recognized it as the same grayish stone that had made up the cliff face.

T. G. shined the light on the places where his kernmantle cord protruded from and re-entered the stone, marveling at the sight. He tugged firmly at the line and it held fast, as he had expected.

Had his rappel taken place minutes ago or hours? Or days? He checked his watch only to find that the hands were frozen. He tried to wind it, but the stem would not turn. Thinking of his compass, he reached into his pocket and held it up into the light. Its needle was spinning wildly counterclockwise, like a propeller, making it, too, of no use.

Remembering the camera in his backpack, T. G. took a flash photo of the rope protruding from the rock, knowing that no one was likely to believe his bizarre story otherwise. A second shot, then a third, and he returned the thirty-five-millimeter camera to its place in his pack.

T. G. hauled his backpack onto his shoulders and took a deep breath. Obviously, only one direction of travel was open to him, and since remaining where he was would solve no mysteries, he set out.

With his first step, a soft, warm light began to glow all around him with no discernible source. It extended some thirty feet before him, dropping into darkness beyond. Intrigued, he began to walk, his boots sounding heavy against the smooth floor. The zone of illumination moved with him. He turned off the flashlight but elected to keep it in his hand, just in case.

He knew enough about geology to know that the sparkly, red marblelike stone could not have been a natural part of the mountain. Who could have quarried and built such a corridor?

Hours passed. He did not know how far he had walked, but he felt certain that the corridor was longer than the width of mountain into which it bore. He felt like a child, one beginning anew in a world where the laws of physics could be ignored, bent, even broken.

If not for the boredom, he would have felt like Carter in Tutankhamen's tomb. He wished for hieroglyphics or wall paintings or even Arne Saknussemm's initials carved into the wall—anything but the same three facets he had been staring at all the way along the tunnel—but there was not so much as a crack in the flawless stone around him. He remembered that even the great pyramids of Egypt showed tooling marks, flaws and signs of their builders, amazing though they were. This corridor was laser-straight, mirror-polished, and exquisite in its simplicity.

For a day and a half he walked, pausing on occasion to rest or briefly sleep as his fatigue demanded. He ate as he walked, and as he chewed the last of his granola bars he looked down at the stainless-steel sierra cup hooked to his belt. Thirst was becoming an enemy, but it was one he had faced before. He pushed the nagging dryness out of his mind.

Finishing the snack bar, he wadded up its wrapper and began to put it in his pocket. He thought better of it, though, and elected instead to drop the wrapper to the floor, where it would serve as a position marker for him on his way back out, giving him some idea of how far he had left to travel.

At least he *hoped* he would get back out.

"So," he shouted, listening to the reverberation of his voice. "I'm going to die in here? Is that it?" His frustration mounted as his mind formed images of a senseless corridor that went on for all eternity, eventually strewn with the desiccated bodies of those who had fallen prey to the same insidious trap.

"Give me a door! Let me out of here!" There was no response but the dying echo of his own voice.

He noticed as he walked that his knee was no longer tender, as if it had never been injured at all. It also occurred to him that for some reason his bodily functions were not presenting themselves as a problem, and for that he was grateful. He would have hated to have to mess up such a nice, spotless, excruciatingly featureless corridor.

Then he paused as he noticed something ahead, something different from the corridor he had followed for so long, something that looked a lot like a door.

He ran to it, his feet aching anew with the increased pounding. Sure enough, the corridor abruptly ended in a deep, triangular doorframe fashioned from the same red stone. T. G. studied it and stared in fascination at the intricate characters carved into its surface. They looked like nothing he had seen in any of his archaeology classes at Cornell, yet he felt as if he *should* have been able to read them. Looking down, he realized that beneath his boots were two carved footprintlike depressions, side-by-side and only a couple of inches apart, that looked almost as if someone had stood with bare feet in wet cement. To each side, at shoulder level, was a handprint of the same quality. He dropped his daypack and took another series of pictures.

Going for broke, T. G. pulled off his boots and heavy socks and enjoyed the feel of the cool stone against the soles of his hot, tired feet. Taking position in the doorway, he nestled each foot into its corresponding depression.

They were a perfect fit. T. G. could feel every nook and cranny of his toes and soles, just as if he had left the footprints himself. Even the crooked, once-broken toe on his left foot was accounted for.

He reached out until his fingers and palms nestled into their carved counterparts to either side. The fit was just as flawless. *How can this be?* He waited.

A gentle vibration ushered up from the floor, moving upward through the walls with a warmth that filled his arms and legs as it flowed toward his heart. Something also seemed to fill his head, something like music but nothing audible—a silent song whose voices were a chorus of harmonious perfection like none he had ever heard, although the song, like the carved writing, was somehow familiar.

With his nose only inches from the door, he watched as the stone before him faded and, in a matter of seconds, simply ceased to be. A new light rose beyond, a light that was pleasing and soft and also had no apparent source. T. G. pulled his hands away from the doorframe, peering with wide eyes into the chamber ahead. He stepped down and in.

The room was circular, with a domed ceiling that reminded him of a planetarium. He estimated its diameter at twenty feet. Looking up, he realized that the gentle light of the room was somehow coming from the veined, pinkish stone of the ceiling, which ended at waist level all around him. At that point a thick, two-foot-high ring of a transparent amber substance protruded from the wall and completely encircled the room. More of the strange language he had seen in the doorframe was carved into the ring. Beneath this, continuing to the floor, was more of the red stone.

Despite a lack of any apparent ventilation system, the air was as fresh and pleasant as he could have asked for.

Walking closer, T. G. realized that the top of the wide amber ring held a deep depression filled with what looked like water. He rushed over, as thirsty as he had ever been, and cautiously sniffed and touched the surface. He brought the wet finger to his dried lips and instinctively knew the sweet liquid was safe. It was indeed water, cool and crystal clear and so pure that it almost seemed to glow. T. G. drank greedily, scooping up the godsend with his sierra cup. He looked up, water dripping from his chin, and saw within the pink wall before his nose a strange translucence unlike any he had seen before. Vague, swirling images were seemingly trying to form within the stone, on a level that was almost subliminal. Were they faces? T. G. stared deeply, trying to pull some concrete pattern or image from the display, but none settled into place before him, and after a couple of minutes the mysterious effect faded altogether. He went back to drinking and his thirst was quickly abated, leaving him satisfied and ready to explore the remainder of the chamber, but not before he paused to refill his empty canteen. Then, after using his camera to take a series of closeup shots of the carved relief in the stone, he turned toward the center of the room once more.

He was startled by the sudden presence of a huge, ornately carved rock pedestal that had been fashioned from the red stone. Waist-high, it sparkled even in the diffused light of the room, and its dozens of raised pictographs seemed to move as T. G. gazed upon it. Their images depicted an odd, artistically melded fusion of forests, waters, warriors, great beasts, and elegantly winged creatures, all beneath a sweeping spread of stars.

Atlantis? he wondered.

On top of this, standing upright in a form-fitting recess, was a flawless cylindrical container formed from the unusual amber. T. G. leaned closer, his breath fogging the side of the vessel, and saw that something dark was sealed within.

"How did you get here?" he asked aloud, knowing that the odd and heightened acoustics in the room should have made any such appearance anything but silent. T. G. walked a circle around the pedestal and examined the object, eyeing both it and the floor around it for any sign of a secret mechanism or trapdoor, but he found none. Turning his attention to the amber cylinder nestled in the stone base, he saw that it had no apparent seams, as if the object inside had been set in place while the yellowish substance was in a liquid state. He marveled at the perfect clarity of the amber and reached to touch it— then paused as he remembered something taught in his archaeology class.

True treasure is often protected by traps. Lethal ones.

His eyes scanned the room again, but he saw nothing that looked as if it were concealing some insidious surprise. He wondered if the entire floor of the room might be a huge elevator, waiting to plunge him into the fiery core of the Earth as punishment for daring to touch the great, lost treasure of the Whoever-They-Weres. He thought back to the cliff wall and to the vanishing doorway through which he had just passed, and he knew that he was seeing evidence of a technology of which modern man could not even dream.

If they wanted me dead, he reasoned, *I would have been by now.*

"Who were you people?" he yelled aloud, before pausing to rethink his question. "Who...*are* you people? Talk to me!"

There was no echo.

He held his breath and reached out. His fingertip touched the gleaming surface of the amber vessel. He yanked his hand back as, at once, a glowing seam appeared, spreading horizontally from the point of touch and encircling the container. T. G. heard a hissing sound as the seam grew longer, and he realized that the amber had just given him an invitation inside. The hiss swelled, then stopped as the seam completed its path around the circumference of the cylinder. The glow vanished.

Vacuum sealed...

He reached out with both hands and slowly lifted away the heavy top half of the cylinder, revealing a leather-encased object about twenty-four inches long and nine wide. He lifted the relic from the remaining portion of the receptacle and found its weight to be roughly that of a loaded backpack. As it cleared the top of the amber shroud, a wide strap of the same leather dropped free and hung loose, swinging as he lifted the treasure clear of the pedestal. He slipped the strap over his shoulder and smiled, hefting its weight.

I can see it now. "*Student discovers three thousand-year-old Atlantean gym bag. Three thousand-year-old unwashed Atlantean sweat socks found inside. Film at eleven.*"

The lighting in the room began to dim. T. G. picked up his flashlight and moved back into the corridor, looking back just in time to see the room go completely dark. The thick stone door rematerialized behind him, sealing the chamber once again. He stood for a moment, looking down at the heavy artifact he now carried, studying its strange leather surface. He felt a strong yet elusive link with eternity, as if the object had been around for a very, very long time.

T. G. quickly slipped back into his socks and boots, then gathered his belongings and began the long walk back. The combined weight of both backpack and artifact was difficult to manage, but he pressed on. Eventually, the weary hiker came upon the food wrapper he had dropped, and he paused to pick it up. As he bent down, he caught a glimpse of something behind him, something lurking at the very edge of his vision. Startled, he spun.

The chamber door was still right behind him, as if he had not walked away from it at all.

He struggled with the image for a moment, knowing that he had covered a great distance despite the evidence of his eyes. Experimentally, he faced the doorway and backed away one slow step at a time. The door silently followed, matching him step for step, stopping whenever he did. When he took a step *toward* the door, however, it did not retreat.

T. G. examined the seams where doorframe met wall, running his fingers along the cool stone. It was a single, homogeneous piece. The veins in the stone were continuous. There were no tracks, no rails, no sliding platforms. No moving parts. No mechanism was responsible. No human was either, he knew.

The corridor was closing behind him. *Healing.*

And once he left it, it would no longer exist at all.

∽o∾

"I packed up," T. G. recalled. "I got back into my harness and hoped somehow I could rappel back out of there."

"We cleansed your memory of the events within the mountain and sent you immediately home," Ish explained. "Your own mind would've betrayed you, had we not done so. Had we allowed you to leave the mountain as you had entered it and then attempt a cross-country trip home, Beltesha's legions would have been upon you before you knew what was happening."

"He found me anyway."

"Yes, but not before we had given you time to attain the inherent instinct of the Guardian, the instinct to protect the Gift at all costs. If you will recall, you twice refused Beltesha's demand that you turn it over to him, though even you yourself did not know why."

"Yeah, well," T. G. admitted. "He hacked me off."

Ish smiled. "It was nothing so simple, but I understand the sentiment. We strengthened you against him, enabling you to choose to defy him. Had you yielded to his demand, you would have been killed on the spot and the Gift would've been utterly destroyed."

"What about that sudden trip I made, the one that saved me from him?"

"At that point, no place on Earth would've been safe for you. Those of the Dark were on full alert, knowing the time had come, that the Gift had been given. Your best refuge was for us to remove you utterly from your world to another, but only temporarily. The time of your task wasn't yet at hand, and you had much left to learn."

"I think I *still* do."

Ish went on. "Then, when the Gift was seen and recognized on that other world, we brought you home again."

"Twenty years later," T. G. understood. "So the trail would be cold. So the heat would be off."

Ish smiled anew. "I wouldn't have put it in those terms, but yes. That's essentially correct. You were safe, but the Egyptian incantation you invoked was like sounding an alarm."

"Why? Those spells should have worked. They apparently did for the Egyptians."

"T. G., those who deal with the Dark in such a fashion are using incantations and rituals *of the Dark's own making*. Men have long sought to accomplish their own ends by employing the occultic forces, while 'protecting' themselves with mock defenses the Dark itself has given them."

"I'm not sure I understand."

"An enemy is never more deadly than when one mistakenly believes that it is under control. For this reason, throughout your world's history, countless hollow spells and powerless commands, to which the Dark and its agents *pretend* to be bound, have been given for man's use. These beings will feign defeat, submission, and utter obedience for a thousand years in order to give men a false sense of power over them…so that at the right time for their purposes they can turn and strike without fear of retaliation. When a man thinks he can fall back upon some spoken incantation or such as his last line of defense, he proudly relies upon his own false devices instead of trusting in the only true defense man has against the Dark…*us*."

T. G. stood and paced for a moment, thinking. It was a lot to absorb. "But why me? What was I chosen to do?"

"There are others whose very lives depend upon the power of the Gift you hold. You must keep it safe and see to it that it reaches them. You're about to play a crucial role in a world's history and help to keep those who would destroy all from doing just that. Beyond that answer, you're not yet ready. You cannot yet appreciate the importance of your task."

T. G. scowled. "You could try me…"

"I know this is difficult. In due course, all will be revealed to you. You must learn patience."

"When I'm done…do I get to go back to my own life?"

"You will be free to do that which you wish."

"Please…just tell me one more thing. Is Jenni alive?"

Ish looked down. T. G. feared the worst. "I understand your feelings for her, T. G. But you must stay focused. Every man has a set amount of time and not one day more…a purpose uniquely his and no other. You have a great task to perform that was declared from the beginning of your world. It is the most important thing you will ever do. All else, even your life and those of your friends, is secondary."

T. G. became angry and stood over Ish. "How can you say that? Nothing's more important to me than the lives of my friends. I'd lay down my life for Jenni and Dave…" His voice dropped suddenly away. He was surprised by the words spilling from his lips, even more so because he knew he had meant them.

Ish looked at him—and smiled. "No greater love. We chose well."

It had taken an extraordinary chain of events, but T. G. had begun to find himself again. His self-pity was all but gone, replaced by a deep concern for others whose importance he had now placed above his own. That part of him that had died along with his parents had finally risen from the grave, dusted itself off, and was readying itself for whatever the future held.

"So you're asking me to trust you…to put my life in your hands."

"Yes, T. G."

T. G. nodded, pacing for several long moments as he considered all he had seen and heard. Finally, he turned to the angelic Ish and spoke. "Okay…I'll do it."

Ish rose, revealing his height of well over six feet. "That's a decision that the T. G. in Colorado could never have made. Your experiences since that time, over this short span of days, have changed you, just as further ones will. Now our forces can amply empower you against any further attacks and give you the capacity to do what you must do."

T. G. was astonished by the fact that, indeed, he did trust the man. "There's something about you…I can't put my finger on it, but…"

"I have something for you," Ish said, reaching into a pouch in his robe. He withdrew a tiny object, which he held in the palm of a closed hand. The man reached out with it, motioning for T. G. to take it from him.

It was a small round disc of sparkling white stone, roughly the diameter and thickness of a checker piece. T. G. held it in his palm and studied it for a moment. Into its face was cut a single word, written in a language he did not know.

"Inscribed upon that is your name, T. G. Your *true* name. All who are ours have one. You cannot yet read it, but you'll know it one day. Keep that stone. Keep it safe."

"A new name? Good. I hate the one my father gave me."

"I know. 'TilGath-pilnezar'…'lord of the Tigris.' A derivation of the name of one of the kings of ancient Assyria. Your father was quite the biblical scholar. You favor him."

"You guys must know everything," T. G. said. "I never told it to anyone. Not Jenni, not Dave…no one."

Ish smiled. "It's time we left this place. You have much to do, and the sooner we begin, the sooner you'll have your answers."

"This other world…?"

"It is the world you visited earlier. Its people call it Noron. This time, however, I'll send you there in a manner of travel more comfortable than the cold darkness you experienced before."

"I hope so. No more falling and crashing into things, please."

"I'm sorry you had to experience that, and the other less-than-enjoyable landings you made. But had I used my full resources, to transport you in the manner in which I myself travel, the power expenditure would have given Beltesha a trail to follow. I sent you along back roads, as it were. Now that's no longer necessary."

"Why not?"

"Because you trust us. That allows you much assistance."

"Once I'm on that planet…how do I find you again?"

"I'll be there."

"Am I going to regret this decision?"

"At times. At first. Until you understand."

T. G. took a deep breath then nodded silently. The chamber filled with the light of the sun, and they were gone.

12

Pretsal was tired, for it had been a long day. The fields had been particularly full that month, their yield increased by a new fertilizer the State had issued. Fertilizer was always coming from the State. This was one of the few times it had actually been fertilizer.

He, like all harvesters, had been working longer shifts than usual. He leaned back in his chair in the gently lit room, trying to unwind, staring at the shadowed swirls in the sculpted ceiling of his dwelling.

He had told the others. Most had doubted. Some had laughed.

Pretsal was not laughing.

He had played it over in his mind time and again and even now was a little shaken by the experience, seven years after the fact. He told himself that the time had come. He did not know exactly what to expect or when to expect it, but he believed in his heart that the time had come.

He had seen the Dovo Kosi.

He was right. The time *had* come.

A dull knock of flesh against wood brought him back to the present. Pretsal reluctantly rose and walked to the heavy door. He was in no mood for visitors, and with each step he framed in his mind the best excuse to send them away. Pulling the door open, the words had already begun to pour from his lips when his eyes fell on the person outside. His voice trailed quickly away. He went silent.

"Hello, Pretsal," T. G. smiled, greeting his friend with the correct usage of his native language.

"T. G.! You have come back!" a suddenly energetic and overjoyed Pretsal said. "I knew you would!"

"I'm glad to see you."

"Please, enter. I hope you find it comfortable." Smiling widely, he watched his guest's every step in amazed wonder and gestured toward a chair.

The big man looked at T. G., at the Gift he still carried. "You no longer make the strange sounds," he observed, sitting nearby. "Was that a real language, the way you spoke before? You speak properly now."

"Yes," T. G. smiled. "I guess I do. A friend…taught me." His knowledge and sudden understanding of the Noronian language had been an instantaneous gift from Ish, a fact that still amazed him.

T. G. got his first good look at Pretsal's home. The last time he had been there, darkness and police hiding in wait had kept him from looking around. To his surprise, he found that it wasn't too different from any apartment he had seen on Earth. Furniture resembling common chairs and a sofa were there, along with what appeared to be a knee-high, three-tiered coffee table.

A low cylindrical object some four feet in diameter and three feet tall stood in one corner. Its upper surface, a flat matrix of metallic blue facets that glistened in the light, was topped with a tall, clear glass dome.

"What is that?" T. G. asked.

"Simulight," Pretsal replied. "It is an audiovisual display system. Through it, we get both entertainment and information."

"Oh," T. G. smiled. "Like television."

The walls of the room were an elaborate combination of hand-cut wood beams and formed plaster. Built-in lighting units were regularly spaced throughout, throwing a gentle, even light. Multicolored tapestries of various sizes, most of which featured sayings of sorts, hung here and there. One in particular caught T. G.'s eye—

All men have but one entrance into the world, and the like going out.

"They told me you were not really here before," Pretsal said. "They told me I was wrong. It has been so long since you were here, I began to fear that they might be right. I wondered if I had dreamed it all. And if it *was* real, I thought perhaps you were not coming back, that it was not yet time, or that perhaps I had done something to offend you, to send you away."

"No, no. Not at all," T. G. assured him, sitting down. "I…had other duties elsewhere. But now I'm here, and I have a job to do."

"Night falls. We must meet with the Twelve," Pretsal said enthusiastically. "We have to go to Darafine. She has to see you, to know for herself. Once they see you, they will believe."

"The Twelve?" T. G. asked.

"Yes—those who await you. Do you not wish to go to them?"

"Yes," he decided, seeing no reason to wait. "Of course."

"We must be careful that the State does not know of our actions," Pretsal went on. "You will be taken into custody if they learn of you." Moving to a large metal plate embedded in a far wall, he momentarily pressed his palm against its brushed-steel surface, touched a fingertip to various points on a jeweled glass circle near one edge, and seemed then to wait for something. T. G. watched, wondering what the gentle giant was doing.

After a moment, a voice filled the air. T. G. could place no direct source for it, but he listened intently as it spoke.

"Prosperity," the male voice said.

"Prosperity," Pretsal repeated. "Honor Pretsal."

"Yes, Pretsal. How goes the harvest?"

"It was a good day. I have called upon you because I *must* share. Tonight. What do you suggest?"

He's on the phone, T. G. realized.

"The nexus," the voice continued. "Someone will meet you."

"All," Pretsal insisted. "All must gather."

"That is unwise," the voice insisted.

"It is necessary."

"Very well, Pretsal," the voice agreed, tinged with reluctance. "Three hours. Prosperity."

"Prosperity." He again touched the plate, apparently turning the phone off. He walked over to T. G. "We should go. It will take us that long to get there. The nexus is the biocenter in Cusira, far from here."

T. G. stood. "Biocenter? Okay. Let's go."

"You should not yet be seen…is that correct?"

"Uh, sure. Why take chances?"

Pretsal went back to the phone.

"Prosperity," a new voice said. "Honor Mathoric Norii."

"Prosperity. Honor Pretsal Jora. I am in need of transit."

"Your location has been noted, Kir Jora," the man said. "All is ready. A conveyance is on its way, and all has been arranged. Prosperity."

Pretsal shut off the phone. "He is a good man," he said. "One of us. He will ensure that no record exists of our journey. We must be careful; your face is known now, as is the existence of the Gift you carry."

T. G. looked down at the priceless object. "You knew what this was," he observed, without surprise. "The last time I was here. And why I carry it."

Pretsal smiled widely. "Of course."

The giant then went to a closet. From there, he handed T. G. a green robe and a large, shawl-like wrap of heavy blue fabric. "Put this over your head," he said. "It will also hide the Gift. You should remain hidden until we have left the city. They will be looking for you."

"Will it fit me?" he asked, slipping into the garment.

"It should. It was mine when I was a child."

"Thanks a lot," T. G. smiled. "You called a cab, right? I guess that's one universal constant wherever you go." Pretsal smiled and nodded, having no idea what T. G. meant.

∽∾∾

The night sky was as brilliant as T. G. remembered it. Sparkling jewels in a rainbow of colors winked as he looked up, his hair blown in the airflow of the car's motion. He had trouble adjusting to the total lack of ground sensation since the car, like the one in which he had ridden during his previous visit, hovered about two feet off the ground as it sped along. It seemed more like an amusement park ride than a form of transportation.

As the hovercab passed near the city's immense central pyramid,

T. G. once again saw the huge, holographic talking head that floated high in the air in front of each of its four sides. He heard it speaking, just as it had done during his first visit. This time, however, he understood its powerful words, an utterance that was repeated again and again.

Obey.

Work.

Serve.

Worship.

Survive.

It was a drummed litany, going on day and night, taking root at a subliminal level, burying itself within them all. Words carefully selected by the State to create a populace of maximum usefulness, one constantly ridding itself of the weak-bodied and the strong-willed.

Finally, T. G. and Pretsal passed through a gate in the city's towering northern wall, left the Luracaynian capital of Keltrian behind, and entered the zone of tropical wilderness beyond.

"It's so beautiful," T. G. said, gazing up into the deep purplish expanse above him. "More so than the sky at home. Much more. I used to love to just lie there at night and look up…thinking of what awaited beyond the world I knew."

"The first time I saw you, I knew from your appearance that you must be from another place," Pretsal commented. "No one I have ever seen looks as you do. You must have traveled far indeed."

"Yes, I did. Very far."

"We were taught that when you came, you would not be one of our own people, but someone sent to us from outside. I do not know why it needed to be so."

T. G. nodded, wondering. Ish had not told him that. He returned his gaze to the myriad lights above, wondering which, if any, was the sun he had known.

The miles fell quickly away as they crossed the dark wilderness. Finally, a new glow of city lights appeared on the horizon. The hovercab slowed as it crossed the border into the first outlying areas, and its speed decreased further as it entered the main walled complex. It was a smaller city than the one they had left, but it was still quite impressive by Earth standards.

"This is Cusira," Pretsal said. "I was born here. I have many friends in this place, but we must be careful. If the Watchers see you before we are able to meet with the Twelve, they will arrest you. That is one reason we meet in the biocenter; it lies on the far fringes of the city, and is not as well maintained as it might be. The Watchers have little interest in it. Nothing important ever happens there...or has before tonight." Pretsal smiled.

"Who are these Watchers?"

"They protect the government. There is much unrest among the people—there always has been. The High Ones leave the people to themselves for the most part, without laws or enforcers to regulate them. The strong and charismatic prosper by preying on those who cannot defend themselves. It is believed that if one cannot protect his life or property, he deserves to lose both."

"Survival of the fittest," T. G. said. "Carried to the extreme. But individuals should be free *and* protected by the law."

"Yes, that is as it should be. Men killing men or taking their wives or property simply because they can is wrong. There are precious few who believe this, however. The world has fallen into a deep darkness, and the worst is yet to come.

"We are left by the State to devour ourselves. But any time a citizen appears to threaten the government or any High One, the Watchers act. Many people have simply disappeared, never to be seen again, for speaking out and trying to change the way things are."

"Those men in your apartment..."

"Watchers, yes. I had been seen as a possible threat to a High One, so I was kept jailed while my daily comings and goings were researched. They found nothing."

"Why did they think you would be a threat?"

"I refused to bow as the president surveyed our fields earlier in the day. He is a brilliant and powerful man. If an alliance forms between Luracayn and Sethii, as is expected, he may well rule all three nations. Kamir has not the military might to defend itself from a takeover, which would surely follow. There would no longer be a land in which to take refuge. Should the whole world fall under the hand of a single man, we would lose what few freedoms we have left. We would become a race of slaves, laboring without payment for the benefit of wealthy and powerful men whose faces we do not even know. President Shass must not be allowed to rule over Noron."

"Shass?" T. G. asked, astonished. "That's right—in your apartment, one of the Watchers said my name! I thought…I wasn't sure…"

"You are of the kindred Shass?" Pretsal asked with sudden concern. He looked at T. G. differently, unsure what significance the revelation held. "How can this be?"

"I just have the same name. No relation, I promise."

"But everyone who shares a name is related."

"Not where I come from. Don't worry, Pretsal. I'm on your side."

"You are the Dovo Kosi. I am here for you. I will keep you safe."

Dovo Kosi. *Voice in the Dark.* Ish had used the phrase as well, but T. G. had thought it merely an expression, not a name.

"How do you know I'm the Dovo Kosi? What are you expecting from me?"

"You carry the Gift. No one else could do so. Through you shall finally come the Awakening." He smiled. "You need not test me. I believe."

Before T. G. could question him further, the car slowed to a stop. Pretsal climbed out and helped T. G. to follow. No sooner had he left the passenger compartment than the hovercab sped away, called to a new assignment.

"You don't have to pay for that?" T. G. asked as the car receded into the distance and darkness. "Don't you have to put money in a slot or something?"

"Normally, for those things that demand a fee, payment is taken directly from my monetary reserve. None was required this time; the conveyance was sent secretly so that no record would be made of our trip here."

"Oh, right," T. G. remembered.

The biocenter was a huge facility, judging from what T. G. could see in the dim purple light of night. It was obviously after hours, for the whole place was darkened and almost vacant. Overhanging trees blocked the stars above, and the sounds of night birds and frogs filled the air.

Moving through a tangle of shadow, they walked through the cut-stone entry gate and into a wide entry pavilion. From there, Pretsal led T. G. aside and down a rarely used and overgrown cobblestone walkway. Hidden floodlights fairly illuminated the massive surrounding buildings of stone and metal, throwing odd shadows. The foliage overhanging their path grew ever more dense as they moved deeper into the biocenter, giving the impression of a trail cut into the lush growth of an untamed jungle.

A deep bellow sounded, its direction of origin indiscernible. There was another then, a reply to the first, it seemed. As T. G. listened, other animal noises became apparent in the still air.

"This is a zoo," T. G. guessed. "Right?"

"A zoo?"

"A place where you put wild animals so people can look at them."

"Ah, yes, it is then. This biocenter is one of the oldest in Luracayn. I used to come here as a child. Here, this way."

They took a side path to the left. The trail grew darker than it had been, but only for a moment. It quickly opened onto the wide ring of the main concourse, which surrounded a vast circular stone wall of about waist height. The outer periphery of the donut-shaped clearing was dotted with terraced enclosures, each of which was set back into the tropical growth and held a different type of animal. T. G. saw common tigers, wolves, and hyenas, as well as a few predatory mammals he had never seen before. Other huge pens seemed to contain only foliage, their animals hiding from view. There were no bars on the enclosures, but a chasm separated each habitat from the concourse, preventing escape and protecting visitors.

It appeared to T. G. that Noron was populated with a fauna almost identical to that of Earth—had these creatures been brought from there?

He and Pretsal cautiously approached a man just ahead of them, who stood at the wide central wall, dressed in the familiar colorful wrappings. His dark hair hung to his collar. He wore a mustache and beard that, for T. G., immediately brought the Sheriff of Nottingham to mind. They walked up to the tall, dapper figure.

"This is Josan Lorana," Pretsal said to T. G. "He will take us to the others."

"Pretsal," the man whispered loudly in retaliation, obviously uncomfortable that his own name had been spoken aloud. "I have been watching. No one has shown any interest in the three of us. It is almost after hours, and few remain here. What is the reason for this meeting you have called?"

Pretsal beamed. "He is among us once again, Josan. As I told you before. I have brought him to you…the Dovo Kosi. He is ready now to reveal himself to the world."

The man looked down upon T. G., whose head was still covered by the cloth. "This?" he asked, almost mockingly. "This child is the Dovo Kosi?"

"I'm no child," T. G. said, pulling the hood back. "And I *have* been sent here."

"*You* have come from the Creator?" Josan said, shaking his head. "How can one such as *this* change the world, Pretsal? His voice is not mighty. His flesh holds no strength. Such a small one as this…"

His words fell away as T. G. pulled back his robe to reveal the Gift. The man's eyes went wide, filled with amazement and awe.

"He carries the Gift," Pretsal pointed out, smiling widely.

Josan extended a hand to touch it, as if to prove to himself that it was real. "It looks as though it is...please. Forgive me. I did not know."

"Don't worry about it," T. G. assured him. "I'm just here to deliver this to those who need it."

T. G. had the sudden uncomfortable feeling that he was being watched and felt a nudge. Slowly turning to look over his right shoulder, his eyes met others.

They glistened like wet gold and were huge, no more than four feet away. Between them, atop a squarish head, flexed a short, elephantine trunk, which sniffed curiously at the air near T. G., who could only stare—at once shocked, amazed, and delighted at the impossible sight. He moved to one side and closer to the wall, where he could look over and down into the huge pit where the animal lived. A smile filled his face as his eyes traced the graceful lines of the animal's long, leathery neck, from its gentle face down to the massive body beneath. *Of course! It had to be!*

It was a dinosaur.

On Earth it would have been called a Brachiosaur. Its green-gold skin almost sparkled in the gentle light of the biocenter, adding to the dreamlike quality of the moment. T. G. looked forty feet down to the hay-covered floor of the huge concrete pit and saw the creature shuffling its tree-trunk legs. As the beast moved, a second, much smaller creature was revealed beneath its wide abdomen, an infant of the same species that never strayed more than a few yards from its mother. T. G. smiled.

That trunk, he wondered, as his gaze returned to the head of the adult. *They missed that little detail back home.* But then who would possibly have guessed that elephants had them as well if *they* had been an extinct species, recreated solely from their fossilized skeletons? Soft tissue structures leave few traces in fossil beds—

"What do you call this animal?" T. G. asked excitedly.

"That is a lorotha," Pretsal answered. "The largest of beasts, yet the most gentle. You do not know?"

"They call them something else where I come from," he said, daring to reach out and pet the animal on its snout. He knew that many a scientist, Professor Kerrod among them, would practically give his life for the chance to do what he was enjoying.

"The others are waiting," Josan said. "We should go."

They moved on, reluctantly in T. G.'s case. He looked back over his shoulder as he walked, watching the impressive creature as it lowered its head and turned toward the other side of the wide pit.

"I can die happy," T. G. said to himself under his breath.

The three entered a small maintenance building just off the main concourse. Inside, Josan led them to a concealed, rarely used trapdoor.

"Down here," Pretsal directed T. G.

A ladder led some five levels down into a dark place, one where T. G. would have been most uncomfortable had the two giants not been with him. At the base of the ladder, what appeared to be a concrete maintenance tunnel stretched in opposite directions. They followed one branch for a hundred feet or so before Josan stopped at a large, reinforced metal door with an access plate much like the one outside Pretsal's apartment.

"This way," he said, completing the access code. The door swung noiselessly open and he went in first, followed by T. G. Pretsal, bringing up the rear, took a last look down the tunnel outside before closing the door behind them.

"No one follows," he said. "It is safe."

The trio walked down a short, darkened hallway, which opened into a wider passage some fifty feet along. A loud, repeated rumble sounded.

"We are beneath the lorotha pit," Josan explained as they walked. "It is the great beast walking around above us. Nothing more."

Momentarily, the men stopped. "We have come," Josan called into the darkness. Suddenly, a single subdued light snapped on overhead and T. G. saw before him a large, round chamber with a waist-high circular platform at its center. An ornate, stone podium was

mounted atop this, bathed in the warm, orange light. At it stood a figure in a dark red robe whose face was hidden by the deep shadow of
a wide hood. The light spilled softly out into the remainder of the
chamber, falling away with distance, only barely revealing the others
who had gathered.

To one side, behind the rail of a large protruding alcove similar to
an earthly jury box, stood eleven others, all similarly garbed in red.
Their hooded faces were also concealed in shadow, but they looked
directly at T. G.

He felt their eyes. Silently, unmoving, they stood. Waiting.

He turned to find Pretsal and Josan donning similar robes of
brown, which had hung on a wall-mounted rack just behind them.
Pretsal handed one to T. G.

"It is customary," he explained. T. G. quickly slipped out of the
robe-and-shawl wrap he had been wearing and into the new hooded
one. The three men then moved deeper into the room, approaching
the podium.

"I call to order this gathering of the Twelve," a woman's voice
sounded from atop the central platform. T. G. looked up to see the
mysterious figure standing with her hands upon the symbolically
empty podium.

He recognized the red polished stone of the podium as being
identical to that in the hidden corridor and chamber from which the
Gift had come.

The woman spoke again. "As the Eleven have been, as the One
will be, as the Twelve are…we come together to keep alive that which
alone is life and the Door to life, preserved for the day in which the
Promise is fulfilled."

"Blessed is the truth," spoke the others in the chamber, in unison.

The woman on the platform turned to face the newcomers.
"What urgent matter have you for us to consider, Pretsal? So sudden
an assemblage is dangerous. We were unable to take the appropriate
safeguards."

"He has returned to us," Pretsal proudly announced. "The Dovo Kosi walks among us once again, just as he did seven years ago."

A murmur filled the room. The figure at the podium reached up and pulled her hood back, revealing a face of stark beauty. Her long, deep brown hair shone, and her cheekbones were high and pronounced in the direct overhead lighting, her eyes sparkling in the shadows.

"Indeed?" she asked, doubt in her voice. "Come forward…into the light."

T. G. looked to Pretsal, who motioned him on. He tightened his grip on the artifact beneath his robe and walked up to the platform. "I am T. G. Shass. I was sent to you by Ish."

"Ish? The Angel of the Creator?" she asked suspiciously.

"You do not look like a prophet," a voice called out from the shadowy periphery of the chamber.

"I *alone* will address him," the woman stated firmly, staring intently at T. G. "Kir…*Shass?*"

"No relation, I promise you. Pretsal told me about this leader of yours."

"We await the *true* prophet promised us by our Creator," she went on, a stern tone of warning in her voice. She placed a hand reverently upon the empty podium and looked upon its polished face. "Many have claimed this role for themselves in an attempt to infiltrate us. All have proven false."

"I was sent here. I am to deliver this to your people." He pulled his robe back to fully reveal the artifact to her. A susurration of voices rose anew in the chamber.

"You carry the Gift?" the woman asked. "Bring it." T. G. walked forward and climbed the few steps up to the platform. Shedding the outer robe, he let the loose garment fall to the floor and slipped the leather strap from his shoulder. He held the artifact out for the woman, and she took it from him, eyeing him suspiciously.

"This empty podium awaits the true Gift," she said, great skepticism in her voice. "It has for centuries, Kir Shass. Nothing else may be placed upon it—or ever has been." As she began to study the ancient object she now held in her own hands, her expression rapidly changed to one of surprise and reverence.

"It...*is* the Old Tongue," she said in amazement, seeing the tooled writings. Those standing in the shadows again responded and walked forward, moving into the light. As they dropped their hoods, T. G. looked upon their faces and saw a group that appeared to vary in age from early twenties to late nineties. All had a deep hope etched upon their faces that, for a moment, rose above the deep pain in their eyes.

"Where did you get this?" the woman asked, running a gentle finger along the tooled hide, feeling its amber gems. "There have been many forgeries...the Watchers have sought to deceive us, to draw us out by creating them. Many have died, having fallen into such traps. But this is by far the most exquisite...and never before have they dared to employ the Old Tongue."

"It is no forgery. I came to you from an angel named Ish. He sent me to bring this to you. Look at me...my skin color, my size, my eyes. They are not like yours. I'm telling you the truth. Pretsal knows. Just open the Gift and you'll see."

There was a renewed, anxious noise from those in the chamber.

"He is false!" a voice called out in a doubting tone. "If it is the true Gift, only the true Dovo Kosi can open it!"

Another voice, rife with accusation. "Only he to whom the Gift is given can reveal it. How can he not know this?"

What? I have to do what?

"They are right," the woman said. "If you are the Dovo Kosi, no one but you can open this." She studied T. G. for a moment, then held the Gift out, offering it back to him.

"Open it," she ordered, with an almost imperceptible nod.

He walked into the light and took the artifact from her. There was a deep and enduring hope in her piercing, learned eyes.

The Dovo Kosi, trusting in Ish and trusting that the Gift he held was true, turned and gently placed it upon the podium.

The eruptive sounds of disbelief and sudden anger filled the darkened chamber. *How dare he! Heretic!* The woman motioned for those gathered to remain quiet, but their indignation would not be completely stilled.

"It is no forgery!" T. G. insisted again, more loudly. "I've come to you from Ish!"

"Then open it," the woman repeated, her voice grave.

It had defied a scalpel, x-rays, a tempered-carbon saw blade, sulfuric acid, and the searing, white-hot flames of a crematory. It seemed that no method known to man could force it to reveal its secrets.

He did not know how to open it.

Come on, Ish! What do I do?

"You must do as they say, T. G." Pretsal frantically warned. "They will kill you if you do not."

"The Twelve must be protected!" a voice called out.

"Open it," Pretsal warned. "Please," he pleaded.

T. G. stood waiting, growing more nervous. There came a sudden familiar hum and a crackle of static in the room, and he knew that a weapon like the one he had seen kill a man in the streets had just blazed to life. Cold sweat broke out on his forehead. Again he looked upon the artifact, just as he had done hundreds of times. He saw nothing new and began to panic. The hum grew louder, closer. The leathery enigma remained lethally silent, sealed, and impregnable. He shut his eyes and prayed for inspiration.

It came.

One last time, his desperate gaze danced upon the tooled contours of its surface as they so fruitlessly had in the past. Suddenly, as if seeing it anew, his focus fell upon a small, unobtrusive symbol nestled among the many-tooled characters on its surface. There was something remarkable about the tiny oval marking, something that cried out to him. T. G. drove a hand into his pocket, withdrew the small white stone Ish had given him, and brought it up into the light. Onto its face, in the Old Tongue of Noron, he now knew, had been inscribed a single word—his true name.

His name. It was the same word imprinted into the symbol on the artifact.

T. G. reached out. With a deep breath, he pressed his thumb against the oval shape in the leather and held it there for a moment. He felt a warmth beneath his touch that seemed to swell into his hand, his arm.

Thousands of years of waiting were over. Now—not a second too early, not a second too late—*it was time.*

He jerked his hand away and stepped back as, to his astonishment, the impervious Gift peeled itself apart, opening like a rose and rolling in red carpet fashion from one side of the podium to the other. The enigmatic artifact finally and willingly revealed itself, as T. G. watched in amazement and breathed a heavy sigh of relief.

The woman, her mouth agape, stepped closer in stunned silence, her eyes locked upon the unveiled mystery.

T. G.'s mind wandered as images of 1975 and home filled his thoughts, the reward he anticipated for a job well done. *It's over! Now, I can go back home. Tonight I can sleep in my own bed. I'll get my twenty years and my life back. And Jenni…*

His heart leaped with joy. Now, finally, his life would be his again.

As he gazed upon the smiling faces of Pretsal and Josan, T. G. realized he had forgotten to take a look at the great weapon the Gift at last had revealed. He first looked up into the exquisite face of Darafine, who stood at the polished marble podium, her eyes drinking in the ageless object before her—the object for which a tiny, surviving remnant of her people had waited for millennia. He then followed her gaze downward and found something he had not anticipated.

There, inside its tooled outer sheathing, was the treasure he had safeguarded, the Gift he had almost died for, the ultimate weapon he had been told would turn the tide of war for the world of Noron.

It was a scroll.

Large and thickly wound, it had filled the artifact to the limits of its leather casing. Encircling two spools of masterfully carved wood, its mottled, tawny pages were densely covered with handwriting in the same language as that tooled into its casing. The vellum showed only a hint of its age, a slight chestnut discoloration along its upper and lower edges.

Darafine began to wind the scroll from left to right, her eyes scrutinizing the precise handwritten script before her. After reading but half a line, she *knew.*

"You are the Dovo Kosi!" she finally spoke without looking up, her quivering voice a loud whisper. Utterly absorbed in the words before her, she did not see the odd look upon his face, the conflict in his eyes. "Please, forgive me…forgive us all. I am Darafine Elesh of the Twelve, Kir Shass. We welcome you. We are humbled. All we have is yours."

She silently moved from page to page, her gaze embracing the ancient lettering upon each like a starving beggar might look upon a sumptuous banquet, her hands trembling almost imperceptibly with astonishment and awe. Through tear-curtained eyes she looked upon its pages, a surge of bridled emotion swelling within her as passage after passage unfolded before her, words she had heard but never seen, words that for so long had been her very reason for living. A strong woman who had seldom displayed anything but rigid determination before her own, she found herself fighting a losing battle to contain a tearful, irrepressible, inundating joy.

She suddenly cried out, her voice breaking with the sheer magnitude of the moment. *"This is the day! The Promise has been fulfilled!"* She began to weep, overcome by the moment.

In silence, those in the room trembled beneath their robes, their heads bowed, their eyes closed, their lips soundlessly uttering words of praise for their Creator.

Josan rushed up the steps to look for himself, to let his own eyes drink in the sight. Gathering herself, Darafine turned to him and nodded in wonderment, then took several deep breaths and returned her eyes to the beloved words written before her.

T. G. also looked down at the ancient manuscript, but not in awe. It was not joy that had been swelling within him at the sight of the revealed Gift, but frustration. That burning chagrin had quickly intensified into anger, and hard words rose to the surface, taking command of his lips as had happened too many times in the previous two years—words without thought, words without basis, spoken in haste and without compassion. Words that cut like knives.

He did not understand.

"A scroll?" T. G. almost shouted, incredulous, his judgment clouded by his rage. "All this was over some old parchment? I went through all of that for…for *this?*"

The outburst took Darafine and the others by surprise. She spoke in a soothing tone, facing his anger though she did not fathom it.

"It is the Time of the Awakening," she said to him, her eyes wet. "Surely you know…"

"Do you know what you did to me? Do you have a clue what I went through?!"

"You have come to us as was foretold. This," she indicated the scroll, "this is the Truth. You will go before us, leading the way, spreading this Truth to all of Noron, and it will fill the world again."

"Hold it," he said, backing away, his hands up, not hearing her. "I'm not staying here! I'm done! You don't get it…I didn't ask for this. I went through Hell getting that here…and now I find out everything that happened to me was just so you people can fall back on some old spells or proverbs or wisdom or whatever to get you through hard times?"

"It is not as you say—"

He cut her off. "Look, I was sent here to deliver this thing, that's what Ish told me. I did that, and I'm glad it's what you people were waiting for. *But my part is done.* I'm getting my life back, and getting Jenni back! I'm going home!"

"Without you, the people will not listen. The prophecy was specific…only the Voice in the Dark can ready Noron for the coming judgment."

"No! I said, I'm going home!" He turned and stormed off, his hands signaling resignation in the air as he walked.

"Your 'part,' as you put it, has only begun," Darafine called after him. "Surely you know this. You have come from the Angel of the Creator. You are *chosen*."

Pretsal and the others, puzzled by T. G.'s outburst, watched their prophet stoop to pick up his robe and shawl as he headed toward the exit tunnel. There was hurt and anger on his face, a deep disappointment that Pretsal saw but did not understand.

"T. G., please. This is not how it was to be," Pretsal pleaded. His words fell on deaf, incensed ears.

They're wrong. I'm done. I've done my part. You told me to deliver that so-called Gift to their world, Ish, and I've done that!

As T. G. entered the tunnel, words rang out in Darafine's voice, echoing powerfully along the cold concretelike walls. He did not want to hear them, but he could not stop it. Like a scalpel, they cut through his rage, piercing his mind, his will, his heart—

Behold, I have not forgotten you. For there shall come, in the darkness of the last day, one unlike any, My messenger. And he shall be for you My Voice in the Dark, one of pale countenance and childlike stature, bearing My Truth kept safely for you. And he shall go forth into the world, declaring that the Day has come upon you, leading you against the Dark.

And his visitation shall bring light to the blind, and music to the deaf, and My Truth shall return to Noron. For I have kept My word, given at the beginning of the world, that One shall be given for you, the Son of Man, and word of His victory shall come to you through My Voice in the Dark.

T. G. stopped cold and closed his eyes. Like a flame doused in water, his anger was dying away. He tried to hang on to it, tried to keep his ire burning, but he could not. Unseen, Ish was there, his hand upon T. G., calming him. Slowly, reluctantly, the unwilling prophet turned, walked back to the tunnel entrance, and looked up at the platform where Darafine was reading from the scroll.

> *And it will come about in that day that all the world shall hear, and many who sleep shall awaken, and the dead shall be made alive. Those who are My sheep shall listen to My voice, and come into My light. Do not be afraid.*

"Athanarius, the twenty-third chapter, verses seventeen through twenty-one." She lifted her gaze from her reading and turned toward T. G. All eyes in the room were focused upon him as he stood at the tunnel entrance, his mind racing.

"You could have told me," he whispered to Ish, not knowing he was there with him. "I might have done it anyway," his lips said, but he knew it was not so. As he again looked into the expectant faces of those who for more than five thousand years had awaited him, he alone heard a voice, a whisper in his mind.

No. You would not have. Only now, in this place, can you begin to realize the importance of the task for which you have been chosen.

T. G. swallowed hard. He walked languidly back into the hushed room, feeling the weight of every eye. A rumble sounded as the huge animal above moved around, each booming footstep resonating ominously in the chamber, punctuating the moment. Reaching the platform, T. G. stopped and looked up at the woman. A tear streamed down his cheek.

Though he had never before heard the words the woman had read, he knew the voice behind them, the voice of He from Whom they had come. He had heard it again and again throughout his childhood, inherent in words so often read aloud by his father. It was a voice to which he had not listened in a long, long time.

"It's a Bible," he soberly realized, looking into her wet pearlescent eyes.

"It is the Truth, given us by our Creator," she nodded. "The handwritten original, which alone survives, its words inscribed by the Voices of Light chosen by our Creator. It was hidden over five millennia ago from those who would destroy it, to preserve it for the last days when the chosen Voice in the Dark would return it to us."

Chosen. It finally became real to him.

He was an average college student from Ithaca, New York. He had eaten at McDonald's, attended public school, played football, shopped at Kmart, and had driven an old Chrysler with bad paint and worn tires. He had always been as average as an American kid could get, or so he had thought. Yet he had been chosen.

Chosen to leave his life behind. Chosen to play a pivotal role in the redemption of a world. Chosen to walk into a land he did not know and face a living Darkness that had held it prisoner for more than five thousand years.

Chosen—*by God.*

"You've been waiting…all this time. For me, for your Scriptures," he stammered, the enormity of the fact overwhelming him. "And then I come in here like this and…" He paused, looking upon the gathered faithful, finding in their eyes the flicker of hope he had unwittingly brought them. "Forgive me." He gathered himself, seeing a kindness on Darafine's face that spoke of a deep and boundless understanding.

She smiled gently. "At first, *no* prophet embraces his destiny."

Prophet? Me?

"How did you know where to find that prophecy so quickly?" he asked.

She stepped from the platform and walked to him. "The Old Tongue was once the only language this world had ever known. When the High Ones came to power and the Truth was all but eradicated, the Old Tongue was outlawed as well. A new language was taught to our children, and all writings from before were destroyed. Anyone found reading or writing in the Old Tongue was executed at once, without trial, and many of the faithful died. But they could not destroy our memories…what we have had of the Truth has survived the centuries by no more than oral transmission.

"There were once hundreds of thousands of smaller, printed copies, distributed for the faithful, but only one original…the Gift you were given. Each Voice of Light passed the Gift along to the next to be chosen, and each added the words then given him by the Creator. Always, in making copies, the original was referenced directly, for our Creator's law demanded…*demands*…that any written copy of the Truth be impeccably accurate. Not one word, not one letter may be put down incorrectly. That eliminated the possibility of our writing a copy of the Truth from memory, and no original remained to draw from. So, in each successive generation, a few such as myself were chosen to memorize its words as best we could, to pass them along, to keep them and their original language alive.

"But these last ten decades or so, the High Ones have instituted a system of memory tampering, which is spread through a method we do not know. The memory of all but those things that are reinforced by the senses day after day fades. Our minds no longer function as they once did…with each new sunrise I find I can remember less, and then only the most vivid of the Truth's passages, such as those speaking of the Voice to come. We have forgotten so much, and this generation was doomed to be the last that would remember the Truth at all. The Dark had almost won…until tonight, when the ancient Promise was fulfilled."

"You are blessed above all men, T. G.," Pretsal said. "You have been sent to reignite the fires of Truth, to free the people from the Dark, and to prepare the way for the coming Awakening."

Abraham. Moses. David. John the Baptist. Paul. So many others.

T. G. had been called into service, just as they had. Chosen as a voice in the ultimate war—that of light versus dark, life versus death, with entire worlds hanging in the balance. The crushing weight of the realization was almost too much for him to bear.

"I've seen *The Ten Commandments* a dozen times"—his voice went quiet, and he ended the sentence under his breath—"and I never even began to realize what Moses must have gone through. Now I know."

"Moses?" Darafine asked.

"A prophet of my world. He was chosen by God…told to defy a powerful ruler and lead a people out of slavery. Any sane person would have thought the task impossible. Moses did at first. But it all came to pass, just the same."

You were right, Doctor. Everything the Scriptures speak of is true!

"Your task, as well, will not be easy," Darafine said. "You, too, will have a powerful ruler to defy and a people to lead."

"I know that now." He looked again at those all around him. "I'll do my best for you," he called out, determination filling his voice.

Everyone in the room suddenly knelt to him. "Great Dovo Kosi, we pledge our hearts to you," one voice called out. "Command us."

"Get up, please," he said, uncomfortable with the adulation. "I'm just a messenger. I was sent to bring this to you, and that's what I did. I know now that there remains much to do…and with Ish's help, the prophecies will be fulfilled."

A cheer went up in the room, a song to the Creator. Then all who were there climbed the steps in turn and approached the podium to look upon the Truth with their own eyes. It had not been seen by their fathers or their fathers before them. Its ancient handwritten parchment almost glistened in the light, the words inked upon it declaring the faithfulness of a Creator Who had never let His people down.

No one living had ever before seen the Truth, but it would soon be witnessed by all the world.

The Dovo Kosi—and Ish—would see to that.

Part 11
THE ANCIENT

13

I t was called a celethene.

T. G. looked upon the great beast in amazement. He had come often to the biocenter since his arrival, and he always marveled at the diversity of flora and fauna on the planet. Most of the creatures in the biocenter, whether dinosaurs, birds, or mammals, were as brilliantly colored as gems. The plants were of the greenest greens he had ever seen. All of them made life on Earth seem muted gray by comparison, and he found himself falling in love with nature all over again.

Despite his preoccupation with his new role as prophet, T. G. thought often of Jenni. More than once she had dragged him to the zoo back home, buying them both season passes and using them often. Her love of nature had been unlike any he had ever seen, for she could sit for hours, it seemed, just looking at a patch of wildflowers or listening to the rain or watching birds in the sky.

I wish you could see this place, he caught himself thinking, before remembering that she possibly had. Yet there had been no sign of her at all on Noron, and Pretsal and the Twelve had even checked their underground resources to see if anyone else like T. G. had been reported anywhere on the planet. She was nowhere to be found—and with each passing month, T. G. began to accept that she simply was not there.

He missed her. He loved her.

He stood at the edge of the pit, gazing at the huge three-horned dinosaur—the triceratops of Earth—its skin a dull orange mottled with brownish purple along its upper back and on its belly. Watching it move about as it used its nose horn to root among the woody plants of its enclosure, T. G. was reminded of *The Enormous Egg,* a boy-meets-dinosaur story that he had adored as a child. He could still see the pen-and-ink illustrations in his mind, and he smiled at the comparison.

"I think I'll call you Uncle Beazley," he said with a smile, drawing the name from the dinosaur in the book. He still carried an affection for the childhood story, but more significantly, Uncle Beazley was an animal much like the one whose skin had made up the Gift's outer sheath. He had grown quite fond of the creature and visited it often.

The gentle beast had a distinguishing attribute that allowed T. G. to recognize it at once, even to the point of picking it out of a herd. Upon its powerful right shoulder it bore a vivid purple crescent-shaped mark, outlined in dappled red.

Dinosaurs still flourished on Noron, both in the wild outer forests and in zoos. From tyrannosaurids to sauropods, ceratopsians to pterosaurs, the entire prehistoric cast of characters memorized by every child on Earth still walked the land, side by side with the elephants and lions and apes.

It was an incredibly complex chain of life to which the great creatures contributed. To his surprise, T. G. had learned that the fearsome, red-and-golden-skinned Tyrannosaurus rex was not usually an active hunter, despite its terrifying appearance and virtually every theory of Earth-bound science. The long-necked sauropods with their huge appetites kept the lush, worldwide plant life in check, but their massive remains after death presented a problem. The carnivorous tyrannosaurids and their smaller cousins, acting as scavengers, made quick work of the giant plant-eaters' huge carcasses when necessary—preventing the huge body masses from decomposing over the lengthy periods of time that would be involved—and then left droppings that were optimally balanced to nourish the plant life upon which the sauropods fed.

Design and execution, a symphony of life.

Via the simulight unit in Pretsal's apartment, T. G. accessed a great amount of basic physical data about the world of Noron. The planet had but a single supercontinent upon its face, which was divided into three large nations that had warred for most of the planet's recorded history. The largest of these was Luracayn, which covered almost the entirety of the continent's northern half. Sethii, located primarily to the southwest, was the next greatest in size and economic influence. The smallest of the countries was Kamir, which occupied just under one-eighth of the area available on the continent and was landlocked.

The planet had no great mountains or mountain ranges, only high, rounded hills a few thousand feet tall. It had never known quakes or volcanic activity, since the planet's crust was intact and its internal pressures were contained. Noron's single ocean was smaller than its landmass, with small, shallow secondary seas dotting the landscape. Wide rivers coursed from sea to sea and finally out to the great ocean, where they emptied.

Interestingly, Noron was missing the vast fossil beds of Earth. *Why should it be so?* T. G. wondered. *How could it be so?*

He stayed in the shadows of the planet, hidden from the Watchers, as he learned of the world into which he had come. Disguised well enough to blend with the public, Pretsal always at his side, he traveled by day throughout the city and the surrounding countryside. Body makeup gave him the same skin tone as a native Noronian, and special contact lenses, which T. G. hated wearing, covered his normally brown eyes with the pearlescence common to the planet. Pretsal's old robe completed the effect, and a "chuni"—slang for "child"—was born.

From time to time Ish privately appeared to T. G., giving counsel and new revelation as the student was able to comprehend it. Specialized skills that were quite out of the ordinary became his to master, gifts of Ish. He matured quickly under the burden he had undertaken, learning to ask Ish not for a lighter load but for a stronger back.

They had indeed chosen well.

The Dark knew that the Truth had returned to Noron, but Ish kept it safe through his strengthening of the Twelve. Darafine labored day and night to translate the scroll into the language all of Noron now spoke, but the going was slow. The languages did not mesh easily, and her love for the scroll's message would not allow her to hurry. No word, no syllable, no inflection could be lost. No Noronian still living knew the Old Tongue but she, leaving her to carry out the privilege alone, but the rest of the Twelve did all they could to aid her and keep her as comfortable as possible as she worked.

When the time came, the Truth would be ready for its new audience. T. G., waiting for that day, hoped *he* would be as well.

Also aiding the Twelve was a faithful underground of those who had awaited the Awakening—small in count, numbering no more than a few thousand, but spread across the planet's face with an established base in practically every major city. They, too, would be ready to move when the time came.

It soon would.

∽◦∾

"What is it? What did I say?" T. G. asked, puzzled.

"You said you were twenty-four," Pretsal replied, swallowing a bite of grilled locust. They sat at a shaded wooden table in the food court of an outdoor marketplace, enjoying the regional fare as they took time out for lunch. The place was crowded and obviously quite popular.

"You may look like a youngster as we walk the streets," he continued, "but you forget that you are not one in reality."

T. G. thought for a moment. It had never occurred to him that a year on Noron probably differed from one on Earth.

"How long is a year here? How many days?"

"Three hundred sixty."

"That's pretty close…shouldn't matter that much. How old are you?"

"I have seen the Feast of Rebirth fifty-two times," Pretsal said.

"No way."

Pretsal smiled, slightly amused at his disbelief. "Yes. Fifty-two."

"Pretsal, no way!" T. G. began to laugh, thinking his new friend was pulling his leg. He went back to his meal of red locust, sliced fruit, bread, and grape juice. After a few moments, he went on. "Come on now…really, how many years old are you? You don't look fifty-two."

"I should hope not," Pretsal smiled, taking a bite.

"I'd say you're thirty, maybe thirty-five tops. Why did you say you were fifty-two?"

Pretsal's face become puzzled. "I do not understand. I did not say that."

"You said you saw the Feast of Rebirth—"

"T. G.," Pretsal corrected him, "that feast comes every six years."

"What?"

"I am 317 years old."

"What?"

"What?" Pretsal echoed.

T. G. saw the serious expression Pretsal wore. "You really aren't kidding, are you? You're serious!"

"Why would I joke about that? It is not funny."

"So how long do you guys live, anyway?"

"It varies," Pretsal casually answered. "Eight hundred…nine hundred years." He pointed at the remaining locust drumstick on T. G.'s plate. "Are you going to eat that?"

"Have at it." An astonished T. G. slid his plate toward his friend. He had gotten used to locust, and even liked it, but he had had enough. As Pretsal ate, the young prophet looked upon him with new eyes. *Three hundred seventeen?* He did some quick calculating in his head. *You were born almost a hundred years before the start of the Revolutionary War?*

T. G. was stunned. "Imagine all you could accomplish with a life span like that! There'd be no limit to the advances you could make."

"One would think so," the giant nodded. "But such has not proven to be the case. Complacency is most seductive, T. G. My people have, in the past, traveled in space, explored the depths of the sea, and accomplished great things in medicine, structural engineering, and physics."

He paused to take a drink, swirling the juice in his cup as he considered a history he knew too well. "For thousands of years now, though, things have remained virtually unchanged. Ours is a stagnant society. Even most of those who had ventured into space returned here long, long ago, abandoning the bases we once built on other worlds simply because it was *easier* to live here."

They left the food court and headed back toward Pretsal's apartment. Questions formed in T. G.'s mind as they walked, and as his friend closed and locked the door behind them, he plopped onto the heavy wood-and-leather sofa and renewed their conversation.

"About what you said before," T. G. began, "I would have thought your race too intelligent just to sit here and rot like that. I mean, what about the future? When history looks back—"

Pretsal took a seat, his expression far from one of pride. "Intelligence has no bearing upon it...and our history is not a proud one. Our minds, once noble, became clouded by a vicious moral decay. Over time the mental skills that built our great cities turned in their entirety toward creating newer, better, and more inventive forms of depravity. Cruelty of an intensity you cannot imagine swept the world. Each man's hand was raised against his neighbor. Sexual atrocities that would sicken any sane person became commonplace."

He hung his head. "We almost destroyed ourselves. Weapons of incredible power wiped out whole cities...whole nations...whole cultures. Unceasing warfare laid waste the entire world. Mutations were born. Huge men, violent, disfigured giants without compassion or mercy exploded exponentially into the populace and struck terror into all who saw them. The monstrosities roamed the land in huge numbers, killing and raping and maiming. Because of their wickedness, severe and fatal birth defects took more than half of the newly born. Combined with the losses due to war, our population, once numbered in the billions, plummeted until there were no longer enough living to bury the dead."

Realization struck T. G., and he considered the intricate murals of ancient bloodshed in the hallway outside in a new light.

"Those carvings out there," he said, "in the entry hall…they aren't mythological, are they? They aren't just legendary or symbolic. Those were real people, and real battles, and real monsters…"

"Yes," Pretsal nodded. He rose and walked over to an ornate storage cabinet set into one wall. As its doors swung open, T. G. saw a glimmer of polished metal and formed glass upon the tall shelves within. Pretsal reached into the cabinet and withdrew a large, roughly rounded object, and only after he turned around and began to bring it closer did T. G. realize it was a helmet. A very old one.

"This belonged to my triascendant," Pretsal began. "He wore it in battle many times. As you can see, it saved his life."

"Triascendant?"

"The father of the father of *my* father."

He handed it to T. G., who was surprised by its great weight. It was about eighteen inches from side to side, and somewhat longer front to back. Its polished surface caught the light hypnotically, even centuries after its manufacture. It was lined with leather and a firm, black gel-like material he did not recognize. As T. G. struggled to heft it into better position, Pretsal indicated a long, deep indentation along its upper right side.

"A blade fell here," he said. "One wielded by an enemy long ago on a battlefield far from here. And here…" He indicated a pitted burn mark on its other side. "Here a ripcharge struck. Either of those blows would have been fatal…and I would never have been born." He smiled. "I suppose I owe my life to this helmet."

T. G. looked at a huge, curved trail of rounded indentations that ran down the left side and then up near the back. After a moment, what they were dawned on him.

"*Toothmarks?*"

" 'Monsters,' as you call them." He took the helmet from T. G. and returned it to its place. "Hell truly lived on Noron. The stench of billions of dead filled the air. Corpses covered the land, the streets, the hidden places. Still men fought. Still they slaughtered each other without mercy. Finally, so few remained that our extinction seemed certain."

"What stopped it?" the transfixed student asked.

"We do not know for certain. At the last possible moment, some measure of sanity returned to the planet suddenly and without apparent cause. The few who remained, scattered across the planet's ravaged face, turned from their relentless fury and stopped the killing. Still, they were wicked…but their wretchedness was no longer made manifest in its *totality.*

"As time went on, new nations were founded, rising from the rubble and debris of the old. Unfortunately, our moral depravity still runs deep…only those few who have clung to the Truth and have looked toward the coming Awakening have not succumbed. For most, this is still a world without hope."

The words drove home for T. G. the vital reason for his being there. It was a world of great physical beauty, but it was spiritually, morally dead. The eyes and senses were fed to satiation, but the soul starved to death.

∽◦∾

Only in the final days had a glimmer of light returned, as the dwindling few who still remembered awaited the Voice in the Dark. And even as that Voice stood at the doorstep, waiting for the final sign that he should make himself known to all, the horrifying moral decay of the planet intensified.

An Awakening was at hand, the only hope for Noron.

A defense against it was in place.

T. G. was expected—and he could not be allowed to live.

14

I must go to the Temple of Passage today," Pretsal told T. G. as they ate their morning meal of sweet fruits, meat, and bread.

"Why?" he asked, his mouth full. Noron shared many of the same fruits as Earth, only somewhat larger, and many Earth had never known. Grapes were the size of plums, and oranges were as big as cantaloupes. T. G., a fruit connoisseur from childhood, had found that particular aspect of life on Noron to be one of the most enjoyable and one he would miss greatly once the purpose for which he had been chosen ended.

"It is required by law. The eldest son of Kir Tosa-Crethan has died. He is my supervisor in the fields, and all those beneath him are forced by law to partake in his grief. It is the word of Drosha."

"Oh, that religion of yours," T. G. commented.

"It is not mine. You know that."

He swallowed the last of his mouthful. "I know. Sorry. I meant Noron." He looked up at his friend and saw that he was truly reluctant to go. "Let me go with you."

"That may not be wise. I have only been required to attend one other, and that is fortunate. It isn't pleasant."

"I need to learn, Pretsal. I need to see as much firsthand as I can. I've been to funerals before, trust me."

"Not like this, I would wager."

Working hand in hand with the government, Noron's theological leaders had long before crafted a false faith that guaranteed maximum financial gain for both the High Ones and the Priesthood, while at the same time keeping the population so morally empty and self-centered that no organized overthrow could ever be possible. The teachings of a mother goddess named Drosha and her child-husband-god filled schoolbooks and popular literature with urgings toward drug use, spiritism, and self-deification, guaranteeing that all would go to their deaths believing that spiritual paradise awaited them, provided they had kept up on the payments.

All would eventually attain that paradise, they were told, following a second, less tangible, more ghastly stint on the planet.

Most of those who walked Noron were not alive. They were apparitions of lost loved ones, "renewed from beyond," conjured to resume their places within their families. The whole Renewal idea was something that had always made Pretsal most uncomfortable, but the law was the law—and he could ill afford to bring the Watchers down upon himself and, as a result, upon T. G. as well.

Wearing their finest robes, Pretsal and T. G. entered the towering doorway of a large, domed building of black stone and dark wood, the Temple of Passage. Immediately, the young prophet was struck by the fact that the gathering was, in appearance, much like any Western funeral on Earth. Somber music played, filling the cavernous hall with strains of sorrow.

One remarkable difference, however, was that the deceased was laid out not in a coffin but upon a padded crystalline altar, clad in his best clothes and wearing every piece of jewelry he had owned. Around the altar were piled all his worldly possessions of value, sorted by worth. Those filing by could take for themselves anything they wished as the "mortician" stood by and smiled. As T. G. watched in disbelief, the attendees attacked the body like vultures, fighting each other, greedily stripping every last vestige of jewelry, clothing, and property from one for whom they supposedly had cared. The ceremony stunned T. G. in its sheer materialism. Had the sight not been so repugnant, he might have laughed.

Afterward, the body, no longer considered of any value, was taken away—not for burial or cremation, but for "processing." T. G. did not know exactly what that implied, and he did not want to know.

After the funeral, the family and attendees drove in procession to a second location, an immense edifice that resembled a cathedral as it towered against the pale sky. Hideous gargoyles peered down from far above as the mourners made their way inside. Huge lancet windows, crafted of a red stained glass that glowed as if ablaze, towered a hundred feet high. As T. G. and Pretsal followed the crowd, they were led into a large, circular inner chamber with a high-vaulted ceiling. Huge spirelike objects of crystal and wood jutted downward like stalactites, hanging menacingly above the attendees as they took their seats in the circular pews. An odd scent hung heavy in the air, at once perfumed and smoky, oppressive in its presence. At the center of the room, atop a high wooden platform, a massive, ten-foot wide, black marble basin stood next to an altar of rough-hewn stone. Upon the altar had been placed a large, jeweled goblet of pure gold.

It was a dark, hideous theater-in-the-round, and the show was about to begin.

Once everyone was seated, a man in a black robe with a large, stylized animal-skull mask on his head walked down the aisle to the applause of all but T. G. and Pretsal.

"Prosperity, one and all," the man said in a deep, resonant voice that echoed unsettlingly in the cavernous room. "Today we celebrate the Renewal of Rothalar Tosa-Crethan, who has left the realm of pain!"

There was a reinvigorated cheer. T. G.'s blood ran cold.

The black stone basin at the center of the room suddenly roared to life as flames burst from it, climbing high into the air, throwing a dancing, golden light upon the attendees. The austere figure placed the goblet out of sight behind the altar, then stood to one side, arms raised, looking upward.

He was a necrolink. This was the most important and cherished part of the funerary process, for it was here that the departed was returned to his loved ones, albeit in nonphysical form. Necrolinks were the most powerful nonpolitical figures on the planet, and they were also the wealthiest. Few in number, they were paid almost anything to bring back those who had died.

They alone, of all on Noron, had a labor union.

"He is Khorr Hallesa," Pretsal whispered to T. G., whose eyes were locked upon the man. "The world's leading necrolink. The deceased man's father is most influential. Most people can only afford to use one of the common, local practitioners. Bringing in Kir Hallesa must have cost him half a year's wages. Watch," Pretsal gestured.

"O, Mighty Keeper of the Gate," the necrolink began, "we seek one who has come unto you. His weary form no longer burdens him, yet he has much still to contribute among his people." Hallesa reached into a pocket, then threw a palmful of a glittery, powderlike substance up into the fire. At once, with a roar, it flared more brightly.

"Ladies and gentlemen, Harry Blackstone Jr.," T. G. whispered to himself.

The man went on quite theatrically. "We summon Rothalar Tosa-Crethan back to his home. Do not stay him, Mighty Keeper; return him to those he loves."

The words rang with uneasy and terrifying familiarity in T. G.'s ears. *I can't believe I actually did that,* he shuddered, recalling the incantation he had performed at the funeral home on Earth. *How could I have been so foolish?*

A beautiful woman who could only have been Hallesa's assistant appeared behind the gathered crowd, carrying a tiny days-old infant in her arms. A new round of applause sounded as she began walking down the aisle toward the center stage. Her slow walk was obviously one of ritual significance. Her flowing red hair shone in the firelight, and her gauzy white gown fluttered over the tops of her bare feet as she drew near the ritual flames. Her eyes were fixed and cold. After finally ascending the few steps leading to the stage, she handed the baby to the necrolink, turned, and immediately disappeared down a hidden staircase in the floor of the platform.

Placing the silent, well-behaved child upon the altar, the robed man looked upward, arms wide. "The balance must be maintained! O Kudis, auditor of souls, accept this creature as a substitute for our friend, with whom we wish to walk again. Let this blood fill your goblet, let this flesh feed your hunger!"

You don't mean...dear God! No!

It was horrible and sudden. T. G. wanted to look away from the sickening atrocity that assaulted his eyes but did not. Knives flashed, sectioning the infant alive as a butcher might dress a chicken for frying. Blood coursed down a channel built into the top of the altar and drained into a small hole at one end. T. G. fought back a wave of nausea. His eyes filled with anger, and he looked up at Pretsal, who hung his head as if ashamed for his people.

"It is done!" Hallesa cried, raising the sacrifice's tiny, walnut-sized heart high into the air for all to see. An explosion of applause filled the chamber. The necrolink then lifted the bloodied knives high over his head, and a new wave of acclaim broke out as if the audience were enjoying a magic show or a one-act play.

"O Kudis, this child I present to you! As has been for all time and ever shall be, we triumph over death through sacrifice. Return our beloved friend as was destined to be!"

Many of the spectators turned to each other, commenting in highbrow fashion on the fine job the necrolink was doing. T. G. noticed that those in the deceased man's family, sitting in the front row, were laughing and shouting for more.

Hallesa reached behind the altar and withdrew the goblet. He carried it ceremoniously down to the first row, to where the Tosa-Crethan family sat: father, mother, brothers, sisters. One by one, he paused before them, holding the goblet of human blood out for each to sip from. T. G. looked away, seething with anger and disgust. The ghastly ritual took several minutes. Hallesa finally resumed his place atop the platform and spoke again, tossing what remained of the infant into the fire.

"The contract is fulfilled. The sacrifice is made. We await!"

A cold wind filled the room, swirling for a moment before mounting toward the ceiling. The icy gust whistled and howled amid the huge spires above, which creaked and swung slightly as an odd, pulsating glow intensified around them, whirling like a glowing mist. It began to coagulate into fixed patterns, becoming a gathering of luminescent, indefinite forms that slowly descended to the altar below as the winds died down. Nearing the floor, the forms became increasingly identifiable human shapes, a cluster of beings. Arms, legs, torsos, and faces became obvious, particularly those belonging to the central figure, who was apparently carried along by the others.

Red eyes flared to life. All around T. G., applause broke out again, louder this time.

The central being was gently taken to the floor and released. The other angel-like escorts immediately left the stage, soaring upward and vanishing in a new swirling light that flared brightly against the ceiling then was gone. All eyes were upon the pale, translucent figure left standing on the platform, which gazed around him at the standing ovation he was receiving. His red eyes glowed dully.

"Welcome back, Rothalar!" Hallesa triumphantly said, his deep voice only slightly muffled by his mask. "Your family awaits you!"

The thunder of applause swelled even louder. T. G. desperately wanted to leave. "Let's get out of here…now," he said to Pretsal, who could barely hear him over the crowd. The two of them wove their way through the jubilant throng, along their pew and up the aisle, never looking back.

Just outside, next to the wide, closing door, T. G. fell back against the building as if exhausted. He could still hear the cheers and wild applause continuing inside, and he shook his head. After a moment, he slammed a fist against the wooden doorframe in anger.

"How can a place be so beautiful yet so utterly rancid?" he demanded rhetorically, still shocked by the murder he had just witnessed. "This place is like a mausoleum…the whole planet…all nice and neat and pretty on the outside, with nothing but death and decay just beneath the surface."

"It has always been so," Pretsal said.

"That was the most disgusting thing I've ever seen," he growled. "If it was up to me, this cursed planet would go straight to Hell right now."

"I am sorry," Pretsal said sadly. "I hate it too. None of us who await the Awakening ever attend this ritual unless forced to. We believe the dead should be left in peace and the living should live, as in the old days."

"At least that poor child is free of this place now," T. G. said, looking out over the city, at the multitude of renewals walking its streets. "Millions of them out there, Pretsal…billions…and a child died for each one." He wiped a tear away then continued, looking up into the pink sky. "When did they start doing this Renewal thing, anyway?"

"The first necrolink was Dondol Gorth. He died about twelve hundred years ago. He instituted the idea, and the State embraced it fully. It became official law, and the dead have remained with us ever since."

"It figures the State would love this," T. G. nodded in disgust. "The whole thing is just unreal. If those people had any idea what they were really greeting in there, they'd run for the hills and never stop screaming."

Pretsal looked puzzled. "What do you mean, T. G.? That wasn't Kir Tosa-Crethan we saw returned to us?"

"Pretsal, when you die, you don't come back. You don't come when called. You don't hang around, haunting the place where you died. You leave. You go to what awaits you. We have no choice in the matter. And the necrolinks, for all their power, have no choice in the matter either.

"Look…out there," he said, pointing down to the city street in the distance. Hundreds of the phantom citizens moved about, accompanied by the living. "Every one of those renewals you see is an impostor. They're agents of the Dark, posing as dead loved ones. Invisibly, each of them stayed close to the person they'd one day pretend to be, learning their mannerisms and everything the person knew. Your whole planet has been duped. Your people never once asked questions—they didn't want to—and instead bought the whole deal and believed each of those beings was 'the former so-and-so' just because the cursed thing claimed to be."

"For what purpose?" Pretsal asked, alarmed by the revelation. "What is their gain?"

"Everything. This is war, Pretsal, and they're the enemy. They're infiltrating you, watching you, and studying you. They reinforce the public's belief in the false State religion, that 'mother-child-oneness of the universe' concoction your government created. They keep you distracted from true spiritual issues by clouding things with a counterfeit afterlife."

He shook his head. "How could we have been so foolish?"

"Don't feel bad. You aren't the only ones."

T. G. had learned from Ish that these same agents of the Dark had long since infiltrated Earth as well, from ancient times, though to a much lesser extent. The stories of haunted houses and supernatural encounters that T. G. had grown up with were accounts of their work, actions designed to create "evidence" contrary to biblical truth. The demented things had fooled proud men into believing lies, keeping the deluded souls wrapped around their putrid, deathly fingers. Only the direct intervention of the Comforter had held the things in check, keeping their deceptive activities within limits.

He went on. "The Dark has a grip on your world that will be almost impossible to break."

"But you must! The Awakening…"

"I said 'almost,' " T. G. half smiled. "What's really scary is that there must be *dozens* of those renewals walking around for every living person on the planet. Probably more…and that's just the ones you can *see*. You're up to your chin in vipers here, and nobody even knows it."

Pretsal looked upon the spectral men, women, and children with new eyes. "Ish told you this?" he asked, horrified.

"Yes. That's why those things flipped out the first time I was here.

They realized that the Gift had been given, that the time of the Awakening was upon them. Their time is up."

"What can we do?" Pretsal asked, his voice filled with concern. "No one knows of this, not even the Twelve."

"I know, but the time has come for them to be told. I haven't said anything before now because your thoughts are not kept secret from those things."

"It cannot be!"

"Anything you or the others think can be overheard by any one of those renewals out there if it gets close enough to you. Just be careful. Don't say anything concerning me or think too overtly of my mission here when you're in their presence. They can't read *me,* not anymore. Ish has given me the ability to close off my mind from them. He's also now shielding the Twelve, and those places where they and the underground meet. That's how Darafine's been able to carry out the translation without being attacked."

"What would happen if they knew *your* thoughts?"

"They'd find the chinks in my armor. We all have them, even me. *Especially* me. The Awakening is on a definite timetable, but until the Truth is released to the people, they're all practically defenseless. Darafine will soon be finished with the translation, and a lot is going to happen in a very short period of time."

"What? What will happen?"

"I don't know exactly. But Ish knows, and he'll tell me when the time comes. He's told me that everything is on schedule."

"I knew the Dark had been working through our leaders, but to see now that it's been living in every house, in every family...it's terrifying."

"For all practical purposes, we're behind enemy lines. We must never forget that. *Always* remember that this is war, Pretsal, and we must win. And as in all wars there will be casualties."

Pretsal nodded. Suddenly his world was not the same. It never would be again. "We're ready," he said firmly. "I think we have been for a long time."

"I know."

It was growing late, and night was falling. The sky had begun its daily transition from light pink to dark magenta, and the sounds of the nearby forests were changing as nocturnal creatures awoke. T. G. and Pretsal walked back into the city proper, headed for a rendezvous with Josan and others of the underground. As they made their way through the crowded streets, a brilliant light flared from an empty alleyway. T. G., shielding his eyes at first, turned to see Ish standing there. Joy filled him as he approached the luminous being.

"What, T. G.?" Pretsal asked, realizing that his friend saw something he did not. "What is it?"

"He can't see or hear me, T. G.," Ish said, the light around him fading away. "It's not yet time that I appear to him or his people."

T. G. nodded, motioning for Pretsal to follow. "It's okay, Pretsal. It's Ish."

The giant's eyes went wide, and his expression became childlike and filled with wonder. "Here? Now? He's really here?"

"Yes," T. G. smiled. "He really is."

They walked deeper into the dark alley, where the figure stood waiting.

"I saw the Renewal ceremony," T. G. told him. "I wish I hadn't."

"I know," Ish said. "It grieves me deeply that the Dark has resorted to such methods."

"Hello, Ish," Pretsal said meekly, aiming the greeting in the general direction of the place Ish stood. He felt an electricity in the air, an intangible wonder that set his senses ablaze. "I hope I've served well."

Ish smiled. "Yes, dear Pretsal. You have indeed."

"He says you have, Pretsal," T. G. repeated.

Pretsal grinned widely. "I wish I could see him."

"You will, Pretsal," Ish nodded. "One day."

"I'll wait over there," the giant said, pointing to the alley's entrance. Walking on air, he moved away, looking back over his shoulder once or twice.

"T. G.," Ish began, his tone more serious, "the time has come. It begins tonight."

"What am I supposed to do?"

"You will encounter Paull Shass and his family. He's a crucial part of what is to come, and you and he must now cross paths. It is the first phase of what must be. Your part in the chain of events will quickly become apparent to you."

"The president? But I'm not ready…"

"You have reached the level of readiness you need to begin, and through continued contact with me, you will endure, mature, and grow stronger. You must now become involved in the political realm of Noron, for only through this conjunction can the battle lines be clearly drawn and allies established. Use the gifts we have given you carefully…and be keenly aware of the movements of the Dark. It encompasses Kir Shass at all times, oppressively so. Keep your eyes open and don't become sidetracked. Don't allow yourself to be distracted by any of the opulence or emotional clutter that will surround you; doing so could prove fatal."

T. G. looked into the radiant face before him. "What's going to happen, Ish? I mean, I know that *you* know what's to come…" He paused. "Please, will I be around to see this whole thing through to the end?"

Ish smiled. "You will walk the green and flowering fields of a new world."

T. G. nodded with a slight smile. "Where do I go to meet Kir Shass?"

"I'll send you there. We have at this very moment given you the ability to travel by will to any location you can envision, but since you do not know of the place where it begins, I must send you there myself."

"Travel on my own? How?"

"Focus. Concentrate. Think of a place, will yourself across the distance, and you'll be there. We will empower you. But be careful;

each time you travel, you will tire somewhat. Doing it too often will exhaust you quickly. All of your new talents will manifest themselves as needed, and they will, at first, be a strain upon you. But as you repeatedly use these abilities, they will grow easier. Like working a muscle; at first, there will be pain, but you will gather strength."

"So just by thinking, I can shift from place to place?"

" 'Shift'…an excellent description, T. G. Yes. Through our empowerment, you can shift at will. But keep in mind that every time you travel by such means, the Dark will know…and will most likely follow. It takes a great deal of energy to move from place to place in this fashion—energy that we will provide—and as I told you, such expenditures of power leave a distinct trail behind them."

T. G. nodded. "Okay, I'll be careful. But first, before I go…" He ran over to his waiting friend. "Go on without me, Pretsal. I have things I need to do now. Keep the appointment with Josan. Tell him it's begun."

"You'll be safe?"

"Hey, I'm in the best hands I can be in. Don't worry."

"Will I see you again?"

"I guarantee it."

Pretsal reached out and bearhugged T. G., then nodded, trying with limited success to conceal his emotions.

"Take care of yourself, buddy," he said with a grin, using a phrase he had learned from his friend. "We'll be waiting." Then the kind-hearted giant turned and hurried away into the crowd.

T. G. watched him until he vanished into the throng, then he walked back to Ish. "Okay. I'm ready."

"Watch. Listen. Use the discernment we gave you. Do not lose focus. The situations and people you are about to deal with will prove intensely dangerous if you do not handle them properly. I will help you if you call upon me. Now, it is time."

In a blink T. G. found himself in a dark place. No falling, no cold, no sudden stop. Just a change in lighting, a variation in acoustics, and the realization that he was not where he had been. What little light there was came from beneath a door that stood some eight feet above, set into a rough brick wall. A damp, almost suffocating scent of mildew, mingled with the pungent odor of an unknown chemical, filled his nostrils.

Arms out, he cautiously groped for something that would tell him where he was. Almost at once, he encountered a stair rail that led upward, from the stone floor where he stood to the door above. For a moment, he considered climbing the steps. As his eyes began to adjust to the meager light of the room, he could make out multiple sets of footprints in a deep layer of dust upon the stairs. The prints led downward into the room. None led out.

Those who made them were still down there. Somewhere.

Then there was a sound. Up the stairs, beneath the door, he could see a shadow of movement, of someone just beyond. His first instinct was to hide, but there was no time. He froze.

The door began to open.

15

Josan looked upon the woman, watching as history was made. They huddled in the lamplight, concealed in a small room far beneath the blackened carcass of a ruin that no longer held any interest for the world.

Darafine completed the final word. It had been written by hand, just as scribes had done more than five millennia before and just as tradition demanded. This time, however, a rotating staff of assistants had simultaneously typed the scriptures into a private and secure databank as she read them aloud. They would be printed for mass distribution. The woman set her pen upon the wide wooden desk and smiled, almost too exhausted to do so.

"It is finished," she said joyfully, looking upon the ancient parchment she had translated. "The Truth has returned to the people."

"Such a wondrous thing you have done," the final assistant said.

"I was an instrument," Darafine corrected her. "I provided a means. Nothing more."

"The Creator be glorified," Josan smiled.

"We must get this onto the infolink as quickly as possible," Darafine instructed the assistant. "Transfer the data to our friends in every city. Tactile copies must be printed at once. Tell them all to be ready to go with worldwide distribution on my signal." She turned to Josan. "Find Pretsal. Tell T. G. that it is done, that the time of his unveiling has arrived."

"They were to have gone into the city today," Josan said. "Pretsal had to attend a Renewal."

The woman shut her eyes in pain. "The blood of so many is upon us all," she quietly said.

"It must have ended by now. I was to have a meeting with them this night. They should be here at any time."

As if on cue, the door to the room burst open and Pretsal entered. He was excited, the others all saw, and alone.

"Pretsal!" Josan began. "The Truth is—"

"Ish appeared to him!" he shouted, cutting Josan off. "He said it begins tonight. The Voice has been called to undertake that for which he came among us!"

"The Truth has been translated," Darafine said. "We are ready; soon all will hear. Ish must have known this. Did you see him?"

"No. Only T. G. saw and heard him. But he was there—I felt a presence. It's something I cannot explain, but it was wonderful."

"Where is T. G. now?" Josan asked. "The Voice in the Dark must speak to the people. They must know that the Awakening has come."

"I don't know. He sent me on to meet with you, as was planned. I don't know where he went or when he'll return, but he said he would be back as soon as it is possible."

"At a moment's notice, we must be ready to send the Truth out among the people. When T. G. makes himself known, the Truth must be there with him." She turned to Josan once more. "Contact Carastine in Tonash. Tell her to oversee the printing of the Truth. I want millions of copies loaded on carriers and ready to go as soon as the time comes."

"Yes, Darafine," he said, and ran from the room.

"I cannot believe that it's finally happening, and in my lifetime," Pretsal said. "Such a wondrous thing…"

"The Creator is faithful even when we are not."

The woman carefully rolled the ancient scroll back into the same tight, heavy cylinder that had first emerged from the artifact and laid it atop the unfurled leather wrapping. Almost at once, the tooled hide soundlessly wrapped itself around the priceless Truth, enveloping it, sealing itself once more into an impervious whole.

Darafine and Pretsal looked upon it in wonder and turned their eyes upward. It was the night they had awaited all their lives.

The Gift had been given—to all the world.

∽o∾

A huge black form stood silhouetted in the open doorframe.

T. G. crouched to one side of the steps, hoping the darkness would provide enough cover. Holding his breath, he watched as the man slowly began to descend the staircase, peering into the dark and moving cautiously as if expecting trouble. In his right hand was one of the lethal energy weapons that seemed to be the firearm of choice on Noron.

T. G. did not move, did not breathe.

"You there!" the man barked, leveling his weapon at T. G. It crackled, charged and ready. "Don't move! Who are you? Where is Grodnal?"

His cover blown, T. G. stood up in the shadows. "I, uh, I don't know…"

"A chuni?" he asked, surprised. "Look, son, you had better tell me. Where is he?" he demanded, his finger twitching against the trigger.

"Who?"

The man descended the steps, never taking his eyes from T. G. On even ground, he towered over him. T. G. got a better look at his face and recognized the Asner-like features of the Watcher who had been in Pretsal's apartment the night he had been arrested.

"You?" the man said. "I remember you. How did you get out of that cell?"

A voice boomed out of the darkness, startling them both. "So despite my warnings, you tried to rescue him anyway, did you?"

The Watcher swung around, seeking the source of the voice but found none.

"Grodnal?! Where are you?" he demanded. "Show yourself!"

A dim overhead light flickered on. A laugh filled the room, and at the top of the stairs a dull blue flash flared to life with the dry crackle of unleashed energy. A dense, man-sized cloud of black smoke billowed out of the flash, out of the nothingness. The Watcher instantly fired his weapon at it, sending a white hot bolt of lightning arcing upward into the thick gloom. There was another laugh, and a human shape began to coalesce within the cloud. In moments it attained solidity, and the smoke was gone. T. G. sensed a great evil, a tangible threat as real as the shadowthing had been. He tensed, trying to ready himself for anything.

"You, Kir Hervie," the man said to the Watcher. "You should have known better than to come here, especially after what you saw."

"Where is he, Grodnal? What have you done with Kir Shass?"

The dark figure came down the stairs. He was draped in a deep blue robe, one covered in what appeared to be occultic symbols.

Hervie backed away, leaving himself room to use his weapon. "I am giving you one last chance to surrender, Grodnal…"

The man only laughed. "Toys, Hervie. You threaten me with toys."

Again the Watcher fired. The bolt, deflected, returned and blasted a sizable pit in the rough brick wall beside Kir Hervie.

"Enough foolishness," Grodnal demanded, his voice threatening. With a sweep of his left hand, the weapon flew from the Watcher's grip. It exploded in midair with a loud concussion and a shower of sparks.

T. G. looked up into the Watcher's face and saw a blank expression suddenly come upon it. The man's eyes seemed unfocused, staring at nothing. "Now, Hervie," Grodnal boasted, "you shall see your master. Walk."

The Watcher turned to his left and slowly began down a long stone-and-mortar corridor that ended in a wide, metal door. After pulling the door open, he disappeared beyond it, and it closed behind him with a deep thud.

Grodnal turned his attentions immediately to T. G. "So, young one…you are with Kir Hervie?"

"No. I don't know him. I don't know where I am, either."

He eyed T. G. suspiciously. "Who are you? I do not know you, and I know many."

Before he could answer, T. G. felt an odd sensation deep within his head, almost like an intense itch, and it was spreading. At once he found that by willing it to cease he caused it to do so, though he had to continue concentrating or it would return.

"You tell the truth," Grodnal said, eyeing him. "Then you block me."

So…he reads minds…and I can resist him!

"My name is T. G.," he said, nodding.

"Grodnal Vord," the odd man said, bowing his head. Still tall by Earth standards, he was shorter than most on Noron. His face was round and dark, with small, close-set black eyes and a flat nose. His cheeks sagged, giving him a perpetual scowl that was intimidating. "Your name is Shass," he continued, "yet you are not related to Paull Shass."

How much did he learn in three seconds?

"No, I'm not."

"Nor are you a child."

"No."

"Come," he said, starting down the corridor. "Follow me."

T. G. stood his ground, letting the man walk away.

"You do not trust me?" Grodnal mockingly asked.

"Of course not," T. G. answered with as authoritative a voice as he could muster.

"Then stand there. It makes no difference."

Mystified by the turn of events, T. G. decided to trail the man at a distance. The dark corridor sloped downward at a difficult angle. The smell of mildew became stronger as he walked, as did the pungent fumes that hung in the thick, oppressive air. The steel door swung open for the man without his touching it, and both he and finally T. G. entered the damp, cavernous room beyond.

There in the flickering torchlight that splashed upon its stone walls, T. G. saw a room like a medieval torture chamber, complete with hanging chains and a hot coal fire into which irons like a blacksmith's had been placed. An array of rough-hewn wooden workbenches rested in the center of the room, on top of which were books, small cauldrons, and glass containers filled with colored liquids. A wide, deep pool of glowing water bubbled at the far end of the wide floor, directly across from the door.

Kir Hervie and another man were pinned to one wall by heavy shackles. As T. G. entered, both of the imprisoned men looked up at him, and he saw that the now-chained Hervie was no longer in a trance.

"A bit theatrical, I will admit," Grodnal said, spreading his arms to encompass the room. "But I like it."

"Who is he, Grodnal?" the unknown prisoner said, straining against his chains. "Hiring help, are you?"

Grodnal smiled. "Charming. Your reputation is well earned."

"They are working together, all right," Hervie said, nodding toward T. G. "I found him lurking down here when I came in."

"I am *not* working for this man," T. G. said, answering Hervie. "I don't even know him. I just sort of *stumbled* into this place."

T. G. studied the other shackled man on the wall more closely. His clothes were dirty, his black hair disheveled. Several days' worth of beard darkened his face. His expression was one of defiance, his eyes ablaze with anger.

"So I am to die at the hands of a fanatic astrologer?" the prisoner asked, glaring at Grodnal. "It ends here, and I have to look upon the likes of you—"

"Never!" Hervie shouted bravely, struggling against his chains. "You will not die! My men and I are sworn to—"

"My dear Kir Shass," Grodnal interrupted, his tone one of mock assurance, "you worry so. The burdens of office are many, are they not?" The magician turned to face T. G. "Make yourself useful. Go outside and tell the Watchers that they may come in and take the president in five minutes. I will offer them no resistance. Any sooner and both of these men die."

The president!

It made no sense. Why did the magician not simply release President Shass, if that was his intent? T. G. backed away from them, then turned and passed through the doorway. Halfway up the corridor, he stopped. Something did not feel right. Impending death permeated the very air around him. It was not intuition, he knew, but something more.

I'll give you specialized skills, Ish had said, *that will manifest themselves as needed…*

T. G. made a conscious effort to block his mind from Grodnal, then turned and crept back to the door, hugging the cold wall. As he grew closer, he heard the sound of chains rattling and the rustling of clothes. Peering in, he saw Hervie frantically struggling to speak, yet no words came from his lips. Grodnal leaned over the chained Shass, almost blocking him from view.

In an instant, a huge knife flashed high into the air, then sliced sideways into flesh with a sickening sound. From the doorway, T. G. reached out with his right arm, palm down, as if to take hold of Grodnal and pull him away from the bloody president.

"No!" he shouted, his voice booming with a sudden power.

Grodnal whirled, the dripping knife in his hand. To T. G.'s surprise, an intense heat suddenly swelled in the tissues of his arm. A deep, aching cold filled its bone, and a blinding, roaring intensity burst from his spread fingertips—a shock wave of light and heat that seared the hissing air as it struck the magician with full force, throwing him to the floor. Hervie's head slammed into the wall from which he hung as the air in the room rushed outward, away from the blast.

"You cannot stop me!" Grodnal roared. His clothing singed and smoking, he rose and angrily fired back at T. G. with a savage black lightning. The impact hit the prophet full in the chest, smashing him into the wall and knocking the wind out of him, but even as he fell T. G. managed to launch a second attack from his aching arm. The scorching burst sang out and caught Grodnal squarely with wrecking-ball force, heaving him through the air and into the circular pool.

It was over in seconds.

Grodnal did not resurface. Gasping for breath, T. G. wearily struggled to his feet, made his way across the room and peered into the phosphorescent water. There was no sign of the sorcerer, for which T. G. was thankful—he doubted he could survive a second blast. His entire body ached deeply, making any movement, even breathing, extremely painful. His head pounded with every beat of his heart. His arm was so sore he could not move it, and it dangled feebly at his side.

He looked down at the arm. *Ish, what was that?*

Hervie, suffering a concussion and on the verge of unconsciousness, had seen the whole thing. His voice, slowly returning, croaked at T. G. "What…are you?"

T. G. did not answer. He focused instead on Shass, who was not moving and hung limply on his chains. Bright red soaked his chest and side, glistening in the torchlight, flowing profusely from the wound. T. G. looked more closely and saw, to his horror, that the side of the man's neck had been opened to the bone. Every major artery and vein had been severed.

"Get…help," Hervie begged before passing out.

T. G. moved as quickly as he could. Every step was agony. Up the ramped corridor, up the steps, then down a wide hallway and up a second flight of stairs. He nearly tumbled through the building's outer door, stumbling out into the night. Instantly, brilliant white lights fell upon him, blinding him.

"Do not move!" an amplified voice commanded. T. G. heard the electric sound of weapons charging up and dropped to his knees.

"Shass…he's in there. Some kind of deep cellar…he's hurt…"

"Where is Grodnal?" the voice demanded.

"Gone…hurry! The president's dying."

Weapons in hand, a dozen Watchers swelled past T. G. and into the immense, ancient house. Two others stopped and shoved him to the grass, kneeled on him, and pinned him there. One began to pull the jeweled sphere from his pocket.

"No. That is not necessary," a woman's voice said firmly. "Leave him alone." The Watchers rose to their feet at her command and rushed into the imposing edifice.

T. G. moved his head and saw the feet of a well-dressed woman standing a few feet away. Struggling back to his knees, he looked up at her. Her face, partially obscured by a veil, was kind, her features smooth. Her honey-blond hair was long and draped gracefully upon her shoulders. He did not know her.

"Thank you," he quietly said.

"You are hurt," she said, seeing his burned robe and his struggle to remain upright. Turning to the dozens of vehicles that surrounded the building, she motioned for medical attention. At once three men with a levitating, man-sized platform ran up to T. G.

"You will be all right," the woman assured him as they lifted his aching form onto the floating stretcher. "Prime care," she ordered as they guided him back to a waiting ambulance. "On my authority."

A Watcher called frantically from the dark doorway of the ominous, castle-like abode. All eyes turned. "In here! We need medical! Now!"

A second group of emergency attendants rushed with stretchers and medical kits toward the building and through the door as T. G., drifting in and out of consciousness, was loaded into the back of the ambulance. A variety of glass and metal objects connected by tubes were attached to his head and torso by a medtech who hovered over him, checking his vital signs.

The man pressed a metal-mesh sensor net against T. G.'s forehead and felt something oddly slippery there. He pulled his hand away and looked at his fingertips.

They were covered with makeup. Looking down at the patient once more, he saw small, light areas where the body paint had been wiped away, exposing lighter flesh beneath. With a puzzled, crinkled brow he cleaned the makeup from T. G.'s forehead and reattached the sensors, closely studying the face of the small man beneath him.

T. G., lapsing into a dreamlike state, barely felt the glass-smooth acceleration of the hovervehicle as it sped from the secluded house. In mere seconds, the ambulance put miles behind it and was hurtling surely along the dark forest road, racing toward the distant walled city.

16

Concealed behind a magnifier mask, his face dripped with a sweat borne of intense concentration. His sausage fingers worked swiftly beneath thin rubber gloves, delicately manipulating fine tools that decades before had become an extension of himself, working miracles time and again.

But not today.

The chief surgeon backed away from the operating table, knowing that the battle was lost despite his precision and experience. The still form upon the table would never again move or speak or look upon the natural beauty of the world that had given it birth. Several of the assisting surgeons and nurses around the table, knowing that all hope was gone, hung their heads and looked away.

"Take him out of here," the chief surgeon ordered. "Make the preparations."

Leaving the dying man to the others, the weary healer left the operating theater and stripped away his mask and gloves. After changing out of his bloodied blue coveralls, he walked out of the sterile healing complex and into the crowded lounge where so many waited for word of his success or failure. He spotted the stunningly attractive woman he sought, whose lovely face was only partially concealed beneath her sheer veil. The veil was customary, a symbol worn only in public, distinguishing its wearer as the wife of someone high in the government hierarchy.

The man wove his way through the sea of family and officials and walked up to her, carefully forming words in his mind, words meant to deal a severe blow as painlessly as possible.

"Kira Shass," he began, speaking slowly and reluctantly, looking into the eyes behind the veil, "I am sorry, but I have failed you. I was able to repair the extensive muscle and tissue damage done by the knife...and if that were the extent of his injury, he would be able to walk out of here tomorrow with barely a scar to remind him of this night. But your husband lost almost half of his blood volume and suffered massive brain damage, due to the blood flow being cut off when a main artery was severed—"

"Healer Sora," the woman interrupted, her eyes filled with tears, "is my husband dead?"

"No. But soon, yes. There is no brain function. He is being kept alive artificially at this moment. The neural regeneration we attempted was insufficient; too many critical areas of his brain have suffered irreversible cell death."

Several government officials overheard the exchange and at once scrambled for the exits. With Shass' death, a reorganization of the government would immediately commence as others in power played musical chairs for his position and those of his cabinet members. Some of those rushing out into the night were already joyfully anticipating what they would strip from his body as it lay in state.

A second healer appeared at the door through which Healer Sora had come. "You had better hurry," he said to the doctor and Kira Shass. "The life sustainment is failing."

They rushed to the postoperative room where Shass was lying, his body almost hidden within a vast array of bright metal-and-glass machinery that droned quietly with an even, low-pitched hum and the sound of circulating liquids. A crowd of healers and government officials stood by, watching helplessly. The life-giving apparatus completely enshrouded Shass' bed, save for a small area on his left side where a person could attend to him—or say good-bye.

Hervie, already treated and released, stood nearby and looked sadly upon the slain president as he slipped away. Other Watchers were gathered there as well, knowing that they were losing the man they had been sworn to protect.

Kira Shass kissed her husband one final time, tears streaming silently down her cheeks.

"Be certain to record the time of death as soon as he passes," Healer Sora said quietly to another healer beside him.

Kira Shass turned and walked away from the bed, pausing momentarily to lean on Hervie as she struggled to gather herself. Wiping away the tears, she took a deep breath and turned with great nobility toward the door. Hervie watched as the strong woman departed.

"The announcement should be made immediately afterward," he said, turning to an associate. "A great man has left us…see to it that the people are made aware of that."

"Yes, Kir Hervie," the younger Watcher said, heading toward the hospital's media center.

∞∞∞

He still felt a bit weak, but T. G., lying in a wide bed, was emerging from the haze. Looking around, he found that the room around him was fairly similar to the one he had seen in the doctor's office during his first visit to Noron. The antiseptic smell that hung in the air confirmed that he was in a medical facility of some sort.

Must every hospital on every planet smell like this?

His bed was surrounded by unfamiliar pieces of equipment, reflecting a healing science unknown to Earth. Brightly colored crystals embedded in small chromed devices spoke of an almost magical ability to heal. Sculpted glass shapes with no apparent internal mechanism glowed with colored displays that T. G. hoped were normal for a person in good health. There was a lot of red within the readouts, much more than T. G. felt comfortable seeing.

Is red bad? It usually is, at least at home. But I feel okay…don't I?

On the wall directly facing him, life-sized, was a rather disquieting real-time image of T. G. that revealed all of his inner workings. He looked at it with in both fascination and disgust. Like an x-ray, but in full color and in three dimensions, his bones and internal organs were displayed for all to see. He waved his arms, moved his head, mouthed words, and watched as the image did it all. As revolting as the sight was, he could not look away. Lidless eyes in bony sockets stared back at him. Pinkish gray intestines coursed back and forth amid wet, pulsing organs. He watched his heart beating for a count of five, then finally averted his eyes and fixed them upon something else. Anything else.

Voices sounded beyond the translucent blue door of his room, drawing his attention to the hallway just outside. Hazy figures moved there as well, seemingly in conversation, until one reached out for the door handle.

T. G. watched as the door soundlessly swung open to reveal the woman he had seen outside Grodnal's ancient mansion. In her slender hands she held the veil he had seen her wearing earlier. Her hair was like spun honey, just like Jenni's. She wore a beautiful, pearlescent wrap dress that shimmered like silk and showed her every curve to its best advantage. No one on Noron had ever invented the high-heeled pump, so the women there, like the men, wore only flat-soled shoes of fairly conventional design. Her jewelry—a delicate necklace and bracelets of jeweled gold—sparkled in the light. She approached him, her beautiful, towering form seeming taller still as she grew close. He saw that her face had been stained by recent tears, and her eyes were still slightly red.

"You are awake," she said, smiling slightly as she took a seat next to his bed. "I am glad to see it."

"Only now," he replied, rubbing his forehead. "I feel like I was hit by a truck."

"A tarruk?" she asked, puzzled by his mention of the roselike flower.

"Nothing," he smiled. "Never mind. Just an old expression." He glanced again at the image on the wall, then called the woman's attention to it. "Can you turn that off or put a sheet over it or something? I'd really appreciate it…"

The woman reached over and touched a plate to one side. The image disappeared.

"Thank you. It was getting to me."

She sat in a nearby chair. "You were injured at Grodnal's fortress. Do you remember?"

T. G. thought back to what he had seen in that awful chamber, to his battle with the magician, and to his encounter outside.

"Yes. I remember. You were there."

"Who *are* you?" the woman asked, obviously noting his pale skin and oddly colored eyes.

"A friend." He smiled. Then, thinking that secrecy was unkind given the circumstances, he opened up a bit more. "T. G....T. G. Shass."

"Shass? You mean…"

"No," he smiled anew. "No relation."

"Everyone who shares a name is related."

"I'm from very far away," he tried to explain. "I'm a different… kindred."

She smiled. "Well, it is nice to meet you, Kir Shass. I am Sereen Shass, Paull's wife."

"You told those men to help me. Why?"

She smiled. "I do not know exactly. The moment you came spilling from that doorway, I knew there was something special about you. I felt compelled to help you. I cannot give you a better explanation than that."

"Well, thank you, in any case," he said, smiling in return. "What was that all about, anyway, with that Grodnal person? Where am I now? I don't remember everything."

"This is a private government hospital," she said. "You were brought here a few hours ago, along with Kir Hervie and the president." She looked down at her lap, her mind obviously troubled. "Paull was kidnapped from our home. I do not know how, with our high security. But Grodnal managed it…and now…" She hung her head.

"Kir Shass…is he…?"

"For all purposes, my husband has died," the woman bravely said, taking a deep breath. "He is on total life sustainment, and it is rapidly failing. I came here because I wanted to thank you, while I still had the opportunity, for your attempt at saving him."

T. G. admired her for her obvious inner strength. "I'm sorry. I know what it's like to lose someone you love."

"Kir Hervie described what you did in that chamber under the fortress. He said you risked your life to defend Paull…that you fought and killed Grodnal."

"Too little, too late. It wasn't enough."

"It was courageous, nonetheless, and will not be forgotten. I am grateful and in your debt, T. G." She looked upon him with wider, clearer eyes. "To have shown such power, you are special indeed. Few sorcerers can do what you did, and none so young. And I see now that you are not like most men…you look quite different without the makeup and eye lenses."

"Oh," he uttered, looking again at his arms and hands. "That. It's kind of hard to explain."

"No need," she smiled, rising. "The healers say you sustained no lingering injury. You may leave any time you wish. Some wanted you detained for interrogation, but I carry my husband's authority, at least for the moment. I suggest you leave this place quickly."

He looked at her, momentarily distracted from her words by her beauty. She was seven feet in height and perfectly proportioned, as lovely as any woman on Earth, only larger. "I will," he finally answered. "Thank you for your help."

There was a sudden rush in the corridor outside. Turning toward the sound, T. G. and Sereen both saw the blurred shapes of several men as they ran past, all headed in the same direction. One paused long enough to poke his head through the door.

"Kira Shass," the Watcher said to her, "come with me."

She followed, leaving T. G. alone to search the room for his clothes.

∽o∾

Puzzled by the commotion, Sereen stood in the open doorway of the postoperative area where she had last seen her husband. *Can you not leave him in peace?* she wondered. The room was filled with dozens of healers, all huddled around the bed where her husband lay dying, uttering medical phrases and astonished speculations among themselves.

Overhearing fragments, the woman allowed herself a flicker of hope. The flicker then swelled into a tiny flame, and holding her breath, she stepped forward.

As the healers gazed upon the bed, blocking it from the woman's sight, she moved slowly closer, forcing her way through the throng to reach the place where she had given him her last kiss. Turning to see the woman behind him, a healer yielded his place to her, allowing her to the bedside.

Her amazed eyes filled with tears of joy as they beheld her husband's smile.

"Hello, Sereen," he said. No longer prone, he was sitting up in the bed, apparently fully recovered. "What is all this fuss about?"

"Oh, Paull!" she cried, leaning in and embracing him.

∽o∾

The nation of Luracayn rejoiced, and the entire world of Noron stood looking on in utter amazement. Paull Shass had all but died, the victim of an attack that should have ended his life forever, yet now he lived again. The healers speculated about his recovery during simulight broadcasts, all of them left with little explanation for what they had witnessed firsthand. His lost blood volume had suddenly returned. His severely damaged brain had healed itself in mere minutes. He was whole again and no worse for wear.

Surely Drosha had blessed him, the world knew. *Surely this is a sign that he is to lead us. Surely he is chosen.*

Surely.

The world fell at his feet.

Sereen Shass, grateful beyond measure, invited T. G. to come and stay in her home, where she could ensure he was properly rewarded for saving Paull's life. Since Ish had told him that involvement with the Shasses of Noron was the next phase in what he was to do, he agreed. Sereen treated T. G. like something of a lucky charm and enjoyed keeping him within arm's length.

Upon leaving the hospital, he was whisked immediately to the president's home and treated like one of the family. Given his own room and command of the house servants, T. G. found himself enjoying the greatest luxury Noron had to offer—the best foods, the best drink, the best clothes, the best of everything. His relatively short stature and other obvious physical differences were certainly noticed but ignored by those around him, for Sereen's blanket acceptance of him demanded the same from those in her employ. He quickly grew to enjoy the luxuries Noron now offered him, and he even gained a few pounds. The opulence of the State was stunning, a different world from the one he had known on the streets.

Sereen had every luxury any woman could want. Her clothes, her jewelry, her every possession spoke of a wealth made available to only a few. She had servants ready to act upon her every whim and was pampered constantly, with a trained staff standing by each day to dress her and do her hair and makeup. Noron's cosmetics fascinated T. G. from a scientific standpoint, for much of what the planet's women did in beautifying themselves seemingly spoke of magic rather than science. They used conventional makeup and artfully crafted gadgets as pleasant to look at as they were functional. One seemingly unpowered device—a five-inch chrome rod called a colorwand—was rare and especially puzzling to T. G. Merely by stroking its sides down the hair's length, a woman's hair color could be varied to any she desired. As her houseguest watched one day, Sereen gave him a demonstration during which she went from blonde to brunette to redhead in less than a minute, then back to blonde again, for that was the way Paull liked it.

Coming and going on the Shass' property as he pleased, even his former life on Earth began to pale for him and the good life took its toll on his mind, if not his body. The house was a palace, a place of beauty and great contentment. The lush garden was an exquisite dance of color and life. He looked forward to his numerous conversations with Sereen, and found her to be a brilliant and pleasant companion. He came to enjoy getting anything day or night simply by asking the servants for it. In a short time, he got used to having all his needs and appetites met, all his wishes granted. He felt safe and comfortable and content.

After a few weeks in the president's home, T. G. decided it would be a good idea to learn more about Paull Shass. Exploring the house library, he discovered scrapbooks, recent histories, and periodicals pertaining to the president's career. He spent many afternoons building a clear mental portrait of the man who was his host.

The Paull Shass T. G. read about seemed a highly ambitious man, driven by a raw hunger for the power that high political office provided. His rise through the political maze of Luracayn's governmental structure had been meteoric, breaking all convention as he went from novice to Napoleon virtually overnight. Many had died or been ruined by scandal during his climb, as was the rule—the history of Noronian government was primarily one of advancement through assassination. Many more had found a way to grab onto his coattails, rising to power with him and making sure that nothing and no one got in their way.

He had married Sereen just after his entry into politics, at the suggestion of his advisers. Servants told the new houseguest that Paull had always spoken down to the woman and largely ignored her, which angered T. G. He felt Sereen deserved better than to live merely as an abused ornament on the president's arm, particularly since there was little doubt in his mind that she genuinely loved Paull.

∽०∾

It was the event of the season. Hosted by Celestte Gesbal, the queen of Luracaynian society and widow of a former high official, the party was a celebration of Paull's recovery, and only carefully selected prominent figures were there. Government officials, government-supported entertainment personalities, government-supported drug designers, and government-supported musicians were invited to share in the joy of the moment. Held only two weeks after the attempted assassination, it was a celebration as much of the coming world unity as it was of the miraculous recovery of the president—and one T. G. Shass was on the guestlist.

The hovercar silently came to a stop before a palatial house bathed in red light. Never had T. G. seen such a place—set well back from the street, behind huge statues of two of Noron's more ancient military leaders, its elegant lawn was artfully manicured with broad-branched trees, low hedges, and impressive sparkling fountains.

"Here we are," Sereen whispered to T. G., smiling. As alert and visibly armed Watchers surrounded them, the president, his wife, and their guest stepped out of the vehicle and made their way toward the thirty-foot-tall chiseled double doors that were the building's main entry. The man's black robes spoke of power. The woman's emerald wrapdress glistened, as did her sheer veil. T. G.'s blue robes, custom-tailored, suited him well.

Like something out of a DeMille vision of Heaven, the mansion was Celestte's home, boasting all the opulence that her late husband had been known for. Ever the dutiful politician's wife, Celestte had let him have his way with the house—although she secretly found the decadence *much* more enjoyable now that it was entirely hers. Its exterior resembled an Egyptian temple, with immense pillars and walls of a glimmering white stone covered in muralistic carvings. As the heavy main entry doors swung open, the pink marble walls and floors inside glistened in the light of immense crystalline chandeliers. Music spilled out into the night, in flowing yet oddly discordant tones that sounded to T. G. like those produced by a theremin. Thousands, it seemed,

had gathered inside already, packing the floor and lining high bal-
conies, milling about amid huge stone sculptures of heroes, monsters,
and gods. A bluish smoke hung in the air.

"Paull!" Celestte called out, personally welcoming them as they
passed beyond the maze of security men who guarded the entry foyer.
She held an intricately decorated golden chalice in her hand, sipping
from it as she grew closer. "Sereen, I'm so happy to see you." She
looked down at T. G., cocking her head slightly to one side as she
studied him. "And this must be T. G. Welcome—I have heard much
about you." She placed her free hand on his shoulder, and he returned
the gesture—it was Noron's equivalent of shaking hands.

"Thank you for inviting me," T. G. smiled.

A cheer went up in the room as the crowd saw that their man of
the hour had arrived. Several women came up and kissed Paull in a
far-too-familiar fashion, to Sereen's visible displeasure. Obviously
thrilled by the adulation, President Shass was quickly swept away into
the crowd, which longed to look anew upon Noron's chosen savior.
Through her long, side-swept veil, T. G. saw the hurt on Sereen's face
as she watched her husband disappear from view.

"This…is amazing," he commented, trying to divert her attention.

"Oh, yes," she nodded. "I have never seen a larger gathering, not
in a private home."

"What do you say we take a seat somewhere and relax?"

"It looks like there are a few empty chairs over there," Sereen
pointed, indicating the far side of the room. Just then a waiter with a
tray of drinks walked up, and Sereen took one. T. G. did as well, not
wanting to appear rude. But before they could sit down, a persistent
woman insisted Sereen join her for a moment and drew her into a
small crowd.

"Find a couple of seats," Sereen told T. G., gesturing toward the
chairs as she turned to follow the woman. "I will be right there." Then
she was gone, vanished in a sea of giants.

Following her suggestion, he made his way deeper into the cavernous ballroom, trying to stay near the outer walls so as not to get swallowed up into the throng. He was amazed at the naked, garish excess that surrounded him. No emperor of Rome knew greater luxury than that upon which his eyes now looked. Gold was everywhere. Set into a far wall was a huge band shell of silver and inlaid pearl, within which the live electronic music was being played. Those in attendance were dressed in robes of the finest make and material, a sign of their lofty stations in life. Many of the women in the room wore veils similar to that of Sereen, for their husbands, too, were high members of the Luracaynian government.

T. G. finally made his way to the small row of plush chairs, carrying his unwanted drink. He was thirsty, but not for alcohol, and he was sorry he had taken the glass. He set it on a small, low table next to one of the chairs and sat down, still trying to take in the ostentatious display all around him.

He had never been very comfortable at formal occasions, preferring more relaxed and casual social interaction. He was made even more uncomfortable by the drug use going on all around him, watching as some of the other guests inhaled blue smoke from crystalline things like those he had previously seen in the city streets. The planet's most common diversions were the purely physical and very temporary pleasures of sex or drug abuse, and markets on almost every street corner featured a wide variety of alcoholic beverages, chemical stimulants, and narcotics.

Many who passed him looked him over curiously, never introducing themselves but stealing second and third glances as they moved farther away.

T. G.'s attention was suddenly drawn upward by color and movement that startled him. Dozens of phantom, fluid shapes filled the air high above the ballroom floor, and to his surprise, the spectral objects were greeted by a sustained round of enthusiastic applause. Holographic and brilliantly colored, glistening like an odd combination of gelatin and the aurora borealis, the huge, glistening, random forms writhed and danced in time to the ethereal music as they orbited the main, central chandelier. Organic in character, the shapes struck T. G. as being alive—and for a reason he could not pin down, he found himself uncomfortable in their presence.

It then occurred to him, as he took a verifying look, that there were no ghastly renewals in the room. Neither had he seen any in the hospital or in the Shass' home. Were they restricted to dwelling only with those of the lower class, where despondency and hopelessness had forced the people to cling desperately to the few familiar joyances their lives already knew?

After a short time, the music changed to a more pleasant and melodious piece dominated by stringed instruments. The colored shapes vanished as quickly as they had come, and sounds of disappointment briefly filled the room.

Sereen emerged from the crowd with her drink, a deep, rich wine. She had pulled her shimmering green veil back, exposing her loveliness. She noticed that T. G.'s glass, on the table, was still full.

"Do you not partake?" she asked him, sipping from her own. "I do not think I ever asked before."

"Not usually," he admitted, "but I didn't want to be rude." He picked up the glass, took a taste, and found it more viscous than normal wine. It clung to the inside of his crystal glass like cough syrup, and burned his throat and sinuses going down.

"On…on second thought," he coughed, his eyes tearing up, "perhaps something else would be better." *What is this stuff?* "I don't suppose they have Dr Pepper here?" he kidded, smiling in turn at the woman's questioning expression. "Never mind," he assured her. "I'll find something."

She sat next to him. He turned to her, making a circle high in the air with his finger. "Those colored things…what were they?"

"Those were the joylights," she smiled. "They appear anywhere people are gathered to enjoy life, to share in the moment."

"Joylights?" he puzzled.

"That is what we have come to call them."

"What do you mean by 'share in the moment'?" he asked, seeking confirmation of his own impressions. "You mean they're alive?"

"No one knows. They come and go in their own good time, and they always have. No man has ever laid a hand on one, and they never make a sound. They act as if alive, though, and everyone has always assumed they are."

He looked up at the now-vacant space above him, considering her words. On Noron, only the wealthy and powerful ever celebrated life in such a manner, and he doubted that anyone of the lower class had ever seen the joylights. He himself never had, and surely Pretsal would have mentioned such a phenomenon at some point over the past year had he known of it.

Sereen smiled. "I have to find Paull. But the serving counter is right over there." She pointed. "Perhaps they have a drink you would like."

"Thank you. I'll check it out."

As she slipped back into the noisy throng, T. G. set his still-full glass back on the table and stood, scanning the room for the counter Sereen had mentioned. It was hard for him to see beyond the crowd of giants, and after a moment he gave up and started moving in the general direction in which she had pointed. He felt like he was back in the dense forest again, weaving his way through towering pines in colorful robes and fine dresses as they moved all around him.

Finally, T. G. found the bar. He could still feel the burn in his throat from the viscid wine. Climbing into a seat at its high counter, he asked for a glass of ice water and got it. Thankful, he drank and watched the other guests as they mingled, laughed, and indulged.

As the evening wore on, many of the guests openly disappeared into the surrounding hallways and plush sleeping chambers beyond, led by beautiful women or handsome men who were obviously there by hire, not invitation. There were dozens of these so-called pleasurers available to the guests, as any good Noronian host or hostess would provide. Watching as guest after guest vanished into the bed-rooms, T. G. began to count them to pass the time, losing interest after sixty-three. A woman's voice spoke his name.

He turned to see Celestte standing close, her arm intertwined with that of a man he did not recognize. He was shorter than most, only six-foot-ten or so, and wore a midnight blue, wraparound robe. His brown hair was close cropped.

"This is Cordan Barthos," Celestte announced. "He is President Shass' second-in-command, so to speak. He wanted to meet you. Cordan, you know who this is."

T. G. looked up into the man's eyes. He had a kind face and smiled widely. "I certainly do. Prosperity, T. G. May I sit with you?"

"Sure," T. G. nodded.

"I will leave you two to get better acquainted," Celestte smiled, sipping anew from her goblet. "Take good care of him, Cordan," she almost sang, her voice a gentle melody, "He is a Shass, you know." She vanished, leaving the two men alone at the bar.

The servant at the counter placed a glass of wine before Barthos. "The world owes you a great debt, T. G.," he said, taking a sip of his drink. "I shudder to think what might've happened to Paull or to our great nation had you not stepped in and stopped that insane sorcerer before he could kill the president."

"I've been wondering about that. I'm not sure Grodnal wasn't fin-ished with his attack before I acted. The way he was just standing there, and the way he talked just before…" He shook his head. "I don't know. Struck me as weird."

"Well, in any case, your courage shouldn't go unrewarded." He took another sip. "I have a proposition for you. I've arranged for you to take a position in the Shass administration, if you want it. Everyone thinks you are related to Paull, so no one will question your appoint-ment. The president wants very much to improve the quality of life for the citizens of this country, and we feel that you're just the person to head up that project."

T.G was flattered but surprised. "Why me?"

"You carry an inherent authority, despite your stature. Paull recognized it right away and I, too, can see it. It's in your eyes, in the way you show concern and compassion for others. You are not a common man, T. G. You are special somehow, very special, and uniquely qualified to help us help the people."

T. G. was intrigued. Concern for the common man had not been a part of Noronian government for millennia. "*Paull* wants to help them?" he asked, a bit skeptical. That did not sound like the Paull of whom he had read. "How?"

"Well, that would be up to you. But we were thinking that it might help to set up some kind of localized subgovernment, one that would allow the people to govern themselves."

"A city government?" T. G. asked, shaking his head. "I think the problems out there may be beyond the help of weekly town meetings."

Barthos smiled. "As I said…that would be up to you to decide. The president wants to abolish the class system and open the doors of opportunity that have been sealed for too long. We'd like you to help set up a research project on the subject, see what conclusions you can put together in a period of, say, six months. Then give us a report, and we'll go from there."

"I've done my homework. Paull rose to power by removing those in his way. Some died, some were disgraced, and others haven't been seen since going up against him. Why should I trust him to help anyone?"

Barthos looked down at his drink, then into T. G.'s eyes. "Unfortunately, what you say is true. I'm not proud of that, and neither is he, but you have to understand that such was the way things were done for thousands of years. Now things are different."

"Different how?"

"Since his miraculous recovery, Paull's come to realize that such a system is wrong, very wrong. He's grateful for his life and wants to change things, to make life better for everyone. He also knows that change like this can only be carried out from within. That's why it's so crucial that he becomes the leader of the entire world. All of Noron must change, or the change will not last. He's a new man, T. G., and a wise and brilliant leader. He wants to lead all of Noron into a glorious age of prosperity and peace."

So, he's seen the light, huh? T. G. swallowed some water and looked hard at Barthos. He got no instinctive feeling that the man was lying. Perhaps it was all true. Perhaps Shass was a changed man. Perhaps not. But miracles had been known to do that to people...

"What do you think? Will you help?" Barthos asked, hope in his tone.

T. G. looked away from the handsome man, wondering if perhaps this was a part of the "new Noron" of which Ish had spoken. Anything that brought a lasting peace and a better quality of living to all must be good, he reasoned. What better way to spread the Truth and word of Ish's coming than by giving everyone a better world to live in? Thousands of years of oppression and suffering would end. And through his office, T. G. could even spread the truth about the Renewals that walked the planet, helping to get rid of them forever. They would have no place on a happy Noron, where the people could look to their futures with hope and get on with their own lives, rather than dwelling on the past with stand-in loved ones. Perhaps this new and kinder Noron that Paull Shass envisioned was the Awakening for which the Twelve and their followers had been waiting.

Looking into the man's eyes once more, T. G. made a decision. "Okay," he nodded. "It sounds like a good idea."

Barthos extended a hand to T. G.'s shoulder and received T. G.'s in return. "I'll send for you next week, and we'll get started. Paull will be happy to hear of this. It's a glorious time to be alive, T. G." The man rose and walked away.

T. G. swirled his water a bit, clinking the ice floating there, and drank the glass dry. Smiling, he looked up to the ceiling and winked at the absent Ish. "Looks like we're going to pull this thing off," he spoke quietly. "I saved Paull, you healed him, and now all the pieces are falling into place. I guess you were right in choosing me, after all." He held his empty glass out, saluting Ish, then gestured to the servant for a refill.

Surely, Ish had blessed Paull Shass, T. G. knew. Surely, this was a sign that he was to help the president lead the people. Surely, Paull, like T. G., was chosen.

Surely.

17

F ar from Luracayn, in another place, another country, President Shass was *not* considered a miracle man, nor blessed, nor chosen.

An older, strapping, slightly balding man, Victus Torboul sat alone in his darkened office, hunched over the heavy wooden desk he had come to know so well. Exotic hand weapons and huge murals of great military battles, bathed in the focused light of ceiling-mounted fixtures, surrounded him, silently fueling the inspired pride he felt for those victories. Immense stone portraits of past leaders, carved into the walls millennia before, stared from the shadows with unseeing eyes at the man as he bore the burden of his office.

Mounted on the wall above him, huge silver wings were spread wide, the insignia of the most powerful man in all of Sethii. He had fought hard to gain those wings, and he had fought even harder to keep them.

Torboul had been Sethii's unquestioned ruler for almost seven decades. Under his leadership, the country's military had grown stronger and its borders had become more secure than at any time in its history. The wealthy had prospered, bringing him the support necessary for political survival, yet he had gained many enemies as well. Dozens of attempts had been made on his life, both by those who wanted his position and by those who wanted his country—all of them falling short. He had been the Sethiic leader for longer than any other man, and he had built a tremendous political machine around himself in the process. His protection was impeccable, his men among the most loyal on the planet.

That night, Grand Premier Torboul sat looking over the thick pile of documents he would sign in the morning. Things were working well in Sethii, and the last thing he wanted was to have to answer to a single world leader.

"Drosha has chosen him," some people had insisted, looking on in amazement as the miracle man, via the media, declared that under his leadership the entire globe would thrive.

The former ruler of the neighboring country of Kamir, King Daricis, had died only days before under mysterious circumstances, leaving his underlings to founder in a flood of indecision and fear. The tiny, financially struggling monarchy, suddenly without direction, had bowed to the pressure Luracayn was exerting, giving its support to Paull Shass and his one-world movement. Sethii would not make the same mistake, not while Torboul was in charge of things. His vision for his nation left no room for shared power.

The newly created proclamation that he held before him, once ratified and made law, would ensure that the government of Sethii would continue to function as an independent entity. He had labored on it for months, ever since Shass had intensified his unified-world campaign with persistent innuendo that military "persuasion" of the other nations was not out of the question.

Torboul hoped, despite the audacious man's bravado, that Sethii's armed force was such that even the mighty Luracayn would not risk an attack, not when the backlash would be so severe. The last war between the two countries, some three centuries past, had ended in a Sethiic victory and territory gained. That was a great source of pride for the leaders of the smaller nation, and Torboul had no intention of lying down and letting anyone else rule his country, now or ever.

Secure within the walls of his fortress capital of Arcania, Torboul rubbed his tired eyes. He knew that there were those, even within his own government, who had come to support the Shass concept of world unity. Fortunately, they were few, and those loyal to him had pledged their lives to his leadership.

He looked at the massive wood-and-reinforced-steel doors of his office, knowing that just outside, ten heavily armed soldiers stood guard, their weapons at the ready. Beyond them, near the perimeter of the complex, hundreds more kept watch. Torboul suspected Shass of ordering the death of Daricis, and he had stepped up his personal security as a precaution against a similar attempt on his own life. It appeared Daricis had died of a brain aneurysm, but the timing of his death was unsettling and suspicious—and during his many years of Noronian governmental involvement, Torboul had learned one thing above all else: *Trust no one and suspect everything.*

Here, deep within his extensive underground bunker, no assassin could reach him. No bombing raid, no heat weapon, no shock-charge barrage, no ripstick could touch him. Secure, he rubbed his weary eyes and looked toward the following morning, when his weekly simulight broadcast would announce his decision to keep his nation independent at any cost.

He rose to his feet and stretched, running a hand through his white hair. It had been a long day, and the comfortable bed just down the short hallway was calling to him. Following a nightly ritual, he paused to press a jeweled plate on his desk and closed his eyes, listening to the gentle recorded music that flowed from the speakers. Soaking in the melody, a piece he had enjoyed all his life, he leaned his head back and let the tensions of the day drift from his body. The air from an overhead fan bathed him in its gentle caress.

Opening his eyes as the piece drew to a close, he was surprised to find a joylight hanging high in the air, far across the room, near the door. It pulsed in blues and purples to the beat of the music, slowly rotating as it so gracefully danced. Torboul smiled, delighting in the sight, and could not help but laugh. He had not seen one in years, not since the celebration of his youngest son's marriage, and he held his hands out in welcome.

"Greetings, my friend," he spoke. "I trust you are a portent of good things to come, yes?"

The joylight moved closer, all the while maintaining its rhythmic, flowing waltz. The music ended, and Torboul sadly expected the visitor to depart.

It did not. It only stopped moving, as if waiting.

"You want more music?" he asked it, pressing the activator plate again. The melody sounded anew, filling the cold stone room, yet the joylight did not dance. Puzzled, Torboul moved behind his desk and stood waiting.

"Some other music, perhaps?"

Without warning, the joylight blazed angrily with pulsing reds and yellows. A thin, incorporeal pseudopod lanced out, striking Torboul in the chest. He was knocked back into his chair as it burrowed deep into him, not breaking the skin yet entering him all the same, in search of its target. Other, larger tentacles sprang down and held the man motionless, burying his face beneath their smothering embrace, muffling his screams. As he writhed helplessly, his heart was constricted by the crushing grip of the joylight until it could no longer function. The intense pain of cardiac arrest wracked Torboul's body as his hands spasmodically clutched at the nothingness that pinned him.

Deprived of blood, his brain shut down. The last thing he heard before his ears went deaf was the music he had loved, and the last thing he saw, through plasm-obscured eyes, was the face of his predecessor's stone likeness as it stood silently by, watching. Then it was over.

His body slumped backward, leaving sightless eyes wide with terror, staring up at the spectral assassin. The next morning he would be found, and his mysterious death would be attributed to natural causes.

A glistening tentacle reached down and touched the disarrayed documents Torboul had so carefully crafted, words meant to inspire all of Sethii toward continued autonomy. They ignited, flashing into ash in seconds, then went cold again. Another gelatinous finger touched a crystalline data-input plate on the desk and wiped the file memory from the building's datastore, ensuring no cybernetic backup. All that remained of one man's dream were charred cinders and a faint vestige of smoke.

Its work done, the joylight withdrew its tentacles from the lifeless man and floated higher, pausing for a moment to enjoy the music that still played in the room. It had removed the final obstacle to Paull Shass' destiny and decided to celebrate that fact in a beautiful, post-mortem symphony of blues and greens. Then, as the music ended, it vanished, leaving the guards standing dutifully outside as they protected their leader from any conceivable threat.

His was the best-guarded corpse on Noron.

18

The War Circle.

For almost four thousand years it had stood at the southeastern edge of the city, a monument to the smothering shroud of creative barbarity that had darkened Noron's history. It was the largest single structure on the planet, a ring of reddish stone and glistening steel, more than two miles wide and 650 feet high at its rim. It seated more than four million, both living and Renewals—and rarely was there an empty seat to be found.

The closest thing Earth had to offer was the comparably tiny Roman Colosseum. Yet that great ruin of antiquity, only half the age of its Noronian counterpart, would have fit into the space occupied by the War Circle seven hundred times over.

Herds of massive tyrannosaurs and other great beasts, held alone in underground pits and starved for weeks beforehand, ripped each other apart as they were released all at once into the arena. At other times, whole armies of chrome-armored warriors, complete with battle gear and fighting vehicles, fought upon its broad, blood-soaked plain, leaving hundreds of thousands littering the ravaged field once the battle was finally won and the slaughter ended.

At its least brutal, its displays surpassed the cruelest, bloodiest battles of the American Civil War, waged again and again. At its worst, it was a nightmarish vision beyond Dante's imagination, and with a paying audience. That audience, aroused by the bloodbath before it, always created tens of thousands of casualties of its own during the drunken riots that inevitably broke out in the seating ring.

T. G. took a seat within the huge, open-faced President's Box. The scale of the arena stunned him. As he looked out over the expansive field of battle, he saw not a grassy plain but something like a small sea. The pit of the circular arena floor had been filled with water to a depth of nearly a hundred feet in preparation for the event, leaving T. G. to wonder what was about to unfold. Events were held only twice a year, for the sheer magnitude of each simply would not allow for any more. Months were spent in readying the arena—more were spent afterward in removing the physical aftermath of the carnage.

Without fail, Luracayn's wealthy and powerful turned out for each spectacle, sitting not among the throng but in private boxes passed from generation to generation. It was an envied status symbol to be able to claim lifelong attendance at the War Circle, and those with the opportunity took it. For the lower classes, however, the experience was a rarity. The wide, multitiered ring filled rapidly with common spectators for the day's contest, some of whom had saved for years and had waited a century for the opportunity to be in that place on that day. Few would live long enough to get a second chance.

"This is for you," a pleasant feminine voice said. T. G. turned to see a glass being held toward him. He reached up and took it, looking at the bubbling brown liquid it held. Its fragrance was familiar.

The young brown-haired woman took a seat next to him. She was Tonie Alexandrya, T. G.'s assigned personal assistant. Her pleasant, smiling face, her gentle perfume and generally happy demeanor had been a comfort to him through the pressure and frenetic pace of his transition to government service, and he was continually amazed with the speed and thoroughness with which she saw to his every need. Like most Noronian women, she was quite attractive, despite her height, and T. G. had often found himself just looking at her, admiring her statuesque beauty—while trying not to let her catch him doing so.

He had been working for the Shass administration for several months from a spacious and luxurious office suite high in the pyramidal capitol building at the center of Keltrian. It was not just a job, it was an adventure—and he did not even have to get his feet wet.

He took a sip of the iced drink and had barely swallowed when a broad grin crossed his face. Tonie, watching, enjoyed his response. "Dr Pepper?" he wondered, surprised. "How? I mean, where did you get it?"

"Kir Barthos said it is a rare drink," she smiled, "and that it is called 'jocala.' Apparently, it originates in Kamir. It is not familiar to me. He must have had it prepared especially for you. Just enjoy."

"Is there more of this?" he asked, examining the fizzing treasure.

"All you want, T. G.," she replied. At once, he gulped it down, draining the wondrous elixir until bare ice rested cold and wet upon his upper lip and nose. He then held the empty glass out for her, and she gladly took it.

Smiling over the sudden reacquisition of that little piece of home, T. G. surveyed the arena anew. It was nearly filled to capacity now, and the remaining seats would be occupied soon. Watching the huge crowd with his powerful binoculars, he thought of how he had recorded and analyzed their comings and goings, their behavioral patterns, and their commerce, such as it was. No census had ever been taken, but records existed since most were tied into the communications link through their telephones, and nearly all were in the employ of the State in one way or another. Putting his little-used poli sci academics to the acid test, he had worked hard, with Tonie's help and that of his small staff, to develop a plan whereby the city would break up into small sectors. Each would be governed by a separate sub-administrator and would have its own law-enforcement unit. New legal codes would be drawn up and strictly enforced, and the streets would be made safe for the first time. He looked upon all the people, knowing that their lives would soon be changed by the policies and laws he would soon help the president to enact. No more slave wages, no more unrestrained crime, no more unfulfilled wants. Soon, very soon, there would be plenty for all. Noron would gain a social paradise to match its physical splendor. The Wellsian utopia would become a reality, albeit on a world a universe away from Earth.

Then the Awakening would come, and the true faith would return to feed the spiritual famine that had been killing the masses for millennia.

Tonie returned with a fresh glass and gave it to T. G.

"Thank you," he said. "I was told the president won't be attending today."

"No. I understand that he has come to find all of this, well, something less than entertaining."

"Then why did he want *me* to be here?"

"He felt there would be some value in your having the experience. Further motivation in your work, I suppose."

As she once more took her seat beside him, sweeping her long hair back out of the way as she brought her binoculars up, a cheer washed over the crowd. T. G. looked out into the wide arena, his attention drawn by a motion to the left and the glint of metal. Colossal doors ten stories high were opening, and as he watched, something began to nose its way through them.

Then, some distance away, a second door slowly opened, and a third. Then more. In all, six objects, equally spaced, took position for what was to come.

The massive objects were warships.

They bristled with weapons of a configuration unknown to T. G. The crowd was to be treated to a full-scale naval battle, with tens of thousands of sailors fighting for their lives. Each crew on each ship knew that victory in the arena was their only chance for survival— anyone left alive after the combat and what was to follow, except for the crew of the vessel judged to be the champion, would be put to death before the next sunrise. That system guaranteed that the spectators, wealthy and poor alike, would get a good show.

This was, after all, entertainment.

The ships neared the center of the arena. They had no sails, for Noron had never known wind, nor was any other motive power apparent to T. G. He assumed that each had propellers or some such gear, as had been the norm back home, but he saw no churning of the water aft of the vessels. Their general shape reminded him of ancient Viking ships, but on a larger scale and combined with the features of the steel-hulled frigates used by the U.S. Navy. Huge, seemingly fragile spires of chrome and crystal rose high into the air above each ship—serving a purpose T. G. could not guess—with flowing, metallic superstructure just beneath. Beautiful as vessel designs go, all of the warships had high, carved figureheads at the fore, each depicting one of the demigods of the Drosha cult. Just below these rested an angled, razor-like bow that seemed designed to ram other ships. The powerful vessels glistened in the light, sculptures of metal and glass on water, like floating jewels bound for collision.

The combat began. There was a flash, followed several seconds later by a concussion that echoed throughout the War Circle. Lightning arced from the towers of one ship, lancing out against its nearest opponent, which suffered an explosion amidships. Other vessels fired, not merely with those brilliant bolts but with dark projectiles that trailed arrow-straight fingers of smoke and detonated on impact.

For more than an hour, T. G. could only watch, mouth open, eyes wide, as the war game continued. Following maritime strategies conceived many centuries before, the ships moved in graceful arcs as they jockeyed for attack position. Small glowing objects of varying colors were dropped into the water, objects that proved to be mines as other vessels, unable to steer clear, slammed into them. Blast after blast sprayed water and debris hundreds of feet into the air with deafening reports that cracked and echoed again and again.

T. G.'s eye was drawn to motion elsewhere in the water, nearer him. Wakes arose at the water's edge, far from the ongoing battle. Swift, dark gray masses surfaced momentarily, fins and humps that broke the surface just long enough to be seen before disappearing back into the depths. They looked to be better than fifty feet long.

Things were out there. Terrible things.

An explosion drew T. G.'s attention back to the warships. One of them had sustained a critical hit and was taking on water, its stern dipping deeper into the dark sea. Fire swept its hull even as the other ships, seeing its perilous condition, leaped upon it like wolves on injured prey. White-hot bolts and more missiles flared into existence in rapid succession until the damaged vessel lost its forward momentum and stopped dead. Seconds later, a fast-moving ship rammed it in its port side, its momentum carrying it through its victim. As the wreckage began to sink, its crew, uniformed in white for maximum visibility, spilled over the sides of the ship into the black water.

There was a new thrashing some distance away, as the glistening shapes broke the surface again and turned toward the site of the battle. They gained speed for a moment, heading for the sinking ship, then dove again, leaving deceptively tranquil waters behind them. Whatever the things in the water were, they were fast and there were easily a dozen of them. The crowd cheered anew as they reacted to the sight, their cruel ovation heard even over the roar of the artillery.

Another ship was in trouble. It began to list to starboard as it tried to circle the main group and get clear for another run. Unable to move fast enough, it was cut off with a barrage of lightning fire and burst into flame as it passed, black smoke billowing from its deck.

The sinking vessel had slipped almost entirely beneath the surface, leaving its crew swimming for their lives as they fought to cling to any floating debris they could. T. G.'s binoculars locked on one sailor, a man with red hair, who had managed to climb atop a small section of deck planking. He fought to keep his place as others, fearing the water, tried to dislodge him and take his place of momentary salvation.

It mattered little. T. G. saw a huge, thrashing shape rise up with a white spray. Teeth flashed as wet, rubbery skin glinted in the light of the continuing explosions nearby. The man with the red hair and those around him had nowhere to hide. White uniforms went red.

T. G. heard no screams. He was too far away.

But they were there.

The enormous kronosaurs, their powerful jaws eight feet long, struck at the panicking men, swallowing some whole and dragging others beneath the surface, locked into jagged vises of savage, razor-sharp teeth. The dead and the dying, the whole and the dismembered, were thrown into the air as a feeding frenzy erupted. The ships still fighting steered clear and carried on some distance away, vying to avoid the fate of the unfortunate hundreds already in the water.

T. G.'s drink shattered on the floor as he quickly rose from his seat and, in a single motion, spun and headed for the door. Tonie, still watching the unfolding drama, paused momentarily before setting down her binoculars and following him out of the box.

∽∽∽

"It can't go on," T. G. muttered as he stood looking out of the high panoramic window of his office. "It has to stop. Not only the War Circle, but the whole Renewal thing too. There's no possible justification for such horrendous atrocities. Someone has to listen. We have to push for a new set of values and bring an end to this bloodthirsty way of doing things."

"It has been going on forever," Tonie commented. "The people want it."

"Then we need to change that! Give them something else—anything else—and get them out of this mind-set that life is worthless and death is entertainment."

"Changing such ingrained conventions will not be easy."

"Well, that's what I'm here for." He surveyed the city below, which spread before him as far as he could see. Within his view, a hundred adamantine towers soared to dizzying heights, some even surpassing the 250-story level where T. G.'s office was. Small one-man vehicles, called hoversteeds, and other larger flying machines buzzed to and fro, like flies above a vast carcass.

"As for the War Circle, professional football might do it…I don't know. Something similar to what they want, but short of lethal. Something they could still channel their aggressions into, but without the killing."

"President Shass wants the same thing. But altering the mind-set of thirteen billion people will take time. It will be a daunting task, to say the least. That was why the added motivation of witnessing the

War Circle's violence was deemed necessary for you. The president was afraid you might give up too easily."

"Well, tell him it worked. I'll never get that image out of my head."

Cordan Barthos walked into T. G.'s office, carrying a long, rolled bundle of papers.

"So," he asked, smiling as he approached the desk, "what did you think of our War Circle?"

"I think you know," T. G. said, still looking out the window.

"Yes," Barthos nodded. "I take it you feel a new urgency in bringing such things to a halt? The president was hoping that further inspiration would come from your visit there."

"No need," he answered. "I already know how rotten things are and how much better they must become. You can tell the president for me that I'd be out there personally, tearing that place apart stone by stone, if I thought it would get this planet out of Hell's ghetto any faster."

Barthos smiled, nodding in agreement. "I'll pass that along. Your work has been invaluable, T. G. Without you right here, doing what we need of you, our reshaping of the world would be much more difficult."

"I wish I could do more."

Barthos set the papers on T. G.'s desk. "These need your approval …they designate enforcement zones and manpower allocations for the proposed police sectors. We'd like to meet over these in three days. Will that work for you?"

"Sure," T. G. nodded, walking over to look at them. "I'll take them home with me tonight and give them a once-over, then I'll get with you tomorrow so we can set something up."

Barthos smiled and walked back toward the door. "I trust you'll be at the treaty signing?"

"Wouldn't miss it," T. G. answered. "It's a day we'll all look back on as a turning point in our lives. I'm sure of that."

"Indeed. You, too, Tonie…I'd like you there with T. G. One day, you can tell your grandchildren that you were there in the room when the world turned onto the road to peace and prosperity for all."

"Thank you," she smiled. "I was hoping to be there."

"Listen," Barthos said. "Why don't we all go to dinner tonight? I think it would be good for us after a day like today. We'll even call it an early celebration of Kir Shass' ascension."

"Tonie?" T. G. asked the woman.

"That would be very nice," she nodded.

"Okay, then," T. G. agreed. "Where will we go?"

"Nowhere but the finest the city has to offer," Barthos smiled. "Leave that to me. I'll pick you both up this evening around sunset. Until then…" Barthos left the room, closing the door behind him.

After a moment, a slightly puzzled expression crossed Tonie's face. She cocked her head slightly. " 'Football?' "

"Just about the greatest sport you ever saw," T. G. smiled, remembering. "Ten minutes with the Dallas Cowboys or the Miami Dolphins, and you guys would never go back."

"I have not heard of it. It must not be very popular."

"I suppose not, come to think of it," he smiled. "Never mind."

He walked over to the huge wall map opposite the window, which at the moment was filled with a glowing overhead view of the city. It had been divided into tiny, differently colored squares, sectioned to follow the main city streets. By touching any one of them, he could enlarge it to fill the entire wall in all its detail.

"Lot of people out there, Tonie," he commented, focusing his gaze upon the tiny sector where Pretsal lived. "With so much violence, how many fewer will there be by this time tomorrow?"

The girl looked away, through the window. The rhetorical question hung heavily in the air. T. G. moved the roll of papers on his hand-carved, blond-wood desk and sat down in his chair, the most comfortable he had ever experienced. He had often wondered how he might take it home to Earth, once his work for Shass and Ish was done and the Awakening was a reality.

"Tell me, Tonie," he began. "I don't think I ever asked you. How did you come into government service? How long have you been here?"

"Until three years ago, I was a servant in Kir Barthos' home. He brought me here as one of his assistants, and I was such until he told me that I now was yours."

"Just an assistant? Nothing else?" T. G. asked, having seen how such things were handled there. Women on Noron were second-class citizens and never held positions of power. Even the wealthiest of them were seen only as reflections of their husbands, through whom they maintained their status. The others were treated as little more than property, to be used as the owner saw fit.

"Yes," she quietly answered, averting her eyes downward and to the side. "Just an assistant." He dropped the subject, seeing her great reluctance to carry the discussion any further.

"It's been quite a day," he said, standing, watching the relief on her face. "I think we both deserve to cut out of here a little early. Why don't you go on home. We have the signing of the Unification Treaty in a couple of days, and since we'll both be there, a little extra rest would probably do us some good. I'll see you tonight."

She rose, nodding in agreement. "T. G., may I ask you something? I mean, if it is too personal, you do not have to answer."

"What is it?"

"Well, why do you look different from other people? I do not mean any disrespect, but I have been wondering. Is it something medical?"

He smiled. "Long story, too long for the end of the day. Ask me again some time."

∽∘∽

It was called Derakiin's Paradise, and it was one of the most exclusive restaurants on Noron. Only those in power and the very wealthy could even think of dining here, and the place was crowded every night. Reservations had to be made months in advance, unless one was of a high enough station—such clients were seated at a moment's notice and were given every luxury the place had to offer, without hesitation. The restaurant's management had learned long before that causing discomfort for those who ruled Luracayn could be very bad for one's health.

Cordan Barthos was of a high enough station.

The restaurant, like most such places on Noron, was immense and overwhelmingly ornate. Most of those in twentieth-century America would have labeled it as gaudy and overdone, from the gold inlay coursing throughout the floor and walls to the huge portraits that silently observed the diners. An indoor waterfall streamed over an artistic arrangement of dark, smooth rocks and crystalline formations, sending a soothing white sound adrift throughout the establishment's two main dining halls. The lighting was gentle and warm, with large open portals in the ceiling that allowed the stars to shine inside.

The place smelled wonderful.

Looking down at his place setting, T. G. again took note of the fact that dinner forks did not exist on Noron—the primary eating utensil was a small, narrow set of tongs, something like hinged chopsticks with pointed paddles at the tips. Their version of the spoon was a perfectly round, shallow bowl with a very short handle, and steak knives were serrated on both edges. Also, Noronian etiquette called for eating utensils to be placed centrally before each person, on the opposite side of the plate, which was always oval. These differences were small but constant reminders that T. G. was not in Kansas any more.

Dozens of circular tables were filled to capacity with four to six patrons each, all enjoying the culinary adventure offered that evening. Wine and water were the only beverages available, both of which were supplied via a low, multiheaded, flowing sculpture of a spigot at the center of the table. Holographic menus akin to fine art were mounted on opposite ends of each dining room, from which all guests made their selections.

T. G. had learned enough about Noronian cuisine to know what he needed to order if he wanted beef, fish, pork, or any of the vegetable side dishes to which he was accustomed. Many of the items listed, however, he did not know, and he was grateful to Tonie for her instant answers to his many culinary questions. Most of Noron's dishes were heavily seasoned, usually far more than T. G. liked, though since his arrival he had been able to adjust somewhat to the overpowering use of spices and herbs. Their confectionery desserts were overly sweet, and they had never known chocolate, which T. G. fondly missed. For the most part, having grown accustomed to what foods Noron had to offer, he preferred to stay with fresh fruits and breads with the occasional giant locust thrown in for good measure.

He noticed that several of those around him were enjoying a meat dish served on a unique, crystal-covered green dish. It smelled wonderful, and every time a servant passed with a tray carrying the entrée, he turned to hang onto the scent for as long as possible.

"This is a famous place," Barthos said, almost proudly. "It was established after the Crolean War by one of the former top commanders. Seems he had been so unhappy with the food served to the soldiers that he vowed never to eat like that again." He chuckled, as did Tonie.

"It is so hard to get a table here," she said.

"When was that?" T. G. asked. "When was the place opened?"

"Oh, well before I was born," Barthos said, thinking back. "Back in 4253, wasn't it, Tonie?"

"Yes," she agreed. "I believe so."

"More than seventeen hundred years ago," Barthos affirmed. "My grandfather actually served under Warlord Derakiin in that war. He made the Barthos family name great through his bravery."

T. G. nodded his appreciation then glanced toward the kitchen. "I'm so hungry," he smiled. "I wasn't so much a little while ago, but the smell of that dish that everybody seems to be ordering is incredible. What is it?"

"On the green platters?" Tonie asked.

"Yes. What is that?"

"It is called 'sholari,' " she said. "Derakiin's is famous for it. People come from all over the world just to get it here. Many other places have it, but they do not have the special preparation secret that only Derakiin's uses."

It was not a food that Pretsal had ever mentioned, with his limited income and primarily fruit-filled diet. T. G. had never seen it for sale before. He scanned the menu and saw that sholari was the single most expensive item listed. Not just more expensive—it was more than twice the price of the next closest entrée.

"That's almost a day's pay," he said with surprise.

"Would you like to try it?" Barthos asked. "Better than the best rib-eye you ever had…I guarantee it."

"Gee, I don't—"

"Go ahead. It's on me." He lifted a small door in the tabletop, revealing a dataplate beneath it. "I'll order." He pressed the proper buttons. "Okay, sholari for T. G. and me. What would you like, Tonie?"

"Just the fruit combination and bread for me," she smiled.

He completed the order and closed the little door. "There. It should just take a moment. Here, T.G, hand me your glass."

He passed it to Barthos, who filled it from the glistening fixture before them. "This is a very good wine," he commented. "I know you don't generally drink, but you really should try it at least once."

"Okay," he conceded, deciding that just once would not hurt. He took his glass from Barthos and sipped the dark liquid. He did not know enough about alcoholic beverages to be impressed. *It's wine. Big deal.*

Only four minutes passed before a group of servants arrived at the table with trays of food. The green platters with their luscious portions of sholari were placed before T. G. and Barthos, and their covers were removed to reveal what appeared to be four tiny steaks spread upon a bed of reddish pasta. Tonie's fruit platter was set before her, with a bowl of small breads placed to one side. The servants asked permission to leave the table, and Barthos nodded.

"Enjoy," Barthos smiled at T. G., taking a bite of his meal.

T. G. sliced a piece from one of the sholari steaks and took a bite. It was incredible—more tender than any meat he had ever eaten and far tastier. It had a sweetness that T. G. could not recognize. As he chewed, he could only close his eyes and enjoy, moaning his pleasure.

"Good, huh?" Barthos grinned. Tonie smiled also, pleased to see her boss enjoying his food so much. "Did I lie?"

"Wow," T. G. managed to say, swallowing the first bite. "This is incredible. What is a sholari, anyway? What kind of animal?"

"Silly," Tonie laughed. "It is not an animal."

T. G. was confused. It *was* meat. At least he thought it was. "I don't get it," he said.

"Sholari," she went on. "Nonborn."

"What?"

"Surely you know," she said. "Nonborn."

The woman saw the lack of comprehension on his face. "How can you not know?" she smiled, surprised by his reaction. "It is genetically conceived on special farms and harvested at an age of eighteen months."

Barthos eyed the exchange with great interest. T. G. glared at Tonie, then at his superior, who went on eating as he watched the rising apprehension in T. G.'s eyes. "Nonborn...*what?*"

"Children," Tonie stated matter-of-factly.

T. G. went white.

"What is wrong, T. G.?" she asked, genuinely puzzled by his reaction. "It is not as if they had ever attained viability or consciousness or contributed anything. They are grown for food."

He turned away, sickened. Convulsions racked his gut, and it took every ounce of willpower he could muster to keep from becoming violently ill at the table. He leaped to his feet and ran for the restroom, knocking his chair over backward in the process.

"What is wrong with him?" Tonie asked Barthos.

"Too spicy for him, I suppose," Barthos said, taking another bite. "Must be an acquired taste."

∽◦∾

T. G. had difficulty getting past the nightmare at the restaurant. Noron had surprised him again with the extent of its barbarity, which always seemed clothed in a facade of normalcy, even elegance. He did not go to work the following day.

The rolled police-distribution plans Barthos had given T. G. were strewn across a tabletop and on the floor around it, but they did not have his attention at the moment. A sporting event not too unlike the decathlon was playing itself out beneath the transparent dome of his large, top-of-the-line simulight unit, and he sat studying it, trying to decipher its rules. Cold drink in hand, he watched the show, drawing constant comparisons with sports as he had seen them broadcast back home. While he appreciated the competition involved, T. G. really missed the team sports he had grown up with and seriously considered introducing American-style football to the people of Noron. *With their size and athletic ability…well, the mind staggers!*

As he watched, curled into one end of a huge sofa, he fondly recalled the way he and his father had spent Sunday afternoons watching football, with plenty of chips, dips, and soft drinks to go around. A loneliness once again began to grow within him, as it had many times, and the face of a friend appeared in his mind. With all that had transpired since his parting with Pretsal, T. G. had never once paused to contact the gentle giant. So much had happened so fast. The time spent in Pretsal's apartment seemed years away. Earth was barely a dream.

Ish had told him not to get distracted, not to lose focus. Because of that, he had tried hard to set his friendship with Pretsal and his ties to the Twelve aside, working instead to focus entirely upon Paull Shass and the task at hand. He had not spoken to Darafine or any of the others since taking his government position, but as he sat watching the games he found himself missing Pretsal badly.

Why not? he wondered. *What could it hurt?*

He reached over and touched the control plate of his telephone, manipulating the jeweled buttons as he had learned to do. After a few silent moments, a familiar voice sounded in the room.

"Prosperity," it said in a low monotone.

"Hi, Pretsal...it's T. G."

The voice came to life. "T. G.! It's been so long. Where are you? What are you doing? How are you? Is Ish with you?"

T. G. laughed at the barrage of questions. "Slow down, buddy, one thing at a time. I'm fine. I just wanted to see how the translation was coming along."

"You have not heard? It had just been finished at the time I last saw you, and distribution has begun. We have been waiting to hear from you, to learn what we are to do next. All is ready for the next step...as it has been for *months*."

"I'm sorry I haven't been in touch, but so many things are happening," T. G. continued. "Tremendous things. I can't really get into it all right now, but tell everyone that incredible changes are about to sweep the planet. Paull Shass is a part of it all. He's the key to a whole new world, Pretsal. Ish healed him so that he could usher in a new age of peace on Noron."

"Ish did this?" Pretsal asked, surprised. "We all heard of the miraculous recovery, of course, but did not realize—"

"Yes, Pretsal. The Creator's plan is unfolding. Tell Darafine—tell the others—be ready. The time is come...the president is about to bring in the Awakening. I don't know when I'll see you again, but it should be very soon, I promise."

"I hope so."

"Take care. I'll get back to you as soon as I can. Prosperity, buddy."

"Prosperity, T. G."

"I just want you to know it's really good to hear your voice again. When I finally do see you, the jumbo barbecued locusts are on me," he said. After a moment, he added something else. "And whatever you do, stay away from the sholari."

"Be careful, T. G., there's much at stake. Take care, buddy."

T. G. closed the call, smiling, and took another sip of his Dr Pepper.

∽◦∾

"Pretsal contacted me," Josan said, descending the stairs to the deep basement level of an abandoned building where the Twelve and their followers had relocated their operations. To ensure security, the bio-center meeting place had been abandoned shortly after T. G.'s departure, and a new meeting location, a complex of storerooms far beneath what had once been a city library, had been chosen for its extreme isolation.

Jerithia had once been a proud, productive city, thriving with industry, creativity, and life. Its streets rang with the sounds of joyful neighbors and playing children. Its people had once been among the most productive on the planet, long before, in the days before the State took power. Under its oppressive fist, however, the human spirit had been crushed first into reluctant submission and later into abject slavery. Then, almost mercifully, came war, one of the thousands that had marred the planet throughout its bloody career—and the once-shining city of Jerithia had been put out of its misery.

Too near the Luracayn-Sethii border, it had been burned to the ground when the mammoth Sethiian army had invaded, leaving most of the eastern part of the country razed and afire. Heavy black smoke, visible for a hundred miles, blocked out the sun as it rose high into the sky. Much of the blackened, smoking territory was later reclaimed after the war, but large pockets were left as part of an abandoned Fire Zone, as it had come to be known. The surrounding jungle growth had quickly filled most of the area, but sections of Jerithia were spared by a series of wide stone streets and towering walls that isolated its northernmost section from the encroaching wilderness beyond. Superstition about the area quickly became a part of Luracaynian culture, as tales of evil spirits and certain death for all trespassers swept government schoolhouses and street corners. Few ever ventured there, and it had been that way for three hundred years.

The Twelve counted on that.

"The Voice has spoken to him just today," Josan continued, walking up to Darafine.

"What did T. G. say?" she asked, sitting at a wide table in one corner of the dimly lit room. "What is the delay?"

A small lamp burned, throwing a wash of warm light across the Truth as she studied the pages of her handwritten translation. The original had been safely hidden, protected from those who would silence its words.

"All is being readied," he replied. "Much has happened these past few months. Paull Shass is in position to take the position of world leader. He can then bring in the Awakening, with the help of the Voice."

"What?" the puzzled woman asked. "The Voice said *that?*"

"Yes," Josan assured her. "All things are to be made new. Our oppression will end. It was for this that Ish healed the president."

"T. G. said this?" she asked again, rising to her feet, stunned.

"He did. He said that Paull Shass is bringing in the Awakening, that it is the Creator's will."

Darafine looked sternly at the scriptures laid out before her. She considered the new information for a moment, weighing all the data, and slowly shook her head.

"He is wrong," she firmly stated.

"What?"

She sat once more, lightly running a caressing hand across the open spread of the Truth. "The blade is being forged in a crucible of white fire. I do not envy the Voice what he has endured, nor that which is about to happen. He does not know, Josan. He has not yet read the words of the Truth. He assumes too much. He does not understand what is to befall him…the burden he must bear." She looked with tear-filled eyes upon the scriptures as Josan, following her sight line, did the same.

"What is it? What does it say?" he asked softly.

"There are several specific prophecies here pertaining to the Voice in the Dark, most of which we had forgotten long ago. One is most grim. Upon first translating it, I had hoped it was allegory, or that it had already been fulfilled in the past. Yet it is not, and it was not."

"Grim? What? What is it?"

She looked up at him. Before she could speak, screams and unintelligible shouts rang out above. An explosion roared violently, then another, shaking the walls. Soot and plaster dust showered them both. The ceiling weakened and began to fall away in ragged chunks.

More screams. More loud, muddled voices, in tones of warning. Another explosion. Darafine hurried to gather the Truth into her arms as Josan used his cloak to shelter her from the debris that rained down upon them both. They tried for the stairs, but a powerful concussion threw the door above from its hinges and flames poured into the room.

A loud chorus of dry crackles sounded above—one that could only come from government ripsticks.

Darafine and Josan tried again, headed toward a side tunnel that carried into a neighboring sub-basement. Just as they crossed its threshold, another explosion rocked the walls, collapsing the tunnel ceiling in a thundering cave-in. Falling debris, blinding, choking dust, and the noxious clouds that filled the air separated them. Darafine called for Josan, but he did not answer.

She fell back against a partially collapsed wall. Off balance, she managed to throw the precious translation into the rapidly spreading blaze and watched as its pages were consumed, sending aloft billows of white that swirled and mixed with the heavy black smoke.

The State could not yet be allowed to know the Scriptures existed, that even at that moment the Truth was waiting, worldwide, to be made known.

The thick haze stung her eyes and burned her throat. Trapped, she fell back into a corner and huddled low in an attempt to find air. The sound of menacing voices and the sharp, lethal discharge of dozens of ripsticks grew louder and more immediate, and she knew that death hovered only seconds away.

There was nowhere left to run.

19

It was unheard of, a first in the long history of the embattled world. The president of Luracayn, the new king of Kamir, and the new grand premier of Sethii all sat down at the enormous table in the lavish Ceremonies Room of the Luracaynian Capitol. There was a huge crowd gathered, dignitaries and press from all the nations of the world, looking on as the course of events took a hard left turn, changing all their lives forever. All eyes were on Paull Shass.

No one in the audience really knew the names of the other two men. It did not matter.

The room looked like a combination of the Hall of Congress and a grand throne room suited for the coronation of kings. T. G. wore formal purple robes and sat in an assigned box next to the one shared by Sereen Shass and Cordan Barthos. Tonie sat next to him, also wearing her most colorful finery, her hair elegantly styled. T. G. cut a sideward glance at Barthos, who sensed it and smiled back, raising his little finger in the Noronian equivalent of a thumbs-up sign. The press was everywhere, taking photos and transmitting the event live, by simulight, to all the world.

A trio of aides, one from each nation, brought a circular, cut-crystal disc some two feet in diameter into the room. It glinted blue in the chandelier light, catching and holding it somehow, creating a glowing effect that was breathtaking. Those in the room broke into applause and rose to their feet at the sight, an ovation that lasted a full minute. The disc was then set upon a velvet drape before the first of the three leaders, who sat side by side at the huge table that dominated the center of the room.

The first man picked up a metal stylus and began to sign his name upon the disc. A bright orange light flared at the point where silver met crystal, scribing his signature indelibly onto its surface. Both disc and stylus were then passed to the man to the right, who repeated the act, then sat back as the final leader of the three—the man of the moment—readied himself for his turn.

Shass picked up the stylus. Pausing dramatically as he looked upon the document scribed into the face of the disc, his face a solemn mask, he brought the stylus up and signed his name in the appropriate place.

And became something new, something Noron had never had before.

Prime Lord of all the world.

Instantly, the room broke into wild applause, a standing ovation that sent chills up T. G.'s spine. The significance of the moment was overwhelming, the drama palpable. Shass rose to his feet.

The whole world of Noron applauded its single, sovereign leader. Its first.

All trade barriers, with the final signature, fell. All national borders opened. All armies of all nations became one. All loyalties merged into one, and one alone. There was only one world. There was only one law. There was only one people.

Sereen Shass, beneath her crimson veil, wept tears of pride. Barthos applauded loudest of all, it seemed. T. G. and Tonie lauded the new world leader too, as the thunder continued. Shass saluted the gathered assembly, then spoke a few carefully selected words.

"My friends," he began, pausing a moment for the applause to fall silent, "this day has dawned on a new world, one unlike that of our fathers…a world of unity, and prosperity, and very soon, peace."

A new round of applause sounded. T. G. looked around the room, soaking in the sight of the people as they honored their miracle man. He felt pride for the part he had played and would continue to play as Noron continued toward the full realization of its Awakening. He saw that many of the lower class were present, a representative group chosen by the Prime Lord's publicity staff to show the world that he was serious about eradicating the class system, making opportunity and resources available to all.

"We have plotted a new course, a new destiny, a new purpose. Soon, through a system of public participation that will quickly come to full realization, you, too, will become a critical part of the drama that now unfolds before us. The class system we have known—a great wall that has thrown a shadow upon the people of this world for long enough—will be abolished. I promise you now...I will lead you into a new dawn of joy and plenty beyond your greatest hopes."

New applause arose. As T. G. stood adding his manual praise to that of those all around him, he realized that it would most likely be a very long speech—and nature was calling. He turned to Tonie.

"I need to take care of something," he said, trying to be heard above the roar. "I'll be back in a minute." She nodded.

T. G. passed the Watchers standing just within the doors of the Ceremonies Room and walked out into the surrounding concourse, heading toward the closest restroom. The concourse was empty since all were inside the hall, enjoying their former president's finest moment to date. A new thunder of applause boomed from within the marble walls, signifying another wondrous promise made by Shass, and T. G. smiled as he realized that politics were politics, whatever planet one was on.

He entered the large, opulent restroom. More like a hotel suite than a sanitary facility, it reflected the upper-class view of nonmoderation in all things. A small flowering garden with a trickling fountain was set to one side of the large high-ceilinged room, the sky stretching wide and ever-pink beyond the angled skylight above. A row of marble basins lined the wall to his right, and as he passed them, making his way toward the privacy stalls at the back of the room, he looked into the wall-length mirror above them.

Local boy makes good, he thought, looking upon his reflection. A kid from New York becomes a prophet and government official on another world—imagine. *Happens every day.*

It had taken him months to get used to the Noronian concept of a toilet. Within a stall, he hung his robe upon a hook, then looked at the reason he had come into the room in the first place. It was not so much a seat as a saddle, something to be mounted rather than sat upon or stood before. Porcelain, metal, and stone, the toilet was as cold as any toilet seat on Earth—that was one constant T. G. could have done without.

Finished, he once again wrapped himself in his robes, washed his hands in the warm flowing water of one of the basins, then dried them and headed back out into the concourse, toward the Ceremonies Room. No sooner had he stepped out of the restroom than he saw a renewal, the first he had seen in months, no more than ten feet away. He stopped, watching as it passed, waiting for the inevitable terrifying reaction.

It had the appearance of a child, a little girl dressed in the common robes of the lower class, and it clutched a worn, ragged doll. Its face bore an innocence that was obscene, considering its true nature. It made its way slowly past, in no hurry, headed toward the doors of the Ceremonies Room, where it apparently was a part of one of the attending lower-class families.

It turned and looked at T. G., never breaking stride. He held his breath and braced for what would surely come next—but no evil, glaring eyes burned through him. No shrill, Hell-born scream filled his ears.

It *smiled* at him.

T. G., stunned and bewildered, watched as the translucent child-thing walked casually away. It entered the Ceremonies Room, and as it passed through the momentarily open door of the chamber, another explosion of acclaim sounded.

T. G., his mind already struggling, barely heard it.

Why? Why didn't it…?

And then, he knew.

No! How could I have…no!

His mind raced. Driven almost by instinct, he ran toward the elevators and pressed his palm against the summoning plate. Seconds later, the car arrived and he lunged into it, hurriedly pressing the destination panel inside. The doors closed—too slowly.

"Come on!" he quietly screamed.

Then he was on his way. Not up, toward his office far above, but down. Down toward the parking area, where his car waited. In mere moments, the antigravity elevator carried him past hundreds of other levels, toward that which he sought. But as the door opened, he froze.

No, not the car. They'll know...

He stood motionless, picturing his house, trying to shift there. In a panic, he caught himself and stopped, his heart pounding.

If you shift, they'll know!

Breathing heavily, he pressed the command plate again and the elevator fell a few levels farther, moved sideways for a while, then dropped once more before coming to a stop. His heart pounded in his throat as he entered a security code. *Will it still work? Do they know?*

T. G. breathed a sigh of relief as the door obediently and uneventfully opened once again, and as he cautiously stepped out into a wide familiar foyer of deep-red marble he began to believe he would make it. His reflection alone danced in the polished stone all around him as he moved—no one else was there. A warm light splashed upon him from directly ahead, and with his heart pounding he ran toward it. His heels sounded loudly, too loudly, against the cool floor as he dashed forward. *Someone might hear!* Without slowing, he slammed into a wide glass-and-metal door, shoving it open as he spilled out into the light.

And onto the street.

He ran anew, headed toward the massive and distant city wall. In planning the proposed law enforcement grid, he had come to know the layout of the streets, the general arrangement of the city, the areas to avoid. Block after block fell behind him.

How could I have done this?

The streets were crowded as always. They were less imposing by daylight, but he knew that danger waited everywhere. He would have to be careful.

How could I have been so stupid?

The high oxygen content and doubled barometric pressure of the Noronian atmosphere helped him, allowing him to run farther and with less fatigue than he ever could have on Earth. His legs did not cramp. His lungs did not ache—not yet. He remembered his frantic run through the woods of Colorado, David at his side, and he knew that the danger now facing him was greater. Much greater. Lethally so.

∽o∾

Shass was into the final stanzas of his speech almost an hour after it had begun. It had gone well. The world was in his pocket.

Barthos had noticed T. G.'s departure, and the still-empty seat worried him. He made his way over to the waist-high divider that separated his box from that to his right and leaned toward Tonie.

"Where's T. G.?" he asked quietly.

"I do not know," she answered, also in a low tone. "He said he would be right back, but that was a long time ago."

Barthos turned his head toward one of the Watchers at the door, then nodded and pointed, indicating the concourse beyond. The man understood and immediately left the room.

Another round of applause. Barthos returned to stand before his seat and joined the ovation, yet his eyes remained fixed, unmoving, upon the door.

∽o∾

T. G. had been running for hours, weaving his way through the maze that was Keltrian. He was astonished that he had gotten so far without incident.

He made his way along one of the city's secondary streets, knowing that the high city wall was still many miles away. Beyond lay open wilderness and dense forest. And cover.

A place he could stop and think.

He moved carefully, huddled over, trying to stay out of sight of the masses all around him. It was vital that he remain unrecognized by the ghostly renewals in particular, for he realized that one sighting might immediately flash his position to those from whom he fled. Whenever possible, he moved through the city's underground tunnel complexes, where power links and sewer lines were run, but he found them more populated by the itinerant than he had expected and had to move carefully to avoid detection.

The tunnels were ancient and mazelike, a dank, subterranean puzzle that made it difficult for T. G. to keep his bearings. As he moved quickly and quietly along, he smelled something ahead, something unusual for a sewer—not the usual oppressive, heavy scent of the synthecrete and steel tunnel, but that of a backyard barbecue. For a moment, pleasant memories of summer cookouts filled his mind. A pall of smoke hung high in the air, hugging the ceiling, stinging his eyes. Carefully, he rounded a bend in the sewer and came upon a scene that both sickened and horrified him. As he hid in the deep shadows, his body pressed against the wet, slime-coated wall, he saw a group of disheveled men and women huddled among several small fires, preparing their meals.

They were working to dismember several human bodies. Using small flameblades, the ghouls were portioning them out, muscle and sinew and organs, to those excitedly gathered to watch. Small, drum-contained fires flared beneath ragged metal grids, providing grills upon which much of the ravaged flesh was cooking. Some ate greedily as others prepared their portions, their demented eyes glistening wetly in the firelight. Knee-high piles of grinning skulls and stripped, gnawed bones littered the tunnel all around them and well beyond, a silent testimony to the horror that had befallen hundreds of fallen, forgotten people.

T. G. fought the bile rising in his throat as he backed away, into the darkness. He doubled back some fifty feet down the tunnel before choosing another route that appeared to end in a narrow shaft of pinkish light, far ahead and above. Horrified, he now longed for daylight as never before—he had no desire to end his career on Noron as an entrée. Making his way up the first access ladder he came upon, he found himself in an open alleyway, where he wearily fell back against a wall and grabbed a moment of rest. Several deep breaths helped to clear the disgusting smoke from his lungs, but he could still smell it on his skin and robes. He yearned for a shower.

After a brief interval, he covered his head with the tattered remnants of a cloak he found discarded in the alley and pressed on, keeping his face out of sight, hoping to attract no attention at all.

He was not so lucky.

Running at full stride, he rounded a corner. In a blur of frenzied motion he was slammed violently and without warning against the dense stone wall of an abandoned storage building. Dazed, he fell hard to the ground, landing awkwardly upon a jumbled tangle of broken machinery and garbage. Losing his grip on the cloak as he fell, he saw two men towering over him, their expressions angry, their fists clenched. Both were well over seven feet tall.

"All right, chuni," one of the men growled. "We have watched you sneaking along for the last couple of blocks…what are you hiding under that robe? Give it up! Now!"

"What?"

"Nobody moves like that unless they are carrying something they want to keep. Give it to me!"

He shuddered at the phrase. Falling back a few steps, he brought his arm up, pointing it at the men, fingers spread. "I don't want to hurt you," he warned shakily. "Leave now…"

The men laughed. "What are you going to do to us?" one asked, feigning fear and stepping closer.

T. G. tensed the muscles in his arm and waited for the aching cold, the searing heat. And waited.

And waited.

Nothing happened.

The men were upon him in a second, their fists pounding him. As T. G. again fell to the ground, one of the assailants ripped the cloak away, revealing that he carried nothing of value. "Nice clothes on this one, eh, Rodlan?" he asked, rifling T. G. for anything he might be carrying. "Looks like a rich one."

"Well?" the other impatiently asked. "What does he have on him?"

"Nothing!" the man said in frustration. "It is just a stupid chuni!"

The other man landed a few final punches and threw T. G. to the ground once more, tearing the bleeding man's clothes in the process. The two brutes then turned and walked away, laughing.

"If your robes fit me, I would take them," one threatened, dismissing T. G. with a wave of his hand. "But since you are just a chuni, I am feeling generous today. Next time, you are dead!"

Finally alone, T. G. rolled painfully onto his knees, then braced himself against the wall and rose to his feet. Picking up the cloak, he wiped the blood from his mouth and nose and stood for a moment, breathing heavily, arranging his robes.

Why didn't it work? he wondered. *Didn't I hold my arm right?*

After several minutes of standing there in pain and humiliation, wondering if he would see a friendly face ever again, he made sure the coast was clear and headed back out into the streets.

For a day and a half he pressed on, running and hiding, staying in the shadows and remaining as invisible as possible. He found water at a small public fountain and drank until his intense thirst died away. The sun set and darkness fell upon the city, creating new shadows for him to hide in. Hours passed, each moment holding the threat of new danger. Finally, after cutting down a last, confusing network of cluttered alleys, he came to one of the many gates in the towering city wall and passed outside. The darkness gave him the cover he needed—the sun would not rise for almost two hours.

Outside the gate, he left the road at once, cutting across a grassy meadow toward the dense forest in the distance. The grass grew deeper and thicker as he got farther from the busy road, but he struggled on, having to raise his knees higher as he ran.

The forest loomed closer, towering over him like a cluster of green skyscrapers. He knew there were probably animals in there that would very much like to eat a little earthling, but he also knew that nothing in there could be worse than what lay behind him. He pressed on, passing the first of the towering trees, into the deeper darkness of the tropical timberland.

He stopped to rest at a point deep enough that he was sure he could not be seen. Breathing heavily, leaning against a tree trunk, he peered between the trunks behind him and scanned the clearing between himself and the city. No one followed.

The last time he had found himself running through the woods, he had not been alone. Now he had no knowledgeable friend to fall back upon, no seasoned woodsman whose experience might mean the difference between life and death. *David, I sure could use your help right now…*

He turned and ran deeper into the thick growth, the sounds of his breathing and his footsteps pounding in his ears.

20

Where is he, Beclan?"

"We do not know," the security man reluctantly replied, standing before the desk of the new chancellor, the second most powerful man in the world. "He slipped out during the speech. I sent men to his office, his house, and everywhere in between, but there is no sign as yet."

"What about the gates? Has he left the city?"

"He has not used a vehicle, Chancellor. We know this, and it would be certain suicide to go into the wilderness on foot. He could never make it to another city."

Barthos angrily shoved a stack of papers to one side. "Why did he run?"

"Again, I do not know. Nothing in the speech could have caused it, and nothing else happened to tip him off. At least, not on our part."

"Maybe he just got smart. He knows now. Somehow he knows."

"No…we had him. There is no way he could just—"

Barthos exploded. "He was chosen!"

"But, Chancellor—"

"We're not talking about your average idiot, all wrapped up in himself! This kid, from among trillions, was chosen as the last of the Guardians…do you understand? The chosen Voice in the Dark!"

"Yes sir."

"I knew he wouldn't completely lose sight of that. I wanted him kept close, Beclan, close! Because at the first sign that he'd figured it out, as soon as it looked like he wasn't going to discredit himself, we'd have to take our chances and martyr him. And it was *your* job to stay on top of him!"

"Yes, Chancellor, but there was no sign that he would run."

Barthos took a deep breath, calming himself. He smiled slightly at the shaken man, reassuring him.

"Well, these things happen. I'm sure you'll succeed next time, right, Beclan?"

"Yes sir. We will find him. I promise you this."

"I know you will. You always have. How long have you been with me?"

"Twelve years, sir. Since your days as a Watcher."

"How is the wife, Beclan? And the girls…your three daughters?"

"They are all well. You are kind to have asked." The man breathed easier. "I will report back on the hour. He will be found."

Barthos nodded and sat back down, dismissing his Chief Watcher with a wave of his hand. He immediately focused his attentions upon the paperwork on his desk, sorting the varied sheets in order of priority. He did not look up as he heard his office door open and close again. Nor did he look up when he heard the electric scream of weapons fire just outside.

After a few moments his door opened once more, and Barthos, still looking down at the papers on his desk, spoke to a man he did not see, but knew was there. "It's been taken care of?"

"Yes, Chancellor Barthos," a new voice answered.

"You are now Chief Watcher. Find T. G. Bring him back here, to this office. I trust you will not disappoint me."

"I will not fail you, sir."

"Clean up the hallway," Barthos casually ordered. "I'm expecting guests."

The door closed. The temperature in the chamber fell.

A wet, raspy sound of breathing echoed in the room.

"You heard?" Barthos asked, not looking up, still concentrating on his work.

"I did," a deep, reverberating voice answered.

"Find the Voice," Barthos demanded. "Silence it."

CNOW

He missed his daypack.

T. G. walked through the heavy forest, pushing past tangled vines and the jagged leaves of large cycads as he wove between the trunks. Flowering blossoms of red, yellow, and purple threw a splash of color everywhere. He had slowed his pace considerably, feeling a certain safety now that he was away from the city, and he took the luxury of caution as he moved along. His thirst had been growing constantly worse since leaving the lethal city of Keltrian, and he thought fondly of his canteen—but it was on another planet.

His torn formal robes and light dress boots were hardly suited for heavy trailblazing. At least he would not have to deal with cold or rain or hail. He used the sun to gather his bearings whenever a break in the overhead canopy of foliage would allow it, but it had been almost thirteen hours since he had left the city, and the sun was setting, depriving him of his only compass. The stars, as bright as they were, would be of little help, for he could never see enough sky to use them.

T. G. was headed for the biocenter in Cusira, more than three hundred miles away. It would take weeks to get there by foot, he knew, but his single hope for survival was that, once he reached the biocenter, the Twelve would still be there. Pretsal's apartment, back in the city, might as well have been a million miles away.

He had been lucky so far. One did not go hiking through such wilderness without becoming prey, for the predators were many. He might make it through one more day, or even two, but anything more would be unlikely considering the abundance of wildlife on the planet. He hoped that some form of deliverance, anything, would make itself available.

He was certain Ish would not be there for him. He had allowed himself to be seduced by the world and was no longer a threat to the Dark, nor was he of any use to those who had chosen him. The child-like renewal he saw had known that. They all knew.

They had won. With his eyes wide open, he had let them.

Angry at himself, he continued deeper into the wilderness. If only there were some other mode of travel open to him, he might make it. But there was not. All cars were monitored. All flights were monitored. All phones were monitored.

But his feet were not. He pressed on.

Darkness fell, the odd, rosy darkness that Noron knew. The same forest that had been so silent by day now burst into a cacophony of sound, filling with the calls of night birds, frogs, insects, and many others he could not identify. His ankles and legs ached, and each step became more and more painful. He would have to rest somewhere.

The sound of running water caught his attention. Stopping to determine its direction, he found that a turn of his head indicated several apparent sources, a result of echoes caused by the massive tree trunks surrounding him. He chose the one that seemed the loudest and, energized by his thirst, began to run. A hundred feet fell behind him, and he began to think he had chosen the wrong direction.

Breaking into a dead run through a dense wall of foliage, the ground beneath him suddenly vanished and he found himself falling, his pumping legs treading only calm air. The slow motion of sheer terror gripped him.

You'd think I'd learn!

He could barely see the night-shrouded forest before him and nothing at all beneath him. Panic struck before he realized his altitude, and in a trio of seconds he plunged some twenty feet into a body of water. Instinctively, his lungs clung to what air they held as he disappeared below the surface, his heart still pounding, his mind filled only with the scramble of self-preservation.

Recovering quickly from the surprise fall, he gathered his wits and surfaced, finding himself in a cool, gently flowing river. He cheered aloud, drinking deeply and splashing his face, enjoying the mild current as it moved past. After several minutes of such water play, he swam to the narrow gravelly shore and collapsed onto the bank. He lay there for a time, his weary arms spread, looking into the starry sky. Tears filled his eyes. He rolled over onto his hands and knees and sat up, kneeling.

He determined that he had not been able to defend himself against the thugs in the alley because he was alone. He could not have shifted from the elevator to his house had he tried, because he was alone. And now he would die in the wilderness because he was alone.

Alone.

A grief too deep for words tore at his heart, for he knew he had betrayed those who had chosen him. He had let the world seduce him into the embrace of other arms. He began to weep bitterly and loudly, eyes closed, his lonely and painful lamentation echoing from the wall of the riverbank as his heart cried out, deep in agony.

He was heard.

∽◌◠

"I knew it was only a matter of time."

Confined to one of the sunken cubicles of the government prison, Darafine looked up from the cot where she lay. Barthos, outside the locked door of her cell, stood peering down at her. His smile belied a heart of darkness, a soul of cold emptiness.

"Congratulations, Chancellor," she replied. "You will forgive me if I do not grovel."

"I would never expect that of you. Not that it would hurt, if you felt so inclined."

"Not that it would help either."

"You're only alive because of me. If you tell us what we want to know, you'll stay that way."

"And what is it you wish to hear?" the woman sarcastically asked.

"The 'Truth'…we know there is a finished translation. Where is it?"

Her answer was one of silence.

"I can't hear your thoughts. You're being shielded."

"Good thing. You might think less of me if you heard my choice of language."

He smiled, overlooking the comment. "How does the underground operate? Who are its leaders—other than yourself?"

No answer. She rolled over, turning her back to him. He continued, forcing his cruel presence into her mind like an unstoppable nightmare.

"I hope your threshold for pain is high," he threatened. "More importantly, I hope that your friend's is higher."

She sat up. "Friend?"

"You weren't captured alone, you know. He hasn't given us a name, not yet. But then, he still has a few fingers left."

Josan?

Darafine looked away, struggling to shut out the image. She knew that nothing she could say would stop Barthos from torturing them both. Like the conquerors of old, he did it for pleasure, not gain. His motives were beyond the worldly, transcending mere greed or the desire for power. His was an ancient evil, fed by the prolonged agony he inflicted on others, not by the riches or worldly authority given him by his position.

Darafine was prepared for death. She always had been. Protecting the Truth and its still-tiny core of followers was more important than any of their lives. Josan knew that as well as she.

"Very well," Barthos said. "We'll see how willing you are to talk once your friend and the others have been parceled out to the dogs. This will be interesting…just how much of a person do you have to leave intact for him to remain a person? At what point does one become…furniture?"

"Leave him alone, or I will never tell you anything."

"Not that you would, anyway. Am I right?" He smiled again, shaking his head. "It never ceases to amaze me the way your kind clings to this 'Truth' of yours. What good has it done you? Has it ever brought you anything but pain? Has this 'Son of Man' you so vainly await ever so much as shown his face? And this 'Voice in the Dark'…so small, so sickly, so easily corrupted."

"The end is upon you," she insisted. "You know that. Your time is short. Soon the Awakening will—"

"The Awakening will not take place. If it was going to happen, it would have done so by now. Come on, you're smarter than this. Why suffer for a lie? Give up this delusion of yours and face reality." He leaned closer to the bars, his breath fogging the cool, polished metal. "Come on, Darafine, it doesn't have to be this way. You are an intelligent and beautiful woman. You know how to get things done. Think of it…I might just have a place for you."

"Yes," she agreed. "You do. The pit of Hell."

∽◌∾

As the sun rose, T. G. began to stir from his hard sleep. The cool water flowed through his fingers as he awoke to find himself face down on the bank, small pebbles pressed into his flesh. He began to remember where he was and how he had come to be there, and he shook his head to clear the mental cobwebs. The deep despair that had torn at him the night before began anew.

He saw a mist rising from the floor of the forest all around him, as if installed sprinklers were gently nourishing the planet's dense plant life. It was a wondrous system—the waters rose each morning with the precision of a jeweled timepiece, feeding the creeks and rivers and sending gentle mists out onto the remainder of the world's surface. The underground reservoirs from which the waters came were kept heated and pressurized by a precisely balanced arrangement of radioactive elements deep beneath the planet's crust—a natural breeder reactor.

T. G. rolled onto his side, leaning on one elbow, scratching his head as he searched for the energy and the will to face the new day.

Then he noticed a sound.

It was beautiful, softly filling the forest all around him, a symphony of shifting chords in a major key, a music unlike any he had ever heard. The sound came from beneath him as well, he realized. Pressing his ear closer to the riverbank, he swept the few inches of gravel aside and found pure white sand just beneath.

It came from the sand. Amplified by the crystalline canopy above, the natural stellar and planetary radio emissions common throughout the universe were being picked up by the sand and its hydroponic sublayer, transforming their signals into audible music when the angles of solar energy and stellar radiation against the canopy were just right. It was as if the planet were a huge crystal radio set.

Each daybreak, if one only paused to listen, the morning stars sang. T. G. had spent almost the entirety of his stay on the planet within city walls, where synthecrete, steel, stone and common city noises had so muffled the musical wonder that he had never heard it himself.

He sat and listened as the sun rose higher, transfixed by the elegance of it all. The pure river, the towering trees, the gentle mist, it was—paradise. Not even the Garden of Eden could have been more beautiful than the miracle all around him. Then the music fell silent, leaving a disappointed T. G. with only the sound of rushing water in his ears.

A short distance away, he noticed a plant bearing a type of fruit he had come to enjoy. He rose and walked over to it, then plucked a fruit from its branch and ravenously ate it, for he had not eaten for almost three days. Called kerali, it was an odd sort of fruit by Earth standards—shaped like a pear, flavored like strawberry mixed with pineapple, colored like a peach, and peeled like a banana. He ate several, filling his stomach until it no longer scolded him. Then he resolved to set out toward his goal once more.

T. G. followed the river eastward for a few hours, then turned aside at a convenient dip in the river wall and headed back into the woods. Huge emerald leaves eight feet in diameter constantly surrounded him like a draped blanket, overlapping each other as they cut his line of sight to mere feet. The dense underbrush crunched beneath his boots as he tried to avoid the deepest and most dangerous extremes of the dense wilderness, choosing the path of least resistance. There the going was faster, for the foliage was somewhat lighter, and he could see the sun well enough to know he was headed steadily northward, toward Cusira. He passed several clearings but avoided them during daylight so he could not be spotted from the air.

At midafternoon, he came upon the carcass of a huge bear, one that appeared to have been killed within the past couple of days. It had been largely eaten by whatever had brought it down and probably by smaller scavengers as well, for very little was left of it. He looked cautiously around, moving slowly and quietly, trying to avoid ending up as dessert. The bellow of some creature deeper in the forest forced him to change his course slightly, hoping to maintain a greater distance from whatever it was. He had done little research on the actual distribution of animal life on the planet, so he was unsure whether the dominant predators in the area were lions, wolves, or worse.

Along the way, as the hours passed, he saw several species of monkey in the branches above. An odd, loud buzzing surrounded him all of a sudden, causing him to dip and turn in a single motion, peering upward in search of its source. Mere feet above, his stunned gaze fell upon a trio of dragonflies, each with a wingspan some three feet across. He dove to the ground, fearing attack, but the colossal insects darted past in search of other food. He stood up once again and brushed the mud and moss from his knees. *If the dragonflies are that big....* He found himself newly aware of spider webs.

Owls' nests and those of other birds were everywhere. Mindful of snakes, he usually kept his eyes to the ground and kept clear of fallen debris. At one point a motion caught his eye some forty feet above and to his right, and he realized with horror and fascination that a huge, shiny green constrictor more than fifty feet long was moving among the heavy branches in search of food. And another and another—and he realized dozens of massive snakes traversed the intertwined branches high above him.

Once again, it grew late. With daylight fading, he decided to find a good place to stop for the night, assuming there *was* a good place. The forest ahead of him began to thin considerably, and within a few minutes he came to a wide clearing irregularly filled with thick, knee-high grasses.

Stone rubble spread before him in odd, evenly distributed piles, beginning just within the forest growth and extending for as far as he could see into the meadow. Finding the uneven remains of a low stone wall partially hidden within the tall grass, T. G. wearily sat down and rubbed his feet, pondering the site, wondering if it would make a safe stopping place for the night. He had not had a drink since leaving the river and his dry throat ached, but he knew that the morning mists awaited and he could find water then.

A large, dark, squarish form just ahead drew his attention, rising from the sea of grasses. From a distance, he studied the granite pedestal, some eight feet high, broken and spotted with gray-green mosses. An intricate and ornate legend had once been carved into its forward face, he could tell, but the wording there had been brutally defaced and was now illegible, save part of one line:

IN SAFETY SHALL MINE DWELL

From atop the fractured, rectangular block rose a beautifully carved pair of sandaled feet and the lowermost part of a pair of armored legs, amputated unevenly just above the ankle. Rubble surrounded the pedestal, hidden within the tall grasses, the apparent, pulverized remains of the statue itself. T. G. estimated that the ancient and long-forgotten sculpture must once have towered some sixty feet into the air, dwarfing whatever other structures had filled the clearing.

Looking down, he studied the scattered fragments of rock debris nestled amid the grasses and clover. He wondered what battle, what war had created the destruction around him.

It was then that he noticed something else. An object rested immediately to his right, leaning against the broken rock wall upon which he sat. It had not been there a moment before.

It was the Gift.

"You?" he asked aloud, picking it up. "Why?"

T. G. held it in his lap, seeing that it was fully sealed once more, just as it had been long before, on Earth. He looked up at the darkening sky and the emerging stars.

"Why?" he asked, his eyes moist. "I don't understand…I mean, I ruined *everything*. I don't deserve this…"

Then he understood. He had not ruined everything. He had not given the Dark a final victory.

He had been forgiven.

By grace, he was still the Voice in the Dark, despite everything.

As he studied the tooled leather of the artifact as if seeing it for the first time, T. G. became aware of a subtle noise behind him. It was an odd sound, a living hiss of air.

Air within nostrils. Big nostrils.

He slowly turned and looked back. And up. His heart pounded. His face went ghostly white. His mind froze.

Less than five feet behind him and eight feet above, the enormous toothy head of a golden-skinned carnosaur hung, sniffing him curiously as if struggling to identify a possible meal.

T. G. stared, petrified, into the wet, yellow eyes of the Acrocanthosaur that considered him. The clawed, two-legged beast began to breathe through its mouth, clouding the air around T. G. with the damp, oppressive stench of rotting flesh. Scattered shreds of sinew hung between its teeth. Faint stains of blood smeared its enormous snout.

It had just eaten *something*. And it was still hungry.

After a beat, the huge creature looked away, flexing its three-clawed hands, as if feigning disinterest—in a test to see if its potential second course would make a move.

It did.

Blood flowed back into T. G.'s brain and he leaped to his feet, prompting an immediate response in the monstrous animal. Its jaws opened as its powerful, ground-shaking, seven-ton bulk suddenly lunged forward, snapping shut dead on target—

—but catching only air.

In surprise, T. G. watched as the great hulk nosed around the stone wall for a few minutes, roaring again and again, trying to dislodge its meal from the grasses. The man had shifted instinctively and found sanctuary on the other side of the clearing, where he crouched behind a tree trunk. The massive beast, now more than three hundred feet away, snorted and bellowed in confused frustration before giving up and disappearing into the forest from which it had come.

I shifted! T. G. realized.

A close call, but it was over. T. G. began to breathe again, sweating profusely, jelly-legged, hands shaking, taking the next twenty minutes to lie there and recover. He wanted to run, to keep moving, but his body cried out in protest and fought against him. The stars grew brighter. The night grew deeper.

If you shift, the Dark will know!

A new sound filled the air, an electric droning like the buzzing of a massive swarm of bees. T. G. looked up to see hundreds of silvery hoversteeds coming over the treetops, taking position, settling onto the far side of the clearing before him. He had seen the things many times before. They were the Watchers' personal air-assault vehicle of choice, a flying motorcycle more than anything else. Upon each rode a government soldier in light combat armor, black-lacquered and menacing.

They had seen T. G. already. There was no point in running. The hoversteeds were too fast, and another shift would only draw them to his new location.

Most landed, but some remained airborne. Hundreds of glaring floodlights blazed to life, clearly revealing the huddled fugitive to all.

In the distance, one soldier, their commander, a Deathlord, dismounted. He walked forward a few steps, facing T. G., and stood his ground.

"T. G. Shass," his magnified voice boomed. "You are ordered to surrender by order of the Prime Lord."

As the hunted man crouched, considering his next move, a voice softly spoke within his mind.

The time has come to face them. I am with you.

He momentarily closed his eyes in praise. Then, taking a deep breath, he stood on wearied legs and began walking toward the commander, the Gift slung upon his shoulder. He continued into the lights and approached the helmeted leader of the force, walking between the low, overgrown piles of stone rubble and past the Watchers parked far to his left and right. The hoversteeds that had been holding station among the stars overhead landed behind him as he moved deeper into the clearing, cutting off his only physical lane of escape.

He reached the center of the meadow and stopped, his jaw rigidly set, ten feet from the huge, imposing Deathlord facing him. The armored warrior, his hardened bodysuit glistening an oily black in the cold light of the hoversteeds, stared at the Voice from behind the glowing, electric red lenses of his helmet.

The more curious of the mounted Watchers looked upon the ancient stone pedestal and the huge, dismembered feet atop it, and read the remains of its inscription. Its significance was lost on them. They did not understand and could not hear. Their world had forgotten. Silently, the stone sentinel stood by and bore no witness to them of another day and another showdown, a final confrontation that, even then, had set in motion the final judgment of their world.

The Dark had lost that day.

"Give me the Gift," the Deathlord demanded.

T. G. heard the crackle of hundreds of ripsticks charging up.

"And you'll let me live, right?" T. G. mockingly stated.

"You have been sentenced to death for crimes against mankind. You are a false prophet, inciting insurrection and treason against the Unified World."

T. G. stood firm, gripping the Gift a little more tightly.

"Leave now," T. G. admonished them all, his voice stern and level. "While you can."

The Deathlord looked at his second-in-command, who stood off to one side, ripstick drawn. "We have a funny one here," he said. Turning back to T. G., he impatiently held a hand out. "Enough. Do as I command."

The Voice did not move. Anger boiled within the Deathlord. *How dare he defy the Prime Lord!* He stepped closer, his hand still out. "Give it to me!"

"Last chance," the absurd warning came again from the little man. The warriors advanced.

I am with you!

T. G. felt a rush of warmth within him. His senses were heightened. The world fell into slow motion.

The Deathlord lost patience and grabbed a ripstick from another soldier, whirling in the same motion to level it at the Voice.

It was his last act.

T. G. threw his head back and his arms out, fists clenched. The chilling cold and searing heat instantly filled not only his arms but his entire body, locking every muscle into rigid stone. A crushing pressure against his chest and ears built with every passing microsecond, making it impossible to breathe or hear. His eyes, shut tight, nonetheless knew a brilliant glare that flooded them, growing brighter and more intense with each beat of his racing heart.

It lasted only moments.

The pressure vanished. The light faded. T. G. felt a hot breeze and began to breathe again. His arms fell. His muscles went limp. He opened his eyes.

What he saw dropped him to his knees. An intense awe totally overwhelmed him. Shaking, struggling, he began to wail, sobbing uncontrollably.

He had not moved, but the spot upon which he knelt was now a tiny plateau, the six-foot-wide summit of a ten-story spire, the central peak of a circular pit that surrounded him for a width of 300 feet and to a depth of 150. The chasm was lined with the thick, irregular glass of fused, melted sand, which glowed a dark, dull red as it cooled. Only the plateau under him had been left untouched, its grasses blowing in the gentle breeze. Wisps of acrid smoke rose into the gentle night air.

The soldiers, the hoversteeds, the clearing, and what remained of the statue and the ancient village were all gone, utterly consumed by the same infinite power that once had called their world into existence.

After a time, T. G. stood, gathered himself, then shifted to the outer edge of the huge pit. The voice of Ish then spoke within his mind, and he turned and began toward a new destination.

As he did so, a pair of glowing blue eyes watched him from the shadows of the surrounding forest. The owner of those eyes knew that a window of opportunity had passed. It was too late.

The Voice walked away into the darkness.

W hy?"

Cordan Barthos paced nervously before the panoramic
window, looking out over the lush gardens behind the Shass
home and into the night sky beyond. Despite the dozens of armed
Watchers stationed all around the house, his world suddenly felt
less secure, less controlled. A contagion had been freed and was out
there somewhere, a disease that would infect the entire planet if not
contained.

It was the only disease utterly fatal to the Dark.

"Why, Cordan?" Paull Shass repeated angrily, looking up from his
plush living-room chair, where he sat waving a stack of papers in the
air. It was after two in the morning, and the Prime Lord was tired. "As
far as I can see, T. G. was doing exactly what we wanted him to do.
These reports all indicate that. Why did he run?"

"I don't know. Something woke him up."

"You should have killed them all, Cordan," Shass said, tossing the
documents onto a low table and rising to his feet. "As long as *any* of
them live, they are a threat to everything we have built and everything
we still must do. I do not know why I let you convince me otherwise."

"Bargaining tools," Barthos insisted. "It *will* come down to that.
I see no reason to destroy a weapon simply because it could conceiv-
ably be used against us. If we're careful, it will do far more damage in
our hands than it would in theirs."

"It is too much of a risk!" Shass replied. "Once the Gift was
given, a countdown began. The Elesh woman knows too much of
what is to come, and we do not know how much of the Truth got
out. If she managed to complete a translation…no! I want her dead!
Now!"

"The Voice will move against us…and soon. We must keep our

heads and keep the tactical advantage. We will force him to limit *himself.*"

"And how do we do that?"

"By exploiting his weaknesses. But Elesh may provide an additional assurance that things will happen as we wish."

"All right, then," Shass angrily conceded. "Keep her alive. But I hate this, Cordan…that woman could still be the key to this god of theirs becoming known to the world again."

"Drosha still reigns, and everything has been carefully orchestrated to create the appearance that she has handed dominion over to you. You are 'chosen' now in the eyes of the people, and from there it's a short step to godhood. The whole world sees you as its savior now."

Barthos calmly took a seat, continuing to reassure his superior. "We have to stay with the plan. We give the people just enough so that they will trust in you and will follow you blindly. We continue to create the illusion of an impending end to the class system, throwing bones to those who think a better world is on the way. By the time they realize that it isn't going to happen, it will be too late. You will have total power and will be unreachable. Those with any ability to marshal forces against us will be kept happy, or they will be eliminated. There can be no overthrow. With a single army and a single union of nations now before us, there is no longer anyone left to challenge you."

"We must accelerate our timetable. We no longer have the luxury of letting things unfold naturally. If T. G. reveals himself to the world as the Voice in the Dark before we can silence him—"

"Using the information we found, a systematic search is underway for those who followed the Twelve. They should be eliminated within the month. The Voice will find no ear to hear him if we handle this correctly, so leave it to me. All who know that the Voice walks among us will be dead before he has a chance to threaten us. He cannot defeat us alone."

The men continued to discuss their rise to power, their voices carrying farther than they had intended. They did not know that another set of ears, awakened from sleep, had been standing unseen and unsuspected, listening in stunned and fearful silence to the monstrous words of the supposedly noble leaders.

Tears streamed down Sereen's cheeks as she quietly slipped away down the long hallway and back into her bedroom. She would not be seeing her husband that night—he seldom slept at home. When he did, he bedded down on a couch in his office, at the far end of the house. She slid back into bed, wide awake, unable to stop thinking about all she had heard.

The husband she had known and loved was dead to her.

Worse than that, she now feared him—and for her very life.

Her world had been torn apart, shredded, by Paull's words. She cried again, burying her face in her pillow, weeping until she was exhausted and could weep no more.

Her final thoughts, before sleep closed in, were of the one person to whom she could turn, a person she had not spoken to for a long, long time, a person who now needed her as well. She wanted to bolt, to run from the house, to go at once to her port in this storm. But she forced herself to stay put for the moment. She could not risk raising suspicions. She could not let the Prime Lord know that she *knew.*

Sleep finally came, sleep that she was going to need.

There was much to be done.

∞

The ground was blackened. The heavy odor of burned wood hung in the still air, reminding T. G. of burning autumn leaves. The scent had always been a happy one for him, but no more.

Now it smelled of death and stupidity and betrayal.

He stood surveying the ruined library, deep within the Fire Zone, far from the clearing where Ish's power had been made manifest. What plant regrowth had once surrounded the building was gone, leaving newly charred remains that betrayed the attack that had recently taken place there. With the artifact slung over his shoulder, he walked slowly through the debris, kicking stone fragments and carbonized lumber aside in frustration, knowing that he may as well have torched the place himself.

"I killed them," T. G. thought aloud, his heart heavy with the realization.

Finding a stairwell into the stone foundation, he carefully proceeded downward, descending only as far as the available light would allow. The room below dropped away into darkness, and the part of it he could see was no more than a clutter of fallen timbers and chunks of plaster. A light pallor of smoke still hung tenuously in the air.

The burden of what he had brought about through his pride and foolishness weighed upon his shoulders, far more than the artifact ever had. All he saw were the faces of the Twelve in that underground chamber that night, as they had looked upon him in the wondrous realization that their Voice had come. Faces. Eyes. He could not shut them out. And then, despite all T. G. had done wrong, Ish had still come to him in the forest, saving his life twice—once through a burst of majestic power beyond T. G.'s comprehension.

He walked back up and into the gentle morning light to find Ish sitting to one side on the former library steps.

"I did this," T. G. mourned. "You sent me here so I could see for myself."

"When one becomes a part of the light," Ish began, "he illuminates those who follow him. Should he turn away from that light, he blocks it instead, casting darkness upon the others." He paused a moment, letting T. G. think about that. "Your position carries a vast responsibility. You must never forget that."

"People died. People who looked to me, trusted me. People who waited all their lives for me to show up. I'll have to live with what I've done for the rest of my life."

"Those who died are in no pain. They are with *us.*"

"I can't believe I was so foolish. I let myself trust the Dark. I fell for it all…hook, line and sinker. They used me, and I never even suspected it." He looked at the seated figure. "Why didn't you tell me I was going wrong?"

"You never asked me. Not once, during all those months, did you call upon me. I was with you, yet you were not with me."

He knew Ish was right. He hung his head. "I was so sure. Of everything. You're right. I never thought to check with you. I assumed you had a hand in everything that was happening because it all seemed so perfect." He sat beside his blue-robed friend. "So you didn't heal Paull Shass after all?"

Ish shook his head. "You would be amazed by the 'miracles' the Dark can perform. Many things we do, it can counterfeit. It will heal, grant wishes, or bestow wealth or worldly pleasures—and these 'miracles' are usually presented as if they had come from us. The Dark will even praise the name of the Creator if its purposes demand it."

"I figured Paull was too important to die," T. G. said. "I was sure you'd done it. I never gave his recovery a second thought."

"Healings are not given based upon any measure of personal merit, but only in accordance with the will of the Father. Even among those who belong to us, not all are healed of their afflictions, for differing reasons. For some, their sufferings or deaths lead to the eternal salvation of others whose lives they have touched. There is a plan in place, T. G., and each life has a part in that plan.

"It is difficult for human pride to accept the fact that, although all prayer is answered, sometimes the answer is 'no.' That which a man thinks he wants is seldom what he really needs. Too often, when a believer is given that which he desires, he becomes too comfortable, loses focus, and immerses himself in the world around him. The Dark knows this well."

The young prophet was humbled. "Well, I sure fell for it." He paused, considering what he had done. "No, I didn't fall for it. I walked right into it with my eyes wide open."

"Mankind usually does. There's nothing new under the sun, T. G.

Your senses overrode your judgment. You heard what you wanted to hear, and you were given your every desire. You filtered everything that subsequently happened to you—everything you heard, everything you saw—through a bias you let them create within you. It has happened time and again throughout your world's history, and millions have been deluded and have lost their lives as a result." He nodded sadly. "You are not the first. You are, however, among the last."

"It had to be the phone call," T. G. realized, thinking of the raid on the library. "I should have known better than to believe that Paull Shass had changed his stripes. They must have been waiting months for me to contact the underground. I led them directly to Pretsal, who led them to the Twelve." He fearfully looked to Ish. Hopeful words stumbled from his lips. "Pretsal…where is he? Is he safe?" His tone dropped into one of dreadful expectation. "Or did I kill him too?"

"He is in hiding, safely making final preparations, along with others. You will see him shortly."

T. G. breathed a heavy sigh of relief. "Some Voice in the Dark I turned out to be. Well, I won't make that mistake again."

"Moses made mistakes. David made mistakes. Peter made mistakes. All serious, all with their consequences, and often others suffered or died because of them. Yet all those mistakes were forgiven and overcome, and great things followed. Yours have been and will be too. Mourn, but make an end of your grief. There is much to be done, and you must remain focused."

"I trust you with my life," T. G. swore, clutching the artifact tightly. "Ask anything, and I'll do it. I will *not* serve the Dark again."

"I know."

He considered the Gift. "Why do I have *this* back? I mean, Darafine finished the translation, and surely copies have been circulated by now."

"Credentials. No one but the Voice in the Dark can carry that among the people. Once the Truth has become known to all, they will know from its prophecies that I have sent you. Just as it was a sign for the Twelve, it will be a sign for all." He smiled. "You may even wish to read it. I have given you the gift of the Old Tongue."

T. G. looked down at the artifact, seeing it with new eyes. Suddenly, the words tooled into its surface were plainly legible.

The Truth, written that man may know the love of He Who made him.

He looked aside, turning his gaze away. "I'm…sorry, Ish. I must have disappointed you so badly. You trusted me…"

Ish smiled. "We do not remember what you did."

"I don't know how you put up with me," T. G. commented. "Are you my guardian angel or something? I never really asked. I guess I've been taking *everything* for granted lately. Please. I'd like to know."

"T. G.," Ish said, rising to his feet, "it is time you knew me."

A burst of new light flared into existence around Ish. T. G. leaped to his feet and backed away a few steps as the man became engulfed in the fiery brilliance. It was like a second sunrise. Watching, transfixed, T. G. squinted and brought his hands up as the light against his eyes became heat against his face as well.

He fell to the ground, covering his head and face. He felt the pinprick warmth of the infinite yet contained power as it played upon his entire body. An unearthly electricity crawled like thousands of hurried ants upon his skin. He could not look, could not speak, could not move. His heart pounded, leaping against his breastbone so hard it hurt. His tightly closed eyes filled with light.

And he *knew.*

"Rise, T. G.," a resonant, infinite voice said. "Look upon me. Don't be afraid."

Slowly, he rose to his feet, soot from the ground blackening his clothes, arms, and face. The blinding glare no longer hurt his eyes, and its warmth even became comforting. Within the radiance he saw a gently smiling face, and his eyes beheld the man's hands as they were held outward.

Something was there upon them, deep scars etched by the cruelty and hatred of men who knew not what they did.

The figure stood patiently, letting his chosen prophet have all the time he needed. T. G. finally found his voice.

"You're...I mean, you're...you're..." The words struggled from his lips. "You...you...*are*..."

"Yes, T. G. *I am.*"

The words were powerful, knocking T. G. backward with a tangible force. He ran them again and again through his mind, weighing the full implication of the simple statement.

I AM...the self-spoken name of God.

The chosen prophet took a few steps closer to the Figure and looked into the unfathomable wisdom of his Lord's eyes, not knowing what to say next.

T. G. struggled to fully seize upon the fact of just Whom it was Who had chosen him. It was too big. "It was You, wasn't it...Who spoke to Abraham...and Moses...the burning bush...and David ...and...Paul..." He paused in wonder. "And...raised the dead, and..." He trembled in awe. "And...died..." He gazed into the loving eyes, then at the wounds in his hands. "Crucified."

His voice trailed off, becoming a shaky whisper, and he wept. "Forgive me. I was so wrong...when I—"

"Losing your parents hurt more than you could express, I know. You suffered much, and your pain made you doubt Me. You believed, in your youth, but after your parents' deaths you were angry. You turned away. Yet I stayed with you through it all, for you were Mine, and I *never* leave My own."

Ish then reached out, and T. G. went to Him. The comforting embrace he found in those arms—the very arms that had forged the universe itself—swept away his sorrows, his pain, his doubts.

Ish looked down into the face of His chosen. "You are My prophet, My Voice, chosen before the foundation of the world was laid. You always will be."

After a few moments, the embrace ended. The glow surrounding Ish faded, leaving a momentary warmth in the air. T. G., his knees weak and unsteady, lowered himself to the stone library steps and sat at the feet of his Lord. After a few moments, Ish joined him.

They sat there for nearly half an hour before a humbled and astonished T. G. could formulate another question or utter another syllable.

"Ish, where do I go from here? What do I do now?"

Ish stood. "You are ready. You will go into the world, and tell them that the Awakening is upon them."

"But I blew it. They'll kill me. The second they see me, they'll kill me."

"What happened at the clearing was only a foretaste of what now follows. You are Our witness. Henceforth, no harm can befall you that you do not allow, so long as you continue to draw upon Me. Those who would see you killed cannot take your life from you. You are immune to their attacks. The forces of nature and all power are now at your disposal. Use them wisely. You have a mission, and you will complete it. The time has come to bring the people back to the Truth. You will personally lead the world away from the Dark. Nothing will stop that."

T. G. looked down at his hands, flexing his fingers as if testing them. "I can't be killed? I don't feel any different…"

"Feelings mean nothing. Your senses mean nothing. I have told you the truth, and it stands alone. Without corroboration. Without majority approval. Without compromise."

Several silent moments passed, and T. G. took one last look around. With new resolve, anchored in the knowledge of Who was with him, he took a deep breath of the cool air and looked up at the pink sky.

The war had escalated—and not for the last time.

∽∘∾

The elevator dropped soundlessly deeper, headed toward the buried complex of sublevels where the government prison lay. The car slid down a heavily reinforced synthecrete-and-steel shaft that was impenetrable, with a single door at the top and one at the bottom. Two hundred feet, then three hundred flew by before the car finally and gently slowed, coming to a complete stop thirty-four levels beneath the foundation of the World Capitol.

It was the most secure penitentiary on the planet. One way in— one way out.

As the elevator doors slid open, Sereen Shass took a deep breath. What she was doing was risky at best, suicidal at worst. But she had to try, for she believed that only in succeeding here did her planet's salvation—and her own—lie. It would be her only opportunity to act, for both Barthos and her husband were out of the country, on an inspection tour of a new industrial complex in Kamir. They would be back in two days.

If all went well, she would be gone in one.

She stepped out of the elevator and into the heavily guarded lobby. Watchers at the security station recognized her immediately, rising to their feet in respect as she approached. She wore a draped gossamer veil of sunburst yellow over her head and face, and carried a small matching purse. Her body was wrapped tightly in short silken robes of green and yellow that hung only to midthigh. Her honey hair shone in the controlled light.

The men looked upon the woman's classically exquisite form as she neared them, walking as only a beautiful, confident woman can. Their lustful thoughts were held somewhat in check by the fact that her husband could end their lives with no more than a nod.

Sereen casually surveyed the bank of circular monitoring screens that lined the wall behind the security desk. Each was assigned to an occupied high-security cell and provided a constant two-dimensional image of anything a prisoner might say or do.

"Kira Shass," the security chief said. "We were not expecting you."

"Prosperity, gentlemen," she said, her voice heavy with the authority of her position. "I have come to see the Elesh woman."

"Forgive me, but we were given a general order to hold her in isolation, with no visitors."

"I am well aware of that. My husband does not want her bizarre ideologies infecting any of the other prisoners. How anyone can be as deluded as she, I do not know," she said in a heavily disapproving tone. "I, however, am immune to the disease she carries, and I wish to speak to her. I want this heretic to know that her feeble attempts to undermine my husband's authority will not go unpunished."

She saw doubt still playing upon their faces and addressed the security chief more directly. "Tell me, Maran, when was the last time one of my husband's general orders applied to me?"

"Well…"

"I intend to go in there, say my piece, and be gone. I have an appointment for dinner in one hour, which leaves me little time to stand here arguing with you. Must I contact my husband and bring him into this?"

At that the chief nodded and one of his subordinates motioned for the woman to follow. He led her down a stark, cold corridor, lit only by the chill of pale blue light strips. Their footsteps echoed as they took a right turn and entered the Isolation Unit, which, like the entire facility, had been chiseled directly into the thick layer of black granite bedrock upon which the city rested.

The Watcher pointed to a plate on the wall, next to a reinforced door. "Place your hand there, Kira Shass," he directed. As she did so he simultaneously pressed his palm into an identical plate some ten feet away. The door slowly swung open. "The security system has memorized you now. You have full access within this block for twenty minutes. I would suggest, however, that you not open the door to her cell."

"Do you think me a fool, Garthon?" she asked in a highly irritated tone, subtly reminding the man that she, and therefore her husband, knew his name.

"Oh…no, Kira Shass," he almost pleaded. "Not at all. I am sorry…it is simply that—"

"What else, Garthon?" she asked, feigning the regal impatience the man expected from her.

"By pressing the plate just inside the cellblock door, you may leave anytime you are ready." He pointed into the block corridor. "Elesh is the only one in there…she will not be hard to find. Do you wish me to accompany you?"

"No. I do not need my hand held. I have a great deal to say to that woman, and what I say is for her wretched ears alone. I want complete privacy, which means no monitoring in this section. No sound, no picture. Especially no sound. Is that understood?"

The order was unusual, but she was who she was. "Understood, Kira Shass," the man said, nodding in respect. "It will be as you say." He turned and walked away, leaving the woman alone to enter the cellblock.

Upon his return to the security station, the Watcher reached over and touched a jeweled plate, disabling the audiovisual monitor.

"What are you doing?" the security chief asked. "You are shutting down surveillance in that whole block!"

"Kira Shass ordered it for the duration of her visit."

"Why?"

"I would assume that she intends to say a few choice things to the prisoner, using language that would be considered somewhat beneath her station," the man smiled. "She is not in the best of moods."

"I do not like it."

"Then *you* go tell her that."

The monitor stayed off.

Sereen made her way along the bare corridor, peering into each cell as she passed. All were empty. Finally, she found the woman she sought, and lifted the veil from her face. She noticed that the tiny blue indicator light on the monitoring unit, high on the wall within the cell, was dark. No one was watching.

Elesh was huddled over the basin, drinking from cupped hands. Sereen silently stood for a moment, watching, allowing the prisoner time to notice her.

Darafine turned and caught sight of the woman's bright clothing from the corner of her eye. Turning fully in surprise, she wiped the water from her chin with the back of a hand. She brushed her dark hair back out of her face. Their eyes met and locked. No one spoke for several uncomfortable moments.

"Hello, Janella," Sereen said, looking upon the woman's tattered, sooty robes. "You look well, considering."

"I am surprised to see you," she replied. "And it is 'Darafine' now."

"So I understand. I must say, I knew you would end up in here, sooner or later."

"Everyone keeps saying that."

"How long has it been?"

"Forty years."

"It seems longer. I am only sorry that it took a situation like this to force…" She paused for a moment. "Janella, there is something that I need to say—"

"Darafine."

The blonde woman nodded. "Darafine," she began again. "I hope you can understand. I have given this much thought. Because of your personal convictions, I think I have always known that something like this would be necessary, one day…"

She reached into her purse.

Fifteen minutes later, those at the security station watched as the influential woman nodded and walked past, headed toward the lone elevator. Discreetly, they continued to watch her curvaceous, fluid form from behind, greatly enjoying the feminine vision their eyes beheld—the short figure-hugging robes, the sexy veil, the flowing blonde hair, those long, luscious legs. Rank did indeed have its privileges, for she was, without a doubt, a woman fit to be seen on the arm of the leader of the world.

The security chief reactivated the monitoring units in Elesh's cell-block. The assigned screen was instantly filled with a view of the prisoner as she lay huddled on her cot, her unkempt brown hair hanging in her face. *What a waste,* the man thought. *That one is not so bad looking, either.* His primal mind filled with images as he leered at her—brutal imaginings of having his way with her, there in her cell and unseen by anyone, her screams unheard as they echoed down the cold stone cellblock.

The powerful woman disappeared into the elevator, and the doors closed. At once, chatter about her obvious physical attributes broke out among the men, who laughed and shared comments as lewd and suggestive as they each felt they could get away with.

In her cell, the other woman thought about what she had done with her life, about the events and the decisions that had landed her there. There was no going back, not now. What would befall her, she did not know for certain, but that was secondary. She knew that she had done what she had to do, that her secret had remained secure. She lay still, listening for alarms or some other sign that something had gone wrong. None sounded, and a joy filled her as she came to realize that none would.

Sereen faced away from the monitoring unit, not moving, feigning sleep. Her hair, now dark, hung in her eyes. She hoped they were watching her, so arrogant and so sure of themselves, never suspecting a woman had deceived them. The longer their masculine pride swelled within them, the more time Sereen would be able to buy.

Her sister, now free, would need it.

∽✺∾

Pretsal carried the huge wooden crate over to where the others had been stacked and set it down. It was all there—power cells, focusing crystals, lens assemblies, electronics packages, and everything else they were going to need for the next battle in their war against the Dark.

The relocation of the underground forces had gone smoothly. Darafine's knowledge of the Old Tongue had allowed her to interpret a small cache of historical military documents discovered by the Twelve centuries earlier, giving them the locations of several long-forgotten installations spread across Noron's single continent.

The room, nestled within the lower levels of a former munitions complex deep in the northern wilderness, was slowly becoming the nerve center of operations for both the Twelve and the Truth. It had lain empty for millennia, forgotten after an ancient war, situated next to a clearing beneath the dense, overspreading jungle forest above. The facility, built underground and well hidden, was heavily rein-forced and constructed of cast synthecrete, cut stone, and steel. It was perfect for the electronic assault the Twelve was about to launch against the Prime Lord.

"Is that the last of it?" T. G. asked, walking into the room, the Gift hanging from his shoulder. "When will it be ready to go?"

"This is all," Pretsal nodded, slapping his hands against each other. The heaviness of centuries-old dust filled his nostrils. "Josan will have to oversee its construction…he once worked in a schooling center, where equipment like this was used. I would expect that it will be a couple of weeks before we are ready."

"And this will take us worldwide, right?" T. G. asked, walking up to him. He set the artifact on one of the crates. "Everyone must hear."

"We'll use the atmospheric canopy as a reflector, as the simulight broadcast centers do. By bouncing the signal that way, it will be picked up by the relay grid used by the government. We can even use the World network frequency if we choose, but I would suggest we not do so for too long at a time. They may be able to set up a trace."

A blonde woman in green and yellow entered, pulling her veil away as she approached the two men.

"Sereen…?" T. G. puzzled aloud, a bit fearfully. *They found us! How did they find us?*

She grew closer. The woman's smile was a wonder to behold.

"Darafine!" T. G. joyfully realized. He rushed forward and embraced her. "I thought you were...I thought the worst."

Pretsal extended a comforting arm, and she hugged him as well. "We had heard horrible things," the gentle giant said. "We feared you had been killed along with the others."

"No," she said. "Not dead, just shaken. I surely would have been, though, had Sereen not freed me." She looked around. "I hoped you had relocated here. Of the possible sites we discussed, this is the most secure. We should be safe."

"Sereen, you said?" T. G. asked, surprised. "*She* freed you...?"

"Yes. She smuggled a colorwand into my cell, and we exchanged both clothing and hair color. She used her palm print to open the doors to the cell and the prison block for me, before sealing herself in. I took her place, and she took mine."

"That took guts," he said.

"You must go to her, T. G. You alone can help her. They will kill her as soon as they discover the deception. I am sure of it, and many hours have already passed." Her glance fell to the floor. "They tortured the others. They may be dead by now. Poor Josan. To have suffered as he did..."

"It was only a broken leg," a calm and familiar voice said from behind, "and barely a limp to show for it, thanks to our good doctor. Good as new."

Darafine spun to see Josan and several others walking into the room, carrying boxes of perishable food supplies. Noron's medical science had allowed his broken tibia to knit in minutes, making a cast or crutches unnecessary. Momentarily confused, she could only stare at his handsome smiling face as he approached on two good legs. She ran to him and held him tightly, as she had thought she never would again.

"Thank the Creator you are safe," he said, returning her embrace. "We were fearful that you would be tortured...and worse."

"But how? How did you escape the prison?" She grabbed his

hands and held them up before her, finding all ten of his fingers healthy and intact.

"Prison?"

"Yes. Barthos said—"

"They did not capture me. They did not know I was there and did not conduct much of a search. The soldiers all seemed to be in a hurry to get out of the library and out of Jerithia for some reason. Perhaps angels scared them, yes?"

"What *did* happen?"

"After the corridor collapsed I was pinned there, under a pile of debris and fallen ceiling beams. I would still be there had Pretsal not come to the Fire Zone, or had he not been so thorough in his search of the library's sublevels. Those were fifteen hours I would not like to live through again."

"Barthos…that monster!" Darafine said. "He lied. Made me think they had captured you and were torturing you. He tried to use you as a weapon against me, and he did not even have you!"

"Sounds about right," T. G. commented.

"As you can see, I am quite safe," Josan continued, "and we have no missing friends. Everyone we lost has been accounted for." His tone became more serious. "Twenty-six were killed in the attack, and the soldiers left them lying where they had fallen. We brought them here, where we can give them a proper and grateful farewell."

"At least Barthos can no longer hurt our friends," Darafine said sadly.

"No, he cannot," Josan said, missing them. He saw their faces in his mind, their smiles. "Despite the chancellor's words, it would appear that only *you* were captured."

"Please, help Sereen," she implored T. G., turning to him. "You have to save my sister."

"Sister?"

"Please, T.G, you have to help her," the woman pleaded. "Go to her."

"*Sister?*"

A voice sounded gently in his mind, not audibly yet clearly.

Sereen is to join us, T. G. She has turned from the world, as you did. She saved her sister at the risk of her own life, as was meant to be. The spiritual shielding that prevents the Dark from sensing the location of the Twelve will also allow you to shift away from this place and back without detection. Go to Sereen. Bring her home.

"Okay," T. G. said. "I'll bring her back here. Pretsal, would she be in the same prison where you and I were jailed on my last visit?"

"She would have to be, yes. There's only one government detention facility in Keltrian. She's probably in the high-security section, though...two levels beneath where you and I were held."

"Yes," Darafine confirmed. "Cell 1102. Sublevel 3."

T. G. took a deep breath. "Okay," he said. "I'll get her. Josan, get your people busy assembling this equipment. The sooner we start, the sooner we can get on the air."

" 'On the air'...I like that," Pretsal smiled.

"It will be done," Josan answered, nodding in respect.

"On the air," Pretsal repeated, tickled.

"Watch my stuff," the Voice said with a smile, indicating the artifact. Then he was gone, as if he had never been there at all. The eyes of the others went wide.

"That is a bit unsettling," Josan admitted. "Seeing him just vanish like that."

"You would be surprised what one can get used to," Pretsal said, gently resting his hand on the artifact. "Doesn't bother me at all."

Josan turned to Darafine, his eyes studying her with some amusement. "Hmmm," he mused.

"What?" she asked.

"I think I *like* you as a blonde."

∽◊∾

Seven long hours had passed since Darafine's escape, and it was after midnight. A weary Sereen stirred, always cautious to keep her face angled away from the monitor. Hours before, food, such as it was, had been left at the top of the steps leading down into the cell, and it was only her extreme hunger that finally compelled her to eat. A hard roll and a few strips of dried meat were the entirety of her meal, accompanied by water from the wash basin.

Just as she forced down the last of the dry, flavorless bread, she suddenly became aware of another presence in the cell. She turned to see T. G. standing there, a smile on his face.

"T. G.!" she cried, startled. "How did you…?"

"Hello, Sereen," he said, beaming at her, so proud he could burst. "Ready to come home?"

"Home…" Her voice trailed off as she understood. "It is all true. You *are* who they said you were. They said there were prophecies, but until now, I did not really…" She rushed to him. As they embraced, her attention was drawn to the monitor light. "They will see and hear us. They will know you are here."

"No, they won't. Trust me."

She relaxed a little. "Darafine reached safety then?"

"Yes, she's fine. I came for you as soon as she told us how you'd freed her. We're all very grateful for what you have done." He smiled anew. "Sounds like you've had quite a day. You shake your personal Watchers, enter the most secure prison in the world, get them to shut off the security system, and pull the old 'switching clothes' trick. Jim Phelps would be proud. Good thing you're on our side."

She smiled. Once more, he was taken by her beauty.

"You and Darafine look so much alike," he observed. "I never noticed it before, but I can really see the family resemblance now that I know. Especially with your hair dark like that. Sure fooled the guards."

"I had to get her out of here. I did not know how or where to find you, but I knew *she* could, if anyone." Sereen glanced downward, remembering. "Janella and I last saw each other so long ago…before she changed her name to protect the rest of us. My family disowned her. Forgot her. Now I know she was right. I heard Paull and Cordan talking about her…and about you." She smiled, lighting up the cell. "She *was* right, T. G. You really are the Voice in the Dark that she always said would come."

"Yes, Sereen."

"And *I* was right," she said, recalling her first conversation with him in his hospital room. "You *are* special." She paused for a moment, thinking. "You must have known Janella was here. If you can move anywhere at will, as it would appear, why did you not just come here and free her yourself?"

"That was for you to do, and you did it. And now you're with us. You are set apart, Sereen. Few women on this world have your compassion or your conscience. And you are a woman of courage. You knew going in that they might well have killed you, had they found you here—Prime Lord's wife or no."

She shuddered, tears welling in her eyes. "How could I ever have loved him, T. G.? The things I heard him say the other night…how could I have been so deceived? It was as if the Paull I thought I knew was dead."

"The Paull you knew may well be." T. G. took her hand, comforting her for a few quiet moments, then he changed the subject. "What do you say we blow this joint and grab a pizza?" He enjoyed her puzzled expression. "Never mind," he smiled. "Come on…friends are waiting."

"Who is Jim Phelps?" she asked.

They vanished in the twinkling of an eye. Several minutes later a young Watcher—a poor soul who as a result would lose not merely his job but his life—would discover the impossibly empty cell.

22

Are we ready?"

T. G. walked into the crowded chamber and found himself before a complex arrangement of polished crystalline forms as beautiful as they were intricate. Sparkling swords of emerald and ruby lanced toward him, glowing with an odd iridescence that splashed shifting rainbows upon his face. The precise collector matrix would gather the myriad patterns of information necessary for T. G.'s image to be broadcast as a true, fully dimensional representation. A crowded tangle of glowing conduits led from machinery bank to machinery bank, linking the varied components of the simulight system by a method that, to T. G.'s mind, could most kindly be referred to as jury-rigged.

"In just moments now," Josan replied, making adjustments to a similar array nearby. "It is almost ready. I apologize for the delay, but to assure worldwide transmission without detection, we have had to integrate several systems that were not designed to be used together. I have never known these varied components to be joined in such a fashion, but they should give us both the reach and the secrecy we need. The signal will constantly remodulate at a precise, random rate, allowing the simulight units out there to switch automatically as the signal does, yet prevent a trace from being carried out. As long as we do not transmit for more than six minutes per broadcast, our position will remain secret."

"Great," T. G. said, studying the array. "This is incredible. A whole different technological path from the one I know."

The prophet watched as Josan labored over the controls, his brow knitting repeatedly as he glanced again and again at small readouts and a simulight dome to his right. He seemed perplexed, possibly getting a response from his machinery other than that which he expected.

"Something wrong?" T. G. asked, rising to go to his side.

Josan made another adjustment and watched as some of the crystals jutting from his board changed color. "Nothing, really, I suppose. Nothing that will prevent what we are trying to do."

Pretsal walked into the room, taking large bites from a huge apple. "What is it?" he asked as he chewed, having picked up the last few words of the conversation. "Something wrong?"

Josan indicated a pattern on the display. "I am picking up an unusual effect as I skirt the upper fringes of the electromagnetic spectrum." He pointed to several indistinct anomalies in the energy patterns being read. "Do you see this?"

T. G. studied the display, unsure of what he was seeing. "What is it?"

Josan spoke deliberately, choosing his words. "It would appear that what we have stumbled upon is not a signal itself, but the *effect* of something upon the extreme upper limit of the EM spectrum... like a shadow."

"The shadow of what?" Pretsal asked.

"I do not know."

"Whatever is casting it lies far outside of any frequency range used for communications or industry anywhere in the world. I doubt it is natural. Odd how it seems to just barely whisper into the known spectrum, as if it lies primarily elsewhere. It is just a fluke that we found it at all."

"Elsewhere...where?" T. G. asked. Josan shrugged.

"Beyond the EM spectrum?" Pretsal asked, offering a bite of fruit to T. G., who declined. "Is that possible?"

"I've learned that there's very little that isn't," the prophet commented.

"What lies out there? What kind of energy?" Pretsal asked.

"Thought itself, maybe," T. G. speculated. "Consciousness. The intangible link between minds." He turned to Josan. "I mean, we know our thoughts are open to the Creator as well as to the Dark."

"Fascinating," Josan uttered. "You may be right."

"Where's it coming from? Any particular direction?"

"No way to know. Even though it is subtle, it is bathing the whole world, I would say. It may be coming from deep space, from outside. To lie where it does, above the upper threshold like that, I doubt the canopy would even slow it down." Josan scrutinized the erratic pulse more closely, frustrated that he could not discern its purpose. "It almost acts like some form of interference, the way its shadow lies upon the spectrum. I know that makes little sense."

A light bulb flared in T. G.'s mind. "Can you block it?"

"I do not know how we could," Josan replied. "I am beginning to doubt it is even part of the physical universe. It would take massive amounts of power to neutralize it, provided we could even construct the equipment necessary to do so, and that is not likely. But why jam it? It seems harmless enough, and since it is well beyond the frequencies we will be using, it is not in our way."

"Well, I'll be," the prophet smiled. "I think it's in *everyone's* way. Almost everyone's, anyway, except for those at the top. And I'd bet it's being generated right here on Noron, probably in the pyramid."

"What?" Pretsal asked, tossing his apple core into a nearby receptacle.

"At least now we know." He pointed to the display. "I'll bet you dollars to donuts this little squiggle is the reason you've all been losing your memories…and why your people can no longer reach their full mental potential."

Josan and Pretsal looked at each other. Was it really possible?

T. G. tapped his temple. "You're being jammed."

∽◦∾

It had been two weeks since the disappearance of the Voice.

And it had been almost that long since anyone had seen Kira Shass. Her last known act had been a puzzling visit to Elesh in her prison cell, after which she had departed alone. Mere hours later, the prisoner had also vanished without a trace. There was a connection there somehow. There had to be.

Cordan Barthos knew that the Voice had been behind the freeing of Elesh. No one else could have done it. Afterward, while trying to keep the loss of the prisoner quiet, Barthos had sent his agents worldwide, searching for any evidence of the vanished prophet or the two women. There had been no sign at all, and that worried him incessantly.

You're out there somewhere...waiting...

An angry Shass, as Barthos expected, had taken his wife's disappearance as an irritating distraction—aside from running the world, he now had to expend the time and energy necessary to appear as the concerned, grieving husband all of Noron expected him to be. He was far more worried that Elesh was free again, screaming repeatedly at Barthos that they should have killed her when they had the chance.

Barthos shrugged it off. He was concerned only with the Voice.

Somewhere out there, the contagion was increasing in power, spreading to others, biding its time. It had gone deep into the underground, where it was gathering its forces anew. The hunt for those sympathetic to the Twelve had not gone well—while some had been captured and executed, others had simply vanished, presumably to join in the swell of discontent that the Voice would soon fuel. But they would surface sooner or later.

And when they did, they would die. The Voice would be silenced.

Other things, however, were indeed going well. The public relations machine created by Barthos had moved at an incredible pace, bringing the whole world to the verge of Shass worship. Statues of the Prime Lord had been erected worldwide in every city center, in every Droshan temple. His handsome, caring face was everywhere. All of Noron loved him.

One more miracle, and Shass would become their god. And with the adoration the people felt for him, a card trick would do it.

Barthos stood watching as the Prime Lord addressed the world from the broadcast studio within the renamed World Capitol. The charismatic speaker stood behind an official government podium, reciting his well-rehearsed words with practiced vigor. The speech was carried via simulight and dealt with the new, combined information and economic system being instituted planetwide.

"I acted as I pledged to do, and you responded," Shass stated. "You have chosen to do your part in bringing about the paradise Noron can be. Just as I swore to give you the world you deserved, you have sworn loyalty to me and to your world by accepting the crystalline data implant we have devised for your security. Never again can your assets be stolen from you. Never again will your loved ones vanish, victims of the crime that has plagued our streets, for now any missing person can be located within seconds, anywhere in the world. As one people, we can now, for the first time in our history, work together to bring an end to the burdens that have kept our society from achieving the greatness for which it is destined.

"The World has instituted the bold, new method of recordkeeping and trade I promised you. As of sunrise this morning, we have activated, for each citizen, a single, fully active account in the new, worldwide UniLink data system. All of you, whoever you may be, can rest secure in the knowledge that both your personal records and your hard-earned monies are being kept safe for you. The tiny implant you have received is now active and is the only access to your information and assets, and that implant, no one can steal.

"Through the implant, you have taken my name for yourselves, becoming my family, and I am sworn to protect you…and that I will do."

Barthos listened as the highly charismatic man went on. *Such fools! It was all too easy!*

The crystalline implant the government had designed, encased within a pea-sized capsule of polished metal, had been planted within the skull of each recipient, under the left temple. The tiny scar that invariably remained following the procedure was covered by a small mark, a tattoo bearing the emblem of the office of the Prime Lord—

an open hand, palm up, upon which a dove was about to alight. Such a grand symbol, depicting a world of tranquillity.

What the people who had taken the implant were not told was that the same numbering system that now guarded their records and finances also controlled them. Without the assigned numbers programmed into the cranial implants, they could be cut off from financial dealings of any kind—meaning no food, no medicine, no job.

And that assigned number also gave the World immediate access to the entirety of the populace, tracking their movements and their dealings. No man, woman, or child could hide from the forces of the government, for the transponder built into each implant would reveal that person's location almost instantly. Every facet of the Noronian people's individual existences had become an open book. Their lives were no longer their own.

Shass *owned* thirteen billion cattle, all of which now bore his brand.

More importantly, the data implant was something that the followers of the Truth would never take, Shass and Barthos knew, for doing so was tantamount to making a pledge of loyalty to Shass and the World. And without the financial resources, which were available only through the implant, they would be driven into the open, where they could be dealt with. No one on the planet could buy, trade, or sell without it. And if anyone who already carried the data implant decided to switch allegiances and follow the Voice, the traitor could be found and eradicated swiftly and easily—and might even lead the vigilant Watchers to the Twelve.

Simulight domes to one side of the sound stage bore the image of the Prime Lord, displaying the signal being beamed to all. Shass continued his oration as Barthos proudly looked on, occasionally cutting glances at the Watchers posted at every entrance to the room. All was going well.

Then, suddenly, it was not.

The three-dimensional image of Shass in each of the simulight domes began to distort and break up, disintegrating into more and more random sparkle with each passing moment. His voice, as well, became increasingly garbled and finally vanished altogether, replaced by the roar of static. A murmur began among the offstage technicians as they searched for the cause.

"What's the problem?" Barthos called to the technical crew, keeping his voice as subdued as possible. "Do something! Fix it!"

Their hands flew over their control boards, trying adjustments and filters again and again, in various combinations.

"It is not coming from here," one of the technicians replied. "It seems to be some form of outside interference."

Barthos whirled and watched as the random pulses within the domes began to settle once again into a clear image.

"It's getting better," he commented. "You must have done something."

As the interference slowly faded away, a human figure became clearly visible once again, standing behind a red marble podium.

It was not Shass. Or rather, not the Shass they expected.

"Noron, I greet you," the figure said. "I am the Voice in the Dark, sent to you by the one, true Creator...whom you have forgotten."

A clock of a thousand days began to tick, counting down.

Right on schedule.

∽०∾

A time passed, and a new class of people emerged on Noron.

There were, as always, the wealthy and powerful. Then there were the masses, willingly existing more and more under the thumb of their Prime Lord with each passing day.

Then there were the living.

A father and his family sat huddled at the center of a small stone storage cellar that was not their own. The tiny room was lit by a single lamp, which hung low from the ceiling. In the warm light, as they sat upon the floor, the man read aloud to the fascination of his wife, small son, and two daughters.

For man is not a creature like the predators of the sea, or the winged things of the air, or the behemoth," he read, "but was created in My image, with My life within him. His heart and mind still cry out for Me, for only I can give him the joy and the life for which he longs.

For apart from My love, there is nothing that can sustain him.*

The man looked upon his family. Their lives had become a difficult daily struggle merely to remain alive, for they could no longer buy food or maintain any other means of survival. Only the pity of a few friends had kept them fed and housed, for the man had illegally left his forced job as a crystal worker, fearing discovery that he had not taken the implant. As a result, he and his family had been forced to flee their government-assigned home. They were fugitives, hiding from the authority intent on seeking them out and destroying them.

But they would not bow to Shass, even to save themselves. They had learned the Truth.

The father smiled despite their physical circumstances. He closed the book, and they bowed their heads.

"Beloved Creator, we thank You that You have brought Your Word back to us. Through your Voice in the Dark, we have seen that our ways were wrong, that they were not Your ways—"

They were surprised by a sudden explosion at the door. It burst open, showering them with splinters as the doorframe yielded to the force outside. Watchers in glossy black armor flooded into the room, cruelly shoving the man and his family to the hard, cold floor, pinning them there. One soldier reached down and violently pulled the woman's hair back from her left temple, then lifted the heads of the others in turn, inspecting them all.

"No mark."

Another Watcher held out a palm-sized device of sparkling metal and red jewels, pointing it in the direction of the victims on the floor.

After studying a readout on the device for a few moments, he turned toward another Watcher and shook his head.

"No implants," he said in a deadly monotone. The soldier then reached down and tore the Truth from the father's grip, kicking him aside in the process.

"Here, sir," the Watcher said, addressing another man, his voice augmented by the facial armor he wore. "Another one." He handed the book to his superior, a huge man dressed in heavy protective regalia that left no doubt as to his rank.

Through tinted eyepieces the Deathlord quickly scanned the book's cover, then tossed it to another soldier. He had seen the words printed there far too many times in far too many places. The soldier dropped the book into a large sack, one already heavy with confiscated Truth. Without a word being spoken, the Watchers began a procedure that had been performed repeatedly.

No warning. No trial. No mercy.

Ripsticks brutally forced against the necks of the crying children were discharged, filling the air with horror and ozone as their flameblades ignited.

"No!" the father cried out, pleading through tears as his wife screamed and began to sob hysterically. The small helpless bodies contorted, ruptured, and went still.

"They were only...children," the father moaned.

"Where are the Twelve?" the Deathlord impatiently asked, gripping the man's head, twisting it so he was forced to look upon the burned bodies of his three children. No answer came from the man's lips—he did not have the information the soldier wanted and would not have revealed it if he did. Silently, he closed his eyes and prayed for strength.

Another crackle filled the air, and the woman's frantic tears fell silent. The man did not have to open his eyes to know that she breathed no more, that he alone remained. Tears streamed from his tightly shut eyes. He prayed harder.

"One last time," the cruel, impatient voice boomed. "Where are the Twelve? Where is the Voice in the Dark?"

He remained silent. The last things he felt were the cold tip of the ripstick against his throat and the intense heat of the discharge as it tore into his nervous system, igniting it, overloading and destroying every muscle and nerve in his body with white-hot violence.

They had uncovered so many traitors, so many misguided idiots who had refused the cranial implant and, as a result, had committed sedition against the Prime Lord. The Deathlord, disgusted, shook his head and pushed past the dozen soldiers of the Treason Squad, who then followed him out.

Why choose certain death over loyalty to the god-man whom Drosha herself chose to lead us? He simply could not understand how the false faith of the so-called Awakening could lead to such sacrifice. He had served first his State and then his Prime Lord for many decades—but never had he seen such dogged adherence to an ideal, a man, or a god.

"The fools," he muttered in frustration, stomping from the house. "Will I have to kill them all?"

23

I t was a capacity crowd. But then, it always was.

The War Circle rocked with anticipation, for those in attendance had been told that, on that day, their Prime Lord was going to show them the new world they were about to enter. It was a special, unscheduled show, one that had been made available to the public at no cost. Everyone gazed out into the immense circular arena in the pale pink light of midday, waiting, watching, wondering. Listening for any word from their leader.

Their messiah. Their god.

No renewals were present. They did not need to be. Those in attendance were already utterly dedicated to the exaltation of the Prime Lord. To the Dark.

Dozens of simulight cameras, stationed all throughout the Circle, came to life and began to broadcast their signals to the world. All of Noron—not just those who had obtained a coveted seat—would witness the triumph of the Prime Lord.

The murmur of the crowd grew louder as the waiting continued. The anticipation was tangible. No one among the throng was quite sure what to expect. All had heard of the spectacle of the War Circle, but this—never had such a monumental event taken place.

God incarnate on Noron!

But one man, sitting alone in a private box above them all, knew exactly what to expect. Barthos sipped his icy drink, looking out upon the empty grassy plain, mentally counting down to the moment when it would happen. *Let them wait. Create the mood, the anticipation, the hunger!*

It angered him that the display was necessary at all. That the Prime Lord should have to stoop to theatrics to get the attention of the people galled him to no end. But the accursed Voice had transmitted dozens of messages to all of Noron over the months since that first interrupted broadcast, creating hesitancy and doubt in the minds of many of those who heard him.

Thousands had been arrested and killed as the government's continuing suppression of the Truth went on, but none of those taken into custody had provided leads as to the location of the Twelve or of the Voice himself. Despite the efforts of the Watchers and Barthos' handpicked best, no clue had turned up concerning the location of the underground's new base of operations. That meant they were being hidden spiritually as well as physically. The Light was rising, and Barthos worried. *The Awakening*—

As Barthos surveyed the vast circular plain of the arena, he knew that the entire world should have been Paull's long before now—but absurd words of salvation and Truth had mired much of the planet in a thick, disgusting hope that Barthos had labored long to destroy. The Prime Lord deserved better than to be paraded like a mere politician before the pathetic cattle of Noron!

Music rose throughout the War Circle, signaling that the moment had arrived. All of the coverage cameras finished their sweeps of the spectators and swung to take in the arena before them. It began.

The crowd of millions hushed as a huge swirl of color grew in the center of the arena, a rising column of rainbow mist or light or something that seemed to take on increasing corporeality with each passing heartbeat. Hundreds of feet into the air it grew, gaining stature as it attained its own reality, taking on a form known to all those who stared in wide-eyed wonder at the vision before them. They were infants in its shadow, insects to be crushed or spared at its whim, yet they leaned closer, gazing in adoration, anxious for what was to come.

The image soared higher, finally reaching a height of half a mile before settling into a form that stood triumphantly and towered above the people, arms spread wide, eyes sparkling as they swept the crowd. Its hair moved as if in a rising, caressing breeze, a phantom wind that stirred its robes and added false drama to the vision.

"Prosperity, my family," it welcomed them. At once, like a single organism, the gathered multitudes broke into wild applause and thunderous cheers, honoring the likeness of their Prime Lord.

"This day is not like any other, for I have come before you to show you what paradise truly is. Drosha has chosen me, and I in turn have chosen you. I will lead you into the wondrous new world I will create for you, and together we shall embrace a totality of life of which this planet has never dared to dream."

More applause, deafening this time. The millions peered up into the smiling visage of Shass, loving him, wanting him.

Glorifying him. Barthos smiled.

Sparkles appeared beneath the outstretched arms of the god-image, coalescing into a dimensional, panoramic vision of breathtaking beauty. Crystalline mountains twinkled in the distance, and rivers of flowing gold spread to a pseudohorizon dotted with dense forests of glittering jeweled foliage. Millions of people were shown resting in meadows of silken grasses, their clothes a symphony of precious stones and shimmering fabrics. All were happy, all were content. None had to labor, none had to want. All got anything they desired.

"Follow me, my children," the Shass-image implored with a fatherly gentleness rarely seen on Noron. "Follow me into this land of dreams, where all of you will know peace in your hearts and a joy you have never imagined. Turn away from the lies of confusion and deceit you have been hearing. This so-called Voice in the Dark would lead you into a bottomless chasm of despair and heartache. Come, my children, come with me."

The masses adored him. Barthos applauded, laughing at the sheer idiocy of it all. The rivers of gold had been his idea. He looked down into the faces of the cheering crowds beneath him, delighting in the ease with which they allowed themselves to be led.

Then a movement caught his eye, something out on the arena floor. Something minute, something barely discernible, a good half mile away.

Someone was out there, walking calmly, patiently, toward the towering display at the center of the arena. Barthos' mind raced—there was only one who could be so suicidally bold, so fatally disrespectful, so unafraid of death as to try such a stunt—

No!

He lunged for his binoculars, knocking his drink to the floor with the motion, shattering the glass. Ignoring the cold splattered liquid upon his legs, he put the optics to his eyes and hurriedly trained them upon the laughingly tiny, still-advancing figure. It was an ant challenging a colossus, daring to defy one who would surely crush it.

With a flip of a switch, the magnified image within his field of view became larger. Barthos made out a figure with robes of blue, hair of black, and flesh too pale to have been born of Noron. It carried something.

The chancellor was surprised, yet prepared. He had known the Voice would surface somewhere, somehow. He had hoped it would not be this day in this place.

Yet he was ready.

Anger flooded him, and he reached aside for a communications panel. "Now!" he ordered, as frantically as his Chief Watcher had ever heard him speak. "He's out there! Release them now!"

T. G. walked closer to the incredible image hovering above him. He was not even half as high as the soles of its sandals. The crowd began to murmur as more and more of the spectators became aware of the man on the arena floor, pointing as they watched him draw near their new god. The vast image soundlessly took a step back, turning to look down at the mere insect approaching from its right.

"Ah, my children," it boomed. "Look upon he who has spoken to you these last few months, he who has woven a pitfall of lies in an attempt to keep you from the paradise you deserve! But do not look upon him in fear, for this Voice is hollow. His threats are empty. Fear not, I have been sent unto you, and I shall protect you."

With that the vast likeness swept a hand in a summoning gesture, and gates all around the arena swung open. The colossal image then morphed into a gargantuan purple joylight a half mile in diameter and withdrew into the air high above the arena. There it pulsed and watched and spoke.

"Now, my children, you shall see this false Voice in the Dark fall silent, and the path to eternal joy will be laid wide for all."

A new round of applause and adoration swelled and soared outward from the crowd. Then, with millions of expectant eyes upon them, two dozen tormented and starved tyrannosaurs, separated from each other by almost a quarter mile, suddenly burst onto the grassy plain. They scanned their surroundings, bellowing into the air as they sought the scent of food. Almost as one, their golden eyes trained on the sole occupant of the arena, who cast them a sideward glance and continued walking toward the center of the coliseum.

The great beasts charged at a dead run while the bloodthirsty crowd cheered. They were less than one-quarter mile away from T. G. when he reached the center of the arena, where he stopped, stood, and raised his arms. He knew that every eye, every pair of binoculars was trained upon him. *Perfect.*

"People of Noron," he spoke in a voice that boomed from above as if coming from everywhere. "Your salvation shall not come from him who has deceived you, the false god you have begun to worship. I am the Voice in the Dark. My coming was foretold thousands of years ago, yet the news of this has been kept from you until now." He looked down at the artifact he carried. "Once again, the Truth is known throughout Noron, and you shall this day see firsthand the power of He Who has sent me to you—your Creator."

Barthos burned with anger as he listened to the speech. Glancing upward at the glistening, hovering shape, he was sorely tempted to call it down, to bring his own forces against the Voice. But those had to be held back until the time for them had come. Perhaps the Voice was not as powerful as he feared.

Wait...

The carnosaurs descended upon T. G. with fury, their tails fully extended as a balance as they leaned forward, jaws snapping as they ran. Their great weight came down hard with each lunging step, their eyes trained upon the lone figure who stood ahead, only seconds away. The prey remained motionless, watching the nightmarish monsters rapidly close the last few hundred feet that separated them from their first meal in weeks. The crowd roared at a fever pitch, cheering for the massive beasts, their only regret being that there were not more victims out there to be devoured.

Then the crowd fell quiet.

The hulking tyrannosaurs, their combined bulk shaking the ground beneath T. G., suddenly struggled to a stop and halted in their tracks a mere thirty feet from their target. Nostrils flared and snorted, and the loudly panting monsters considered him. The man only stood there, looking into the eyes of the great carnivores that surrounded him, watching as their animal minds heard commands they had never known before, words beyond mere language, words their ancestors had once heard and understood and obeyed each day— before those words fell silent.

Words spoken by the One Who had given them life.

T. G. lowered his arms and held a hand out toward the leviathan directly before him, the largest of the pack. The huge creature stepped forward and came to a stop an arm's length from the tiny robed figure, then lowered its head and allowed T. G. to reach out and gently stroke its reddish snout. He felt its rough, warm hide against his fingertips, scratching the massive head as he would a dog's. The beast closed its eyes, seemingly enjoying the attention. The prophet broke into a huge grin, knowing that not since Adam had any man been able to do what he was doing.

After nuzzling its newfound master, the huge beast stepped back and spun toward the others, roaring a guttural bellow to which they all responded in kind. Then, in unison, like some impossible, antediluvian drill team, the beasts turned their backs to T. G. and faced the audience, roaring a prolonged warning, surrounding their Creator's chosen prophet with a toothy, physically impregnable ring of protection. The beasts were his.

"These majestic creatures know me," T. G. spoke to the gathered millions. "They also know their true Creator, and their true place in this world. Look upon them…and remember."

Barthos screamed in anger, throwing his binoculars against the wall. He slammed his fist against a jeweled plate, which then flashed red. Immediately, the roar of massive engines was heard and the most powerful armored battlewagons Noron had to offer moved onto the plain. First dozens, then hundreds of them advanced, their armored hulls gleaming pearlescent in the light of midday, their bristling weapons primed and ready as they hovered toward their target. T. G. looked upon the dinosaurs surrounding him, knowing they had served their purpose, and knowing also that mere flesh, however fierce, could not stand up to heavy artillery. With a kind sweep of his hand the tyrannosaurs vanished, shifted into the jungles and forests of Noron where they belonged.

Again the Voice stood his ground alone. The war machines grew closer.

Let's not do this again, shall we? T. G. mused, shaking his head. He had seen enough of this tactic with the hoversteeds and had no desire to repeat the performance. Yet the people had to see, had to know Who was calling them back to life again.

He looked up into the colossal joylight hovering above, not knowing whether it remained up there out of fear or overconfidence. No matter. The day was his, and T. G. knew it.

He dropped his head back and closed his eyes, arms upstretched. He had been given control of the natural realm of Noron and was about to push that power to its limits in order to do that which was desired of him.

He felt something he had not felt in a very long time, and it caressed his cheeks like an old friend. His robes fluttered, his hair was tossed.

Wind.

The gale built in the arena, in gusts that grew colder by the minute as they swept through the vast ring of spectators. The people looked up, never having known wind or weather, and saw something dark begin to swirl high above. The gray mass grew, billowing into a greater threat each second as it churned and spread across the entirety of the sky. Its shadow blanketed the War Circle, and those below began to fear as it grew darker still. Small, scattered drops of cold water, carried in the cool wind, struck their faces.

"Stop him!" Barthos screamed into the arena. They could not lose it all now, all of that which they had gained—*the Prime Lord must triumph!* "Destroy the Voice!"

The war machines all opened fire sooner than they might have, still far from their target. From all directions, blue-hot bolts shot out at T. G., searing the air, only to halt short of their mark. Like water against glass, they splattered into suspended dishes of spectacular, brilliant color, denied the target they sought.

The black swirling storm above descended. Lightning lanced out, striking the ground with searing heat and painful, sharp claps of thunder. Rain began to fall in earnest, for the first time in the history of this world. T. G. looked up into the storm, not fearing this tempest as he had the one that had threatened David and him in Colorado. Torrents began to spiral out of the center of the storm, sending sheets of hard rain against the war machines that still advanced upon him, and as he watched they slowed, losing visibility. Hail fell, smacking the ground and the vehicles like hammers, a barrage of milky ice.

The hovertanks took aim once more. As one, hundreds of missiles streaked into the air in a barrage that should have leveled whole cities, aimed at the solitary man in the center of the arena. Leaving tracers of white in their wake, they soared in flattened arcs at almost the speed of sound, locked hard upon the unmoving figure that stood waiting for them.

Thundering shock waves slammed against the spectators as the warheads, like the energy weapons before them, struck a solid, invisible wall that would not allow them to pass. At first, the crowd cheered as huge balls of flame and dense smoke concealed the result of the attack. Quickly the smoke trailed off into the building winds of the storm, revealing that the untouched Voice was alive and well. The masses gasped, stunned by the impossible impotence of the mighty government forces in the arena before them.

The lightning increased in both frequency and intensity, striking war machine after war machine yet never nearing the gathered audience, which looked on, terrified by the roaring maelstrom before them. The sharp, unceasing thunder was jarring and relentless as it struck the crowd. Some turned and tried to flee, but most peered upward to see a trio of huge, evenly spaced bulges appear at the base of the storm, swellings that dropped silently downward as they spread wider. Then a deep howl built in the arena, an odd sound that engulfed all others and was felt as much as heard. Three vortices dropped from the wall clouds that gave them birth, moving with the total storm in a huge clockwise rotation centered within, and limited to, the arena. They roared like living things, malevolent mountains of mindless and total destruction, cutting violent, half-mile-wide swirls into the grass of the arena plain.

Tornadoes. Brutal black winds devastating everything they touched, traveling in a tight circular path around a common axis—the Voice.

As rain pelted his face, Barthos gestured wildly at the hanging joy-light, screaming in an attempt to be heard above the din. His spoken words were swallowed up, yet his thoughts were heard.

They cannot be allowed to see us fail! We cannot falter in their eyes!

Yet to make a direct attack was to risk utter defeat in the view of all—

The joylight acted. Reassuming its previous form, it walked past the sweeping cyclones and out to the very edge of the arena, where it towered over the throng. Barthos spun and fled the presidential box, twisting his knee in the process, desperate to get out of the War Circle.

The simulight cameras failed, showering sparks on their operators as their intricate crystalline arrays burned and melted. The people held their arms up to their Prime Lord, looking into his smiling countenance, pleading with him to save them. The image held its hands out over the drenched multitudes and swept past them as it walked the full circle of the coliseum. Loud, panicked cries of confusion ensued in its wake, but with the torrential rain and the chaos of the surrounding storm, T. G. could not see or hear the distant spectators well enough to understand why.

Then the tornadoes intensified further still and swallowed the attacking vehicles, mangling them with screams of tortured metal, sending debris and the bodies of their operators flying. The image of Shass whirled in the midst of this and advanced on the Voice, its eyes flaring with the terrifying red light the prophet knew so well. Being immaterial, the colossus was not affected by the storm and effortlessly slipped through one of the rushing tornadoes as it roared past.

"Come on, pal," T. G. challenged the ponderous figure. "Let's do it."

The Shass-image threw a massive, searing energy bolt at the Voice, who momentarily vanished within the flaring incandescence as it struck. As the glare faded, the colossus saw that its hated target had stood his ground as the soil was violently shredded and burned to a crisp all around him. Peering up from the midst of the steaming, smoldering turf, T. G. shook his head.

"You're going to have to do a lot better than that," he shouted, bringing his right arm up in a wide arc to point at the skyscraper image towering over him. "Like this."

An immense, blinding orb instantly sang out and struck the

image, engulfing it, searing the wind with a crackling roar that would have vaporized any mere man as near to it as was the Voice. It was the very essence of infinite power, a pre-elemental force that knew only one source but many conduits. Tens of thousands of separate screams burst from the Shass-image as it flew apart with the intensity of the impact, disintegrating into the smaller spectral beings that had comprised it. Some of them were consumed utterly by the blinding fireball, while others, seared and crippled, fled into the storm above.

"Welcome to the Awakening," T. G. said, watching the retreating phantoms. His spent, tired body ached badly, every muscle, every hair.

But it was a good tired.

The Shass-image had vanished utterly, leaving the Voice alone upon the storm-soaked plain. T. G. motioned and the cyclones lifted, unraveling into scattered wisps of darkness, disappearing into their parent storm more quickly than they had appeared. With another sweep of his hand the clouds parted and cleared away altogether, dissipating as if they had never formed at all, leaving the rain-drenched War Circle, the white mottling of melting hail, and scattered piles of tangled wreckage as evidences of their existence. Bodies were strewn everywhere, silent and awful, saddening T. G. as he walked between them and across the littered plain. There were hundreds of them. They wore uniforms. They had families. They had names.

Now they were lost forever.

The winds vanished. The scents of fresh rain and wet grass hung heavy in the air. Only a light stirring of breeze moved within the arena. The quiet was overpowering. T. G. looked up into the pink sky, which shone once more with the gentle radiance of the sun above. Calm had returned.

Yet only he was aware of it.

The millions of gathered followers in the seating ring, groping in silent panic as they sightlessly trampled each other, had been struck forever blind, deaf, and dumb by their god. There would be no witnesses to the events of that day.

∽∾

"He is not like the other Guardians, Cordan!"

Paull Shass threw a book at Barthos, striking him squarely in the chest with a sharp corner of the hardened leather binding. His anger burned deep and unquenchable. The booming words echoed within the cold, polished walls of his palatial office, magnifying the wrath being directed at his second-in-command.

"You said we could handle him!" Shass went on, spinning in his chair to peer upward through the expansive window of his office and into the night sky. "You said history showed that his powers would be limited! If that is what limited is, we may as well leave the planet right now!"

Barthos angrily threw the book to the ground, leaped from his chair near the massive hand-carved desk where his leader sat, and limped toward Shass. "You do that again and—"

"And what? *What will you do?*" the Prime Lord demanded, his eyes wild with rage.

Barthos backed down, turning away, trying hard to contain the seething fury within him. *Too soon…*

"Nowhere do the ancient scriptures say that the Voice was to be so powerful," Barthos slowly said, as calmly as his restrained anger would allow. "All of the power is attributed to the Truth itself, to its spiritual awakening of those fools out there. There are no specifics concerning the level of power granted to the Voice in the Dark…just prophecies that have been interpreted dozens of ways."

"Well, now we know!" Shass grumbled. "How could we have been caught so unaware?" His voice became heavy with sarcasm. "I thought you knew all there was to know about this 'Awakening.' "

"I *do*," Barthos said through gritted teeth. "And I know that the Truth is not as truthful as that sanctimonious, egomaniacal Ish would have everyone believe…most of its prophecies are nothing but wishful thinking on His part."

"Well, true or not, right now, out there, that Truth of His is being circulated. It is giving the people a solid hope, not just the trappings of wealth or the creature comforts that we offer. People are starting to listen, Cordan, and every day I can feel thousands of them slipping away, slipping through my fingers, diminishing me! I will not have it! What the Voice did to my men…hundreds of my best men! And not just today, but before…when we had him…when he was surrounded out in the wilderness…wiped from the planet as if they had never existed!"

Barthos looked away. "We weren't ready then."

"And we are *now?* The power of one man…as if the entire clearing had simply vanished! And that was nothing next to what we saw today!"

"Today's display was unprecedented. Not even the most powerful sorcerers of history were capable of such things. No past Guardian was ever given power like that. Never! They preached and ran and hid from us, and then sometimes, *sometimes* they were granted special power for personal defense. But this Voice in the Dark is something new altogether. I've never seen direct empowerment of this magnitude. What happened out in the wilderness was unparalleled, and I had hoped it had shown the very limits of his power. We could have handled that, had it occurred again today. We were ready. But his authority has passed beyond that of a mere Guardian or prophet now, almost as if he's the direct embodiment of Him."

"They do not work that way," the Prime Lord corrected. "You know that."

"I said 'almost.' This Voice is something new—a manifestation we haven't seen before."

"I was humiliated out there," Shass shouted in an accusing tone. "That 'Voice' handed us our heads before we knew what hit us! And if not for that deaf-and-blind solution your 'friends' brought to bear, the whole world would have seen it!"

"We controlled the situation."

"Did we? Even though we stopped all of Noron from seeing the outcome of today's little adventure and blamed the Voice for what happened to the spectators out there, I have lost credibility! They want to know why I let a false prophet permanently obliterate the senses of millions of my children! The people are doubting me!"

"They mean nothing! They're cattle!"

"If the cattle keep dying at this rate, I will be the ruler of an empty ranch, Cordan! Or worse, they will turn to the Voice and I will rule nothing! They may be worthless, but without them I go down…and so do you!"

"We could not have known that he—"

Shass screamed, cutting him off. "I am the Prime Lord of Noron! I will not be embarrassed by the likes of that prophet or by anyone else! This planet will bow down before me, and I will hold the lives of the people in my hands, and they will be mine to do with as I please…and no power known to man will be greater than mine!"

"You are the Prime Lord," Barthos placated him. "Yours is the ultimate authority in all the world."

"It did not look like it out there today! Just what would you suggest as our next plan of action? What will guarantee that nothing even remotely like this ever happens again? How do we kill the Voice?!"

"We can't."

Shass glared at him, disbelieving, surprised by the admission. "What?"

"I'd say he'd be given any authority, any reinforcements, any amount of power it would take to keep him safe from direct attack."

Shass rose from his desk and walked closer to the vista-window behind him. Angrily, he surveyed the glittering city lights thousands of feet below. "So we concede? We pack up and flee in the night and hide out there in the jungle?"

Barthos stared at the man's reflection in the window glass. "No. He will be ours nonetheless."

Shass, puzzled, turned and walked back toward Barthos, waiting for him to continue. "Well? Are you going to tell me or not?"

"We can't kill him, but we *can* make him come to us, and we can force him to die *willingly*."

"How? If you know something, some way to get rid of him, why have we not done so before? Why did we let him live this long? For that matter, why did we not simply kill him when he served us, while he was here within easy reach?"

"His death would have served no purpose then. He was not yet recognized by the world as the Voice, and eliminating him then would only have forced the selection of another. The Gift would have gone to someone else."

"We had him, Cordan…"

"It is not enough simply to silence the Voice!" Barthos shouted, losing patience with Shass' scolding, questioning barrage. "We must destroy the Truth along with him! The only way to do that was to utterly discredit him before the entire world *after* he had declared himself to be the chosen one. And that is still the way! By corrupting him while he was serving under me, we could have exposed him whenever he came forward…even if he had endorsed you, as we hoped. But something wised him up before it all came together …before the hypocrisy we had built in him could fall into place."

"I want his head, Cordan!"

"You'll have it. And once he and the Truth are both dead, once there is nothing left in our way, the ancient prophecies will unravel and disintegrate like the lies they are—just so much moldy parchment. The people who have listened to him will come back to Drosha and to you."

"I certainly hope you know what you are doing this time," Shass said mockingly. "You let the Elesh woman slip away when I wanted her dead. And now, when we are dealing with a man who holds the power of the universe in his hands, you dare to insist he will come to *us?* And that he will just lay down and die? What do we do, Cordan, ask nicely?"

All of Barthos' remaining patience barely kept a fingertip grip on the boiling anger he felt toward the Prime Lord. "*Your* wife freed Elesh," he reminded Shass with some satisfaction, speaking slowly and deliberately. "We figured that out, remember? And as for the Voice…he holds great power, but there are weaknesses in him, and I know them. I hold the key to his death. He *will* come to me."

24

The Battle at the War Circle, as it ironically came to be known, rapidly became the stuff of legend. The Twelve had done a good job of circulating the truth about what had happened in the arena that day, exposing glaring inconsistencies in the government's version of events. Those who had heard the Truth and had begun to believe saw the confrontation as a sign that the prophesied Awakening was indeed coming upon the world. Others, those who worshiped the mother-son deity of Drosha-Shass, believed every word of the false information being disseminated by the government and used the cruelty of "the Blinding" as a battle cry against the Voice and his followers. The grieving families of those who had been in attendance at the War Circle welcomed the generous offer of medical care from their Prime Lord, who swore he would not rest until the Voice, an evil sorcerer who had "so unmercifully crippled" his "beloved children," had been seized, imprisoned, and executed.

Following T. G.'s first simulight broadcasts, Noron had begun to polarize into two factions, each with a leader empowered by forces beyond himself, forces who had set the scene, forces standing at the ready. The number of those who had heard the Voice and had felt their hearts open to him were small at first, but that quickly changed. Over the following months, the adherents of the Prime Lord diminished in number almost as rapidly as the Disciples of Truth grew in force, indicating a constant and increasing swing in loyalties that angered Shass and Barthos.

Amazingly, to the chagrin of the Prime Lord and the chancellor, those who had first received the implant before going over to the other side had apparently managed to rid themselves of it, allowing them seemingly to disappear from the planet. That meant an undetected medical network was in place for implant removal, a contingency that supposedly had been taken into account in the design of the device. Once implanted, if the tiny, metal-sheathed crystalline capsules were ever again exposed to the air, they would detonate with enough force to destroy both the former implantee and anyone standing within a ten-foot radius.

Many were hearing and heeding the Voice. Too many. The continuing, unannounced, pirate simulight broadcasts by the Twelve and their awaited prophet did a great deal of damage, leaving the Prime Lord in an ongoing struggle to stop the bleeding.

He could not. No spiritual tourniquet could close eyes that had been opened by their Creator. Hundreds of thousands had refused to take the implant and its accompanying mark. Their lives became cruel existences, even for those who had been among the wealthy. The law was harsh and swift.

A commotion drew Kir Hervie's attention to the front of the marketplace. He had just filled a canvas shopping bag, topping it off with a carefully chosen assortment of oranges and dates, when he heard shouts. Walking toward their source, he saw an elderly woman on the ground near the entryway, a heavy boot harshly pinning her head to the cool, polished floor. As Hervie grew closer, he heard orders being shouted, orders that, he knew, meant trouble for the woman.

"Bring the Watchers," a man was saying.

Hervie proceeded to the scene and set his bag on the floor. "I am Watcher Prime Hervie," he said to the market supervisor. "What is the problem?"

"Kir Hervie," the man said, "this thief tried to make off with a few loaves of bread without making payment."

As the huge supervisor kept his boot pressed against the woman's head, Hervie knelt and reached to pull her graying hair out of the way of her temple. She had no mark there, meaning no data implant beneath.

"You have not taken the pledge to our Prime Lord," he gruffly said to her.

She remained silent.

Hervie knew she was a follower of the Truth. Only they, among all on Noron, had refused the mark, and her silence confirmed the fact. She did not beg, did not plead for a second chance, and did not struggle in any way. He had heard other Watchers tell of their encounters with the stubborn, misled Disciples of Truth, though he himself had been too busy guarding Shass and his family to witness such individual defiance firsthand.

Something inside him was…impressed.

"Please, take your foot from her," Hervie asked the supervisor. The man did so, yet the woman remained there against the floor, terrified.

For good reason.

But then a strange calm seemed to wash over her as she gazed up into the face of the kneeling man who loomed over her. Hervie peered deeply into the peace and clarity of her eyes, as she fixed upon his. They were the last things she saw.

He pressed his handheld ripstick against her neck, searing her nervous system, ending her life.

∽∾

It had been a wondrous night. In an athletics arena in the modest town of Meklavil, a farming community near Luracayn's extreme western border, T. G. had addressed a crowd of twenty thousand, all of whom had come to know the Truth. It was one of thousands of pockets of organized worship that had been established in secret worldwide, gathering to praise their Creator and His Truth. As T. G. spoke the people had waved their copies of the translated scriptures in the air, breaking into song, a joyous gathering that had touched his heart. It had been a risky affair, announced only at the last minute and only through underground channels. But the faithful had turned out for it, knowing the risk, knowing that their lives would be in danger if the forces of the Prime Lord raided the meeting. Just as occurred every time the people gathered in the Creator's name, there was a spiritual shrouding of the event, shielding its existence from threatening ethereal eyes. No agent of the Dark would know it had taken place. There were, however, the physical eyes and ears of the Watchers to consider, so the forces of the Twelve were very, very careful to maintain a constant vigil at varying points throughout both the town and the surrounding countryside.

All had gone well. During his brief speech, T. G. had been struck by the event's similarity to the Billy Graham crusades of Earth. He felt honored and humbled to have been chosen for the role. As he spoke, he scanned the audience, seeing their faces, the hope that was there for the first time, the life that shone in their eyes. They in turn looked with wonder upon the Dovo Kosi, the chosen Voice in the Dark, the one whom their Creator, at the beginning of the world, had promised to send to them. Most of the new believers had never known that the Truth existed. Now that they knew, they rejoiced.

It had grown late. Most had left the arena, taking with them an invigorated love for the Truth. T. G. and Pretsal remained backstage for some time, allowing the pressing crowds outside to thin before attempting to leave. They sat, pondering their next move, sharing a carafe of cold fruit juice as they watched a recorded replay of the event.

"It's wondrous," Pretsal commented, watching as the small re-creation of T. G. spoke within the transparent dome of the simu-light unit.

"And just as Ish protected me," the image spoke, "making my way safe so that I could bring the Truth back to you, so He will make safe your path beyond this world and into the next, where He awaits you with open, loving arms. Nothing will separate you from Him…for He never leaves His own."

"Again I thank the Creator that I am alive to see this," Pretsal smiled. "And I am forever grateful to have had some small part in the Awakening."

"Small?" T. G. smiled. "You probably saved my life. Anyone could have found me on that hillside when I first arrived, and there are a lot of folks out there who would just as soon have sold me as sirloin."

"I cannot claim credit for that. It was no accident that of all the people on Noron you were found by a follower of the Twelve."

"Still, you acted. And for that I'm grateful." The prophet smiled at his friend, patting him on the shoulder. "Come on…let's get out of here. You hungry? This would be the perfect time for a Denny's. You guys don't have those here. You'd love Denny's. Late at night it's a nice place to just kick back and talk."

Pretsal, having no idea what T. G. was talking about, smiled as he retrieved the data crystal on which the crusade had been recorded. T. G., the Gift slung over his shoulder, pushed open the heavy outer door of the arena's freight entrance and stepped out into the night. Pretsal followed, close behind. A few feet beyond the door, Josan waited with a hovercar. It was well after midnight.

"I heard it went well," Josan smiled. "I wish I could have seen it. So many people, all sharing the promise, knowing the love of their Creator in such a tangible way."

T. G. stood next to the open car, resting a hand upon its cool metal body. "Thanks for keeping a lookout. No sign of trouble?"

"Nothing. We kept station all through those hills," he said, pointing all around, "and several of us were posted just within the entrances. Still, it is amazing; I had expected problems. Things were almost too quiet."

"Don't say that," T. G. kidded, climbing into the car. "In the movies back home, those would be considered famous last words."

"Where to, gentlemen?" Josan smiled, manning the controls.

"Denn-eez," Pretsal grinned. "So we can kickback."

T. G. shook his head, cherishing his friend's sense of humor.

"Home," he said to Josan, smiling.

The hovercar left the curbside and pulled at high speed onto the main road. Whisper-quiet, the silence of the vehicle allowed its riders to enjoy the sounds of the night creatures in the thick, surrounding forest. Crickets a foot long chirped their song. Frogs croaked deeply, their call resonating against the trees. More distantly, larger creatures wailed and bellowed as they called their mates or signaled warnings of predators or declared a kill.

The car, without slowing, rounded a curve. T. G., cradling the Gift as if it were a small child, glanced up, past the trees, at the single moon and the myriad stars above. It was all so beautiful.

And then chaos.

A blinding flash, a deafening crack, and the prickle of unleashed electricity filled the air. Metal screamed as a violent concussion wrenched the vehicle. Before T. G.'s eyes, everything went into slow motion.

The world turned inside out, and bone-shattering forces slammed him against the side of the passenger compartment before all finally went still. When he could think again, he found himself pinned beneath the overturned car, his chest crushed against the roadway by the weight of the vehicle. He felt great pressure, but little pain—if not for Ish's special protection, he would have been killed.

He flashed back to a cold November highway. Strobing colored lights and screaming sirens blared in his mind's eye, his mind's ear. Another burst of light, another roar of death—his senses fell away as his mind turned inward upon itself, leaving now-detached sounds to echo in the distance and unfocused sights to diminish into gray, confused shadows.

A third explosion not thirty feet away startled him back to reality. A rain of soil and pulverized grasses fell upon him. He heard a shout. His name.

"T. G.," came the cry, panicked and low. "Where are you? Are you—"

Still shaken, he turned his head as another blast detonated just to his left, cutting off Josan's call and throwing light beneath the wrecked vehicle. The mangled car shuddered, freeing T. G. slightly. He swung his loose arm around and threw the car back, casting it aside as if it were balsa and paper, revealing himself fully to whatever was attacking them.

In an instant he was on his feet, looking for the Watcher he knew had to be there. His tattered robes were burned, yet his flesh remained untouched.

The prophet's eyes locked upon his target, even as it acquired him. A hoversteed was some fifty feet away, its weaponry aimed directly at him as it swooped in yet again, its rider concealed in black armor. T. G. lashed out, throwing a searing pulse that detonated on impact and showered the forest with sparks and flaming debris, the remains of the soaring attacker. In the firelight, T. G. rubbed his arm and scanned his surroundings, trying to find his friends as his eyes slowly readjusted to the relative darkness.

The sundered hovercar was in flames, casting a dance of orange light upon T. G. and the towering trees. Josan had been thrown clear and was lying in the deep grass some twenty feet from the road. He was stirring, seemingly intact, trying to sit up. Scanning again, the prophet saw another form lying farther away, well downhill in the meadow. It was not moving.

T. G. ran to Pretsal. The gentle-hearted giant was lying face down in the lush flowering grass, his clothes blackened and torn. T. G. knelt and gently rolled him over, cradling his head, searching for signs of life. As once before—the two of them amid the dense, cool clover, one injured, one reaching out to help.

"Pretsal…come on, buddy…talk to me," T. G. pleaded.

The man's face was badly burned, and huge fragments of twisted, jagged metal and glass glistened where they protruded from his exposed chest. His broken, shattered bones numbered in the dozens. Blood soaked his shredded robes. Slowly, too slowly, his eyes fluttered open, unfocused and searching.

"Famous…last words," the weak utterance came. "That's funny…"

A wetness welled in T. G.'s eyes. "Hang in there, Pretsal…we'll get you to a healer." T. G. threw his head back, his throat constricting. "Ish!" he cried out, fighting tears. "Help me!"

He looked back down at his friend. "It'll be okay…you'll be okay!" It was a command, as if he could force the warm, seeping red life back into his friend by sheer will. His emotions were twisted and confused in their intensity. He felt a flicker of anger against Pretsal for just lying there and dying on him.

Looking down upon the shattered body, a fleeting, wishful thought filled his mind. *I could shift us…I could get him to a healer and save him!* But T. G. knew the wounds were far too extensive to be healed in time, even for Noron's advanced medical technology.

Josan struggled to his feet and approached slowly, his dislocated right arm dangling unnaturally at his side. T. G. looked to him, his eyes begging for help, despite his knowing there was nothing either of them could do.

Pretsal coughed blood. "Hey," he weakly spoke, "it's okay, buddy…I'm ready. It's…my time. I'm…ready…" He reached up, trying to touch T. G.'s face. The prophet helped, taking the man's wrist, pulling the hand to his cheek. "I…can't see you…"

"Hang in there," T. G. choked, his throat knotted. "I still haven't taught you to play football."

Pretsal closed his eyes as a faint smile touched his lips. He coughed again, then opened his eyes slightly and tried to look up at his friend again. He knew his fingers were touching T. G.'s face, though he could not feel them.

"Dovo…Kosi…" Pretsal smiled. Suddenly, his gaze shifted, as if drawn aside by something.

"Pretsal!" T. G. vainly pleaded, tears streaming.

"I see Ish," the dying man whispered, smiling weakly as he looked past his friend, the words coming with his last gentle breath. T. G. turned his head slightly and saw that Ish was indeed standing just behind him. Pretsal's eyes closed as his once powerful arms went limp.

The Voice wept bitterly, cradling his fallen friend. All the grieving he had never allowed himself following the deaths of his parents finally came streaming out. The forest went quiet around him, as if in respect.

He felt a hand upon his shoulder and a comforting warmth, the only kind in all the universe that could reach him. "He is at peace, T. G.," Ish said.

T. G., his sight distorted by a curtain of tears, kept his eyes tightly shut as he clutched Pretsal's lifeless hand.

"He's come home," the Lord gently continued.

Why didn't You save him? T. G. wanted to ask. But he already knew the answer. *Every man has a set amount of time and not one day more…a purpose uniquely his and no other.*

"Pretsal took a direct hit, I think," Josan said softly, cradling his injured arm. He could not see Ish. "It was a Deathwatcher. A government assassin. He may have been stalking us for days. I never saw him until after he had fired."

"What was the point?" T. G. asked, expecting no answer. He gently lowered Pretsal's hand, then wiped his streaming eyes with his robe and gathered himself. He took a deep, staggered, stabilizing breath.

"What do you mean?" Josan asked.

"They can't kill me. They have to know that. Why send an assassin?" T. G., his cheeks stiffening with the salt of drying tears, pulled off his outer robe and draped it over the still form of his friend.

"Perhaps it was not you they were after," Josan offered. "At least…not in that way."

"He's right, T. G.," Ish said. "Barthos is trying to force you into a confrontation."

"They want me mad enough to come to *them?*" T. G. wondered aloud.

"Yes," Ish and Josan affirmed simultaneously.

"Then I'll give them what they want. And when I'm done with him, I swear there won't be anything left standing."

Josan, remaining silent, took a few steps back. Despite their friendship, he was still apparently awed by the mere presence of the Voice, the hugeness of it all.

Ish stepped closer. "T. G.," He began, "the decision is yours. But know that if you go there, you will be entering into the greatest trial of your life."

"No jury on Earth would convict me."

"You know what I mean. What is to come will try both your faith and your courage by fire. Do *not* go into this on raw emotion. You must do so firmly anchored in your trust in Us and in your knowledge of the Truth."

"I trust You. You know that. And I *am* angry…enough to level the planet. Look, I've done what can be done out here, hiding from the Dark and Shass and Barthos. The Truth has been spread to every corner of Noron. Word is out. The lines have been drawn. It's time to go into battle…for real. We can't do what needs to be done by lurking in the shadows. Not any more."

Ish looked at T. G. They had chosen well. He turned, took a few steps away, then faced His prophet once more. "Remember, I'll be with you." And He was gone.

A silver hovercar silently swept up and came to a stop mere feet from the burning, overturned vehicle.

"Kir Lorana! Kir Jora!" someone called. "Is the Voice harmed? We saw an explosion!" Several men and women jumped from the car and ran downhill, toward where Josan stood waving. He walked up toward the road, meeting them.

"We have lost a brave compatriot…and a friend," he told them, a great sadness in his voice. "It is Pretsal. Bring a pallet. We must take him home."

T. G., overhearing, stared into the depths of the night sky, at the spectacular stars embedded there. He took another deep breath and thought of his fallen friend. "He's already up there," he whispered, a bittersweet smile lightly curling upon his face. The stars were bright.

Rest, now, buddy. Have an apple…and save one for me.

25

He is coming?" a dark figure asked as he toyed with a kinetic sculpture in an alcove of Barthos' office. "What makes you so sure?"

Barthos sat at his desk, amusing himself with a Noronian version of solitaire. Rather than cards, however, it involved small, flat, numbered squares of ivory-colored stone, all arranged in a series of circles before him.

"He'll be here," the man said, sliding game pieces from place to place. "Any minute now, my man will…" He checked his timepiece. "Oh. It's later than I thought. It's already happened."

There was a new balance to the tone of the room, one that pricked Barthos' ears and caused him to look up. He lifted his eyes to the door and saw there a still, silent figure cloaked in the darkness of the entryway. It had not come through the door. It had simply—entered.

"I'll be with you in a moment," Barthos said casually, indicating a row of plush chairs to one side. "Take a seat."

"Funny," T. G. said, his tone serious and threatening.

"Did you have an appointment?" Barthos continued. The other person in the room, standing with his back to T. G., stopped playing with the steel-and-glass sculpture and watched Barthos for a cue.

"No," T. G. answered. "But you do."

The Voice stepped forward into the dim light. The click of his heels against the cold black stone echoed throughout the room.

Barthos looked up at the other man in the room. "I believe you've met the Voice in the Dark, haven't you, Kir Vord?"

The man turned to face T. G. His face was round and dark, with small, close-set black eyes and a flat nose. His cheeks sagged, giving him a perpetual scowl. A familiar one.

"Grodnal," T. G. whispered, surprised.

"Ah, yes," the sorcerer said, his rough voice grating in T. G.'s ears. "We have met. But I knew the young man before his career had taken off, back when he was just starting out."

"Such a touching reunion," Barthos smiled.

"Have a good swim?" T. G. dryly asked Grodnal, walking closer. He stopped ten feet from the desk, cradling the Gift before him like a shield. "He works for *you?*" he asked Barthos.

"Oh, well, I suppose so, yes. When I need him, he does. When there's a job to be done that is suited to Kir Vord's special talents...well, let's just say his work has proven most satisfactory."

T. G. shook his head. "So it was a set up. You duped a whole planet into believing in a miracle that *you* engineered."

"Of course," Barthos smiled, sliding another game piece into place. "It's not as if I could have asked Ish to help out, now is it? He seems to have a particular stubbornness when it comes to deceit."

"You attacked and kidnapped Shass and practically killed him. Then you had him healed by the Dark. Seemingly back from the dead before the entire world."

"Thank you," Barthos smirked, faking a bow. "Quite clever, wouldn't you say?"

"And Shass never knew it was coming, did he?"

"Ah! The man knows puppet strings when he sees them, Grodnal. Very good." Vord nodded and smiled, looking at T. G. as if sizing him up.

"So why make Shass Prime Lord? Why not yourself? How does that help you?"

"No, no. That's all for now," Barthos replied. "Ask me again later."

T. G. became impatient. Flexing the fingers of his right hand like a gunfighter, he stared Barthos down. "You wanted me. I'm here."

Barthos tossed a game piece aside and rose from his desk. "T. G., you've become quite a problem for us ever since you walked out. I'm afraid we just can't tolerate your behavior any more."

"Meaning?"

The man replied in a tone of all seriousness. "You're fired, T. G. Pick up your last paycheck and clean out your locker."

T. G. did not smile. His anger built at the man's mocking of the situation, at his lightheartedness after killing Pretsal. His anger even prevented him from recognizing how incongruous—how *earthly*—the comment was.

"Or," Barthos continued, turning away, "we could just kill you."

Instantly, a blunt force slammed T. G. from behind, grabbed him, spun him aside, and drove him unmercifully into the stone floor. Overpowering the force that pinned him, he managed to find his knees and whirled to see that Barthos was no longer in the room—Grodnal alone stood facing him, hands extended, eyes black and wide.

"Round two," the sorcerer spoke quietly.

T. G. tried to stand but found himself straining against unseen hands that gripped his arms, head, and waist tightly, restricting him, pulling against the Gift, holding him motionless. Grodnal calmly walked over, reached out, roughly grabbed a handful of T. G.'s hair, and yanked his head back.

"Pretsal was just the first," the dark man hissed. "They will *all* be dead by morning."

Rage flooded T. G., whose body suddenly wrenched free with a burst of searing white power that hurled the dark forces against the walls. He leaped to his feet, but before he could fire at Grodnal, the sorcerer vanished in a dense swirl of darkness that opened up and consumed him. Deep laughter filled the room as the Voice, giving chase, hurled himself into the dark vortex before it closed and followed the sorcerer's trail.

A black, senses-distorting, cold-as-death tunnel carried T. G. along, slamming him from side to side within the narrow maelstrom before finally and violently throwing him against a hard stone floor. Gathering his wits in a fraction of a second, he was on his feet, arms poised to fire, scanning for any sign of movement near him.

He was in a huge chamber that gave the appearance, more than anything else, of a medieval throne room. Torches lined the walls, the warmth of their dim flickering swallowed by the chill of the viscous dark. Cruel bladed weapons of configurations unknown to T. G. decorated the walls, their designs reflecting untold centuries of battlefield agony and intense savagery. A cold, ponderous scent permeated the room, that of air that had been too still and too damp for too long.

There was just enough light to reveal an arched granite ceiling that hung forty feet overhead, the entirety of its surface covered with carved figures in contorted, agonized poses. Scenarios of war and torture and pestilence danced in the ruddy, fervid glow, adding a sense of motion to the scene—the combined sufferings of human history splashed there in one grisly panorama. To the sides, tall, narrow windows cut deeply into the thick walls at ten-foot intervals, their black glass reflecting the meager torchlight.

Behind T. G., a massive, sealed lancet door of black wood reinforced with hammered black iron soared to a height of twenty feet, its huge hinges forged of bronze. Before him, at the front of the room, was a portal of polished quartz. It portrayed two reaching forms—horrifyingly thin, emaciated bodies, their faces distorted in terror, empty eye sockets staring, their arms and legs forming an archway. Their hands came together in the embrace of a cluster of skulls of reddish stone. Beneath this, at the top of six wide steps cut into and rising from the dark rock of the floor, was an empty platform seemingly meant for a throne.

Across the front of the ebony top step were carved words in the forbidden Old Tongue, characters like those on the Gift, but with a vastly different message:

I WILL REIGN ABSOLUTE
AND THE STARS THEMSELVES WILL EXALT MY NAME

He stepped forward, studying the words, then looked up to the archway and the excruciating pain on the carved faces there. A deep chill ran through him, a chill he had felt only once before.

His guard dropped for an instant as he recalled the frozen tomb his apartment building had become, as he once again envisioned the lifeless, ice-covered form of the elderly woman in her rocking chair. The cold was so deep, so final, so—

Before he knew what hit him, T. G. once more found himself on the floor. The concussion smashed his head hard into the unforgiving stone, a blow that would have killed any mere man, yet T. G. quickly rolled to his knees and fired an energy blast at the point from which the dark bolt seemed to have come. The blast struck one of the lifeless, black windows, which exploded outward—

—and then healed, leaving no sign of the shattering impact.

At the sound of laughter, T. G. whirled and fired again, this time striking the black-robed Grodnal squarely in the chest. With a lightning-quick sideward move, the sorcerer deflected most of the blast harmlessly away. T. G. followed with a second pulse, which also did little more than singe the man's clothing.

"You were lucky last time," Grodnal boasted. "This time I'm ready for you. This time you die." He lashed out with black lightning that swallowed the very air as it flashed to the other side of the room—

—where T. G. no longer stood. Instantly, the Voice was behind Grodnal, his arms wrapped tightly around the sorcerer, pinning his elbows against his sides. A white glow erupted from T. G., enshrouding him in a searing radiance that scorched Grodnal with a power that nullified his black force. Grodnal struggled to break free, but the intensifying white energy, suffocating and irresistible, held him immobile. The sorcerer cried out in a bellowing, inhuman sound that was magnified further by the echoes of the chamber. The screech swelled into a cacophony beyond the range of human vocal cords, filling T. G.'s ears with pain as it became an intolerable din. Grodnal thrashed violently, like a bronco trying to shake its rider, throwing them both against the walls, floor, and ceiling with brutal force again and again. Still T. G. held him fast, squeezing more tightly as the sorcerer struggled to free his arms. The white energy surrounding them both increased to solar intensity. Seconds passed like hours, and T. G., eyes clamped tightly shut, prayed for an end to it.

Then the Voice felt a shift in Grodnal's form as the man's body finally went limp. Still T. G. held him, fearing a deception, but he could feel that the black force within the sorcerer had faded. Slowly he released his hold, tensed for an attack, and watched as the form slumped to the floor, where it lay still.

The white glow surrounding T. G. faded away, and he slowly walked around the recumbent man, watching for any sign of movement. Gaining position to see his round face, he watched as Grodnal's open, black-marble eyes began to glow a brilliant blue. There was a crackling sound from the body, and it twitched slightly as the light in its eyes flared like spotlights. T. G. backed away slightly and tensed his arms toward the fallen sorcerer, not knowing what to expect. He ached all over. His head throbbed.

Like water from a faucet, the blue light drained from Grodnal's eye sockets, spilling out into the air, where it began to take on another shape. As T. G. watched, more and more of the brilliant blue essence filled the air above the body. The temperature in the room dropped sharply, bringing with the cold a dread silence like that created by a heavy blanket of new-fallen snow.

The glowing blue shape became humanlike in form, translucent and beautiful and beckoning, hanging in a cloud of cerulean light before him. The sound of loud, raspy breathing echoed wetly from the cold walls. When the last of it had pulled free of the man's body, it looked at T. G. with hard, glowing eyes, considering the prophet. The apparition appeared weakened, spiritually injured. After a tense moment, with nothing else to lose, it screamed and rushed forward.

Still in pain, T. G. fired. The being was utterly consumed in the dazzling light, which flared out of existence once its work was done. The thing—*the demon*—was gone, returned to the primordial ether from which it had come.

It had been an agent of the Dark, like the renewals and the joy-lights, using the fleshly shell of Grodnal Vord when necessary for the performance of its world-bound duties. A fallen, incorporeal being, it had worked since before the dawn of the world to bring down the light of the Truth.

"I told him it was a bad idea, the one-on-one thing," a voice echoed, filling the room. "But he wouldn't listen."

Breathing heavily, a badly fatigued and aching T. G. turned to see Barthos standing atop the steps, under the portal, dressed in royal robes of red and gold.

"You get demons…to do your dirty work," T. G. wearily said. "You're a sorcerer…you think you're using the Dark…but it's using *you*."

"I tried to tell him that you can't be killed," the man went on, ignoring the comment, "but you know how some guys are. They just have to see things for themselves."

"He saw."

Barthos shook his head in mock sadness. "I really tried. I mean, I told him who you were. I told him you had been chosen and empowered." He indicated the artifact slung over T. G.'s shoulder. "I told him you were the one true Voice in the Dark. I told him—"

"Can it," T. G. interrupted.

Barthos smiled at T. G.'s impatience and took a breath. "Forgive me. You're quite right. Back to business."

"Where's Shass?"

"Not important. Right now, you and I have some catching up to do."

"Not interested."

"Don't be so sure. I know more about you than you think." He reached into a rib pocket of his robe and withdrew a small rectangular something that T. G. could not clearly make out.

"Terrible picture of you," the man smiled, looking at the object. "Doesn't begin to do you justice." Then he began to read. "Shass,

T. G., 325 Brentwood Road, Apartment 304, Ithaca, New York…"
He looked up at T. G. for a moment. "Hair, black. Born November
2—"

"I get the picture," T. G. cut him off. "You took my driver's
license last time I was here. You knew who I was all along."

Barthos casually flicked the license at T. G. It sailed across the
room, landing at the prophet's feet.

"New York, New York," Barthos sang. "A helluva town…"

"Speaking of Hell," T. G. said, too weary to really listen, "What's
up with this grisly excuse for a room?"

"Decorated it myself."

"You would have enjoyed Auschwitz."

Barthos smiled. "I did…very much."

The man began to walk from side to side upon the dais, speaking
as he went, enjoying the sight of the exhausted prophet before him.
"You *still* don't get it, do you? You really don't." He shook his head,
mockingly. "How obvious do I have to get? Perhaps I gave you too
much credit."

The chill once more coursed through T. G.'s body, more severely
this time. Obviously, there was more to Barthos than he had thought.

"What are you babbling about?" he asked, perplexed.

The man held up his right hand and flexed its fingers as if they
were clawed. "I rather miss those talons," he said, admiring his hand.
"Ish cheated, you know, dropping you into that portal like that…you
were mine, dead to rights."

T. G. tensed. Every hair stood on end. Cold sweat broke out on
his scalp.

"*You,*" he angrily whispered, finally recognizing his enemy anew.

Shadowthing. Mortuary corpse. Angel of Hell. And now, the
second-most-powerful man in all the world.

"In the flesh," Barthos laughed, his eyes suddenly blazing blue.
"So to speak." Enjoying the disbelief on T. G.'s face, he went on.
"Could I have been any more obvious?" he laughed. "Dropping clues

here and there…call me a thrill seeker, but I just love seeing how far I can push things without blind fools like you catching on. And you were *so* blinded by pride…I'm amazed you finally wised up to the fact that we were using you."

"What clues…there *were* no clues."

"Come now. At Derakiin's, the night you discovered the joy of cannibalism. I mentioned your fondness for rib-eyes, when I couldn't have known about that. I mean, here they don't even call it *beef.*"

He laughed loud and mockingly, quite pleased with himself. "And did you *really* think that was something other than Dr Pepper you were guzzling?"

T. G. suddenly felt very unsure of himself. "I…I thought…"

"I sent my associates to seize a whole shipment for you, truck and all. Of course, they had to kill the driver, but the smile on your little face when you took that first sip was well worth it. Long way to Earth from here, I must say. You're lucky I don't charge by the mile. Or by the year." He paused. "Or by the death."

"Enough!" T. G. turned away, his pride shattered, trying in vain to shut out the words. *How could I have been so stupid? And a man died!*

"Pay attention, now," the fiend said, waggling a finger in the air. "We're not done yet. You know, I must say…overall, you're really very good. I mean, I've gone up against the best the Creator had to offer. The old Guardians, they all fell to me. One after the other. And the eleven Voices of Light—the greatest of the Guardians, who penned that accursed scroll you brought back to this planet—they died in this very room, most of them. Took a while, I'll admit, and usually only after prolonged torture. Very messy business. I was a Deathlord back then. Not just a job…it was an adventure. The chicks always went for a guy in uniform."

T. G.'s patience was gone. Despite the deep weariness that permeated his body, he extended his hands as if to fire, his muscles crying in protest.

"Hey, look," Barthos said. "You wanted answers, right?"

The young prophet tensed, holding his ground, trying to disguise his pain. Something in him made him listen, made him delay the inevitable.

"As I was saying," Barthos went on casually, "It finally came down to my dear friend, Parmenas. A tricky one, he was. I'd hunted him for years, waiting for just the right moment. When I captured him, he *still* held the scroll, the original. Finally, it was mine! I had won! It was the last copy of the Truth anywhere on Noron, and I was about to have the honor of destroying it once and for all. But there again I was cheated. I stood right there in front of him and saw the thing hanging around his scrawny neck, not even as far as from me to you. I'd won, fair and square. But at the last second, Ish comes and yanks the thing back from the old man. You can imagine my disappointment."

"So how many did you take it out on? How many died?"

"Just a few," he replied, reflecting almost fondly, "towns."

"You're psychotic."

"That's where your little leather pal there came from. It's stolen. From me. Do you see the kind of guy you're working for here? I just thought you should know. He didn't even get you a new copy for your very own. That one you're carrying is *so* old, so *used.* I hate to think of where it's been." He then leaned forward and spoke in a low, mocking tone, as if not to be overheard. "Just between you and me…those old Guardians weren't the *cleanest* people."

T. G. glared, a fierce anger burning within him. He wanted to fire, wanted to end it—but listened. From the deepest recesses of his wearied mind, he sensed *something* in Barthos…or in the room…or in the very stone beneath his feet, an indefinable something that held him in check, soundlessly crying out to him from everywhere at once, fighting to be heard.

"I guess what I'm getting at is that it's just so darned…*inconsistent*…to kill the first eleven bearers of the Gift and let the twelfth one live. That has really bothered me. It's the single black mark on my otherwise stellar career. So I decided, since I couldn't find you, I needed to make you come to me. And since I can't kill you, I need for you to die of your own free will."

"I don't think so," T. G. growled through gritted teeth, reminded of Pretsal's death.

"You are here," Barthos gestured, indicating the oppressive chamber around them, "because I wanted you here."

"Here, there…doesn't matter to me where you die."

"Fine," Barthos smirked. "You're the boss. But think…isn't there one more thing you're just dying to know?"

No…there's nothing that—

But there was.

Panic suddenly filled T. G.'s eyes. Barthos saw it. And smiled.

The man gestured off to the side of the empty cathedra, to a pair of Watchers in a side corridor whom T. G. could not see. The sound of heavy boots against stone filled the air, their harsh rhythm mixed with other, more uneven footfalls. At once the armored men walked out onto the throne dais, their ripsticks held tightly against the throat of the shackled prisoner they held immobile between them.

T. G.'s scalp tightened, his vision tunneling onto the face of the prisoner. The glow faded from his arms and hands.

NO!

"T. G.!" a pleading voice cried out, a cracking voice strained by prior, tortured screams. A voice, nonetheless, that was pure music to the young prophet.

"Jenni!"

Their eyes locked. Her tangled blonde hair was matted with dirt and blood. Her arms were pinned behind her at an awkward angle. She wore a sweater, now ragged and bloodied, that T. G. had given her for her last birthday.

"Oh…you two know each other?" Barthos mocked.

"Let her go!" T. G. screamed. "This is between *us!* She has nothing to do with it!"

"Quite to the contrary…she has everything to do with everything. Right now, she's the reason you are going to die."

Jenni stood in utter confusion, hearing the indecipherable gibberish coming from the lips of the others. She did not have the gift of language T. G. had been given and could not understand why he spoke the odd language so fluently.

"T. G.! What is all this?" the girl cried. "Help me! They're hurting me!"

He stood frozen in indecision. His mind was flooded by too many thoughts, too many factors to be considered. *Can I shift up there and free her? Can I get her out of here before they can act?*

Barthos shook his head. "Don't even try it. You may be fast, but those ripsticks are faster. And as for shifting somewhere else, forget it. You'd only delay the inevitable. We'd follow right behind you and kill her wherever you went. And who knows what innocent bystanders might find themselves in the line of fire? You could, of course, attack my guards. I can't stop that. But ultimately, you will not destroy us without killing her in the process."

T. G. stood silently, fearing for the girl he still loved. He had been ready to die before—were it demanded of him—in a world without Jenni. He had no concern for his own life, short of fulfilling his duty to Ish.

But if Jenni died, that would mean—

Barthos, knowing that questions were flooding T. G.'s mind, turned to face Jenni. While he could not read T. G.'s shielded thoughts, he had seen enough human behavior over thousands of years that he could accurately surmise any person's reaction to virtually any given situation. He spoke to her in perfect English. "Tell me, my dear, do you believe in God?"

She remained silent. The guards jabbed their ripsticks harder against her throat.

"I don't know! What difference does it make?" she cried out, her eyes red, her face still wet with tears.

"Wrong answer," Barthos gloated. He descended the rostrum, chuckling, and took a few steps toward T. G. "No God means no Christ. No Christ means no salvation. No salvation means…" He smiled, shrugging. "…no happy reunion on the other side. She comes to *our* party."

T. G. looked at the girl with pleading eyes. *Oh, Jenni…if only!*

Jenni cried out in confusion and fear. "T. G.! What is all this?"

He tried to present a front of confidence and calm. "It's okay, Jen…I'll get you out of here. I promise."

"Ah," Barthos smiled. "Young love." He signaled his men, and they dragged the bewildered, frightened girl through a massive stone doorway and back down the corridor from which they had come. She called out to T. G. yet again, crying for help, her pleas echoing. T. G. took a step toward her, a step halted by a hard forearm from Barthos.

"No, no," he said. "Mustn't touch."

T. G. shoved the arm aside and mounted the steps. Barthos whirled and called out to him, just as he reached the top. His tone was suddenly grave.

"One more step, and she dies."

T. G. froze, torn between what his emotions screamed for him to do and what his intellect demanded. Livid, he spun back toward Barthos.

"Kill her and you have no control over me."

Barthos shook his head. "I didn't say she'd die this instant."

"All right. What do you want?"

Barthos smiled, his radiant white teeth flashing in the torchlight. "Ah! At last!" He walked up to T. G. and looked down upon him. "Actually, I thought I'd made that quite clear.

"I want you to die. Tomorrow. You lower all your defenses and give up your life…and I'll release her. Once you're dead, I'll send her back home, to Earth, and I'll never touch her again."

"You're lying."

"Well, that's just a chance you'll have to take, isn't it? But think about it…she means nothing to me, not once you're out of the way. I don't need a tool once the job is done."

He thought hard, knowing what he had to do.

The Truth is already out. I've done what I came to Noron to do. The Awakening will happen now, whether I'm here or not. And after I die, I'll be with Ish…and my parents…and Pretsal. But Jenni!

"Take your time," Barthos said calmly. "You have thirty seconds."

For spite, T. G. made him wait the entire thirty seconds.

He closed his eyes. *Ish, be with me!*

A flowing warmth washed over his body and curled deep into him. He was not alone. The sensation swelled into his tired, aching arms, then intensified in his chest, embracing his heart.

Where his treasure was.

He heard a voice, speaking within him, calming him. The words astonished him—*and he understood.*

"All right," T. G. conceded, as if the decision had not been made long before. "You win."

"Excellent!" Barthos signaled, and another Watcher entered with a set of heavy manacles. At his leader's direction, the soldier began to place them on T. G., but hesitated.

"Oh, it's all right. He won't bite," Barthos said. "Will you, T. G.?"

T. G. stood silently as the cold iron shackles closed around his wrists and ankles with a loud series of clicks. There was a grim finality to the sound. The chains were heavy, dragging his hands downward.

"Dramatic, I know," Barthos smiled. "But I love a good show. Like the decor of this room…sometimes, the old ways are the best." He gestured to the guard, who began to lead T. G. away.

"Until tomorrow, then," Barthos laughed, waving as the Voice in the Dark was taken to his cell.

∽◌∾

Ah, the old ways.

It was a dungeon, dark and damp and cold. Straight out of a

Hollywood movie, it was as medieval a place as T. G. had ever seen, right down to the black iron chains hanging from the walls. If he could have stopped breathing, he would have done so to avoid the heavy malodor of mold and moss and rot that was the very air. No other prisoners were in the room with him, but the huge, disjointed skeletons of a few of the chamber's former occupants kept the Voice company, pinned by shackles to the dark stone of the walls or trapped within a caged pit in one end of the floor.

"What are *you* in for?" he asked, looking at a skull that peered up from the pit. Leaning against the cold wall, T. G. sat on a low stone riser, one apparently meant to serve as a bed. One arm rested on the Gift.

Despite his immediate situation, his mind remained focused on Jenni. It had been, ever since he saw her there. *She's alive.* Was she now nearby, confined to the same prison? Or did Barthos have something else planned for her?

"Jenni!" T. G. called experimentally. Only his own voice came in reply, bouncing uselessly from the hard walls.

He looked down at the hardened chains that so theatrically bound him. How easily he could vaporize them with a glance. The massive wood-and-steel door to his cell would be no more an obstacle than if it were made of tissue paper. In seconds he could be free, and nothing Barthos or the Dark could do could stop him.

But no.

"Just get it over with," he whispered, his head hanging limply.

"Strength, T. G.," Ish's voice said, its tone one of shared pain. "Soon the moment for which you were born will come. And it will pass."

The prophet turned to find Ish sitting next to him. "Jenni's here. Barthos has her. Rather, Beltesha does. Barthos is just a shell he's using."

"Yes," Ish nodded. "And he does not understand. His arrogance has blinded him."

T. G. smiled. "Well at least we have that." He looked into eyes of gentle, embracing flame. "This is hard, Ish. Really hard. Harder than anything I've ever done. It's taking everything I have just to keep sitting here like this and not fight back—and not grind that infuriating smirk of his right into the ground."

"I know," He said. "I know."

"I guess You do," T. G. said, disappointed in himself for forgetting to Whom he was speaking. "Forgive me. I know You've been there…and then some. It's just so big. I'm having trouble wrapping my mind around it."

"There is nothing to forgive. I am well pleased in you."

T. G. smiled, then after a few moments thought of the girl. "Where's Jenni?"

"She is here, in another annex. We are in the prison of the country's former capitol. It's a very old structure, older than any on Earth, once a great fortress. Barthos is keeping her here until after tomorrow, thinking that doing so maintains a stranglehold on you. The courtyard where all things will come into focus is here as well."

T. G. looked down. "Will she be okay, Ish? Please…I have to know."

"She has a future, T. G. With Us."

He smiled at that.

"Remember," Ish said, laying a comforting hand upon T. G.'s shoulder, "I will be with you throughout every moment of the trial that is to come. You will not be alone."

The Voice nodded with a faint, determined smile. "I know. I trust You beyond all else, beyond anyone else. If I didn't, I wouldn't be here. To be honest, I'm not scared so much about what's going to happen tomorrow as I am about remembering to trust when the time comes. I'm terrified I'll let You down."

Ish smiled. "I will strengthen you. You will honor Me, and those who follow the Truth, in a way that few men have. This single act will be the greatest thus far in this world's history."

The culmination of it all was almost upon him. T. G.'s hunger and thirst were intense, and he fought to keep his mind off the needs of his body. He recalled his life on Earth. Images of school and friends and everyday life passed before him like a warm, comforting parade. It was so distant now, so ordinary, so unreal to him.

The burden of his own passion finally broke through, and he wept. Too much had happened too fast for his heart to keep up with it all. Despite his faith, he was emotionally unsure of the footing ahead of him—a dark road is a dark road, no matter how many times one has read the map, and fear swelled within him. In mere hours, he was going to leave everything he knew behind and leap into the unknown in its purest form.

Later, his mind calm once again, he recalled something his father used to say, something T. G. had thought ridiculously trite at the time. *I don't know what the future holds, but I know Who holds the future.* Suddenly, as he looked upon the robed Presence seated just a few feet away, the words seemed not so silly.

They weighed upon T. G.'s mind, bringing to light a question.

"Ish...the decision I've made...to do what has to be done. I, uh...I want to understand something."

"Speak."

"Did I decide to do this, or was it preordained for me? If I was chosen before the beginning of the world, as You said..." The question trailed off. "Well, You know."

Ish smiled. "The Father, and I, and the Comforter alone exist outside of time, outside of the limitations of the framework We created for you to live in. We see the entire parade at once, as it were, from eternity to eternity, while you and those of the angelic and demonic realms are bound to a single, narrow vantage point. You must watch the parade as it passes. For Us, there is no past or future. There is only 'now.'

"All choose the path they will take. Man chooses. The Dark chooses. The angels choose. All are responsible for the choices they make. Yet at the same time, the Father is utterly sovereign. All things were decreed by Him, in His good pleasure, before the beginning. Despite appearances to the contrary, free will in the creature and unlimited authority in the Creator are not mutually exclusive. But your current frame of reference will not allow you to comprehend this.

"One day you will better understand. But not now, not until you have been freed from your limitations. You see through a glass darkly. That which is possible for an infinitely dimensional God cannot be fully understood by one who is bound and limited by a four-dimensional existence."

"Four?"

"Time. Bound as such, you cannot grasp the necessary points of reference. It would be far simpler for a two-dimensional listener—constrained by two-dimensional concepts and hearing only two-dimensional terms—to grasp the concept of a sphere. What I can tell you is that all things and all events, even those of evil, are used by Us for good and for the carrying out of the Father's will.

"That is where trust comes in. And trust...simple trust...is faith."

Throughout all of history, men either believed in God to keep His Word or they did not. Abraham had been willing to kill his precious son, Isaac, on a sacrificial altar not because of mere blind obedience to God, but because he knew his Lord had *already* promised that a great nation would one day come into existence through the boy. Abraham believed that God would keep that promise, even if it meant bringing Isaac back from the dead. And Job spoke ten of the most incredible and faith-inspiring words ever recorded by man: *Though he slay me, Yet will I trust in Him.*

Men either trusted Him, or they did not.

They trusted Him, or they turned elsewhere.

And many *had* turned elsewhere, away from the one true Door provided for them, hoping for an easy path or a shortcut of their own design, a self-made salvation that would satisfy their pride. The tragic thing was that none existed.

There was little left to say. Ish sat at His prophet's side, invisible to all others, and would remain there all night. T. G. tried several times to close his eyes, but sleep would not come. There would be none that night for the prophet, nor would there be even the courtesy of a last meal.

T. G. sat quietly, with little choice but to contemplate his situation. That day with David on the mountainside seemed so distant, as did his time in Dr. Abelwhite's lab as they tried to analyze the Gift. He thought back over the past two years, over his life on Noron and the role he had fulfilled. He thought of Pretsal's smiling face, of the crunch of an apple that often signaled his approach. Of Josan and Darafine and that first night beneath the biocenter when the Gift first revealed itself to all.

And of Jenni. His love for her, dormant amid the swirling rush of events since his arrival on the new world, had flared to life again, as vital as it had ever been. He pictured her smile. He wanted her— wanted to hold her, to smell her hair, to gaze longingly into her eyes as he once had, to kiss her and taste her warm, sweet breath and keep her in his arms forever.

But he knew that would have to wait for another time, another place.

Tomorrow he was to die.

26

The sun rose over paradise.

Diffused sunlight sparkled upon the dance of a crystal cool stream, throwing overlapping ribbons of light upon the lofty horsetail reeds along its bank. Jeweled fish of ruby and emerald darted among their roots. A distorted reflection rode upon the surface of the water, the mirrored image of a lush forest of towering timbers that spread to the horizon.

Amid the glorious expanse of life there in the wilderness an immense structure of black stone stood beneath the morning sky as it had for more than fifty centuries. Its six towers stretched toward the heavens, sheltering abandoned ritual altars and astrological observatories within their heavily buttressed walls, concealing vast pits below their foundations where the torn remains of countless living sacrifices had once been thrown. Long ago it had served as the mind and heart of the New Order, a massive edifice dedicated to the extinction of the Truth and those few who still clung to it.

Those who knew it existed called it the Dark Fortress.

For most of its history it had stood empty, passed by as governments had sought more centralized sites and more sophisticated architecture. It was far removed from any human dwelling, left to stand alone against the incursion of nature—forgotten, abandoned for millennia, a mute witness to the coming of the Dark.

But today it was the center of the world.

T. G. sat in his cell, again reading from the scroll he had brought back to Noron, Ish at his side. Ish answered questions as quickly as T. G. could ask them, as a single wondrous story unfolded with each word he read. While the events, persons, and specifics dealt with a different world, he was struck by its similarity to Earth's Bible. *But of course. Though they deal with different planets, the same Author wrote both.*

The sound of footsteps pricked T. G.'s ears. Someone was just outside his cell. With shackled hands he lowered the scroll to the floor, then watched as it rolled shut and once again sealed itself within its impervious leather casing. Voices sounded outside as orders were given. The distinctive whine of charging ripsticks filled the air.

No sooner had the Gift come to rest than the door opened. Several armored guards entered, their weapons aimed at T. G. They did not see or hear Ish, but they sensed Him—an air of surpassing discomfort surrounded them, a hair-raising authority that swept their doomed souls and wordlessly held them in judgment.

"It is time," their leader ordered, visibly shaken.

T. G. stood, dusted off his robes, took a deep breath, and picked up the Gift. He was exhausted, famished, and parched, and he knew his suffering had only just begun.

"Well," he said, placing the wide strap over his shoulder and fishing for something to say. Nothing appropriate presented itself.

He followed them toward the door as Ish stood and watched.

"Be comforted, T. G.," Ish said. "It will be brief…and I will be with you."

The prophet looked into Ish's warm eyes as he passed and nodded. The Voice drew strength from those eyes.

It was then he saw a tear coursing down Ish's face.

∽∾∾

Simulight cameras were stationed at every possible vantage point, their lenses trained upon the center of the wide, unkempt courtyard. Tangled grasses still pushed up in irregular patches through the cut-stone pavement, though most of the foliage intruding upon the site had been cleared away hours before. Towering walls of black stone and dark steel rose into the sky on all six sides of the enclosure, blocking the risen sun, throwing the broad, hexagonal floor of the courtyard into shadow. High portals topped by elaborate arches, separated by columns of marble and bronze, led to dark chambers beyond the walls or to long tunnels leading through the body of the black citadel and to the forests beyond.

At the center of the courtyard a cylindrical pillar of polished obsidian and gleaming metal rose from the stones of the floor. It towered some thirty feet into the air and was covered in glassy rounded carvings. Inlays of silver and gold ran throughout its surface. A large polished ring of pearlescent metal was mounted at a point fifteen feet above the ground, a thick donut-shaped object obviously meant for a specific purpose. Smooth channels cut like screw threads into the pillar, spaced a foot apart. Three metal attachment points were set into the encircling, spiral groove at eye level, 120 degrees apart.

Within an open-air viewing box, Barthos sat high in a ceremonial judgment seat, overlooking the courtyard below like Caesar at Rome. Next to him, on a slightly higher seat, sat Prime Lord Shass, who showed extreme discomfort with the proceedings, fearing another fiasco such as had occurred at the War Circle. The two men sat alone, for no other spectators would be allowed to see or hear the execution firsthand. Only they and a trio of executioners would view the proceedings, and if something went wrong, the executioners themselves would be put to death. No witnesses.

Just in case.

Still the world would be watching. It was to be Shass' moment of final triumph, the verification of his deity, the final nail in the coffin of the Truth.

There was to be a ten-second delay in the transmission of the simulight broadcast. No surprises would meet the eyes of the world. Fully automated cameras—which could be cut off instantly by a single kill switch in the hand of Barthos—would allow the entire planet to watch as the Voice was proven false, put to death by the one true god of Noron, Paull Shass. There would be no broadcast sound in case the Voice had final words to share. All broadcast frequencies were to carry the show, ensuring maximum worldwide exposure.

"You are sure that nothing will happen to embarrass me here?"

Shass demanded of Barthos, doubting him. "You said that before, and—"

"Nothing," Barthos assured him. "It's as good as done."

"You really expect him to just stand there and let us kill him?"

"He took the scourging, didn't he? We pushed him beyond torture…if he was going to defend himself, he would have done so by now. He's thinking only of the girl." Barthos grinned. "Love…such a wondrous, dependable weapon. It always has been."

"Submitting to death and submitting to torture are two very different things," Shass protested.

"Very well, if *you're* afraid," Barthos said with no little sarcasm. He touched a button on a handheld com-unit, calling the detention unit below. "Bring the girl up here," he ordered, then closed the connection and turned back to Shass. "We'll keep her up here where he can see her. Then if he does get any fleeting notions about saving himself, perhaps her presence will dissuade him. In any case, I swear to you, when this day ends, the sun will set on the lifeless corpse of the Voice in the Dark."

"See that it does," Shass warned, his voice one of controlled anger. "If that prophet walks out of here alive, you do not."

Barthos held his rage in check. He silently glared at the Prime Lord, his teeth tightly clenched. *Not yet!*

A movement below, emerging from the shadow of one of the courtyard's entry tunnels, drew their attention. A surrounding company of ten Watchers was leading a man onto the vast hexagonal pavement. His step was uncertain and wavering—it seemed at a casual glance that he was having some trouble keeping his feet, even beyond the encumbrance of the heavy chains that bound him. The light of the sun broke over the high walls and found the floor of the courtyard.

"Ah," Shass smiled. "It begins."

Barthos pressed a switch and dozens of cameras swung into action, locking onto the stumbling man below. Their crystalline mechanisms whirred and spun as they zoomed in, tracking their target as he made his way deeper into the courtyard.

"Showtime," Barthos whispered.

∽◇∾

Josan and Darafine were the last to enter the room. The others were already there, gathered in the assembly chapel they had made of a one-time storage chamber. The room was wide and roughly circular, with a low wood-beamed ceiling from which hung light fixtures of dark metal. The attendees sat on concentric benches, which were broken by a trio of wide aisles leading toward the center of the room, focused on a small altar with a single candle burning upon it.

Sereen Shass and the Twelve sat silently in their dark robes, somberly holding a final, unwanted ceremony that they had been forced to endure all too often. Several Disciples of Truth, their heads bowed, also waited for the proceedings to continue and sat quietly. No one spoke as Darafine walked to the center of the wide room and took her place behind the waist-high altar. Josan moved to his place nearby, sitting before her on the front row.

The seat next to him was painfully empty.

"Our friend has returned to the dust from which he was made," Darafine gently said, her tears glistening. "And now our sacred duty is to continue the work to which he was dedicated, indeed, to which we all have pledged our lives. The Truth must yet be heard, and we cannot rest until every ear has heard the word our Creator has restored to us."

It had been a beautiful burial, held beneath a copse of towering oak trees. The vitally pink sunrise breaking over the emerald greens of Noron had been breathtaking, as it always was, yet a deeper meaning permeated the proceedings themselves and the hearts of those in attendance. It had signified a new beginning for he whom they had most recently lost, a passage from what was to what shall forever be.

"We will miss our friend," she went on, after pausing to draw a deep breath. "As we miss all whom we have lost. Yet we shall see our fallen friends again…indeed, they would not now return to us were they given the opportunity. This world is but a dim reflection of the wonder to come, the wonder that awaits us all in the embrace of our Creator." She blew out the candle and stepped from behind the altar as a tight curl of smoke rose into the air.

"The light that was Pretsal Jora has not been extinguished but has been embraced by the greater light of the Creator. Let us remember him always and look toward the day when once again we know the warmth of his presence."

After those words, the gathered mourners stood and milled among themselves, bringing comfort to each other. The low murmur of their voices was sharply interrupted by a louder, single voice, sounding from the doorway.

"Darafine!" a technician named Andrel called, "you had better come see this!"

Josan and Darafine rushed toward the door and into the hallway, followed closely by Sereen and several of the others. At the far end of an adjacent corridor, on the same level, they followed the tech into the simulight broadcast room.

"Over there," he pointed, indicating one of the domes. "It fills the entire simulight bandwidth…on every frequency."

They moved closer to the dome, to the drama unfolding there. They saw a tiny figure they did not recognize, a person restrained and obviously in pain, struggling to keep his feet. A voice sounded as if narrating the scene. Shass.

"And so, my children," the Prime Lord continued. "Today, I have delivered you from a malignancy that has overshadowed this world for long enough."

Sereen reacted at the sound of her husband's voice. She had seen the monster he had become, the monster he probably always had been, just beneath the surface. She turned from the dome and stood a short distance away, listening, her eyes closed.

"What is this?" Josan asked, angry at the public display of torture. "Who is that? What has he done?"

The group looked more closely at the balding man under the dome. His face was battered, his scalp torn, his clothes ripped and bloodied. His robes hung in tatters, revealing a savaged, glistening back that had been laid open by prolonged and barbarous flogging. As Darafine watched, she came to realize that the man was not bald—his hair had been plucked out by handfuls, leaving sparse, bloodied shocks where a full head of dark hair had been.

"T. G.!" she cried out, realizing. Those in the room reacted in horror.

"No!" Josan shouted. "It cannot be!"

The voice of the Prime Lord went on. "This day, the false, self-proclaimed Dovo Kosi will meet his end. Without fear, we can, with the new sunrise, continue our journey toward peace and plenty, unencumbered by such as this wicked sorcerer."

The camera angle switched to a lower viewpoint, close on the man's face. His left eye was swollen shut, and the white of his right was bloodied red. His battered cheekbones were cut and bruised. His lips were torn. Blood streamed from his nose and mouth, and several of his teeth were missing. Yet beneath the wreckage of his now-inhuman face, the heart of the Voice shone forth in silence.

"We have to do something!" Josan cried in anger. "Where is the signal coming from?" He frantically studied the image of the courtyard. "I do not recognize that place…where is he?"

"I cannot tell," Andrel sadly replied, wishing it were not so. He worked the control array further in what he knew would be a futile effort to isolate the source of the signal. "The broadcast is on every frequency. Every simulight on the planet must be receiving this. It will take some time to ascertain his location…several hours, if ever."

The unfolding image continued. The mercilessly beaten Voice in the Dark was lifted into the air and pressed against the courtyard's central pillar by four of the Watchers while another mounted a ladder and climbed toward the metal ring above him. Darafine watched in silent horror for a few moments, then turned and moved to a stone pilaster near one wall. There she wept, silent tears falling as she had known they one day would. Josan saw her and went to her side.

"We will help him," he said, trying to comfort her. "We *have* to help him, just as he would do for us!" He turned to the gathered crowd. "Who will come with me? We will find him and stop this and bring him home!"

"No," Darafine interrupted, wiping away the tears. "What you speak is not the will of the Creator. You have seen that Ish works through T. G. He could have stopped this at any time. He did not. With but a thought, T. G. could be here with us even now, if he chose to be. He does not."

Josan turned to look again at the image. "But it makes no sense. Why give the Dark such a victory? Why would the Voice have chosen to—"

"Because of who he is," the woman gently said. "Because of *what* he is."

Then Josan remembered and understood. " 'The burden he must bear,' you said. This is what you meant. The Truth…it speaks of this?"

She looked up at him, her eyes wet, recalling the scripture: "And my chosen Voice shall fall silent."

⚭

His torn, mutilated back was pinned against the cold black stone by muscled arms that also held his legs and abdomen motionless. Above, another Watcher on a ladder slipped the chains that bound the man's wrists through the polished ring and reattached them to his manacles, suspending him there by his arms alone. Intense pain flooded him as it had for hours.

Then, as T. G. watched, the Gift was handed up to the man on the ladder. He wound its leather carry strap through the dark metal ring, hanging the artifact from the pillar, above its owner. It was a final insult on the part of Shass, who thereby used the precious Gift as a signpost to brand both it and its prophesied Voice in the Dark as false.

When they had finished, T. G. hung upon the pillar, his feet treading air, his weight fully supported by his aching wrists. As he watched the men walk away, he did not know exactly what to expect, whether it be a further scourging with the brutal whips or a firing squad of ripsticks.

It was to be nothing so pleasant.

The Watchers left the courtyard of the Dark Fortress, leaving T. G. alone there. The Voice struggled to breathe, taking what air he could in gulps. He was in excruciating pain, and the position of his arms made it difficult to get air. Looking up with his lone working eye, he saw Shass and Barthos seated in their box, watching him. He knew his life was numbered in minutes now, but his thoughts were not on himself. Slowly, he scanned the high surrounding walls and windows, searching.

Jenni was nowhere in sight. He feared for her, but he was grateful that she would be spared the sight of his execution. He tried to let go, trusting her life to Ish.

T. G. could feel that He was there with them both.

His attention was then drawn by a great sound, one of muscled tonnage loping heavily against the stone pavement. The crack of whips split the air, and commanding voices broke in. He turned his head slightly and saw a hulking ceratopid being led into the courtyard via one of the long tunnels. A glance to the right showed another, and judging by the sounds around him he determined that still another was being brought up from behind. Watchers led the great orange-and-purple beasts into the arena using a combination of electric prods and whips, bringing the animals into place for something.

T. G. suspected that he was to be intimately involved.

Two triceratops were goaded into position out wide before him, with the third directly behind. The three beasts, spaced equally around him and facing away, stood motionless as great harnesses were brought into the courtyard and thrown over their backs. Their muscular tails slowly moved from side to side as straps were fastened and adjusted on the heavy leather-and-metal fittings.

One of the dinosaurs turned sidewise as its harness was attached, drawing the attention of T. G.'s good eye. Straining to look to the left, the prophet recognized its markings and realized despite his diminished vision that the triceratops was one he had seen before, one he had previously looked upon with great affection.

It was Uncle Beazley, the gentle giant he had so fondly adopted at the Cusira biocenter. Its massive head turned to look at the tiny man lashed to the stone obelisk, and its eye met his. T. G. thought he saw a glimmer of recognition in that kindly eye, yet knew his face had been beaten to the point of being unrecognizable. He wanted to call out to the huge, powerful animal, to summon its aid.

I could will him over here. He could free me! I could live!

He closed his eye and turned away. It was not the course he was to take, and he knew it. His will was failing, and it was becoming increasingly difficult not to shift away or command the dinosaurs to come to his rescue.

Help me, Ish! I…I can't do it!

He clenched his teeth, shoving a loose incisor out of its socket and reopening a deep laceration on his tongue in the process. Throbbing pain and the metallic taste of warm blood filled his mouth anew. He struggled to focus on Ish, on the warm eyes of flame, on the One Who had chosen him, had trusted him, and some two thousand years before had died for him.

The Voice was faltering.

Shouts and a new sound drew his attention back to the activity around him. Heavy ropes three inches in diameter were attached to the harnesses of the ceratopids, one for each of the mighty brutes. The Watchers then struggled to drag the free end of the heavy, organic cables over to the column where T. G. hung.

They wrapped them once around so that they rested against T. G. and within the carved channels on the back of the stone pillar, then attached them to the metal fittings there. Other men standing beside the dinosaurs tightened the slack at the point where the rough, jagged ropes tied into the harnesses, creating even lengths between T. G. and each of the surrounding animals.

He had become the axis of a deadly three-pronged Maypole. The ropes cut across his knees, waist, and chest, binding him solidly against the cold, black stone of the pillar before crossing the distance between him and the huge beasts of burden. As far as T. G. knew, it was like no form of execution or punishment known on Earth, and it struck him as being cruel, yes, but also as highly inventive and incredibly effective.

The Triad. Simple and elegant. It was an atrocity that spoke of mankind's in its purest, fallen form.

Three of the Watchers took their positions next to the dinosaurs, prods at the ready. They were to serve as executioners. The others left the vast courtyard so as to further reduce the number of witnesses, carrying the ladder with them.

A signal came from the Prime Lord. The three Watchers nodded in acknowledgment.

It was time.

∽∘∾

Darafine and Sereen comforted each other as they watched the horror that filled the simulight dome. Josan paced, angrily slamming his fist again and again into anything within striking distance.

"The law is the law," Shass' voice rang again, filling the room. "And this man's crime demands that his execution, by Triad, be slow and agonizing. By decree, he must not reach the point of death before sunset. However, your Prime Lord is merciful…I will overrule the law and allow an expeditious death, so that this sorcerer, his false Truth, and its inherent madness all come to an end as quickly as possible."

"How very charitable," Josan said bitterly. "No one has died by Triad in thousands of years."

Ah, the old ways.

The Disciples of Truth were each huddled around one of the trio of domes in the room, unbelieving, unable to look away. Their faith in Ish and the Truth was unshaken, but their knowledge of what to do next was lacking. Confusion slowly built within them. The Voice had been their leader, their guiding light, their focus. And now he was being taken away, cruelly and suddenly.

They bowed their heads as if one. Silent, fervent prayer filled the room.

∽o∾

The Watchers pushed their prods into the flanks of the beasts, forcing them slowly forward. T. G. watched in horror as what little slack there was suddenly was taken up. The ropes left the ground. He began to feel the pressure of his bonds in earnest.

The world watched on public and private domes, and most viewers were eager to see the prophet fall. As the cameras zoomed in, intent on capturing every sign of agony, celebration ensued among those of the Dark. Those whose minds had been opened to the Truth wept, clutching their copies of the scriptures as they prayed.

The billions who followed Shass and had taken the implant cheered as the ropes tightened. After living entire lives devoid of any sense of justice or compassion, only now had they adopted a superficial sense of social ideology, modeling their new, shallow convictions after the spoken words of the Prime Lord. They cursed T. G. and the Truth, their hearts darkened.

A glimmer of movement above caught T. G.'s attention. Through a stinging, blood-curtained eye he looked up into the wide viewing portal directly opposite him and saw not only Shass and Barthos, but a trace of blonde hair in flurried motion. Jenni, in chains, was struggling against a guard and being struck for her resistance. Something was jammed against the girl's throat. She wept loudly as she looked upon T. G. below.

No! Leave her alone! Get her out of here!

Barthos, next to her, was smiling. T. G.'s anger flared.

When I get you one-on-one...

The ropes suddenly constricted him further, cutting off the thought. He could not move his legs. It was difficult to breathe.

Jenni, I'm sorry, I didn't want you to see this.

He would have cried had any tears remained. The pain increased with every prodding of the dinosaurs, yet he tried to watch Jenni, as if by doing so he could protect her.

"Let him go!" she yelled at Barthos through her tears. "Leave him alone...please...what do you want? Who are you people?" She struggled against the guard and the shackles that held her. Barthos turned and looked at her, smiling in amusement. Shass only shook his head.

"Whatever you want! I'll do whatever you want!" she offered, her voice choking through her tight throat. "I promise...just please, don't kill him!"

Barthos laughed.

"T. G.!" a faint, sobbing music called out, diminished by distance. "I love you!"

The words brought her sweet face to the forefront of the prophet's mind. He wanted to go to her, to shift out of the Dark Fortress and take her to a place of safety, then take revenge and lay waste the entire world for what it had done to them. If not for Noron, it would be 1975 and he would be home with Jenni and—

The ropes suddenly tightened again. T. G. had determined not to give Barthos the satisfaction of hearing any sound from him, but the intense pain overrode his will and burst from his knotted throat in a guttural cry. He began to sob, his chest heaving what little it could beneath the ever-increasing pressure of the unforgiving cordage.

With...with a word...with a thought...I could be free...

More electric crackles sounded, echoing from the black walls. The beasts pulled harder. The ropes compressed him further. An intense, agonizing pressure built in his legs, then was suddenly and sharply released as the bones gave way with a loud crack. He heard and felt a rapid series of snaps as his ribs began to yield.

Ish!

T. G. felt his life draining away, replaced by an agony that flooded every muscle, every bone. He could no longer breathe, his constricted lungs denied room to move. His vision began to tunnel and grow dark, the narrowing image encompassed by sparkles. With his last remaining strength, T. G. craned his neck and gazed at the Gift above him, at the words etched upon its surface. From his low, awkward angle, he could not read them all—but those he did see defined the very reason he had laid down his life…

"…that man may know the love of He Who made him."

Then, within his failing mind came the voice of Ish, piercing the chaos of the pain in his body and the roar of blood in his ears—and T. G. felt himself begin to pull free of the body in which he had lived. The warmth came to him, flooding him, washing over him. Mercifully, it drowned out the final, horrible collapse of his body as it yielded to pressures it was never designed to endure. Blood flowed freely to the ground beneath him as he was crushed into the cold, unforgiving stone of the pillar.

His heart, pierced by the splintered fragments of his rib cage, fluttered for an instant like a fallen bird, then stopped.

He felt a lightness, a swirl of motion. He could no longer feel the ropes around him. He saw a light.

And the Voice in the Dark fell silent.

Part III
THE JUDGE

27

J osan lay on his bed in the dim quiet of his room, staring into the shadows. His mind was burdened and unfocused, a haze of doubt and anger.

The Voice in the Dark had been taken from them. Like scattered sheep in the presence of wolves, the Disciples of Truth were frightened and unsure. For the first time in more than two years, they were without the spiritual leader they had awaited for almost five thousand. A regrouping would now be needed, a rethinking of the strategies they had so carefully and so successfully put into action. All they had done had hinged upon the Dovo Kosi, whose very existence had been the one tangible proof of the validity of the Truth and its prophecies.

Now that credibility was utterly gone. To the eyes of the world, the Prime Lord had become the victor in the war for the soul of Noron. On worldwide simulight, the forces of Drosha, Shass, and the Dark had proven themselves the stronger faith before billions of those who had been undecided or wavering in the placement of their trust.

Josan tried to suppress the anger he felt toward the Creator. He struggled to understand what had been accomplished, to grasp the reasoning behind the torture and murder of the one man who had become the physical heart and soul of the true faith.

It simply made no sense.

Darafine knocked and entered the darkened cubicle. She, too, had questions, but while she did not have answers, she did have her faith. She began to reach for a lightplate beside the door.

"No," Josan said. "Leave it off." There was hardness in his voice.

"Andrel located the source of the signal," she quietly said. "It is coming from a point in the far northeastern section of Luracayn, in the deep wilderness. There is an ancient fortress there...most likely that is the place we are seeing."

He did not respond.

"I just thought you would want to know."

"It is too late," he said, defeated.

"I know." Her head hung low.

"It just does not serve the Creator for T. G. to die that way."

"It would seem not," she replied, closing the door behind her. "But we have to trust Ish. All things happen for a reason."

Josan shook his head. "I have been over it again and again. Nothing I can think of makes his death more valuable than his continued life. Nothing." He choked on the words. "And now they mock him by just leaving him hanging there…like a trophy. It is abominable …as if torturing and killing him were not enough."

"Perhaps his death is an example to the rest of the world. There is no greater proof of love and commitment than to lay down one's life for another…or for the Truth."

"But in the eyes of the world, that expression of dedication comes at the expense of the Creator's omniscience," Josan replied.

"I know," she said.

"This was supposed to be the Awakening. But most of the world is still asleep…and will never awaken now."

"Many have been brought into the light."

"And so many have died. Our friends in Jerithia. Then Pretsal. And now T. G."

She walked over and sat beside him on the bed. "I miss them too," she said, placing her hand gently upon his. Tears welled up, blurring her vision in the already darkened room. "But we have to believe that this is for the greater good. We must now dedicate ourselves that much more toward the establishment of the Truth throughout the entire world."

"Our job has become about a thousand times harder."

"This could never have come easily. You know that."

"But this…it defies reason."

"Our reason perhaps. But we do not think as the Creator does.

We cannot see all things as He does. We have to be patient, Josan."

He considered her words silently. It would take time to get used to the idea that things were not going to unfold as he had expected them to, for his anger and frustration to fade. The woman rose, placing her hand upon his once more in a gesture of reassurance.

She left him alone in the dark.

∽∾

The lost rejoiced. Those whose eyes had been opened wept.

The sun set, and darkness descended. The mortal remains of the Voice in the Dark still hung by chains from the pillar. The ropes that had ended his life had been removed, and the beasts that had mindlessly done their part in the execution had been returned to their enclosures, leaving the courtyard empty save for the black obelisk and the still, tiny form upon it. Rigor mortis had come and gone. Lights flared into existence, throwing their glare upon the vanquished, unmoving figure, ensuring that all the world could see his broken body throughout the night.

On Shass' order, the corpse was not to be removed from the pillar at the stroke of midnight following his death, as was the custom. It was instead to remain in place until the week had ended. The display was a gruesome show of power and utter disrespect, but it made a point to all the world.

The Truth was not worthy of common respect, let alone one's faith.

Shass had declared a weeklong world holiday, for the threat of the Voice in the Dark had been removed from the face of Noron once and for all. The Prime Lord had also ordered that the image of the slain false prophet continue to fill simulight domes for the full duration of that week as a constant reminder of his victory. In homes and public places worldwide, in restaurants, businesses, and hospitals, the grotesque figure of the Voice's crushed, still form was everywhere to be seen. Those of Shass drew reassurance from it. The billions who wavered in their beliefs were confused by it, for the powerful words of Truth they had heard no longer seemed to make much sense.

All across the surface of the planet, parties began and gifts were exchanged. Those who carried the implant and bore the mark of the Prime Lord were given a provision of free credit toward their purchases, and they praised their leader and his kind generosity. All of his people overindulged in drink and drugs and the pleasures of the flesh as they lost themselves in the morass of the single largest party the world had ever known.

The hundreds of millions who had followed the Voice, who had heard him and had dedicated their lives to the Creator of Whom he spoke, were sorely tested. Everywhere, their leader's stilled, broken form hung for all to see.

Yet the believers were not alone. Their young faith, having had little time to grow and mature, was tempered by the hideous situation as if by fire. And in order that their faith be not utterly consumed by those same flames, they were strengthened against the relentless assault of the Dark until they could stand firmly in their knowledge of the Creator.

Their faith, callow though it was, would have to be resolute if they were to endure the still greater test to come.

∽∾∾

One of the larger parties in Luracayn took place in the home of Celestte Gesbal, once the hostess for the celebration of Paull Shass' miraculous recovery. Now she opened her home for a celebration of his ultimate ascension, after which all the world would be his to adore. Thousands came and went as the open-door affair dragged on with a depth of decadence remarkable even on Noron. Few were sober, and even fewer cared.

Celestte glided through the ballroom, seeing to it that her guests sated their every desire. She had brought in a simulight unit for every room, so that at all times her guests could be reminded of the wondrous reason for their carnal joy.

She paused and looked into the dome, wobbling slightly on her unsure feet. A smile crossed her rouged lips as she sipped her drink and gazed upon the remains of the bloodied, disfigured man, drawing extreme satisfaction from the sight. *And to think,* she maliciously considered, *I once let that warped degenerate into this house.*

As she watched, the image began to waver and break up. Another presence began to replace it, coalescing beneath the dome as a new signal clarified itself. It stabilized, forming a noble face with which all the world was familiar, a face that had not been seen in some time yet still carried a measure of authority. Celestte looked upon it, welcoming it into her home.

"Oh, my dear," she said to the lovely image, "where are you? We've been so worried…"

"Prosperity, people of Noron," the woman began, her eyes sharp, her face unveiled. "I am Sereen Shass, the wife of your Prime Lord. I have come to you to tell you that you have been deceived."

The full attention of the room was upon the dome. Indeed, all over the world conversations and festivities came to a halt as the previously popular woman spoke.

"My husband, your Prime Lord, is a fraud. He has never had the best interests of the Noronian people at heart…he has always desired only power for himself on a level unmatched in our planet's history. Now that he has gained this power, he seeks to use it to keep a stranglehold on the entire world. He is not divine, nor is he chosen. Please listen to me…I was not kidnapped or in any way coerced into leaving him last year, nor into speaking these words to you today. I left him when I learned of his government's plan for controlling the people, and I sought the council of those I knew opposed him.

"The prophet who was put to death was true. His coming was foretold thousands of years ago in the Truth he returned to our world. I know this from firsthand experience."

A loud murmur swept the party. Celestte pressed a switch and muted the sound coming from the simulight unit in the ballroom, then called out to her confused guests.

"Ignore her," she said confidently. "She is obviously under duress, saying words prepared for her. I know Sereen, and she would never attack her husband in this way. We have seen the Prime Lord's love for us, and we know what we know."

The party resumed, starting again at a somewhat quieter level. Celestte turned back to the simulight dome and momentarily watched the soundless lips of the woman as she went on speaking. Sipping from her glass again, the hostess reached up and rubbed her temple, and felt the tiny scar there.

∽◦∾

"Get her off of there!" Shass exploded.

"There's nothing we can do about it," Barthos said, watching the dome in the Prime Lord's office at the World Capitol. "But we can control the damage once she has finished. She can't speak for long without risking a trace, so she cannot say too much. Many will not hear her, and those who do will readily accept whatever explanation we give them."

The dome broke into static for a moment as Sereen's signal ceased and was again filled with the image of the dead prophet. She had spoken for only six minutes, but both Shass and Barthos knew that some level of damage had been done.

"Find her and kill her," the Prime Lord ordered. "I do not care what it takes. Put every Watcher in the world on it if you have to! I want her dead before midnight tomorrow!"

"That may not be necessary. The Twelve and their followers must have no direction now and very little public support. Billions who had been undecided have surely come to worship you and will soon take the implant as a sign of their allegiance to Drosha and the Prime Lord she chose. If we let things take their natural course, now that the Truth has been diminished in the eyes of the people, those who still follow the message of the Voice will be driven into the open and exposed. There will no longer be any public sympathy for them. They will now be seen as deluded fools."

"What if they try to steal the body? Perhaps we should have brought it back and put it on display here instead of leaving it in that courtyard."

"Taking it would serve no purpose. The whole world saw him die. Any claim they might make that he wasn't really dead would result only in mockery." He gestured toward the simulight dome. "Besides, I left the fortress heavily guarded, and the whole world's monitoring the body. No one could even make an attempt at it."

"I want the worship of the entire world, Cordan," Shass demanded. "If anyone breathes on this planet, he will do so with my mark on his head. I want the coming Feast of Rebirth to be the day I go before the people and tell them that every living soul on Noron is mine. I will not have my great name assailed in this fashion any longer…do you understand me?"

Barthos thought about that. "The Feast comes in just over two months. I don't know…that isn't a lot of time, Paull—"

"That is the way it will be, or I will replace you and bring in someone who can get the job done properly. Understand?" Shass sat at his desk, turning his attention to other matters. "You may go now."

Seething, Barthos looked away. *Perhaps now should be the time!*

He wordlessly walked out of the Prime Lord's office and headed down the corridor toward his own. Along the way, he toyed with an idea, and the more he thought about it the more it appealed to him.

Barthos took the elevator to the level four floors below that of the executive offices and stepped into the lobby of the Security Section. Walking casually to the door of the office of the Chief Watcher, he peered in and found the man eating dinner at his desk while the body of the Voice filled the simulight dome there. Barthos knocked on the doorframe, and the man spoke without even casting a glance in his direction.

"Yes, what do you want?" he demanded, his mouth full.

"Working late, I see," Barthos smiled.

The Chief Watcher coughed and almost choked as he looked up and realized who he had addressed so gruffly. "Oh…uh, yes, Chancellor Barthos," he said in a suddenly respectful tone, surprised that his superior had come to his office. "There is much to be done."

"Very good. I want you to bring the girl prisoner up to my office. Have her there in exactly one hour…understood? Not one minute later. And once she is there, I am not to be disturbed for any reason."

"Yes, Chancellor Barthos," the man nervously answered, knowing that his superior was easily angered if kept waiting. "It will be as you say."

"Yes, it will," Barthos said, turning to leave. "Do *not* disappoint me."

The chancellor headed back into the elevator. As the door closed, he thought of Jenni's youth, her beauty, her vitality. Almost laughing aloud, he silently congratulated T. G. for his excellent taste in women.

When it came to humans, Beltesha had always been partial to blondes.

∽◦∾

"This is everything I can remember," Sereen said, handing a sheet of paper to Josan. "The duty schedules were always strictly enforced by the Watchers. I was privy to many details of the security system, and these timetables dictated the placement of Paull's top men."

Josan scanned the handwritten sheet, Darafine at his side. "There may be a tiny window of opportunity," he said, nodding and pointing to the paper. "Here…at this point. For almost ten minutes at the shift change. There will be only half as many guards in place. The chances are small, but it is all we have. If we can avoid raising suspicion and prevent direct conflict, so much the better."

"What about the cameras?"

"If this is handled properly, they will not matter," Josan stated.

"I cannot promise that these figures are still valid," Sereen cautioned again.

"We will have to take the chance," he replied, taking a deep breath. He looked at Darafine, gazing into her eyes. "This is far from certain. Yours is the final word. Do we risk bringing him in? Lives may be lost."

"We do," Darafine asserted. "We owe T. G. this much, at the very least."

"And we bring him back *here?* Despite the risk? It could mean giving ourselves away again. We could lose everything, Darafine…and suffer a recurrence of what happened in Jerithia."

"He belongs here," she answered. "He is one of us."

∽◦∾

Jenni sat huddled in her detention cell, still utterly confused about her surroundings. Feeling cold, as she often did, her tattered sweater did little to keep her warm, and she wondered what had become of her long coat. She had convinced herself that everything happening around her was but a part of some strange nightmare, one from which she could not awaken.

It *had* to be. T. G. had died horribly before her eyes.

It had been a terrifying experience—the man she loved had been executed without reason or explanation. She had wept for him until she could no longer, hoping against hope that when the dream ended she could run to him and feel his arms around him and find him alive and well.

It *had* to be a dream!

Of course it was! Dinosaurs pulled those ropes! And since there are no dinosaurs, it must all be a dream! And these other people…they're so big and their eyes are so weird and they speak so strangely!

The cell around her had to be unreal. It was so odd, more of a pit or an animal cage than a jail cell. The bars were up so high, as was the corridor floor beyond them. Reaching out, she touched the hard cold stone of the wall, and wondered at the solidity of her hallucination. The tiny blue light of the monitoring unit on the wall shone clearly. *Are all dreams so vivid, but I just can't remember them? Will I forget this one as readily once I wake up?*

It had to have been weeks since her arrival, she knew. *Can a dream seem to cover weeks? Or months? Or years?* Dreams make their own past, their own prior circumstances, she once had read. She longed for a shower and clean clothes and her own bed.

She tried to retrace her recent past, hoping to understand how she had come to be where she was, if indeed it was reality she was dealing with. She had solid memories of being on the way to T. G.'s apartment, of walking along in the cold New York autumn. She remembered hearing the roar of an airliner passing high overhead, above the cloud deck where she could not see its running lights. Nothing seemed out of the ordinary at all—she loved to walk under the crisp night sky and think about things while the snow sparkled in the streetlights.

But then something odd *had* happened, she recalled. Nearing the Brookfelder Building, she was struck by how dark the structure was. No interior lights were visible. Seeing T. G.'s car in the parking lot, she had decided that he was home, that he had simply forgotten to call her that evening as he had said he would. It was not so unusual a thing; he had often gotten involved in projects or studies and had forgotten dates with her or other get-togethers with their friends.

She remembered climbing the wet, rock-salted steps to the tall, brass-trimmed door of the building. It had been left open, she remembered. But just as her hand had touched its frozen surface, there was a harsh gust of cold wind from just inside and a loud sound like horses stampeding across hard ground. *Something* had then swept her from her feet, something cold and brutal that carried her violently into a swirling darkness, and then—nothing. *Did I fall? Am I unconscious and suffering a concussion? Am I still lying outside T. G.'s building? Am I in a hospital?*

Her next awareness had been of being in the cell, where she had remained except for her brief trip to the fortress where T. G. was killed. They had tossed her around along the way, striking her a few times, but only as if to rough up her appearance. No one asked her any questions nor made any demands.

In the fortress chamber the night before, T. G. had looked so different to her somehow. Perhaps it was the robes he wore—she had rarely seen him in anything but jeans and a flannel shirt—or perhaps it was the way he carried himself, the authority with which he moved.

She thought back to the first time she and T. G. had met—in their elementary-school cafeteria. Walking past her as she ate her lunch at one of the tables, he had slipped on spilled milk and dumped a whole tray of spaghetti on her shoulder, ruining her new sweater. Had he not broken his arm as he hit the floor, she might have been angry with him.

Instead, it was love at first sight. Not that she told *him* that—one had to play the game, after all. A couple of days later, he had given her a card in the school hallway, apologizing for messing up her sweater. She was the first to sign his cast.

And the rest, as they say, was history.

She smiled at the memory. Those had been good times, with good friends and loving family. Her parents had practically adopted him as their own, well before the deaths of his own mother and father.

Other images then intruded upon her, shoving the kinder memories aside. She had watched him die, horribly and brutally. In her mind she again saw him there, tied to that horrid pillar, his blood running in rivulets from its base.

She shut out the image. *That wasn't real!*

Jenni glanced at the empty food tray she had left on the bunk opposite her own. She had tasted and smelled the bread and the odd drumstick of a meat she could not identify. It seemed that all five senses were coming into play in her amazing dream, with stunning clarity.

I dream in color. She smiled.

Seeing no choice but to tolerate the obvious hallucination and ride it out, she sat on her huge cot and leaned back. Her attention was soon drawn by footsteps in the corridor outside, and she looked up to see a huge man in dark gray robes at the cell door, peering down at her.

He looks like Ed Asner, she realized. *Now I know this is a dream.*

The man pressed his palm against a plate on the door, and it silently swung open. He stepped into the eight-foot-high opening, filling it almost completely.

"Setah cree kuda et tuphesa," he said, seemingly giving her an order. He did not shout but spoke with a quiet, determined authority as he gestured for her to come to him.

"What?" Jenni asked. "I don't under—"

The man thundered into the cell, taking note of the active monitoring unit on the wall. Reaching down, he grabbed her by the arm and pulled her to her feet.

"Hey!" Jenni defiantly shouted, pulling away. "What do you think you're doing? I'm not going anywhere with you. I know this is a dream now, *my* dream, so I make the rules from here on out."

The huge balding man looked at his timepiece, then with a sigh he fell back upon a second option. He reached into a pocket of his robe and produced a small gleaming sphere.

"What is that?" Jenni warily asked, backing away slightly.

In an instant, he had pressed the silver object against her neck. There was a small hissing sound. She fell into his arms.

The girl would not give him any more trouble. The guard effortlessly lifted her limp, sleeping form and carried her up the steps and out of the cell, closing the barred door behind him. He walked down the corridor of the minimum-security unit, nervously checking the time again. It was late. He had taken too long—much too long.

He knew that disappointing Barthos was less than wise and that his very life was at risk. But he had made a vow and had a job to do.

The Watcher carried her past the duty station, pausing momentarily to sign her out. The guard behind the desk, laughing at the sight of the girl over the man's shoulder, pressed a jeweled plate and opened the door to the elevator lobby. Still chuckling, he watched as Jenni was carried away.

She was expected.

28

The sky was dark and threatening, as it had been for months. A hard, howling wind swirled, cutting through the tree trunks and porch posts like icy water rushing through jagged rocks. The storms were building again; as they took life, their anger could be felt in the air.

Janice Parklin drove along in her blue late-model all-terrain vehicle. Its rounded metal shell was already dented from the hailstorm of a few days before, and with a wary eye she looked up into the building clouds as she made her way along. Brown, brittle leaves and scattered pieces of litter darted wildly in and out of her path, carried along by the outflow of the descending thunderstorm. It would be upon her in minutes.

It had become a world of upheaval in the decades since T. G. had last visited her. In rapid succession, so much had happened. First, hundreds of millions had inexplicably vanished worldwide. Theories proposed to explain the event, however unbelievable, ran the gamut from massive-scale alien abduction to mass hypnosis to the second coming of Christ.

Then war had ignited on the Eurasian continent, spreading like wildfire carried by the wind. Biological warfare, banned yet instituted nonetheless, had introduced dozens of new plagues into the general populace for which there were no treatments. Quarantines had been implemented and strictly enforced, separating the Western Hemisphere from the Old World.

Then a cluster of small asteroids had impacted the Earth in a damage path stretching from the center of the African continent across India and into southeastern China, throwing thousands of cubic miles of dust and debris into the upper atmosphere.

As a result of the impacts, tectonic plates across the planet had buckled, opening new volcanic fissures, which further damaged the already reeling ecosystem. Weather patterns worldwide had shifted, the result of hundreds of eruptions and a smothering cloud of ash and volcanic gases that dimmed the sun by day and the moon by night. Food production had fallen sharply as crops failed worldwide, and prices soared.

Powerful earthquakes had rocked the world. The cities of Tokyo, Mexico City, and Los Angeles no longer existed. The enormous fault lines running beneath them had opened up and swallowed the great cities, and the tremors continued as the entire surface of the planet suffered. Volcanic activity had increased a hundredfold, burying thousands of square miles under many millions of tons of falling ash, flowing mud, and molten rock.

New wars had erupted in the wake of the onslaught, as some nations preyed upon others whose resources had been compromised. The combined death toll from the disasters, both man-made and natural, stood at well over 1.5 billion—approximately one-fourth of the world's population. In large part, the northeastern United States had been spared the worst of it.

For the moment.

The neighborhoods and streets that Janice knew fell behind her as she reflected on the past. Even before the asteroids had struck, so much had changed in her life. Everything she had held dear had been stripped away by time and circumstances, leaving her alone to struggle through empty days made up of vacant hours and hollow memories. She had lost her husband and her only child, leaving her alone in a house that seemed large even when all three of them had lived there. Its wooden floors and brightly papered walls had become barren and cold. It was an old house where once a home had stood.

Over the years she had picked up books that stood dusty and forgotten on shelves throughout the house and pored through them, finding some measure of refuge within their pages. One night, with the cold snow of January silently piling up outside, she had even picked up a Bible before climbing into bed.

Years ago it had been a gift to Jenni from T. G.'s parents. Now it had saved her mother's life.

So much had happened since—one major world event piled upon another, both physical and political, and the structure of her life was altered yet again. This time, however, the changes were invasive and unacceptable, and she could not merely roll with the punches. She was left with no recourse but to run, to try to stay clear of the new dangers and new ways that were sweeping the strange, new world and to hope she could get by on the fringes, unnoticed and secure in isolation.

She had doubts, but she had to try. The alternative was not an option for her.

The woman had left it all behind, years' worth of accumulation. A few boxes of clothes filled the backseat of the vehicle, along with a handful of mementos. In the seat beside her was her purse, filled with cash she had emptied from her bank account. Paper currency was still worth something, at least for the moment, and if her luck held out it would maintain its value for just long enough. Gasoline had been severely rationed, but what she carried in her tank, she hoped, would also last until she reached her final destination.

She signaled at every turn and stopped fully at every light, making certain that nothing she did called attention to herself. Before long she would be out on the highway and headed toward her sanctuary.

A flash of movement caught her eye. Darting out from between two parked trucks, a man slammed headlong into her front fender, shaking the vehicle. The woman screamed as her brakes squealed and she slid to a halt. She leaped out of the car and ran behind it to the other side, shaken, her heart fluttering.

The man was on the ground, hurt but alive. He was struggling to get to his hands and knees, and as she leaned over him, helping him to find his balance, he looked weakly up at her. He was young, no more than twenty-five. His short, dark, curly hair dripped with sweat. His features were sharply chiseled yet kind, with brown eyes that were soft and wise. He was thin, too thin, as if his meals had come too small and much too far between. Blood ran from a wide cut on his forehead.

"I'm sorry," she stammered, wiping the blood away with a tissue. "I didn't see you...you came out of nowhere!"

He was breathing so heavily he could barely speak, clutching at her fluttering skirt with a weak hand. "Please...help me..."

Only then did Janice see the tiny reddish mark upon his forehead. During the months before, she had seen it many times on the television news, but never thought she would lay eyes upon it in reality.

"Please," he went on, bracing himself heavily against the side of the car as he managed to find his feet. "They are coming...they will find me..."

Janice knew the mark. She knew what it was, what it meant. For him, it meant persecution and arrest and torture.

For her, if she helped him, it meant death without trial.

Her mind raced. She made a decision.

She quickly helped the man into the vehicle, shoving her purse onto the floorboard as she cleared the seat. Once inside, he slumped sideways, bending low to avoid being seen. She pulled dresses and blouses from the backseat to cover him. Satisfied that he was sufficiently hidden, she closed his door and climbed back into the driver's seat, her eyes constantly scanning the houses and streets around her for any sign of his pursuers. She saw none and prayed that none had seen her.

She raced off, her heart still pounding. Something new had been thrown into the mix, something that gave her life meaning once again.

It began to rain.

29

Was there a problem in the cellblock, Kir Hervie?"

"No…and again, I am sorry for my lateness in bringing her to you."

"She is here; that is all that matters."

Jenni, still unconscious, had been placed upon the soft cushions of a bed in a small side room. Hervie looked at the girl, studying her. "She should come out of it at any time…I would have thought she would have already."

Just then, Jenni stirred. The voices had broken through the last few layers of induced sleep that blanketed her mind, and awareness returned. She slowly opened her eyes and realized she was no longer in her jail cell. An instant later she saw the two men standing over her, looking down at her. One of them was the Asner-like man she had seen earlier.

"Welcome back, my dear," the other man said. Jenni could not understand his language, however, and fearfully shrank from him.

A woman entered the room. Her hair was dark, her smile bright. She said something to the men, then took a seat on the bed, next to the girl.

"Hello, Jenni," she gently said in perfect English. "I see you are awake now."

The girl's face brightened at that. It was one of the few times in weeks she had understood something said to her. "Who are you?" she asked, hoping for an answer.

"I am Darafine Elesh, leader of the Twelve," the woman said. She then indicated the two men. "This is Josan Lorana, my chief administrator, and our new friend is Moryl Hervie. It was he who brought you to us."

"But who are you?" Jenni repeated, more insistently.

The dark-haired woman saw that the girl was frightened, and she felt for her. "We were friends of T. G.'s. In fact, it was he who taught me your language. For two years, I have studied. A daunting task, though I was able to grasp the basics quickly—I have always had a gift for words."

Jenni felt some measure of relief, having heard T. G.'s name spoken. "How did I get here?"

"This will make little sense to you, I know, but I will try to explain. Kir Hervie brought you to us…"

Jenni nodded and smiled slightly and looked up at Hervie. He nodded, pleased to have been able to serve his Creator through her rescue. The girl could not know that, unlike earlier when she had seen the huge man in her cell, he now no longer bore the traceable implant once contained within his skull. His presence therefore no longer threatened to lead the government to the Twelve, which was the only reason he dared come to the complex at all.

But it was no human medical skill or hidden surgery center that had removed the tiny device and its overlying mark, despite the theories of Shass and his chancellor. Just as He had done for all who had come to the light of the Truth, Ish Himself had removed Hervie's brand, cleansing him of the lethal thumbprint of the Prime Lord. It was an added gift to those who were His own, a tangible proof of the love that had freed them from the Dark—both spiritually and physically.

"He was a Watcher," Darafine went on, "a dedicated government official and former presidential bodyguard. For many years, government service was his life." She smiled up at the man, whose face suddenly became quite kind as he returned the smile. "But then the Truth, as it does, spoke to his heart and opened his eyes to the light of the Creator. You were supposed to have been taken to the office of Chancellor Barthos last night. Had that happened, I shudder to think what would have befallen you. Instead, and just in time, Kir Hervie used his position, along with information we provided, to free you and bring you to us, as he had promised he could do.

"You are safe now. Following his arrival here, T. G. had asked us to begin a search for you…your safety was of primary importance to him. He insisted that you had to be among us somewhere, so we used every method and every contact at our disposal to find you. However, after many months of looking, we found no sign that you had ever been on Noron and eventually gave up our search. It was not until Kir Hervie contacted us a few days ago that we learned you were indeed here."

"Where is 'here'?"

"We are in a safe place in the extreme northern wilderness."

"No…I mean, what is 'Noron'?" she asked, apprehension in her voice.

"That is the name of this world," Darafine smiled. "I know it is a lot to comprehend…but the Creator has seen fit to bring our two worlds together in this manner to fulfill a promise made to those of Noron long, long ago."

"Dor jaleed crealosa?" Josan asked Darafine. She smiled, replied, and listened as he spoke to her once more. The woman then nodded and turned back to Jenni.

"Josan reminds me that you have been on our world for quite some time," she said. "Kir Hervie has explained everything to us. Apparently, you arrived sometime during T. G.'s first visit here, nine years ago. It saddens me greatly that he did not live long enough to learn you were safe. He loved you very much." She paused, seeing the wetness in Jenni's eyes.

"He said that?" the girl asked, a bittersweet smile on her lips.

"Many times," Darafine answered, touching Jenni's shoulder, giving what little comfort she could.

She looked around, seeing the room for the first time as possibly something other than part of a mad dream. "What do you mean *nine years?*"

The woman went on. "Yes…it must seem a much shorter time to you. Since your arrival, your presence here was kept a secret, and you remained asleep in bio-stasis. It is a deep, induced sleep during which the mind and body remain unchanged. You were reanimated only because Barthos felt the time had come to use you as a tool against the Voice in the Dark."

"The what?"

Darafine smiled. "This will take a little while to explain."

∽∘∾

Barthos slammed his fist against his desk for the hundredth time, infuriated that the girl had been taken from him, apparently by one of his own men.

"Hervie is dead…do you understand me? Dead!" he thundered. "And find those healers! I want to know who's pulling our implants!"

"Yes, Chancellor," the new Chief Watcher nervously said. "We will find Kir Hervie and execute him. And the healers will be found. All will be as you say."

"Go! Get out of here!" Barthos commanded, uncontrolled fury seething just beneath the surface. The man before him was grateful for the opportunity to leave and wasted no time in doing so.

Barthos glanced across the room toward the simulight dome that stood there. The image of the dead, silenced Voice still hung within its crystal shell, the body so much the worse for having spent half a week exposed to the warm, open air.

At least you're out of the way, the man grinned scornfully.

He went back to his work, channeling his anger into an avenue more constructive than assaulting his desk. Reports were coming in from all over the planet that those who had been followers of the Voice and the Truth were in disarray, scattering in confusion as the constant likeness of their slain prophet played before them. The psychological onslaught Barthos had put into play by keeping T. G.'s image before the world was working—and brilliantly. The one-time Disciples of Truth were scattering like sheep with no shepherd.

So he had lost the girl for now. Big deal. She *would* be his eventually, when those who were protecting her fell to the grinding millstones of military action, economic exclusion, and social pariahhood.

And when he did finally have her, he mused, it would be that much sweeter. Perhaps he would have T. G.'s corpse mounted and hung in his office, so that the now-sightless eyes that had once defied him could look on as he brutally conquered the girl.

Ah, the old ways.

Amusing himself with the thought, he continued to look over his paperwork until a motion barely within his field of vision drew his attention. He looked up, expecting to see someone entering the office, but saw no one. He dismissed the movement as a trick of the light, until a few seconds later when it happened again. He looked up once more.

It was not coming from the doorway.

It was coming from the simulight dome.

He watched in horror as the battered face of the Voice he had silenced slowly looked up and stared directly at him. Then, with a piercing whine, a burst of brilliant light swallowed the image, filling the dome.

Barthos screamed.

∾o∾

The two women sat alone in the room that had been T. G.'s. Jenni was feeling better, for she had been able to shower and wash her hair for the first time in weeks and been given clean, soft robes of light blue and white. Darafine simply visited with her, answering her questions, giving her all the time she needed, knowing she had a whole world to get used to.

The girl sipped grape juice from a porcelain cup, assimilating all she heard. She struggled with the possibility that perhaps she was not dreaming, after all, but even when her intellect was satisfied her heart was not. Acknowledging that the place and the people around her were real also meant accepting the fact that T. G. was dead, and that she could not do.

Other worlds, other cultures, and a chosen prophet with whom she had shared many a pizza. The whole thing was way too big and way too strange.

As Darafine sat near her, continuing a brief lesson in recent Noronian history, the door suddenly flew open.

"Darafine!" Andrel called from the doorway, "you had better come see this!" Then he was gone, leaving the door wide open.

The woman immediately leaped to her feet. As she hurried toward the door, Jenni called out to her.

"What? What is it?" Jenni asked. "What did he say?"

"Stay here," she instructed Jenni. "I will be right back."

Darafine ran into the simulight room to find Josan and Hervie already there. Andrel stood at his console, his eyes wide. Josan held a hand out toward Darafine, summoning her closer. "Come and look!" he invited her, his tear-marred face a picture of joy and amazed fascination.

She drew near until she could see the dreaded dome once more. For days it had held a vision of death and defeat, mocking the Truth and all that its followers had stood for. It had become an enemy, a symbol of the Dark.

But now it held light. And life. And wonder.

As they watched, the dazzling light began to dim, revealing in its midst a moving form, one very much alive. When the glow was gone, the cameras revealed that T. G. had been restored. His face was unmarked, his hair once again was thick and dark, and his eyes shone with triumph and determination. His flesh was whole again.

And all the world witnessed the return of the Voice in the Dark.

Jenni, too curious to remain behind as Darafine had instructed her to do, walked into the room and saw her T. G. within the dome, still hanging from his chains.

"No, no!" she began to cry. "I can't watch this again!"

"Jenni, no!" Darafine beamed, rushing to hold the girl. "This is happening right now, as we watch!"

"It's…it's *live?*" a confused Jenni asked, gathering the courage to look into the dome. "But…I don't understand."

Darafine went to Josan. They embraced, their eyes on the miracle unfolding before them. Their joy spilled out into the room around them. "The Voice is alive again!"

Jenni, so happy she could not contain her feelings, began to cry. Even Hervie's eyes filled with tears of absolute joy. He knew he had chosen correctly in believing the Dovo Kosi and in the Truth that had been brought back to Noron. Of course he had. *There was never any doubt!*

But yes, there *had* been, he knew.

Hervie also knew there was one woman who had not lived to see this day. His joy was dampened as he thought of her pressed against a hard and unforgiving marketplace floor. That aged, gentle face—its dignity, its bravery, and its unfathomable peace—had ultimately led to his own conversion. It had been what first put doubt into his mind concerning the godhood of Paull Shass. The woman's eyes spoke of a depth of devotion that no follower of Drosha or the Prime Lord had ever known, and *that* love had nagged at Hervie until finally, stubbornly, he had come to realize that the Truth was *real.*

His face had been the last thing her eyes had seen. Those eyes had stayed with him, judging his heart, right up until the moment his Creator had called him into the light, as one of His own.

He turned and left the room, his eyes still filled with tears, but for a different reason. He was humbled and mystified that he, a man who had killed one of Ish's chosen, could be called to salvation by his Lord. Such grace and forgiveness were beyond his comprehension, and such love he had never known. As he returned to his own chamber, the huge, powerful man fell to his knees and wept, begging the forgiveness of his Creator. Comfort would come—yet the man would carry the image of the elderly woman's eyes with him for the rest of his life.

∽◦∾

Back in the simulight room, the miracle continued to unfold. Josan, his face wide with a beaming smile, turned to Andrel. "Bring the others! All must witness this glorious sight!"

Jenni and her new friends watched as T. G.'s chains melted away and he dropped to the ground, fully intact. Standing at the base of the pillar upon which he had died, the prophet rubbed his wrists for a moment, then appeared to look upon his tattered robes with some amusement.

T. G. turned to Ish, Who stood beside him, unseen by the rest of Noron. Ish had been with him the entire time, through the entire trial, and it had been His voice, His command that had returned His prophet to physical life. The Voice in the Dark looked into those loving, brilliant eyes, eyes now as filled with glory and victory as they had been filled with tears and empathy three and a half days earlier. The Voice nodded, knowing what had been accomplished.

"Welcome back," Ish smiled, placing a warm hand on T. G.'s shoulder. "It is done."

The entire world now knew the reality of the Truth. Through the resurrection of the Voice, they had witnessed the power of their Creator firsthand. Like Lazarus of Earth before him, and for the first time in Noron's history, the dead *truly* had been returned to life.

The image of the risen Voice continued to go out to all of Noron, despite frantic attempts by Barthos to stop the broadcast. Other forces kept the cameras functioning, turning the Dark's attempt to humiliate the Creator into the very vehicle through which His greatest statement would be made to the world.

Other Disciples rushed into the simulight room and quickly came to realize what was happening. The camera angle widened to reveal heavily armed and armored Watchers rushing into the courtyard. They opened fire. T. G. rose to his feet, unharmed, but he took no direct action against them. The Watchers, seeing the invincibility of their target, dropped their weapons and fled the scene.

Finally, as T. G. stood in utter triumph, he spoke to a confused, frightened, and transfixed world. "I walk among you again because of the power of He Who made the universe," he began. "The Creator has sent me to you that you may accept His gift of eternal life. I, his prophet, have been made alive again, and so shall it be with all who believe in the very Son of the Creator, Whom you know as Ish. *There is Life in no other!*

"He Himself has paid the just penalty for your transgressions. Long ago, in another place far from here, He, at once Creator and Son of the Creator, took on a sinless human form and was put to death …taking upon Himself the inflictions due you all. The debt of sin you owe Him has been paid for you in full. You are free now, free to come to Him and accept eternal life in His name."

"Son?" Darafine wondered aloud. "Then…He is no mere angel as we had believed…!" She stood in utter amazement as the totality of the Truth crystallized in her mind. "Of course…it had to be! This unifies the entirety of scripture…the history, the promises, the coming of the Voice…everything!" She excitedly turned to Josan. "Do you not see? That is the answer to the great mystery of the Scriptures! The Truth hinges upon *one* supreme sacrifice…made by *one* sinless man! *Without it, there could be no reconciliation between Creator and Creation!* And that sacrifice was made by the only Being in the universe Who could possibly have made it…the Creator Himself, made flesh! *Ish!*"

"What is it?" Jenni asked. "Tell me, Darafine!"

"The Son of the Creator has returned T. G. to life!" the woman told her. "And now, because of His own sacrifice of long ago, *all* may live!"

"The Son of the Creator," Jenni quietly repeated, her face a picture of new comprehension. The title obviously struck a familiar chord.

Darafine's mind filled with warm, new light as dozens of lines of scripture suddenly sparkled with perfect clarity. One formerly undistinguished verse now sang to her, crying out of a love and a design and a dominion more intricate and complete and wondrous than even she had imagined:

And before all the world, death shall be an enemy fallen upon his own sword; the Son of Man shall raise his Voice, and the sleeper shall arise, and the Truth shall be known.

"We are the sleeper," she whispered. "Of course…"

T. G. went on. "I was sent to you first as the final Guardian of the Truth. But I was also sent so that Ish could display His love and His power through my resurrection. And now, I am here to herald His coming! He will come among you in but a mere span of days, leading a final war against the forces of death and darkness that have had their way upon Noron for long enough! Each of you, wherever you are as you now listen to me, must decide with which side you will stand…and make no mistake: There can be no neutrality in this!

"What you have witnessed today is a display of the *true* power of life in the universe, unlike the false miracle created by the forces of the Dark in the healing of Paull Shass! Drosha does not exist, and the worship of her is a falsehood created by the Dark through the governments of Noron. Look to the Truth, which has been returned to you! Decide…decide with whom you will fight! The hour of the final battle is upon you all! This…is the *Awakening!*"

Jenni had not understood a word he had said. But he was alive again, and at the moment that was all that mattered. She had finally decided that what she was seeing, however fantastic, was no dream, and any power that could have restored T. G. in such a manner was very real indeed.

The Voice and the Gift that had hung above him vanished from the scene inside the dome, as if never there at all. The black stone obelisk stood barren and alone at the center of the bloodstained courtyard, a silent monument to the miracle all had witnessed. Darafine and the Disciples of Truth fell to their knees in joyous prayer, thanking their Creator for what He had done. Josan wept, repentant that so much doubt and so many questions had filled him following T. G.'s death. He had lacked trust, yet from that weakness had now come a stronger faith and an even greater love for the Truth.

Jenni walked away from the others and stood alone near the door, considering all that had so quickly inundated her. Her eyes streamed tears of joy. She had witnessed a miracle. After hearing Darafine's words, she had recognized with sudden clarity the parallel between the Truth and the Christian faith of Earth, and she understood that the one true God was indeed Lord of all worlds and all peoples. Father and Son and Holy Spirit—one infinite God in three Persons, just as she had always heard. She knew Who it was Who had given her beloved T. G. back to her, for her eyes had been opened to the reality of Who Ish was.

The Son of the Creator...Jesus Christ!

She felt a deep gratitude and an even deeper awe, and for the first time in her life she saw her own need for Him. Inaudibly, she whispered words she had never uttered before and made a decision she had never before made.

At that instant her life forever changed. She felt no urge to laugh, knew no tingling sensation, and saw no fireworks before her eyes, for raw emotion was not the foundation of the gift she had just gained— just as it was not the basis of the infinite price that once had been paid for it.

She did, however, feel the warm hand that touched her shoulder. Jenni spun to see a smiling face she had longed for, a face she deeply loved.

She fell into T. G.'s embrace.

As the others stood around them, he held her, cherishing her, feeling her warmth within his arms, smelling her long blonde hair as her head rested against his robed chest. Jenni began to cry anew, drawing from his strength as she finally let go of emotions deeper than any language could have expressed. There was nothing said between them, yet T. G. knew that she had come to know her Creator, that never again would he have to fear losing her.

Unseen, Ish stood nearby. In a few hours much would befall the world, but for the moment a quiet and prayerful togetherness was needed. He looked at T. G. and Jenni and smiled, for He shared their joy and was most pleased.

She had chosen well.

30

It was a new day. All had managed to find sleep during the night, despite the excitement surrounding the return of the Voice. The true wonder of what had transpired was not lost on the Disciples, who tended, despite themselves, to stare at T. G. just long enough to make him uncomfortable. This continued off and on throughout much of the morning, until he reminded them all that they, too, were servants of Ish, just as he was, and that all had their own special roles to perform in the Awakening.

The day wore on, and everyone was thankful for the calm. The interlude was necessary yet doomed to be brief, they all knew. All-out war loomed on the horizon, menacing and inevitable, for the Dark would not accept meekly the resurrection of the Voice. *Something* would happen—and very soon.

For now, they enjoyed a gentle quiet, and something wonderful was allowed to take center stage in their lives, if only for a moment.

In a flowering glade beneath majestic oaks just outside the Twelve's command center, T. G. and Jenni were married in a quiet ceremony. With Darafine presiding, the couple stood before the Twelve and the assembled Disciples of Truth and became one, bound together in love to face what the future held for them. The ceremony involved no ring, no white dress, no throwing of rice—only the modest, symbolic sharing of a single goblet of wine between them, with a simple vow of dedication spoken by each to the other before the gathered witnesses.

They spent the afternoon alone as husband and wife, walking hand-in-hand in the small clearing near the moundlike entrance to the underground complex. Pterosaurs sailed across the sky high above, butterflies fluttered from blossom to blossom, and brilliantly colored birds sang sweet melodies. The newlyweds shared fruits and breads T. G. carried in a leather pouch slung at his waist and drank pure water kept icy by a small synthetic crystalline bottle.

They were as Adam and Eve, knowing each other in the splendor of Eden. It was paradise, and for the moment they were alone in all the world. He held her and she him, each with a new realization of just how precious the other was, how fragile their lives were. They had lost each other, seemingly for all time, yet had found themselves back in each other's arms.

Despite the extraordinary series of events that had transpired since, a single moment in time still gnawed at T. G.'s conscience, one he wished he could erase forever.

"I'm so sorry," he said, watching as an enormous falcon soared gracefully above. "I was so wrong…what I said to you…those stupid things."

"When?" she responded, looking up at him.

"Before," he stammered, looking into her dark eyes. "After I got so upset over your date with Michelle's cousin. I was such a bonehead. I was way out of line to have said those awful things to you. I know you just went out with him because she asked you to…you didn't even know the guy. I just…well, I just…I got so…" He trailed off, lost in a morass of insufficient words. Nothing that could fall from his lips could fully express the regret still in his heart.

But she heard his heart, the silent and painful struggle there. She stepped close and gently spoke four words that healed the self-inflicted torment needlessly burning within the man she loved.

"I don't remember that."

Then Jenni smiled, her face a radiant song that cleansed him, humbled him, forgave him. All he could do was look into her sparkling eyes, thanking Ish that He had seen fit to give such a woman to such a foolish man.

The day went on, and the sun dipped low. The fauna and flora of Noron captivated Jenni, as she saw in them a scale of loveliness and magnificence she never imagined nature could possess. It was beautiful beyond words; yet even with all of the wonder around them, T. G. rarely took his eyes from her.

"What is it?" she finally and impishly asked, noticing his complete attention. "Do I have lobsters coming out of my ears?"

"It's just that I have to keep pinching myself," he smiled. "I can't believe you're really here...or that you're still mine. I thought I'd lost you."

"*You* can't believe it?" she laughed. "If anyone had told me that my wedding would take place on another planet, or that my husband would be a chosen prophet of God, raised from the dead...well!"

"Well, the way *you* say it, *sure,*" T. G. said with mock seriousness. "You make it sound far-fetched or something."

She slapped at him, smiling. "Oh, right...I suppose to you this was all just a day at the office? TilGath-pilnezar Shass, if you try to stand there and tell me that—"

"Where did you hear that?" he interrupted, floored to hear his full name spill from her lips. "How do you know my name? All this time you've known and you never said so?"

She took his hand. "Don't be mad...your mother told me during the party she threw for your dad's fiftieth birthday. She said that if we were going to be married, then I at least needed to know who I was getting saddled with."

He feigned anger. "Oh, just great. What else did she tell you?"

She sidled closer and stood facing him, pressing against him, rubbing her hands up his shoulders and around his neck. A huge smile crossed her face. "Oh, not too much...just that your little hiney was the cutest any baby ever had."

"Please...not the bearskin photo," he moaned with a pained face.

"The bearskin photo."

"Great."

"Oh...don't be such a grouch." She leaned up and kissed him, savoring him, thankful that they were alive and together. They stood in each other's embrace, listening to the insects in the trees and the music of the gentle breeze against the leaves high above them.

∽◦∾

Cordan Barthos sat at his desk, his head in his hands. It all seemed to be unraveling, everything he had worked so hard to build. Worldwide reports indicated that people were staying away from the Drosha-Shass temples in droves, undecided where their loyalties should lie. Every person who turned to the Truth was a dagger in Barthos' chest, and he was ready to put an end to the continuing abandonment, whatever the cost. The implants were vanishing without a trace, and no medical facility for performing the removal procedure on his former followers had been found.

The Prime Lord had taken his staff and gone into seclusion at the Dark Fortress. The last thing he wanted was to have to answer questions or face the public before a solid strategy was in place for regaining the ground that had been lost. His anger against Barthos had become unquenchable. He had voiced publicly that his chancellor was at best incompetent, at worst a traitor.

Barthos knew they had to cut their losses. If the fools would not bow to their Prime Lord, Barthos was determined that they would not bow to the Creator either. If he acted quickly enough, they would remain his for all time.

An empty ranch is better than none at all, Barthos mused, remembering Shass' metaphor. *And cattle are bred for death, after all.*

The rhythmic sound of wet, labored breathing suddenly became apparent in the room and drew closer. Barthos was bathed in a dim blue light. He looked up into glowing sapphire eyes that cowered a bit as they stood before him, some fifteen feet away. The thing dared come no closer.

"We are ready," it said.

"Do it," he said. The entity nodded in understanding and was gone.

⁖◦~◦~◦⁖

The sun had set. T. G. and Jenni lay on their backs on a densely clovered hillside, gazing into the night sky above them. She was astounded at the color and intensity of the stars and at the deep magenta of the sky into which they were set.

"Isn't this romantic?" she asked. "I mean, who gets a honeymoon like this?"

"Well, yeah, I suppose it is."

"Why is the sky that color?" she asked, awestruck.

"Long story," T. G. smiled.

She was fascinated. "It's so beautiful."

"I wish I had a really good telescope right now. I bet some of those higher magnitude stars are really twins. And there are four ringed planets—"

"Romantic to the end," she teased, tickling his ribs with a finger. "Can't you just look at something pretty without being so scientific, for once?"

"Sorry," he laughed. After a moment, something dawned on him. "You know, I've been here for more than two years, and this is the first time I've really stopped and taken the time just to look at the stars. I mean, I've glanced up at them, but not like this…smelling the roses, star-wise."

"I'd say you've been missing quite a show." She thought for a second. "Two years? I thought I've been here for nine."

"Well, I've been here twice…once before, when you wound up here, too, and then this time, with seven years in-between by Noron's reckoning."

"What do you mean, 'by Noron's reckoning'?"

He got up on one elbow, facing her. "Time doesn't flow the same

way here as it does back home. I don't know why or how…but when
I went back home after being here the first time, I found that out."

"What do you mean?"

"I had only been here for a day or so before returning to Earth.
There…" He trailed off, reluctant to continue. Jenni did not know
about her father's death or that she, like T. G., had lost more than two
decades back home. "It's…it's just different. Hard to explain. I don't
really understand it myself."

"My parents must be worried sick," she said. "Nine years…I can't
imagine what they must have gone through all that time." She looked
at him. "I know there are still things to be done here, T. G., but could
we maybe go home just long enough to let them know we're okay?"
She looked into his eyes. "Is it possible? Please?"

He looked away, considering it. Once there, she would know how
much time she had really lost. It would be painful for her. But she
deserved the truth and to see her mother again. *What do you think, Ish?*

*Through Me, you now have the power to shift anywhere you
wish…and back again. Take her home, T. G., but only briefly. The Dark
is on the move.*

"Okay, Jen," he smiled. "Let's go home."

"Now?" she asked hopefully.

"Whenever you want. But we can't stay long…at least, *I* can't."

"Where you go, I go," she said. She leaned over and kissed him,
then lay back in the cool clover again for a moment and stretched,
staring without really thinking at the expanse above.

"Huh," she commented after several quiet moments, as something caught her attention.

"What is it?" T. G. asked, sitting up.

"Up there," she pointed. "Those three stars…that could almost
be Orion's Belt…with the Orion Nebula just below them."

"*Now* who's being scientific," he teased.

"No…really. Look."

T. G. followed her arm up to the formation of stars. There were

---

so many in Noron's sky, thousands more than he had ever seen from Earth, that individual patterns were almost swallowed up in the glittering clutter.

"Yeah, kind of," he replied, "but it can't be. The constellations we know would only be visible from Earth's position in the galaxy. Move far enough away to be on a world like this one and they'd lose their patterns."

"I guess so," she said. "But there, too…look. Those stars could almost be the Pleiades, don't you think?"

His eyes shifted from point to point among the heavens. "You're right. It does look like—"

He abruptly cut himself off, his mind suddenly reeling, and leaped to his feet. The sky suddenly cried out to him, as if he had been deaf all his life and was hearing for the first time. *There's Taurus…and Gemini!*

He whirled to the northwest. *Cassiopeia!* And to the northeast. *Ursa Major!*

It was inconceivable. It was impossible. It was true.

It was Earth's sky.

∽∞∾

The little girl heard a noise coming from her parents' sleeping room, a noise like her friends made when they wrestled in the dirt outside. She rose from her bed, picked up her rag doll and cradled it against her, then walked out of the room she shared with her siblings and into the main area of the house. It was strangely cold and dark enough that she could not see well, yet she made her way along, knowing every inch of every room and hallway.

It had been a loud night. Her parents had gotten into an argument over something, which always frightened her. Their words about a Creator and a Voice and about Drosha were confused and skeptical, filling the house with tension and doubt for most of the evening. Her parents had always told her that Drosha loved her, that the man who had come to be their leader would make sure they would all be happy for the rest of their lives.

Now they were not so sure. Her father had brought home a book, one full of big words and with no pictures, and it had brought questions into the house with it.

The child saw a familiar grayish glow coming from the open door of her parents' room. Stepping into the doorway, she saw her renewed grandmother standing next to their bed, leaning over them as they lay still.

She could not see the contorted, agonized faces of her parents, frozen in death stares, mouths agape. Nor could she see that the gnarled hands of her ghostly grandmother were inside their chests, her cold fingers tightly wrapped around their now-still hearts.

"What is it, Geja?" she innocently asked in her small voice, rubbing her eyes. "Are they asleep?"

"Yes, my child," the renewal answered. "Asleep."

"Why are you in here?" the girl asked, her breath fogging before her. "Why is it so cold?"

The renewal stood up and turned toward the child, its eyes glowing a familiar, soothing blue. It held its arms out to her, beckoning her to come closer.

"Come here, little one," it said. "Come to Geja."

∽○∾

Her eyes fell upon a place that was alien to her, and the nearer she drew the more foreign it became. It should have been very familiar, a place of kindness and peace and gentle memories, yet it was not. Its peeling white trim and torn window screens spoke of neglect, as if it had been abandoned for some time.

Jenni moved cautiously up the walk to the house, her disappointment growing with each step. Her new husband hung back a short distance, remaining near the curb as he watched Jenni come to grips with what Earth had become in their absence. He knew he had to tell her what he knew about the time they had lost and about her father. But he watched and waited, choosing his moment so as to hurt her the least. He could not simply blurt it all out at once, he knew, but he also knew he had to prepare her somehow for what they would surely find.

Neither of them could fathom the abandoned wreckage of their former neighborhood, a place of broken windows, cracked pavement, and overgrown lawns. There was no one to be seen on the entire street. It almost had become a ghost town. The only things missing were blowing sand, tumbleweeds, and the sun-bleached wreckage of a stagecoach lying in the street.

That mental image caused something else to occur to T. G. It was incredibly still, far more so than he could ever remember it being on Earth. The air was warm and stagnant, with no trace of breeze. It was so quiet. No leaves stirred in the lifeless trees, no insects buzzed, and no birds moved in the sky overhead or sang their songs. Though it was only afternoon, the sun was strangely dim, throwing an odd light upon the world. It was as if one were looking through sunglasses, and more than once T. G. absentmindedly reached up to remove eyewear that was not there.

Things had changed, timeless things. The sun had lost its brilliance and the winds had withdrawn from the world, leaving it alone to suffer a fate T. G. and Jenni did not yet understand.

As the young woman mounted the steps to the wide, covered front porch, T. G. hurried up the walk toward her. Dead grasses and weeds well more than a foot high surrounded them. To one side, he spotted the desiccated remains of a small dog, almost completely concealed by the heavy growth. The sight struck him as odd somehow, and it took him a moment to sort out why. *There are no flies...there should be flies!*

Jenni hesitantly approached the front door, extending a reluctant hand toward the torn screen door. The house felt all wrong, as if it had never belonged to her. She glanced up at the metal house numbers, verifying yet again the correct address.

"Mama?" she called, not really expecting an answer. "Daddy?"

The heavy wooden front door was slightly ajar, allowing her to see that the house was uncharacteristically dark and horribly quiet. She halted in her steps, pulling her hand back, and turned to T. G. as he came up beside her.

"What happened?" she fearfully asked, sadness in her voice. "This doesn't look like nine years…this looks like, I don't know, a lot longer."

"It *is* longer," he gently said. "Like I said…the time flow between the two worlds is different and very erratic. When I was here before…after I had been on Noron only a day or so…I found that a lot of time had passed here while I was away." He paused, reluctant to hurt her, but he knew he had to continue. "I'd lost twenty years, Jenni. That's how much time had gone by *then*. Now it could be a year or two later or fifty. I have no idea."

"Twenty years?" she asked, shocked and incredulous. "But…but that can't be, T. G. It just can't…" She looked up at the house again. "My parents couldn't have gone through that, worrying and waiting for me to come home for twenty years! They just couldn't have!"

He held her for a moment, giving her time to cope with the truth. She had handled the revelation pretty well, he thought, but he dared not pile the news of her father on top of that. Not just yet.

"Are you okay?" he asked, looking into her eyes.

She nodded bravely. "Let's…let's just find my parents."

"Okay." He moved past her, pulled aside the screen door, and cautiously pushed the front door open. "No one's here. Come on," he said, confident that it was safe. "Maybe we can get some answers inside."

He took her hand and together they walked into the house. The last time he had been there, Jenni's mother had been alone, living a life of solitude and sorrow. Even then the house had felt much as it had in 1975, still filled with the sounds and smells to which T. G. had become accustomed during his years around the Parklin family. But now all that was gone. The house smelled only of emptiness and decay, and it was so awfully quiet.

Her mouth open in disbelief and sadness, Jenni stared at the broken chaos her home had become. Most of the furniture her family had owned was missing, and what remained stood in broken disarray, toppled, shoved out of place as if ransacked. Drawers had been pulled from desks and dressers and thrown aside, their contents spilled and scattered everywhere. A torn, stained mattress had been pushed into one corner of the living-room floor, where once Jenni's mother's antique piano had stood, and trash and food debris were strewn about the floors. Jenni began to cry as she looked upon the looted ruin her home had become, searching for something, anything, that would tell her where her parents were.

T. G. left his wife for a moment and made his way through the house. His footfalls brought creaks from the scratched, faded floorboards as he kicked empty food cans aside, stepping over and on the widespread layer of clutter on the floors. He walked into the kitchen, remembering his last discussion there. It had been in that room that he had first come to realize that he had lost so many years and that Jenni, too, was missing. Now, as he looked upon the broken plaster of the walls and the ruined hardwood of the floor, he knew that yet again the world that was his home had gone on without him.

He spotted a crumpled, soiled sheet of newspaper and reached down for it, hoping to find its date. To his dismay, however, he discovered that the upper part of the page was missing. His eyes fell upon a small headline:

U.S.–EUROPEAN UNIFICATION PLAN SENT TO CONGRESS

PRESIDENT EXPECTED TO APPROVE U.N. PROPOSAL

He scanned the article for a moment, then dropped the paper, shaking his head. *I wish I could say I was surprised.* The political unrest of Earth had led a war-weary world to accept the idea of a single, one-world government. One man ruling the entire planet. One government. One law.

No place left to hide…

Who knew how old the paper was. Perhaps it had been lying there for decades, and Earth had already suffered under the corrupt and merciless totalitarianism of its own Paull Shass.

T. G. turned and walked back through the house, headed toward Jenni's former bedroom. He found her sitting in a cleared area of the disarrayed floor, leaning against the wall, her face wet with tears.

"Where are they, T. G.?" she asked, not really expecting an answer. In her hands she held a water-stained framed photo of her mother, its shattered glass catching the meager light. She looked around the spoiled, dusty room, trying to correlate the sight with her memory of the warm, comfortable bedroom in which she had lived. *My dresser was over there…my bed was right there. My vanity was there!*

"Listen, Jenni," T. G. slowly began. "I think it's been a long time since I was here last."

"I know," she grimly said. "I found this." She held up part of an old phone bill, dated October 1999, and handed it to him. "It's old. And it's addressed to my mom…not to my dad. Why isn't it addressed to my dad, T. G.?"

He lowered his head, knowing he had to tell her. He saw the worry and confusion on her face and wanted to soothe her, not add to her pain, but there was little choice. She had to be told. He sat down and put an arm around her, trying to comfort her, and told her what he knew of her father's death.

She rested her head against his shoulder and quietly cried, her body shuddering. He held her as she let the grief go. They sat there for a long time. It grew darker outside.

Jenni thought of her father, of the good times she had spent with him. They were times that had been all too brief in hindsight. She now regretted the days she had told him she was too busy with school matters to go to lunch with him. She wished she could have one more day to see him again, to tell him how much she loved him.

Thoughts of her father led invariably to thoughts of death and the afterlife, and she wondered what he had gone through—how he had died, what he had felt, and what he was now experiencing. It dawned on her that the answers might lie just a question away, with one who had died, yet lived again. Her love for T. G. was strong and pure, and she felt ashamed that she had not yet offered herself as one to whom he could open up and share what he had endured.

Jenni reached down and touched her husband's ribs. "I never asked you," she quietly said.

"What?"

"What was it like...when you died?"

He thought about that and smiled gently as he wiped away the last of the wetness on her cheeks. "Well, the actual dying part wasn't so great." She smiled briefly as the joke broke the tension. "The pain was indescribable. But it was only *my* pain."

"What do you mean?"

"I can't imagine the suffering Ish must have gone through, on the cross. I mean, the sheer agony of crucifixion...plus the anguish, the guilt, the sin of *every* man and woman ever to live, all heaped onto His shoulders at the same time. It's so far beyond...anything..." His voice trailed off.

There were a few quiet moments as both considered the immeasurable sacrifice made by their Lord. T. G. held his wife tighter, and kissed her hair.

"Did you see God?" Jenni asked.

"Other than Ish?"

"Yeah. I mean, Heaven and all."

He considered the question. "I remember being somewhere, somewhere very peaceful, but it's all vague, like a dream. Hard to remember. There was light everywhere. And this soothing music I can't describe...it was wonderful. Beyond just musical notes, somehow. I do remember that Ish was there. It's funny, but He's the one thing I do remember clearly, as if He were the focus of all else...the light, the music, everything...as if nothing else really mattered in and of itself." He breathed deeply. "And then, I was back in the courtyard and the pain that had been in my body before I left it was gone…and here I am."

"Here you are," she softly smiled.

"I was dead for more than three days, but it seemed like minutes. I guess time didn't exist where I was. I just…sort of stepped out of the flow for a minute, then back again." He smiled. "Or something like that."

"What you were saying before…about the way time moves and all. Can we go back?" Jenni asked.

"Back?"

"To 1975…before all this."

He held her more tightly. "No. I don't think so."

She nodded, reluctantly accepting the fact. After a few more moments, she spoke again. "What could have happened?" she wondered aloud, looking up at a broken window nearby. "There's no sign of anyone. Where is everybody?"

"I don't know. I haven't seen or heard a living thing since we got here." He glanced around. "But it looks as if *somebody* slept in here not too long ago. Bums, maybe…probably a good bet. Who knows when that was."

"There's just nowhere else to look," Jenni sadly conceded. "If Mama thinks I'm dead, which she certainly does by now, then there's no telling where she might have—"

She cut the words off, in one motion sitting bolt upright and whirling to face T. G. Her face came alive, her eyes sparkling again.

"The cabin! She went to the cabin!"

The possibility had not occurred to him. "Could be…"

"Sure! They were going to go live there when they retired anyway, Daddy always said, and by now…sure! That has to be it! She's there!" Jenni, filled with a new hope, jumped to her feet and anxiously helped T. G. to his. "Come on," she said, still clutching the framed photo of her mother. "Pop us up to Canada!"

He had wanted to check on David, to see how his friend had fared since the last time he had seen him. But Jenni came first, and seeing David at that moment would change nothing.

"Okay," he smiled. "First class or coach?"

"Just do it!" She playfully slapped at him, her face bright with optimism.

"I'm going to have to start charging you by the mile," he teased. Her smile filled his heart. It was all the payment he needed.

31

Small as glacial lakes go, it had been cut into the Canadian soil thousands of years before by the same mammoth sheet of ice that had drastically reshaped the entire landscape. It was a pretty lake, with craggy reefs along its stony shores and still waters that ran cold and deep. Its water was clear and pure at the surface, but an abundance of minerals once carried by rain from the surrounding rocky hills had created a brownish tinge just a few feet below. Abundant varieties of fish swam in its depths and along its shores where tall pines stood, meeting the water's edge with no sandy beach, only broken rock. The dense forest that bordered it on all sides extended for thousands of square miles in all directions, towering so high as to hide the lake's existence from those who were not specifically looking for it. Other than coming in by floatplane, only an old, forgotten logging road provided any access at all—and then only if one had a vehicle tough enough to make it along the narrow, winding, pitted route.

Perfect.

Janice Parklin walked out onto the porch of the huge cabin, taking with her a bowl of small potatoes and a peeler. She had already cleaned and filleted the fish she had caught earlier in the day and was preparing a side dish that had always been her favorite. And her husband's. And her daughter's. There had always been plenty of frozen, canned, and freeze-dried food in the cellar beneath the cabin, enough for a year or more for all of them, so selecting the day's menu resembled shopping at the market more than anything else. An artificially lit garden kept behind the cabin provided fresh vegetables, just as the one she had long nursed in her backyard in Ithaca had always done.

She sat in her rocker and set the bowl in the lap of her blue housedress, then began a recipe she had prepared many times before. A special seasoning and frying method taught to her by her grandmother could transform mere cut potatoes into things of culinary wonder, and as she began to cut and peel she remembered past times and past meals.

It saddened her that the secret would stop with her. She had always meant to teach it to Jenni, but the girl had always been so busy with her friends—

She stopped, catching herself. Even after decades, her heart had never healed and she still agonized for her missing daughter. True, the pain had lessened with time, but it remained nonetheless. No body had ever been found, and T. G.'s visit in the mid '90s had been so brief that she wondered if it had really happened at all. If only—

No. She isn't coming back. Move on—you have other responsibilities now!

She looked out over the lake, at the small, gently sloping trail that led downhill from the house and to the boat dock at the lake's edge beneath her, some 150 feet away. The waters grew dark so much earlier in the day than they once had, she noticed, since the sun had been dimmed by ash. It would be night soon. She longed for the warm, bright sun of a few years before, before the tumult had enveloped the world, when things were still as they always had been.

She continued to peel and cut the potatoes, working without really thinking about the task at hand, glancing up occasionally at the lake. The sound of a fish splashing near the small dock drew her attention to the empty rowboat moored there, the gentle ripples lapping against its sides as it patiently waited for the next time its services would be required. The name 'Jenni Lynn,' though faded a bit, was still emblazoned across its stern, hand-painted in blue.

My Jonathan built that boat—for her—

She looked back down, back to her work. Her hands, she noticed, had become her grandmother's hands. A moment later, her ears were caught by the pleasant sound of a gentle rustle in the trees, a sound she had not heard in some time. As quickly as it had begun, it stopped. She looked up at the pine forest around her, and at the trees along the lakeshore—

—and her gaze was caught by two robed figures standing on the dock, looking up at her as they spoke to each other. One was dark-haired and clothed in blue, the other blonde and wearing white and holding something. Janice had had no visitors since coming to the cabin, and her eyesight, while not as it once was, was still sharp enough to have spotted the strangers on their way in—yet she had not seen them approach. It was as if they had just suddenly appeared on the dock. Fear gripped her, and she wondered if she dared make a dash for the house.

Please—they couldn't have found us! Not here!

Looking closer, she could see that one of the intruders, the blonde, was most certainly a girl. A voice, calling out across more than a hundred feet and dozens of lonely years suddenly broke the stillness.

"Mama?"

Janice stood, knocking the bowl from her lap and its contents to the floor. Her mind whirled upon itself, pulling away from her senses, fighting to accept the possibility and hoping against hope—

"Jenni?" she called, her voice breaking. The robed girl ran toward her. Janice, breaking into a flood of tears as she realized it was true, descended the wooden steps and ran toward her daughter. "Jenni! Dear Lord…Jenni!"

They met on the pathway, embracing and crying, holding each other. Janice kissed her daughter again and again, saying her name over and over as if trying to convince herself that it was real. She caressed her precious Jenni's face, looking at the lovely eyes and nose and smiling lips she still knew so well, crying along with her daughter as their spoken sentiments melted into a muddle of tears and joy and unending thankfulness. Finally, after many minutes, words came once more.

"Oh, sweetheart," Janice struggled, joyously crying and laughing at the same time, "where were you? Why have you been away for so long? Are you okay? Oh, look at you…you're wasting away! Have you been eating?" The questions came like a barrage of machine-gun fire, prompting Jenni to laugh.

"Oh, Mama...I wish I could tell you everything! So much has happened...we were at the house, and I found this..." She held out the old, framed photo. "And when T. G. and I figured out that you'd be here at the cabin, we—"

"T. G.?" the woman asked, remembering that there had been another person on the dock. She looked past her daughter, toward the robed figure standing some fifty yards away. "Did he tell you I saw him after you'd disappeared? He came to the house, but that was years ago..."

"How long have you been up here?"

"Oh...years now..."

Only then did Jenni see the decades that had befallen her mother, realizing that the middle-aged woman she remembered had now far surpassed the half-century mark. She mourned for the years that had been lost in their relationship. Her mother still looked vital and beautiful, despite the fact that her auburn hair had gone largely gray and her face had become gently lined with worry and loneliness. Her eyes still blazed brightly with the same vivacity Jenni remembered, but there was something new there too—a profoundness, a deeper purpose, a clarity of perception she had never seen before.

A spark of eternal life. Her mother, she now knew, had been touched by her Creator.

T. G. stood on the dock and watched them, allowing them all the time they needed. This was their time, their reunion, and he wanted to let them share it alone. He smiled, a tear running down his cheek, happy that the woman's long vigil had ended, that her daughter had finally been returned to her. He would join them, and soon, but first there was something he knew he had to do—and do alone.

As he gathered himself, he paused to look up at the reddish

moon, inching its way downward toward the pines to the west. It had been a long time since he had looked upon its mottled face, and it was one that had become that of an old friend once again. He smiled, and was gone.

∽•∾

Night had fallen. Cordan Barthos, dressed in flowing black robes, stood upon the dais of the throne chamber, looking at the dark stone of the room and thinking. He felt more at home in the Dark Fortress than anywhere else in the universe, and he often came here to clear his head. It was his world to build up or to destroy, and in no way was he going to let anyone undo all he had brought to fruition.

So He threw us a curve. Well, it's nothing we can't handle.

Renewals planetwide were killing any in their families who even hinted that they might turn to the Truth, so Barthos knew it was likely that the proportion of Drosha-Shass followers to those sucked into the Truth would remain constant or better. Who knew? If enough were killed, the ratio of the lost might even hit eighty percent.

Very soon it would be all-out war, and he relished the thought. And best of all, the Voice had gone back to Earth, his role in things fulfilled.

At least the kid has no further role to play. That's one less pain to worry about.

He surveyed the room, remembering. Here Guardians had died. Here the Voice in the Dark had finally been captured.

And I rightfully had him! He was dead and out of the way, and then you cheated and brought him back!

The massive lancet door to the chamber slowly creaked open. A black-armored Watcher entered the room and nodded respectfully. "Yes, Chancellor Barthos? You summoned me?"

"Where is the Prime Lord?" Barthos asked with no little disgust in his voice.

"He is below...in conference in the Hall of Law, sir."

"What's he doing?"

The man suddenly began to shift his feet nervously, obviously reluctant to answer.

"Well?" Barthos insisted.

"He is...well, sir, he is choosing the new chancellor."

"I want him up here. I must speak to him."

"I will inform him of that as soon as the conference has ended, Chancellor."

"I want him here now. Tell him I demand his immediate presence...and in this room...that his future as Prime Lord is at stake. 'Later' will be too late."

The Watcher was caught in the middle, fearing for his life. Whatever happened, it was likely he had seen his last sunset. "I will...I will tell him of this at once, Chancellor. I do not know that he will listen."

"He'd better. Go."

The man quickly left the chancellor. The huge wood-and-steel door shut behind him with a loud *thung*. Barthos glared at the closed door, waiting.

It was time to bring in the heavy artillery.

∽૦∾

It was such a lonely place.

T. G. carried his sandals as he walked across the wide, featureless plain, his bare feet sinking less than an inch into the pleasant warmth of the dusty sands. A brilliant white sun in a deep black sky hovered low above the horizon and cast long, dark shadows upon the desert expanse. It was just as he had always imagined it would be, a place of stark contrast and magnificent desolation.

He drew near the place he sought. Small, scattered fragments of golden material sparkled all around him, shining brilliantly against the dark ground where they had been blown by a burst of fiery gases. Boot prints trailed everywhere, sharp and clearly defined, leaving mute testimony of the coming of two men who had anticipated that single moment for all of their adult lives.

T. G. turned and walked over to the centerpiece of the site, a spindly looking structure of aluminum and Mylar. He moved into its shadow, standing where once another man had stood with the eyes of the world upon him. Tears in his eyes, T. G. gazed upon the curved, stainless-steel plaque attached to the structure, left there to speak for all time of the momentous accomplishment of that day. He read the words engraved there, words he already knew by heart, words that had brought inspiration and hope to a country divided by war and hatred and to the people of the entire world—

HERE MEN FROM THE PLANET EARTH
FIRST SET FOOT UPON THE MOON
JULY 1969 A.D.
WE CAME IN PEACE FOR ALL MANKIND

They were great words, proud words, words that had captured the imaginations of all who had heard them read aloud that Sunday night so long ago. Standing upon the footpad, T. G. reached out and took hold of the lightweight aluminum ladder before him, sensing that he must be the first to stand in that spot since Neil Armstrong had done so at the end of man's first walk on the moon.

In his youth, T. G. had longed to make the quarter-million-mile journey undertaken by his spacesuit-clad heroes. Now, thanks to Ish, he finally had, though not by a means he or anyone else had ever envisioned.

Through Me, you now have the power to shift anywhere you wish— and back again.

He turned his head and looked toward a point just a few yards to the north, a spot that had proven too close when it counted. What he saw saddened him, tearing at the long-held national pride he still felt.

There, a long bronze pole rested against the soil where it had fallen after standing for less than a day. The proud banner it once had held erect was all but gone, broken into dust by conditions it never had been designed to withstand. A lone, small fragment remained upon the soil, protected by a thin layer of gray dust, bleached white where once red and blue had shown.

He slipped back into his sandals and easily climbed the ladder in the reduced gravity. Taking a seat on the corrugated porch above, T. G. paused there and looked down. The sight of the two discarded life-support backpacks near the foot of the ladder caused him to wonder at his continued existence. Those who had been there before him had been forced to rely upon complex, bulky suits to sustain them against the harsh conditions of the lunar surface. But T. G. was breathing, fresh air passing in and out of his lungs. The 250-degree heat of the scalding lunar sun was gently warm against his skin, while the minus-250-degree shadows were only pleasantly cool.

Something that is only there when it needs to be, he recalled of the Gift and its protective layer. He smiled at the comparison.

He craned his neck almost directly upward and looked at the Earth. It was a precious marble of life against the black void, though not blue as it once had been. Patches of dull gray blotched most of the globe, largely hiding its ocean surface and obscuring the warm tones of the landmasses. He had expected as much. The weather he had just seen while there was a far cry from anything he had known while growing up. *Something* had happened to the planet, he knew. Exactly what, he did not.

"You see it as I always have," a voice spoke.

He lowered his gaze to find Ish standing at the base of the ladder. "How can I hear you speak?" he asked. "There's no air. I'm hearing you, and not just in my mind."

Letting the question pass, Ish continued to look upon the world above. "Once blue, but now darkened...a brilliant jewel tarnished by iniquity."

"It's still beautiful," T. G. said, gazing at the shrouded planet.

"Even like that...what's happening up there? When I was at the lake...the sky looked different."

"Our day has begun, as was foretold."

T. G. considered the words for several moments, still amazed at the precision with which God's great plan unfolded. He then turned his attention toward the discarded spacecraft beneath him.

"You know, I really wanted to be an astronaut when I was a kid," he smiled. "To orbit the Earth, to walk around up here. I never thought I had a chance. The odds were next to zero. It was a profession with maybe forty openings, and they were full. But here I am."

He looked upon his Lord, questions on his mind. "Ish...back on Noron, the stars I saw were the same as those here—"

The Son of Man smiled, running a hand along a rung of the lunar module's ladder.

"The answer to that goes back to the beginning of time, T. G. Just as a potter begins with a lump of clay and fashions from it the item of his desire, so the universe was created. Before all things were, there was the 'clay,' brought into being by the will of My Father."

"That's what I saw in that vision you showed me," T. G. recalled. "The beginning of Creation."

"Yes," Ish said. "But once created, much evil would befall the world, including the rebellion of man. We knew this in advance, since We created all the scenarios of history, both possible and actual."

Omnipotence. T. G. nodded.

"The Dark, once temptation had led man astray, did all within his power to prevent Us from keeping the promise We then made to mankind...the promise that We would send into the world One Who would reconcile Creator and Creation. In a very short time, the thoughts and deeds of men became intensely depraved, and no room was left in their darkened hearts for God.

"The Dark and his own swept the world, increasingly defiling it, even to the point of interfering with the physical propagation of mankind. He hoped to corrupt man's lineage to such an extent that the promised Deliverer could not be born. We could not allow this to happen. Our promise had to be kept. It became necessary to destroy your world with water to eradicate the shroud of evil there and preserve a single, untainted bloodline through which the Redeemer would come."

Water, T. G. understood. *Like baptism—a symbol—a cleansing!*

"It was Our desire to show those of Heaven's realm the necessity of this great Flood, this Deluge. By doing so, the Father would be glorified, and His love and trustworthiness would be displayed.

"So before the beginning, the clay was divided into two exact likenesses, and each was set into a separate dimensional framework. Not two halves of a whole, *but two wholes.* They became identical worlds, set in motion simultaneously, lying within different planes of existence.

"One of these is your world. The other is Noron."

T. G. was stunned. An alien planet halfway across the galaxy was one thing, but a dimensional twin, occupying the same space at the same time?

Ish went on. "The people of Noron are descended of Adam, just as you are. We took two of his posterity, male and female, to Noron, well after the Fall at Eden. Within a short span of centuries, mankind filled Noron just as he had filled the Earth. Sadly, the malignancy of sin increased there as well, and the entire Noronian race soon turned its back on its Creator. Only Earth knew the Deluge, however. The depravity on Noron was allowed to continue unabated, until only a handful remained alive. Their corruption was complete. Only the grace of My Father finally restrained them, for without it, man on that world would have perished utterly by his own hand…and so it would have been on Earth."

T. G. was amazed. "So Earth was originally like Noron is now? With the canopy and the single continent and everything?"

"Yes," Ish nodded. "It was as you say. Earth, too, once knew only one race of people. And one language, the Old Tongue, which was given by the Father to Adam. But that was before the Deluge and before the confusion at Babel that only Earth knew."

The Deluge. It was the reason that Earth's surface featured extensive fossil beds, while Noron did not have them at all. The planet's vast layers of sedimentary rock, along with the fossilized remains they bore, had been laid down during one single, catastrophic, worldwide event.

"So," T. G. realized, "through Noah's family, the lineage of the Deliverer was saved...and You Yourself then became—"

"The Redeemer of both worlds. Yes."

The simple beauty of the plan was overwhelming. T. G. sat for a moment, awed by what he had heard. Earth had been given a transitory reprieve from the plague of eternal death. Had the Deluge not come, man would have perished nevertheless—and utterly. The Flood had *saved* mankind, and the intense corruption that had plagued the Earth had been washed away so that all could begin again and God could become Man in order to save him—eternally.

"Those agents of the Dark who had directly interfered in the propagation of man, on both Earth and Noron, were bound and will remain so until the time of judgment. It is they you saw in the form of 'spiders,' there within the Pit."

A shudder swept T. G. "There were so many..."

"What you saw were but the merest fraction of their number. They are as the grains of sand on the shores of Galilee."

T. G. nodded, his mind still filled with questions. Another sprang at once to the surface. "But why the time flow difference between the two worlds?"

"For the protection of both," Ish continued. "We created the stream of time within each plane of existence so that it would run independently of the other, speeding up and slowing down erratically and abruptly, with no parallel along the way. Anyone bound within one of the flows would perceive only a constant and even progression of time...but the flows are in reality drastically disparate. This keeps the forces of the Dark divided. While they can indeed travel between Noron and Earth, they cannot know exactly when they will emerge on the other side, and therefore they cannot plan a prolonged attack and carry it out. At the moment of Creation, the time lines began at the same instant...and they will end at the same instant. But in between, there is no equivalence.

"Beltesha, heeding the prophecies of the Truth, knew that the Voice in the Dark would be chosen from among the people of Earth. Therefore, long ago, he chose to travel to your world and wait for as long as was necessary for the giving of the Gift, so that he could attempt to prevent the fulfillment of the Promise made to the faithful of Noron."

Ish played his fingers lightly against the cool face of the lunar module's dedication plaque, feeling the two hemispheric maps of Earth engraved there, enjoying the inadvertent symbolism of two identical worlds, side by side yet never touching.

"Come," he said. "It's time to be getting back. You must return to Noron. The culmination of all things has begun."

T. G. climbed back down the ladder though really it was not necessary. He paused to take one final look around, picked up a tiny moon rock, and dropped it into his pocket.

And then the moon was lonely once more.

32

Paull Shass pushed open the immense door to the throne chamber, bringing his armed Chief Watcher with him as a bodyguard. The door closed behind them on its own, unnoticed.

It had been a bad night. It was about to get worse.

Much worse.

Shass was livid, his breath coming quickly in loud, nasal bursts. The very idea of his soon-to-be-former chancellor demanding an audience with the Prime Lord of all the world was infuriating. He found Barthos kneeling at the steps to the dais, his back to them, giving no indication that he had heard them enter at all.

"I am here, Cordan," the Prime Lord announced, stepping closer as he left his bodyguard near the door and approached the dais. "What is it? What could not wait until after you had been replaced with someone of competence?"

There was no immediate response, which only made Shass angrier. Barthos continued to kneel, his head bowed, facing away.

"Today is the Feast of Rebirth, Cordan…and I do not yet rule the hearts of all the world. You recall my deadline, do you not?"

Shass scanned the antiquated room, its carved murals and horrifying statuary chiseled above the dais. His eyes then came to rest upon the inscribed letters in the face of the upper step of the platform. It was not in a language he could read, but he recognized its general appearance.

"That is the Old Tongue," he accused. "It is forbidden! What is this place? I have never been up here…I never even knew this room existed."

"It was not necessary that you know," Barthos calmly spoke. "Until now."

"What do you mean, 'not necessary'? You forget to whom you speak, Chancellor!"

Barthos stood and calmly turned to face the Prime Lord. "No. I have not forgotten." He stepped down from the edge of the dais and slowly walked closer to Shass, speaking as he moved. "You see, all has pointed toward this moment. Everything I have done, everything *you* have done, has led to this moment. You're an integral part of what will now come to pass."

The temperature in the room plunged, and a visible frost suddenly formed on the walls, floor, and ceiling. Shass' and Barthos' breath fogged in the gelid air. In seconds it had become painfully cold.

"What is it?" Shass demanded, some level of fear in his voice. "What are you doing?" He backed away from the black-robed figure before him.

Barthos watched Shass with some amusement. "What's wrong, Paull? Don't you trust me anymore?" He smiled. "Oh, that's right... you don't. Well, in any case, you won't be replacing me. I'm afraid it's going to be a Shass-Barthos ticket from here on out."

"You are not merely dismissed from your duty," Shass threatened, "you are a dead man." He gestured for the bodyguard behind him to come forward. After a few tense moments, when the man did not appear, Shass whirled to see why not.

Without a sound, the Watcher had been dismembered limb from limb, his blood and internals splayed wide across the floor and walls, frozen solid. His sightless eyes stared at Shass, frosted white. His mouth was locked open in terror.

"Sorry about that," Barthos said. "I know good help is hard to come by. I suppose you'll be wanting my key to the executive washroom."

For the first time in his life, Paull Shass was truly terrified. Cold sweat soaked his forehead and palms as his mind blanked. Panicked, he whirled and charged the door, clawing at it wildly, tearing his fingernails away in its rough grain. He tried to pull the ice-covered handle, but his sweating hands only froze to the metal. He cried out in agony as he tore them away, leaving his skin behind.

"Now, now," Barthos smiled. "All this fuss. I'm not going to kill you, Paull. You have my word on that."

A roar filled the chamber. Shass put his torn hands to his ears, trying to shut out the painful sound. A great wind kicked up, making it difficult to stand, yet Barthos seemed unaffected. The sound grew still greater. He could feel it in his chest.

Shass stooped over and cradled his bleeding hands, looking up at Barthos. "What is this?" he screamed.

"This, Paull," Barthos answered, a touch of pride in his voice, "is the center of the universe. Watch this. This is great."

A coruscating swirl built upon the throne dais, a ragged cyclone of cerulean light that widened and grew brighter as Shass watched. The roar of a thousand screams echoed from the icy, blue-lit stone walls. Barthos knelt where he stood, facing the platform.

A tremor shook the ancient fortress and the dense timberlands around it, tossing the towering trees and the huge black edifice on a rolling wave as *something* approached, something discordant with the physical world it was entering. As the floor moved, Shass was thrown from his feet and onto the icy remains of his former bodyguard. He screamed and tumbled clear, then tried to steady himself on his hands and knees. He looked up at the dais once again.

Something began to take shape, materializing out of the light. It gathered substance, becoming a dark mass of shapes, taking on a definite form.

It was a throne.

Fifteen feet high and eight wide, it was made of polished human bones fused together into a solid, dark yellow-brown mass with glistening veins of solid gold running among them. The eyeless sockets of burnished skulls stared out into the room from its arms and back. Femurs and vertebrae formed its base. It was hideous.

The glowing blue maelstrom continued, building anew as Shass watched in horror. He began to cry, frightened beyond his capacity to contain the fear that filled him.

"Oh, come now," Barthos teased, shouting so he could be heard above the din. "Be a big boy."

The brilliance of the vortex swelled until it was blinding, and Shass shielded his eyes. Suddenly, the noise and light were gone, and Shass looked in fear toward the throne.

There before him sat—*something*. It was huge and roughly human, translucent and etched in blue light, a full ten feet tall in a seated position. It had eyes of piercing light and an inviting face that spoke of unending benevolence.

It had once been the pinnacle of all Creation.

It was beautiful.

It was Death.

Shass gazed upon it, rising to his feet. He could not look away. Its intense beauty overloaded his mind like a powerful drug, demanding the total commitment of his senses.

Come to me, it said.

Shass stumbled forward. For him, the room, Barthos, and the world no longer existed. All there was, was the figure on the throne. It had become his universe.

Come, it beckoned again. *And all the treasures on all the worlds I rule will be yours.*

As Barthos knelt, Shass moved closer to the throne as if in a trance. He could not look away, could not disobey the voice that spoke to him. He ascended the first step and then the second, all the way up the six steps until he stood face to face with his destiny.

In an instant, with a sharp cacophony of tearing flesh and snapping bones, it was over.

Always use the tools at hand . . .

Shass sat on the throne. His body had been utterly violated, ripped into layered shreds of tissue around shattered bone held together only by his belted robes, then instantly healed again. His flesh had momentarily opened to admit a new tenant, and in that one agonizing moment the man known as Paull Shass ceased to have any control whatsoever over the body into which he had been born. He had been shoved mercilessly into a dark corner of existence—trapped, blind, and deaf, within his own skull. He was fully conscious, yet cut off from his senses and the outside world. He tried to scream again and again, but his efforts were soundless and unheard.

The new owner of the body smiled, holding a bloodied, torn hand to his face, flexing its fingers. His eyes burned a bright blue.

"Flesh," he smiled, his voice an echo of death.

"My Lord," Barthos said, his eyes down. "We are gathered. It is time."

The Feast of Rebirth had seen its final, ultimate realization.

The Dark had been made man.

∾○∾

At night the warm light glowing in the cabin windows made it seem like a most inviting place to be. T. G. walked through the front door and found Jenni and her mother sitting before the cold, dark fireplace, drinking tea and sharing the details of their recent lives. It was a lovely cabin, softly and warmly lit by oil lamps, with walls of flagstone and wood and a floor of polished wooden planks. Heavy wooden beams held up the vaulted ceiling, and ornate iron light fixtures hung from them.

It was a large dwelling, more like a hunting lodge than a simple lakeside cabin, with three bedrooms and a full kitchen in addition to the spacious living area. It was easily as large as the Parklins' house in Ithaca had been, and the cabin was quite comfortable. Electricity for the lights and appliances was provided by a solar array that Jenni's father had installed the year before he had died, including batteries for nighttime use—but the newly diminished output of the sun made it necessary for Janice to conserve her power usage. The furniture was plush and yet rustic. Family photos and mounted fish graced the walls, along with the more feminine touches of frilly draperies and artistic arrangements of dried flora added by Janice during her visits there.

Jenni looked up as T. G. entered, and she smiled, holding a hand toward him, wiggling her fingers, beckoning him to her.

He crossed the room and took her hand, then bent down and kissed her. Janice smiled at that, knowing the love they felt for each other.

"So…where have you been?" Jenni asked. "Take a walk around the lake?"

"Not a lake," he smiled. "A sea…a long way from here."

"What did you get all over the hem of your robe? And your feet…"

"Dust…just dust. Nothing special."

She looked at him with a puzzled brow, then smiled and dismissed the comment as an attempt at humor that she did not grasp. She would ask about it later.

"I told Mama," she smiled.

"Told her what?"

"Come here and let me hug my son-in-law," Janice said. He smiled and went to her, bending over her as she sat in her chair. She patted his back as they embraced. "We always knew it was just a matter of time."

"You have no idea," he smiled.

"Yes, I do. Jenni's told me everything. I'm very proud of you, for all you've endured. I'm honored to know you and honored to have you in the family."

"The honor goes to God." He smiled anew, as did she.

"Yes," she agreed. "I know that now." She indicated a Bible sitting on a small table next to her chair. "I know a lot of things I didn't know before…and more importantly, I know Christ. It's been amazing, watching the things in that book come to pass, one after the other."

As if on cue, someone else entered the room from the hallway. T. G. turned to look at the dark-haired man and at once felt a kinship with him. It was an odd sensation, an intangible link, a oneness he could not explain and had never felt before. T. G. could see that the man felt the same things, judging from his expression.

"T. G.," Janice began, watching as the two men studied each

other, "this is Marcus Levine. He's a friend of mine. He comes to check on me every few months or so."

They shook hands. Something flowed between them, and they looked hard and deeply into each other's eyes. T. G. noticed the seal on the man's forehead.

It was a small oval, encircling something written in the Old Tongue of Noron.

"Where are you from?" T. G. asked, his curiosity intense. "Far away?" *Could this man be from Noron? He doesn't look it, but—!*

"Oh, yes," the man nodded, his voice betraying the barest hint of an Israeli accent. "Far away."

"Luracayn?" T. G. fished.

"Orlando," the man replied.

"Oh." *So much for that theory.*

Janice smiled at her friend. "Marcus is very special, T.G…just as *you* are."

"Special?" T. G. asked.

"Yes," she smiled.

Jenni spoke up. "It's happening here, too, T. G. The 'end times'…the conclusion of human history. Mama's been telling me all about it. Biblical prophecy is being fulfilled here on almost a daily basis. That's why the sun and moon look so odd, and why it's so still outside. It's all part of what was planned for Earth, just as the Awakening was decreed for Noron. Looks like both worlds will end up at the finish line at the same time."

He was amazed at the depth of discernment she showed in that brief observation. Such was indeed what Ish had told him would happen.

"The late, great planet Earth," T. G. said. "The book of Revelation. It's happening?"

"All around us," Janice said. "I've been listening on the shortwave. The world is in great upheaval…it appears that we are well into the trumpet judgments now. This tiny corner of the world has been largely unaffected at this point…and I have come to believe that's only because Marcus is protected and immune from them."

"Protected?" T. G. asked.

"I'm of the twelve thousand of the family of Levi," Marcus said, as if that were explanation enough. T. G. knew there was something he was missing, some piece of the puzzle that he should have known but did not. Marcus went on. "You...you aren't Jewish...what were you called upon to do?"

"Very long story," T. G. smiled. "But we serve the same God and the same Messiah."

Marcus nodded, considering the statement, then walked over to Janice. "I must leave here in the morning." He indicated the world outside. "My place is out there. Lives depend upon me...and I can't let Him down. I'll come back again as soon as I can."

"I'll miss you," Janice said with a touch of sadness.

"And I you."

He hugged her as he would his own mother.

Marcus turned to T. G. and explained. "At one time I was too weak to serve—hunted, malnourished, and very ill. I was inches away from capture and prison. I wouldn't have made it through another hour and would have been silenced. Janice found me and brought me here at the risk of her own life. She nursed me back to health. It took a little while, but once again my voice was strong enough to go out into the world."

T. G. smiled at the use of the word. *Voice.* "You were chosen," he said, understanding. "Sealed. Set apart from the dawn of time."

"Yes," Marcus nodded, feeling the kinship more strongly. "You understand...as only one who has walked the walk can."

"And now you cannot be killed. Nothing on Earth can touch you. You have special protection from the Lord."

"Yes. For now." He looked to Janice. "You'll remain safe here, after I have gone...and until the time of woe has ended. Know that you are blessed, Janice Parklin. You've shown great faith."

He headed toward the door, pausing to retrieve a flashlight from the windowsill.

"I don't mean to be inhospitable," he said, "but if I don't get a little night fishing done, there'll be no fresh fish for your mother tomorrow. It was good meeting you both."

"You too," T. G. said. "Take care." He and Jenni nodded, and the man was gone.

T. G. then took Jenni's hand and indicated with a look that he needed to speak to her. She rose to her feet, and they walked into the kitchen.

"Ish came to me. I have to go," he said quietly, looking into her eyes. "Noron's final event has begun...*their* tribulation. The Dark has escalated the war somehow. I have to be there."

"I know."

"I want you to stay here with your mother. From what Marcus says, you'll be safe."

She stepped closer, looking up into his handsome young face and took his hands in hers. "We've been through this before. Whither thou goest, *I* go," she smiled. "No arguments."

"Jenni, I—"

" 'Once and forever, to remain at your side,' " she quoted, gripping his hands more tightly. "I took that vow, and I meant it. I'm coming with you. You're not going anywhere without me, so get used to it."

"Yes ma'am," he smiled, and they kissed.

She glanced into the other room and silently watched her mother, who sat leafing through the Bible.

"I remember that Bible," T. G. said to his wife, following her gaze. "My mom and dad gave it to you. It was just like the one they gave me."

"I should have read it...and I will. It was a wonderful gift."

"To the whole world," T. G. smiled. "In the larger sense."

Jenni turned back to face him, holding his hands up between them. "Mama will be safe here, and I know I'll see her again. My place is with you."

He smiled, unceasingly amazed that such a woman was his.

33

The world shook again.

Josan braced himself against a table, waiting out the terrifying tremor. He knew the underground complex that was the home of the Twelve was more than sturdy enough to withstand the ground movements, but their intensity was not the most worrisome thing.

Why were they occurring at all?

The shaking slowed and then stopped. At that moment the door to the planning room opened, and T. G. and Jenni walked in. He had learned early on that suddenly popping out of thin air could prove disturbing to others, so he usually tried to materialize elsewhere first, then enter an occupied room through more conventional means, such as a door.

"An earthquake?" T. G. asked, walking up to Josan and Hervie, who had largely assumed the role of security leader for the Twelve. "How long ago did this start?"

"The first tremor occurred a few weeks ago, shortly after you left. We have had many since, each worse than the last."

T. G. tried not to be surprised by the time flow discrepancy—he and Jenni had been gone less than a day by his own reckoning.

"I know of nothing available to the Prime Lord that could cause such an effect," Hervie said.

Josan shook his head. "Our data indicates a distinct first movement. It was centered in the deep wilderness, in the area of the Dark Fortress...the place where you were held and executed. The first tremors were not severe enough to cause great damage, but the effect is spreading. Soon we will start to see a fracturing of the planet's crust...and if that happens..."

"That first tremor had to be a *reaction* to something," T. G. said. "This couldn't just happen naturally. It's physically impossible. Noron's subterranean tectonic layer is still intact." He turned to Jenni. "I have to go check this out. Please, stay here with Darafine."

She nodded. "Just come back to me."

He smiled and stroked her hair. "I've already died once, Jen, and *that* didn't keep me away, did it?"

"That was different," she said, smiling back. "I was dreaming then."

They kissed briefly. Then T. G. turned back to face Josan as something occurred to him. "Has anyone been outside since this began?"

"Not that I am aware of."

"Perhaps we should take a look." Hervie nodded.

T. G. motioned for Jenni to follow, and the four of them quickly made their way down the corridor. After passing through an open set of inner doors, they climbed a flight of access stairs leading to the main entry of the complex, and Josan pressed his palm against a jeweled panel set into the wall. The overhead steel doors rumbled open, sliding back into the ceiling, and an odd, warm light spilled into the corridor from outside. Their nostrils filled with the scent of burning wood.

Something was wrong.

They emerged to find the timberlands around them ablaze, and the air above choked with a heavy pall of smoke.

"Is it a forest fire?" Jenni cried.

"No," T. G. answered. "Nothing that simple."

Motion had drawn his gaze upward, and he peered into the smoke-darkened firmament. There, unseen by the others, darting swiftly among the heavy clouds of black, were millions of luminous winged figures, totally filling the evening skies from horizon to horizon, warring with each other. He heard a sea of angered cries and the sharp electric crackle of elemental energies. The beings fired thundering bolts of white and black lightning at each other and wrestled hand-to-hand, often moving in formation like huge flocks of birds of prey. They covered the entire world, and cities planetwide were falling into ruins under the relentless attack of the warriors of the Dark.

Angelic warfare. It was an awesome sight he could not have described to the others had he tried. The beings, despite their altitude, still conveyed an aura of power that no man-made force could equal. As T. G. watched, he realized he could not tell one side from the other by sight—the fallen ones were still angels, still majestic in appearance, and still very, very powerful. He thought of all the classical paintings he had ever seen of demons, portraying them as hideous, leathery-winged things or emaciated skeletal beings. He knew that those images more accurately portrayed them for what they *were* than for what they actually looked like.

Sin, as it always did, had made them like whitewashed tombs, magnificent and heavenly on the outside but fetid and corrupt on the inside.

"Get back inside and stay there!" T. G. ordered. They hurriedly descended the stairs as he remained behind, peering down at them. "Close these doors! Don't open them for anyone!"

Josan pressed hard against the panel. The heavy, reinforced doors began to slide shut. Jenni tried to run back up the stairs toward her husband, but Hervie restrained her.

"T. G.!" she frantically cried as the doors sealed with a loud *thud*, separating her from him.

"He will be all right," Josan tried to comfort her, but she did not understand. "He is the Voice…Ish is with him."

From among his unintelligible words, she grasped only the name "Ish"—but it was enough. She was comforted, and closed her eyes in prayer. The group left the door and headed back into the inner complex.

Outside, the Voice turned and looked up into the heavens, knowing the sheer power of the forces at war there. Poised for battle, that same power awaited him, if not a greater one—but he knew where he had to go, what he had to do. He pictured the Dark Fortress, ready to shift.

Barthos is there, T. G. knew. *And he's mine.*

❧

Darafine sat in the dim light of her room, poring over the scriptures of the opened Gift that T. G. had entrusted to her, studying its prophecies concerning the last days. Since his arrival, things written thousands of years before had been coming to pass, and the sometimes mysterious words of the final book had become clearer. Placed into the new context of recent history, the verses spoke to her as never before.

Jenni sat in the room with her, on her bed, watching the woman at the table as she scanned the Truth. Darafine sometimes read aloud in English, so her new friend could hear and understand.

"This is from the book of Parmenas," she said. "It is the last book of the Truth…and is largely prophecy." Jenni nodded, listening intently.

And the Dark shall move upon Noron, and the ground will shake with the fury of his footfalls, and he will wage war with the Truth in the air, and his swords shall be legion.

She scanned ahead several pages, seeking those phrases that seemed most relevant.

And fire will burn upon the land, and two-thirds of the trees will be burned, and the sea will be as blood, and the smoke will darken the skies until the light returns. And the light will be seen by all, yet the many will remain darkened and willfully blind.

She stopped reading. Deep concern crossed her face as she stared silently at the scroll before her.

"What is it?" Jenni asked.

She paused uncertainly, then spoke without turning toward the young woman.

And the light will leave the world, rejected by the many, and the final darkness will spread upon the land, and My Voice will be swallowed up, and My Word will fall upon the world unheeded.

Jenni was puzzled. "That can't be right…that sounds like God's giving up."

"I know."

"But it can't mean that."

A tremor hit, rocking the room for the second time in less than an hour. Jenni screamed at the first jarring shock then held the bed tightly and rode it out. The lights flickered and then returned. Finally, it was over, and she went to sit at Darafine's side.

"They're getting worse," Jenni said. "Sure this place can take it?"

Darafine smiled. "I suppose we will find out."

"That isn't very reassuring." Jenni tried not to worry, but her emotions pulled her into a deep mire of doubt. " 'Swallowed up,' " she quietly repeated. "What could that mean?"

"There is another verse that follows," Darafine said. "But I do not understand it. The scripture changes tenses here, only for this verse… and what it says makes no apparent sense."

"What does it say?"

Darafine turned to the scroll again, gazing at it for a moment, hoping that sudden understanding would come. It did not. Still uncertain, she read the words:

And those who are Mine were taken away, and all that I had made was destroyed as by fire, and the Creation became one before Me.

∽∘∾

It was his old apartment all over again.

And then some.

T. G. materialized at the center of the throne chamber. He immediately crouched into a defensive position, arms extended, yet found no one else present. It was like standing in a meat locker. Ice coated everything around him, including the ghastly throne that now towered over the dais at the front of the room. His breath fogged white, falling away as he spun, his eyes scanning the room, searching for any sign of life.

Or death.

His stomach turned as his gaze fell upon the frozen remains of the Watcher near the door. He averted his eyes, not wanting to look upon the mangled, glistening corpse, and turned back toward the platform. The light of the torches flickered, throwing shadows on the walls all around him, keeping him edgy and unsure. He constantly thought he caught movement at the periphery of his vision, forcing him to turn from side to side with every step he took.

Then he heard it. A laugh he knew all too well, rumbling within his chest, echoing from the icy, snow-white walls. He tensed, waiting for the inevitable attack, and moved cautiously toward the dais. The hideous laugh grew louder. Closer.

His senses sharpened as he mounted the glazed steps. He was repulsed by the immense throne, by the thoughts of pain and torture it inspired. He moved around it, deciding it might be a good idea to get behind it and take whatever cover it might give him.

He reached a hand out to touch an arm of the ice-coated seat, as if to convince himself that the monstrosity was real. He was appalled that any mind could have conceived such a thing, but he knew who he was dealing with and would have expected as much. As he reached the rear of the throne, keeping his eyes on both the huge chamber door and the wings of the dais, he stumbled as his feet became tangled in something.

T. G. jumped back, his heart racing, and saw what had almost tripped him. It lay on the floor, hidden in the shadow of the macabre throne, a figure he knew well. Unmoving and covered in a white blanket of frost, it stared blankly up at him, torn open and lying in an awkward tangle like a rag doll cast aside by an angry child.

It was a body, one that had once been a minor politician named Cordan Barthos. But that was then. Barthos had not been merely human for quite some time.

Now what had once been his flesh was an empty husk, hollow and dead, no longer needed. A shell, a tool, spent and tossed away.

T. G. slowly knelt and reached out to touch it. He found it was frozen solid, its arms reaching up as if in a plea for mercy.

The chilling laugh grew louder still.

T. G. stood, unable to discern the direction from which the nightmarish intonation came. Suddenly feeling vulnerable, he bounded down the steps and back into the center of the room.

"Show yourself!" he angrily screamed, whirling in all directions. "I'm here...let's get this over with!"

A motion drew his gaze back to the dais. A black shape moved in the shadow of the wings to the right of the throne—a huge shape, a shape peering down at him with eyes of luminescent blue. The laughter stopped.

He braced, waiting for the shadowthing to move out into the dim flickering light.

It did not.

Pretsal did.

"Hello...buddy," the thing uttered, its voice deep and guttural. It spoke with the broken roughness of vocal cords that had lain still for weeks, decomposing beneath warm soil.

T. G. stood transfixed in silent horror, his muscles locked and unresponsive. He had been ready to fire, but could not. In shocked denial, he stared at a face of death that in life had been that of his closest Noronian companion, its eye sockets darkened, its cheeks hollowed. Its flesh still bore the scattered burns it had sustained in the Deathwatcher attack that killed the man. Its pallor was one of deathly, bluish white and horrid purples. Its hair was matted with dirt and dried blood. It still wore the ceremonial robes Pretsal had been buried in.

It was smiling.

"What's wrong, buddy?" it taunted him. "Didn't you miss me?"

T. G. glared at the obscene visage, horrified that such a display had been created. He knew that the being who was Pretsal was beyond pain and in the presence of the Creator—that the body before him was but the shell his friend had once occupied—but the very idea of such heinous irreverence for the dead left him repulsed and aghast.

"Oh, come now," it continued, slowly making its way down the steps. It held its arms out, beckoning him. "Give your old amigo a big hug."

White-hot power leaped from his arms and hands and hit the corpse full in the chest. Its robes were blackened and burned away at the point of impact, but it showed no other sign of damage.

"Now…is that any way to welcome back an old friend?" it asked.

A dark concussion slammed into T. G., knocking him back into the wall, where he fell upon the frozen remains of the dead Watcher. Dazed, his balance askew, he shook his head and managed to crawl off of the ravaged body. His flesh stung. It had been a more powerful blast than any Grodnal had ever thrown at him.

"You'd think I'd get a little show of appreciation for all the trouble I went to," the thing went on, standing there, towering before him. It looked upon itself, admiring its work. "I did this for *you*, old buddy."

"Stop saying that!" T. G. yelled. "I know you, Beltesha, whatever face you hide behind."

"What's in a name?" it asked, its demeanor changing. "A corpse by any other name would smell as…intensely." It smiled, its mock warmth drenched in smug wickedness. It walked over to one of the tall black-glass windows and threw it open to reveal the warfare filling the reddened, smoky skies all around them. Tall flames rose from the deep forests, throwing their hellish, dancing light against the dense, black pall above them.

"Finally," it gloated. "Finally."

The devastation had claimed much of the planet. Cities worldwide were in crumbling flames, falling under the onslaught of the innumerable dark forces bent on destroying them. Angels of Light had quickly descended upon the destroyers, striving to keep them occupied and away from the population until the last great Dawn, allowing the final few enough time to choose Life over Death. Already hundreds of millions who had chosen Drosha and the Prime Lord for their salvation had died and were dying, their ballots eternally cast on the wrong side, trusting in their false savior even as the blade fell.

A deep rumble sounded. The walls and floor shook, throwing T. G. again into the wall. Beltesha stood solidly at the window, laughing maniacally in the midst of it all. The quake lasted half a minute, thirty seconds that seemed an eternity. Then, as if it had never been, it was over. Silence filled the chamber.

T. G. sensed another presence in the room. He saw Beltesha bow toward the dais, and swung to look at the ghastly throne. It was occupied by Shass, who sat there surveying them both—yet there was something different about him now, something that made the prophet's blood freeze in his veins.

The Prime Lord's eyes glowed blue like Beltesha's. As he looked into those eyes, eyes of death set into a handsome, stolen face, T. G. knew who he faced. Pure horror gripped him. Pure anger filled him.

"So," the Dark began, in an egoistic voice calm with the assurance of victory. "The Voice in the Dark, last of the Guardians. You have caused me a lot of trouble. I'm afraid I cannot allow that to continue."

"It was my pleasure," T. G. grimly said, with no respect whatsoever.

"It is *my Master* who speaks to you!" Beltesha bellowed.

"And me without my autograph book," T. G. shot back. Beltesha raised an arm, ready to destroy the miserable prophet for his insolence.

The Dark calmly waved a hand, stopping him. "No, no…he must not die, just yet…or die *again,* I should say. Very good, young man. Most impressive. Caught me quite by surprise, I must admit." He turned to Beltesha. "You still have much to share with him, do you not?"

The aged demon bowed to the Dark. Then, without even looking, he flipped a hand in T. G.'s direction and again a battering-ram force slammed the weakened prophet into the wall. As moments passed, the Voice steadied himself, shaken, trying to regroup.

"I'll…" T. G. began, his fury gathering again. "I'll *kill* you!"

"Will you now?" the thing with Pretsal's face asked, cutting him off with another blast. T. G. was hurled violently into a corner near the door, his body in agony. His equilibrium was gone, sending the room spinning. He feared his right shoulder had separated, for it screamed in pain and he could not raise it. He considered a retreat, a shift out of the chamber.

The Dark smiled, enjoying the show. He watched as Beltesha circled the fallen prophet like a ravenous carnivore toying with its prey, waiting to make the final kill.

"I knew you looked familiar when first I saw you at your apartment," Beltesha went on, speaking calmly. "We had met before. Don't you remember?"

"Wha…what?" T. G. struggled to say.

"Oh, yes. I was amusing myself while passing the time on your world, waiting for the Gift to be given. Now isn't that ironic? I could have had you then, but I didn't know 'the Voice' was going to turn out to be *you*."

"You make…you make no sense," T. G. weakly muttered, his head down.

"You *still* don't remember me? I'm hurt," he sarcastically pouted, feigning injured feelings. "It was me, buddy, there with you on that lonely stretch of highway in the dark, cold middle of the night."

T. G. looked up at him, his eyes widening with hatred and realization.

No!

"Your father was about to be invited to take a job as a minister at a lovely little church in Ithaca, which would likely have led to the saving of thousands over a relatively short span of years. Such a fervor for his God, your father had.

"But *we* had someone else in mind for that particular position—a man we knew was all wrapped up in law and feelings and the superficial trappings of 'faith,' who wasn't going to lead anyone anywhere. *He* got the job instead…and all who heard him through the years that followed never heard a word about the utter grace of their God, which *alone* could have saved them. They became bogged down in rituals, 'modern' thought, and outward appearances, spending all their free time patting themselves on the back and raising money for new and larger sanctuaries, never knowing eternal life or any personal relationship at all with their 'Savior.' There they were, perfect little 'Christians' who thought the whole time that their outward deeds were impressing their God. We had them right where we wanted them, and there they stayed.

"I…bound…*thousands*," he proudly closed, "all by leading one truck driver…to have one-too-many beers…on one-too-many nights. Now *that's* efficiency."

Anger filled T. G., an anger that forced his limbs into action as he tried in vain to find his feet. He suddenly found himself faced with the cause of all the misery he had suffered—misery that had evolved from a single catastrophic moment on a dark road far from home.

"You killed my parents?"

Through Pretsal's face, Beltesha smiled triumphantly. "There—I knew you'd remember me!"

T. G. cried out in bitter agony, weeping as he brought his left arm to bear on Beltesha. But before he could fire, another dark blast threw him into the frozen adamantine stone. He crumpled into a sobbing heap, his hands shaking, his tears freezing to his face.

Beltesha turned his attention back to the window. The orange light of the sea of flames played upon his cadaverous, borrowed features.

"Glorious!" he exclaimed, watching the combat above. "Soon all the pitiful souls of Noron will be dead, lost forever, cut off from the source of life we all once knew—"

"*Silence!*" the Dark screamed. Beltesha cowered, having momentarily forgotten himself.

"I…I am sorry, my Lord," he stammered. "I meant only that—"

"Be done with him!" the Dark said, pointing at the huddled prophet. "Then join me." Beltesha bowed to his master, who vanished in a swell of darkness, leaving an empty throne on the platform.

T. G. saw Beltesha turn to face him, and he closed his eyes.

Finally, he prayed.

"*Ish…help me!*"

At once a voice flooded his mind.

Why did you wait so long to ask?

T. G. dropped his head, realizing his error. He and his Savior spoke, their communion lasting but a moment in real time.

I…I wanted revenge on Beltesha…for all he had done to me…for all he had put me through. It was all I saw…all I wanted. I forgot You! How could I have forgotten You?

Because you still battle the flesh—and will until you leave that body once more.

Ish paused then spoke again. *As My prophet, you have an inherent power, which I gave you. But you have pridefully drawn upon it alone in coming here. It has kept you alive until now, but it is not enough against Beltesha.*

Forgive me…

You are now and always have been forgiven. Otherwise, I could never have known you at all. T. G.'s senses cleared, and after a moment he heard his Lord speak once more. *Now, it ends—and the vengeance is Mine.*

A power surged through T. G. unlike any he had felt, blazing like an inferno within every cell of his being. But no mere power—it was *alive*, a Person in itself, a direct manifestation of the fullness of God, filling every bone, every sinew as *He* coursed through the prophet like a river of molten steel. T. G. felt his body rise, and suddenly his feet were beneath him. He raised his arms and pointed them at his mortal enemy, spreading his fingers. Beltesha watched in amusement, like a bully watching a weak, frightened child approach, tiny fists raised in futility.

"Ready to join Mommy and Daddy?" he gloated.

Then, suddenly, his pale, emaciated face became a portrait of terror as he watched the eyes of the Voice blaze forth, filled with purifying flame. He had seen those eyes before.

Once.

"No!" Beltesha shrieked, backing into the white-frosted wall. He tried to shift to safety, tried to flee to *any* other place, but could not.

Something held him, kept him pinned there in that room, where ancient Guardians had been tortured and killed by his hand so long before.

Panicked, Beltesha turned and slipped on the icy floor, trying to get away. As he reached the coated steps of the dais, he slipped again and crashed to the hard cold floor. He rolled and looked back upon his onetime victim, only to see the Voice standing firmly in place. He felt those painful, sun-bright eyes upon him, searing him. They were the eyes of his Enemy, the eyes of his Judge.

The eyes of his Creator.

The unwieldy flesh he wore was suddenly too confining, strangling him, weighing him down. Pretsal's body tore apart as the archdemon sought escape from it. Blue light poured from its eyes, mouth, nose, and a wide chasm that spread across its chest. The fallen angel struggled to free himself from the tangled, tearing mass of flesh, as if escape from his final sentence was possible.

His form began to coalesce in the air above the body. Still caught, he stared into those blazing eyes. His intense pride was finally stripped away, and he realized at last that he, like so many on Noron, had cast his lot with the wrong side. There was nowhere to run, nowhere to hide, nowhere to live. A wind gathered within the chamber and rapidly built to agonizing force. A deafening roar like that of oceanic waters slammed into him, tearing at him, drowning out all else.

Remorseless, wailing, he defiantly cried out the name of his Creator. The utterance, engulfed by the intolerable din, was his last.

He screamed in stark terror as all went blinding white.

Beltesha's final, piercing cry was swallowed up in a light beyond light, a sound beyond sound, as the very face of God touched Noron for an instant. Stone vaporized as if it had never been. Elemental energy, devastating in its purity, seared the earth and scorched the air. A shock wave radiated outward at dozens of times the speed of sound, thundering across the entire planet. Trees were felled for hundreds of miles. A violent brilliance stretched out upon the skies and created a false sunrise for much of the world.

Then the light faded away, and T. G.'s eyes returned to normal. A hot, gentle wind caressed him, comforting him, tossing his hair. He trembled slightly.

Around him, in all directions and extending for dozens of miles, everything was gone. The Dark Fortress, the wilderness, everything.

Just gone.

T. G. stood at the bottom of an immense crater of charred, barren ground, mottled with dark, fused glass and scattered small fires. High overhead, the forces of Dark and Light resumed their struggle, having momentarily paused to move clear as the infinite power from below swept past. They knew that its merest touch would have meant final, total annihilation.

The Voice stood amid the sizzling, blackened soil and peered up into the smoke of the night sky, watching as the glowing warriors battled. His body did not ache as it always had before, though his hands shook with adrenaline and exhaustion. His limbs hung limp and heavy and his legs wanted only to remain at rest, but there was no pain. His body was exhausted, as if he had run a thousand miles.

And it had changed. It had served as a direct conduit for the manifest power of God, brought to bear by Ish, through the Person of the Comforter.

"Beltesha?" T. G. asked aloud.

"He is gone," an audible voice said, with great finality.

The prophet turned. Standing next to him was Ish, His robes and white hair blowing in the hot breeze.

"He has been judged," He finished.

T. G. stood for several quiet moments, listening to the warm wind in his ears as he surveyed the smoldering emptiness around them. Since coming to Noron, so much death, so much destruction had flooded his eyes, his senses. A question rose in his mind, an audacious question, a question he had never dared ask before.

The question.

"Ish…why?"

The tall Man cocked one eyebrow as He looked down at His chosen prophet. It was a question that had defied the ages, leaving uncounted philosophers and religious men to debate the issue, while a definitive answer eluded them.

"Why did You do it at all?" T. G. continued. "Why make man or the universe or the angels at all, when You knew that the Dark and his agents and so much of mankind would turn away from You?"

Ish looked patiently into the young man's eyes and smiled gently, his own eyes radiant. "The clay…again inquiring of the potter." T. G. looked away, wishing he had not posed the question.

"I'm sorry," he said. "You certainly don't owe me an answer."

But the Man continued.

"The answers to that are many, T. G., and most would be unfathomable for you or for any man. But, in answer to you, I will say this: The Father is utterly sovereign. Nothing, not even sin, can exist except by Our consent. Over iniquity and all else, We reign. We knew the creation of both man and angels would lead to those who would turn away from Us, deny Us, despite the fact that only in Us is there Life. We chose to create the realm of the angelic hosts, as well as this realm in which you of Earth and Noron live. Just as easily, We could have created entirely different ones…or We could have chosen not to do so at all and remain alone."

He paused a moment, allowing T. G. the time he needed. "We did not wish to remain alone."

The prophet nodded, his eyes wet, understanding. While the infinite God had lacked for nothing and needed nothing to fulfill Himself, He had nevertheless chosen to create human and angelic beings with whom He could share Himself, for His own glory—despite the fact that doing so, He knew, would mean taking on a physical form and suffering an agonizing death upon a wooden cross, upon a hilltop His own hands had formed, upon the very world He had made.

It was all so elegant. It was all so wonderful.

They stood silently for a few moments, watching the skies above them and the conflict there. T. G. knew it was far from over.

"The Dark," Ish spoke, his calm voice barely more than a whisper "has taken on physicality for the duration."

"We have to stop him."

Ish shook his head. "You are My Voice, chosen before the foundation of this world was laid. You declared My coming, and through you We showed the world that We alone hold the Keys of Life and Death. You have served Us, and faithfully, and We are pleased in you. Many live who would otherwise have died.

"But it is *My* battle now, T. G. Where I must now go, you cannot follow, and what I must now do, you cannot take part in. Go to Jenni…comfort her…and wait for Me."

34

The synthecrete was smooth and cool beneath her, pleasantly refreshing against her bare hands and feet.

Jenni sat on the steps beneath the entry doors of the complex, gazing up at them, her mind filled with thoughts of her husband and all he had done. It still amazed her that an ordinary boy from New York had become such an important part of the history of an entire world. When she thought about it, though, it dawned on her that the great figures of Bible history, at least the way she had seen them portrayed in movies, had also been average, everyday people—and sometimes even unlikely candidates—before entering the roles God had set aside for them. Moses, David, the Apostles, all of them.

The spiritual war T. G. had entered into was an old one, and Jenni tried not to fear for him, but with the upheaval sweeping the planet, doubts welled up inside her. As she dwelt upon her fears, tears soon pooled in her eyes and hung wetly on her lashes like morning dew on a spider's web. Perhaps she had recovered him only to lose him again—

Come back to me!

The ground shook again. Jenni braced herself against the wall, waiting it out.

Please…?

As if in reply, there was another rumble. She braced for an instant, expecting a tremor, but instead saw the doors above her begin to open like a sleepy eye. Orange light slowly poured in, and a small amount of dirt and ash rained onto her. She jumped up and backed away from the slowly sliding door, then ran past the corner of the entryway and down the corridor, where she silently and fearfully peered from the shadows. Too frightened to call out, she held her breath as the doors clanged into their fully open position. A wall of warm air laced with the heavy scent of wood smoke washed over her.

The sound of slow, heavy feet against the hard steps echoed slightly toward her. Each footfall came later than she expected it, as if they came cautiously.

Fearing a Watcher, she instead looked up to see her husband move from the bottom step and into the corridor. His appearance had changed, but she knew him at once. A squeal of delight fled her lips as she ran to him.

T. G. smiled weakly as he took his wife into his arms. She detected an odd weariness, a fatigue like none she had ever known in him. His slowed pace down the steps had come not from reluctance, but from exhaustion. Jenni looked up into his face and realized that her husband's young features, while still smooth, betrayed an underlying antiquity, sensed more than seen, as if he had reached out and touched an engulfing timelessness—and been changed. In his crystalline eyes, Jenni saw a depth of clarity she had never seen there before, a wisdom, a peace.

They were one, kissing as he held her close for a moment, sharing the stillness as they cherished each other's embrace. When she rested her head against his chest, listening to his heart, he drank in the scent of her hair, the warmth of her softness against him. Then she looked up at him, her wet eyes glistening in the dim light.

"Look at you," she said, smiling through happy tears, running her fingers gently and lovingly through the snowy locks above his left ear. "Your hair has turned white."

"Really?" he asked, reaching up as if to feel the color difference. "I'm not surprised."

Josan and Hervie rounded the corner, weapons drawn. At the sight of the Voice, both men breathed a great sigh of relief and neutralized their sidearms.

"Well, look who is back," Josan smiled, as the massive door slid shut above. He rushed forward and hugged T. G., slapping him on the back in joy. "What happened? Where did you go? Your hair—"

"I had some unfinished business to take care of," T. G. said, "and it's been dealt with." He pointed back over his shoulder. "It looks pretty bad out there. No picnics for a while."

"English, please?" Jenni asked, smiling. Watching him speak Noronian was something she just could not seem to get used to.

"I think I've done everything I came to Noron to do," he summed up for her.

Jenni laid her head against his shoulder. "So do we go home now? Or at the very least, can you stay here with me?"

He kissed her atop her head. It was all the answer she needed.

"Welcome back," Darafine said, coming up the corridor. "We feared the worst."

T. G.'s expression became more serious. "Barthos is dead. Paull Shass probably is too...but his body's still up and around. The Dark possessed him directly in order to take on physical form. As for why..."

"So it was prophesied," Darafine nodded. " *'And the Dark shall walk upon Noron, and the ground will shake with the fury of his foot-falls.'* That explains the tremors."

"That is not all," Hervie said. "This explains much. Shass...or the thing using him...has been on simulight almost constantly for the past few weeks. There has been something different about him, though...his charisma was high before, but now it has hit the canopy. We have had to forbid everyone, especially the women, from watching any of the broadcasts. It is just too dangerous."

"Yes," Darafine nodded. "Sereen almost succumbed to his charisma. She came to me in tears several hours ago...and she is a strong woman."

"Yes, she is," T. G. nodded, recalling the woman's daring rescue of her sister. "I can understand it though...the Dark was once the most glorious of the Creator's works. His inner and outer beauty were deep and perfect, spoiled only by the fact that he tried to supplant his Maker. At that point, he lost the radiance of fellowship but retained his own inherent magnificence. Nothing since has stripped him of that, nor the seductiveness it carries with it."

"And he is using it to try to draw the final few to him," Josan said. "Shass was not quite appealing enough on his own, I suppose."

"It does sound like a final grab for votes, doesn't it?" T. G. agreed. "That means Election Day is here. Time is running out."

"For all of us perhaps," Hervie said.

Jenni poked T. G. in the ribs. "Either teach me this language or give me subtitles. Or charades. Anything."

He smiled at her. "You up for it?"

"Hey," she said, "I was the one who took French in high school, not you."

"Okay, if you're sure."

"I'm sure."

"This will be tough."

"I don't care."

He held up three fingers, meaning 'three words,' beginning a game of charades.

"No!" she laughed, giving him a playful shove. "The language…"

Josan and Hervie looked on in puzzlement. Jenni smiled, pleased with the fact that someone else wore that expression for a change.

∽✤∼

The sun rose for the last time.

Daylight was just breaking above the horizon of Keltrian, dimmed by the dark, heavy pall in the air. The surrounding forests continued to burn uncontrolled in a conflagration unlike any before seen. Other fires, within the city walls, had spread from building to building, sector to sector, gutting what would burn and leaving desolate what would not.

A tiny figure stood atop the World Capitol pyramid, arms outspread. The building's four sides sloped down and away for a mile, and for most the relatively minuscule ten-foot-square summit on which he stood would have inspired immediate and intense vertigo. Yet he was unaffected, and unconcerned.

The world, he gloated, *is mine.*

The Dark surveyed his kingdom, and the wondrous destruction that was laying it waste. The flames, the smoke, the quakes, and the distant screams of millions were all a symphony of joy to him, proof that he had been right all along. It was unfortunate that the fool Beltesha was unable to join him in his moment of triumph, but the sycophant would have eventually become a hindrance anyway, somewhere along the line.

Better to be done with him now and retain as much of the glory for one's self as possible.

Half the world's population had died already, and of those, three-fourths had chosen Darkness. *A crushing blow to the Creator,* the Dark mused, *to lose so many of His precious physical ones, with so many more yet to die unsaved!* It was glorious!

There was a brilliant flash. A fierce explosion sounded, and a vicious shock wave slammed into the capitol, shattering much of the glass on its northern side. The Dark turned to look upon the small mushroom cloud rising into the air far in the distance, a glaring fireball that had already obliterated the power-generating facility there along with much of the area surrounding it. He laughed, counting another several hundred thousand souls among his spoils.

It was starting out to be a good day.

❧

T. G. sat bolt upright in bed. He and Jenni had gone to sleep only a short time before, and in his lassitude a deep slumber had closed in quickly. But now, like flipping a switch, he was wide awake once more, his heart racing. He had been awakened by a dream—a vivid, waking vision like the one he had experienced in his apartment before his first shift to Noron.

There on the same gray plain he had seen before, Ish appeared, an immense figure towering into the sky, arms outstretched. All around, in a gathering that stretched from horizon to horizon, billions of people walked lovingly toward their Messiah. Then had begun the sound of the rushing waters as before, but this time, there were words within the roar. Three words in Ish's voice.

It is time.

Nothing more was needed, no explanation. T. G. simply knew.

He swung his legs over the side of the warm, comfortable bed, waking Jenni with his movement. She looked up at him and discerned his blurry shape in the meager light.

"What...what is it?" she asked, her eyes barely open.

"Get dressed," he said, grabbing for his robes.

"Why? What's happening? Feels like we just now—"

"*It's* happening!" he almost shouted. "Hurry!"

"I thought you were *through,*" she said sleepily, sitting up.

"Come on!"

Both were quickly into their robes, and with tousled hair and bare feet they moved along the corridors, banging on every door they passed to alert everyone.

"What is it?" Darafine asked Jenni in English, stepping from her room into the wide hall. "What is happening?"

"I don't know," Jenni sleepily replied.

"Follow me!" T. G. shouted, excitement in his voice. "Bring everyone!"

Rounding the final corner, he pressed his palm against the control plate and the overhead door slid open. Before it had reached full retraction, he was up the steps, Jenni in tow, bounding out into the subdued light of dawn.

The beautiful meadows and forests through which T. G. and his bride had wandered after their wedding were gone. The lush grasses and trees all around them had been destroyed, leaving only smoking, charred remains to surround the complex. The air was warm, for the forests in the distance still burned, driving the outside temperature ever upward. If not for the smoke stratifying in layers high in the still air, the sky would have been brighter still. But it was light enough.

Jenni's eyes went wide as she peered into the sky. For the first time she could see the battle being waged there, the angelic war for Noron. In awe, she watched as the luminous beings continued their struggle, more numerous than the stars and brighter still. Like meteors on a summer night they darted, swooping and maneuvering, changing trajectories in sudden, breathtaking moves that would have defied physical law had the warriors been material.

Suddenly, a third of them fled away, seemingly in fear.

Everyone spilled from the stairway and onto the scorched meadow, gazing into the sky. Josan held Darafine as they, like the others, looked into the heavens, recognizing the beings above for the angels they were, the angels described to them in the pages of the Truth. The spectacle brought tears to some, quiet contemplation to others, and awe to them all.

The remaining angels quickly parted like a curtain, gathering into a sparkling ring that surrounded the skies, leaving an immense, open space directly overhead. A few moments later, something began to fill that space.

Lightning flashed silently from horizon to horizon, arcing white across the sky. A resonant sound like that of a trumpet blast echoed across the forests, coming from everywhere at once. It sounded three times, filling the world with triumphant music, heralding an arrival.

It began as a glow, centered directly above the complex, and rapidly swelled until it stretched from horizon to horizon. New shadows fell beneath T. G. and the gathered spectators as the light became brighter. But even as it surpassed the brilliance of the sun, their eyes knew no pain, no heat, no discomfort at all. The intensity increased moment by moment, until it shifted and gathered itself and began to assume a cohesive shape. It took on color and form. A great wind began to sweep the land.

T. G. held Jenni tightly, watching the light above. She began to cry softly, but was unsure why. T. G. did as well, but he *knew* why.

Intense awe thickly filled the air, imbuing all who stood there, transcending their every conception of reality. Their minds, as one, sought something from the comfort of past experience—anything— that could help them identify what was now before them.

From any point on the planet's surface, the same image was visible above. The shape that now filled the sky was a figure—the figure of a man. His eyes were flames of pure, cleansing fire. His hair flowed long and white. His robes were majestic blue.

And all the world looked upon Ish at last.

Those who were His knew Him. Everywhere, all who had chosen the Truth knew that their promised Savior had come and that the Voice in the Dark had spoken truthfully to them. They had heard the trumpets. They huddled together in the open, gazing with love and excitement and awe upon the image of their Messiah, awaiting Him.

Those who had rejected Ish cowered in their homes or hid under anything that would shield them from the agony of those piercing eyes, eyes that saw through their flesh and into the depravity in their souls. They cursed Him, begging Drosha and the Prime Lord to rise up and defeat the hated One Who hung over them.

Everyone at the complex fell to their knees, overwhelmed with awe, with all but one gazing for the first time upon the face of He Who had created everything and everyone they had ever known. Peering up into the gentle face of their Creator and Savior, they humbled themselves, trembling, knowing firsthand the power that had called the universe into existence with a single thought, a single word, a single love.

◠◡◠

One upon the planet did not fall to his knees.

The Dark stood atop the capitol pyramid, his face seething with anger, his fists clenched so tightly that his nails drew new blood from his raw palms.

"NO!" he screamed, livid that his moment of triumph had been overshadowed by such a blatantly egotistical display. He stared defi-

antly into the eyes above him, cursing them, feeling their scalding heat upon him.

"This world will be mine, as will the other!" the Dark screamed, his words cutting through the roar of the winds. *"I will sit upon the throne of Heaven, and my name will be exalted throughout the universe! And these…these of this world…you will not take them unto yourself! They will be mine, or they will not be at all!"*

He held his arms out, his head back. As he continued to stare upward in defiance, something like tears of black oil began to well up, covering his eyes completely before spilling over and streaming over his cheeks. Within moments, the same dark matter issued from his nose, ears, and mouth, spilling outward, coating his robes. The rate at which it poured from him multiplied until it gushed forth, flowing down his torso and legs and onto the top of the pyramid, becoming a rapidly spreading ebony puddle around his feet.

From every pore of his body the blackness came, a darkness infinitely beyond the mere absence of light, bursting forth with the force of water through a shattered dam, an impalpable, slippery torrent. It was a pure nothingness that no mind could envision, colder and more empty than the depths of space and just as pervasive. The substance-without-substance moved as quietly as a low fog, dense and swift and unstoppable, cascading over the summit and down the sides of the pyramid until the monolith's sparkling, mirrorlike faces were lost beneath a glove of gelid black.

With impossible speed the Darkness flowed on, reaching the bottom and spreading outward in all directions, blanketing the streets, buildings, and alleys of the city below as it flowed over and between them. Streaming forth now from the Dark only from his neck down, it increased in size at a rate beyond mere flow, growing exponentially, racing toward each horizon.

It absorbed all light and all heat and all life. Men ran from its black, merciless touch, but fell victim nonetheless as it swept along like a tidal wave, engulfing everyone over whom it passed. It claimed the saved and the lost with equal totality. No closed door, no sealed window, no hidden shelter kept it away. The Dark delighted in the new wave of screams that rose from the city below, knowing that all the world was perishing by his hand. He had sent the Darkness forth not merely to kill, but to annihilate both body and soul, wiping them away as if they had never existed. That which did not live, its black devastation would not harm. That which did would *vanish.*

It was to be an act of un-creation, an unraveling of the very handiwork of God, sucking the breath of life from the world as if it had never lived. Noron would be left desolate, sterile, and unloving of its Creator.

"Look upon this!" the Dark mocked. *"I now leave you what you would leave me…a barren rock unable to praise your name!"*

The Dark laughed, watching as the cattle of Noron simply ceased to be, counting their number as they fell. The sickening, booming laugh built in power until it could be heard worldwide, preceding the Darkness so that the people would know just who it was who had defeated their Creator. There would be no great last call on *this* world, the Dark gloated, no summoning of the saved into the air. If they could not belong to him and would not fall at his feet in ultimate, eternal adoration, then *no one* would have them—*and the jealous Creator will lose the battle he has waged against me since the worlds began!*

As it rushed along, the Darkness smothered and extinguished the fires raging throughout the forests of the world and even consumed those fleeing, panicked animals that managed to evade the inferno.

Faster it spread, coating the world like a blanket of black snow, flowing as deeply as was necessary to ensure that no flesh escaped. Tentacles of deep black reached up out of the spreading mass and pulled birds, pterosaurs, and insects from the air. It filled the rivers, seas, and lakes, killing all life there. Those who fell in its path, man and animal, felt a numbing, choking, leaden cold at first, a cold without light or sound or sensation. There was no air for their lungs, no light for their eyes, no sound for their ears. Just a drowning in blackness as the merciless Darkness filled their mouths and ears and lungs.

Then came nothingness.

❦

T. G. and the 284 Disciples of Truth knelt before Ish in the charred grass, praying to Him. Their robes, hands, and faces were blackened with the soot of the meadow. They watched and waited, looking upon His wondrous visage above them, holding their arms upstretched.

His voice filled their minds.

It is almost ended. Do not be afraid.

Then they heard something else echoing from beyond the horizon. A laugh—an abysmal, wicked, terrifying laugh T. G. knew all too well. Confusion tore at him. He knew that it was Ish's time, that the Dark was finished, and yet—

Movement caught his eye. He looked toward the terrifying black tidal wave approaching from the distant southeast, and his sinews tightened. The laugh that filled the world grew louder, more victorious. The dark wall grew rapidly closer. He looked up at Ish.

What is it? he silently asked his Lord. *What's coming at us?*

The final Darkness.

What do we do? he asked, tensing for battle.

Lie down, Ish replied.

What? the prophet asked, disbelieving, knowing that a great danger was bearing down on them all.

Lie down. Do nothing.

The two commands tore at every remaining grain of human pride within T. G. Every instinct in his body screamed at him to fight, or to take his wife and his friends and retreat into the deep shelters beneath the complex—to save himself and them. He fought the fierce compulsion even to shift away, forcing himself instead to focus upon the trustworthiness of his Lord. He remembered the words of Ish, spoken during the revelation He had given in the dungeon of the Dark Fortress—

All things and all events, even those of evil, are used by Us for good and for the carrying out of the Father's will. That is where trust comes in. And trust…simple trust…is faith.

T. G. decided. He was angered at his own hesitation. How could he have doubted even now, after all else? At once, Ish vanished from the skies, as did the angelic host surrounding Him.

There was no time. The Voice turned to the others, who stared in horror at the rushing Darkness. Its roar became intolerable, as did the dark laughter. Their voices rising in fear, the gathering began to lean toward the shelter behind them, wanting to run, as T. G. had wanted to do. He cried out, halting them.

"Everybody down," he ordered. "Where you are! Leave this to Ish! Get on the ground! Now!"

They all did so, and he was thankful for that. Nearly three hundred souls who had fought the good fight lay in the direct path of the enemy, offering no resistance, trusting the words of their given Voice, trusting in their Lord to protect them. Ish was their only shield, their only armor, their only hope. They lay there, face down against the scorched soil, their bodies pressed together, praying. The roar, the laughter grew louder.

"Are you…sure?" Jenni fearfully asked T. G., curling into him.

"No," he answered. "But Ish *is*."

He lay next to her, his arm over her, her head tucked under his shoulder. Josan and Darafine lay huddled with Sereen. Hervie held his breath, praying silently. No one spoke. No one uttered a sound. There was no time for questions, no time for doubt.

As one, they waited. The last moment ticked away.

A thunderous reverberation like crashing ocean waves filled their ears, and suddenly it was upon them. They felt a great weight of rushing cold, pressing in, churning around them, engulfing them. The unstoppable Darkness swept past, crossing the world, covering it in its entirety in less than nineteen minutes.

And the Voice was swallowed up.

∽∘∽

The Dark stood atop the pyramid at the center of what had once been the city of Keltrian, laughing in triumph, spinning in delight as he surveyed the ruin he had made. He had watched as the beaten Ish had fled away in defeat, leaving the people of Noron in his merciless hands, and now all the world was his to do with as he pleased.

The Dark had been the planet's rightful owner for thousands of years. Now he alone lived upon its cold, silent face, still embodied within the plundered form of Paull Shass.

"Take it!" he screamed to the heavens with a sweeping motion, arms outstretched, his laughter filling the skies. *"It's yours!"*

He was drunk with the madness of self-deification. At one time he had accepted that he was doomed to lose his war, and he strove only to pull as many down with him as possible. But delusion embedded in intense pride had finally so corrupted him that he had actually come to believe he could triumph over his Creator and usurp the throne of Heaven.

Victory!

He roared mightily as the Darkness continued to flow. Then, at the peak of his depraved revelry, his ears detected something. It was a sound, a deep rumble, more felt than heard. His laughter suddenly died away.

For a thousand days it had traveled, undiminished, across interstellar space. It was a word, a single word. A voice.

A judgment.

And the Word fell upon the world unheeded.

It impacted with full force on the other side of the planet and drove deep into Noron's core. Thousands of vast subterranean reservoirs began to boil as 2.5 billion vibrations per second worked against them. As the underground oceans strained against their rocky boundaries, fissures began to open. Noron fought valiantly to resist the internal torture that unmercifully built within it.

For a few precious moments, the planet held its own. Just a few.

A faraway glare drew the Dark's attention to the horizon, and as he watched in stunned disbelief, the planet's crust just beyond his view succumbed.

There, past the edge of the world, dense plumes of white erupted forth and shot miles into the sky with an intensity unimagined. He heard nothing at first.

Then the shock wave hit. Intense, cruel winds immeasurably beyond hurricane strength slammed bluntly into everything in their path, filled with deadly projectiles of stone, wood, glass, and steel. The Dark clung to the twisted metal framework of the pyramid's summit, crying out in terror and rage.

He tried but could not leave. *Something* pinned him there.

More fissures tore open planetwide, throwing plumes of steam into the upper atmosphere with an intolerable roar. The ground rolled as if fluid. The once-solid crust of Noron broke up into thousands of tectonic plates, and its single eggshell continent flew apart. Still the pressure increased, and superheated waters exploded through the narrow openings the preliminary fists of steam had forged.

A prolonged, deafening concussion shook the face of the world as immense blades of boiling water screamed white into the turbulent sky. At an altitude of eleven miles, their forceful, upward rush was momentarily interrupted as they slammed into an obstacle.

The canopy shell shattered like fragile crystal as the searing knives of water tore into it. Millions of icy shards fell into the turbulent maelstrom below, melting back into that which they had once been long before.

And Noron knew rain for the second time.

Temperatures dropped instantly at the poles as the atmosphere vainly fought to equalize itself. Powerful winds well below freezing blasted the once tropical polar forests. Hailstones more than a foot in diameter slammed against anything that stood, breaking glass and splintering timber. Mountain peaks ten thousand feet high were thrown up violently and valleys sank down as the crust beneath them shifted along new fault lines. Scalding mud and water exploded out onto the surface, and the merciless slurry scraped the planet's face, unleashing the power of the planet's inner forces for the first time. A stinging torrential downpour reduced visibility to the grayness of zero and made it difficult even to breathe.

The Dark clung to the apex of the shattered pyramid, watching as the planet all around him tore itself apart. His Darkness had been swept away, lost within the maelstrom. The colossal building upon which he knelt began to collapse upon itself, yielding to forces it was never designed to withstand. The scream of straining, buckling steel filled the air. He stared in horror as he dropped lower and the turbulence below grew nearer.

The Dark suddenly knew that he had *not* won—that he merely had been a part of something much greater than himself. Trapped within his self-imposed shell of flesh, again and again he cursed the name of his Creator. He felt pain and terror and fear—and would continue to for all eternity.

For him, as also for Beltesha and all who had followed the Dark, it would end in a lake of fire, created at the beginning of all things. There was life *only* in the Creator of all life, and those who would not fellowship with Him could not live.

A new roar from his left caught the Dark's attention. Though he could not see beyond the heavy curtains of pounding rain, he turned his head for the last time and listened. He then screamed and wept bitterly in utter defeat.

A wall of boiling mud and water a mile high was moments away.

The planet's rebirth had begun, a rebirth that would result in a single world in which the Dark and his kind could find no place. Noron and Earth were both gone.

But something new would arise from their weary remains.

Epilogue

L ife.

It had come into the universe with so much potential, so much magnificence. It was an eternal gift given to every creature of that wondrous Paradise of so long ago, direct from the hand of a loving God Who wished to share His love. Yet His gift had been rejected when Man proudly chose self and corruption over perfection and the glory of his Creator's presence.

That turning from perfection had left only imperfection in its stead, and all the universe had fallen from grace. Every molecule, every atom was an inseparable part of a physical continuum that had turned its back on its Creator. It was cursed, its fellowship with Life broken.

But no more.

Ish put forth His hand and the universes became that which they had once been, breaking down into their purest essence with a heat more intense than that of a stellar core. Pure energy again filled space-time, the elemental power from which the totality of physical existence had once been sculpted.

In the beginning, God created.

The planes of being melded into one. The energies of both universes, Earth's and Noron's, were combined into a single, continuous whole. No longer was there a need for two. No longer was there a need for the duality that had served well to glorify the Lord Who had created it.

Now there was only one universe.

Now, as in the beginning, there was—*the clay.*

The infinite energies of Creation coalesced once again into distinct shapes, giving birth to the stars and planets of a new cosmos.

But this time, there would be no Fall. There would be no Curse. Never again would anyone be lost.

The price had already been paid. In full.

An infinite God had reached down into the corrupt, four-dimensional prison in which man had bound himself, and through His own death had set him free. Man could never have reached up to God, despite his countless attempts to do so. There was one true path by which man could reach his Creator, and one alone—and the only One Who could have bridged the infinite chasm between them had revealed it.

One Door—one Way, one Truth, one Life.

A new, much larger Earth shone among the stars of space, glistening in the light of a new sun and a new, unscarred moon. As before, the planet sparkled magenta while its wondrous hydrogen ice canopy filled its skies, a pearl set among the stars, a jewel against the velvet black of space. The new world had no ocean, nor did it have need of one.

It was beautiful.

And the world became one before Me.

T. G. and the others looked down upon the new Earth from within the new city Ish had made for them, steadily descending from space above. Soon it would make contact with solid ground.

There to stand forever as the City of God.

Those in the City had trusted in Ish, and He had not failed them. On Noron, He had saved His people worldwide during the planet's final moments, taking them away to safety even as the wave of Darkness appeared to swallow them forever.

Even the unsaved had been removed at that moment to what awaited them, pulled from beneath the viscous Darkness in which they had drowned. They had not ceased to be, had not become as if they never were. The proud Dark never knew, and counted them all among its—*his*—victims, believing to the end that he had undone Creation, depriving Ish even of those who hated Him.

So self-deluded was the Dark that he had come to believe he held the ultimate keys of life and death. He did not. He never had.

He had fought against his Creator on both Earth and Noron, jumping back and forth between the two theaters, carrying out his war against the Light as the time-flow differential allowed. His demonic agents worked hard on both worlds as well, carrying out his will, hoping they had chosen the winning side in the war.

They had not.

For a time toward the end, the Dark had been bound in a great abyss, and Earth enjoyed a thousand-year rest from his attacks. On Noron the interval was but an instant. And once freed, more determined than ever, he and his agents had waged war again, on both worlds, and lost. To the end, his powerful self-delusion was such that he thought he could supersede his Creator and proudly rule in His place. He was wrong.

But that was a part of *what was.*

Now a new glory entered the realm of God's kingdom.

It was called New Jerusalem. For all time, it would be the home of those who had trusted in their triune Creator.

T. G. and Jenni walked along, delighting in the spectacle of the City all around them. Beneath his feet, his eyes soaked in the gleam of a material he knew, one he had seen before only in small quantities, one over which he had puzzled. It glistened in the pure light, its rich amber tone deepening as its depths grew greater, yet always remaining transparent. It made up the very street upon which they walked.

Color was everywhere. Stars sparkled in a thousand hues beyond the crystalline walls. The City was spectacularly beautiful, seemingly more a form of art than a functional dwelling place. Every type of precious stone glittered all around for as far as the eye could see, making up even the very foundations of the immense structure.

They stood upon the wide street of transparent gold, surrounded by buildings of the same flawless material. Light was everywhere, flooding through the glassy streets and walls around them, streaming down from the summit of the great City so high above.

Streaming down from God.

The entire City, almost fourteen hundred miles square and soaring to the same height, was transparent. At no time within its walls would its people lose sight of their Lord. Forevermore they would know His direct presence, and He theirs. Never again would anyone be alone.

T. G. turned to look at Jenni. She wore a seamless, flowing robe that, like his own, was brilliant white. They looked upon each other, knowing they were the same people they had been, yet different.

Upon their arrival in the City, into which Ish had brought them immediately from Noron, each had known at once that the bodies they now occupied were not those into which they had been physically born. In wonder they looked upon their new selves, joyously realizing they finally were as the Creator had always intended them to be. They felt no pain, no displeasure, no discomfort of any kind. T. G. held his hand up, knowing he was as corporeal as ever.

And then some.

He was of flesh and bone as always. Yet there were differences—no longer was the cleansing, nourishing blood of his old body necessary. He would still eat and drink, and with the new City he would enjoy doing so immeasurably, but everything needed to sustain him would henceforth come directly from Ish. He alone was life, pure and free.

He always had been.

They walked along, seeing all around them millions of others who were identically clad. Their fellow citizens were gathered on every story, diminishing to invisibility above them amid the other quarter million levels of the towering City. They numbered some twenty billion, all having their own place, a mansion set aside for each of them.

Jenni was the first to hear it—the roar of cool water rushing past. They rounded a corner and came upon the center of the City, where a mighty river, clear as crystal, flowed from above and outward for as far as they could see. It split into four tributaries, one headed toward each side of the City. Very soon, on Earth, those branches would flow out through the walls and into all the world, where their life-giving, inexhaustible waters would fill the hydrologic needs of the new planet.

Overhanging the river, growing along the esplanade and spreading as wide as a football field, was a lush fruit tree, its trunk thicker and more mighty than that of any sequoia. Its hundreds of thousands of branches lined both banks of the river, hanging to ground level, all laden with colorful fruit. Thousands stood pulling the luscious, juicy delight from its limbs.

One of them was Pretsal. T. G. ran to him and they embraced, their joy flooding outward, almost tangibly.

"Here," Pretsal smiled, handing a piece of the fruit to T. G. "It isn't an apple like you asked for, but I think you'll like it."

"You heard me?" T. G. asked, remembering the roadside words he had spoken after Pretsal's physical death.

"No, but I got a message."

They shared the fruit and Jenni joined them, but all found that they needed only one piece to satisfy their hunger. Neither Jenni nor T. G. really felt thirsty, not yet, but they knelt to drink from the clear, shimmering river. Its almost luminous water was unlike any they had ever known—a pure, liquid life flowing for all to take freely.

There was a joyous reunion as T. G. found himself surrounded by those he loved. Josan, Darafine, Sereen, and the other Disciples of Truth with whom he had shared his adventure in Ish were there with him. Though they, too, had changed, he instantly knew them all and held them close, happier to see them than he had ever been.

Carlene Abelwhite, her face stripped of the effects of age, paused to hug T. G. as she walked past, headed toward her earthly husband, who waited a short distance away.

David, understanding at last what it was his friend had endured and why, sat with his earthly family on the low wall of the riverbank, across the way.

A familiar, long-absent voice called to T. G. He turned to see his father and mother, their arms outstretched toward him, their faces alive with life and light. He ran to them and joyfully embraced them both, treasuring them. His memory of their deaths paled away into nothingness, and the grief it had carried with it vanished as if it never was.

"I missed you so much," he said, filled with joy. "I had thought I'd never see you again...until I learned better."

"We've been waiting," Sarah Shass smiled. "We were told of your special place in the Father's plan...we knew we'd see you again."

"You were right," T. G. said, overwhelmed. "Both of you...about everything. You were so right."

John Shass looked into the eyes of the man he had raised, seeing the life within them, seeing what his son had become.

"We're together now, son," the former minister said. "In Him. Nothing will ever keep us apart again." He delighted in T. G.'s salvation and held his son tightly, knowing what he had endured, sharing the jubilance he now felt. "It is a wondrous new future that awaits us...all of us."

Searching the crowds, Jenni felt drawn to a another group gathered near the great Tree of Life, and there she found her mother. She ran to her and they embraced, looking up into the wondrous light that bathed them all. Janice held her daughter for a very long time, thankful for the grace of their Lord in saving them both.

"I saw Marcus a short time ago," she smiled. "He and his brethren, the 144,000 witnesses of the house of Israel...they spread the message of God during the last days. Look...they've gathered up there." She pointed to a level some twenty floors above.

Jenni looked up and saw the chosen thousands sharing the light, praising their long-promised Messiah for all He had done.

Elsewhere among the billions within the city, looking upward into the glorious light of Life that bathed his youthful face with its warm glow, stood a man no longer in pain, a man whose flesh was no longer marred by the savage punishment of hard decades in the wilderness.

His name was Parmenas.

He delighted in the promised City around him, overflowing with the joy of knowing his Creator's plan had come to fruition, just as he knew it must. He embraced the others gathered around him, the martyred thousands of others who had dedicated their lives to preserving the Truth their Creator had imparted to them. And of those thousands, his eyes sought the ten who, like him, had put pen to parchment in the writing of the books of the Truth—the Voices of Light. Athanarius and Trelivan and the others were all there, basking in the wondrous rest their beloved Creator once had promised them.

Parmenas, delivered by Ish from the torment of his pursuers, thereafter on occasion had spoken humbly with his Savior, learning of the great mystery of the Truth—of the final, ultimate atonement made on another world on behalf of those of *two* worlds, his own Noron and a strange, faraway place called Earth. All of them, the saved of both worlds, now had an eternity to spend together, to share as they never before had been able, and to glorify the One Who had given each of them the greatest Gift of all—Himself.

Parmenas had heard the spreading story of the last Guardian, the Voice in the Dark, whom *every* book of the Truth had prophesied would herald the Awakening of their dying world. *Where is he? Is he among us?* He smiled, praising his Lord and the trustworthiness of his Word, and searched the faces of the gathered Guardians around him. *What is his name?*

They would indeed meet soon and would share tales of their lives as bearers of the Gift and of the honor each knew in serving his Lord. The chosen of all history—the writers of the Truth, the writers of the Bible, and the prophets and apostles of every age—would have untold eons to gather and rejoice and marvel in the outworking of their Creator's plan.

But first there was something T. G. wanted to do.

He left his parents and went back to Jenni's side, then took her hand and looked into her eyes, seeing that an opportunity was slipping away.

"Let's go on down to our new world," he suggested, seeing that the City would come to rest on the planet soon. "I want to watch this place coming down out of Heaven. We'll only get one chance to see it."

"Oh…yes!" her face beamed, imagining the sight.

No longer bound by the physical laws that restricted the old Creation, they soared into the air and out into space, laughing and holding hands as they swiftly headed out over the high City walls.

Ish smiled as He watched them go, delighting in the joy of his Voice.

The stars shone brightly all around them, a trillion worlds waiting to be explored for the glory of He Who had made them. They dove toward the shining planet below, laughing with delight as they soared ever closer to its protective pink shell. Every turn and barrel roll was a wondrous, joyful experience to be shared. The canopy quickly rushed toward them, and just before they reached it Jenni instinctively closed her eyes and squealed. T. G. laughed, squeezing her warm, soft hand tightly, knowing they would pass through the solid, frozen shell as if it were not there.

At once, they were through the twenty feet of pinkish ice and clear of the other side. They felt the sweet air of their new world against their faces and breathed it deeply, enjoying the rich scents of flowering plants and the tropical life it carried. It was a wondrous, virgin world, yet untouched by humankind.

T. G. and Jenni would be the first to stand upon it.

Wide meadows spread below, covered in clover, flowers, and deep grasses. It was here amid the splendor of direct Creation that the faithful of Earth who had died before the Flood of Noah would eternally live, in a utopia even more breathtaking than the fallen Paradise they had known before.

T. G. and Jenni broke into level flight, unfettered by the bonds of gravity. As they swooped low over the lush, green forests of the new Earth, Jenni reached down and brushed her fingertips against the soft leaves of the towering, uppermost branches. She laughed in delight, watching the treetops blur beneath her.

T. G. watched her long hair as it flowed in the wind and gazed upon her radiant countenance, enjoying her, loving her, cherishing her. He humbly thanked Ish for having given her back to him, knowing he might have lost her forever.

Now they had all the time in the world.

Afterword

My goal in bringing *The Last Guardian* to life was to present basic biblical doctrine within an intriguing story framework, thus creating a book that would both entertain and enlighten its readers. Many of the fundamental principles of our faith are not widely understood today, even by many who consider themselves Christians, and without grasping these basics one cannot fully appreciate the sacrifice made by our Lord, nor the wonder of the grace that *alone* saves us. I hope this written "lamp" has helped shed some light and that you have enjoyed traveling alongside T. G. Shass.

This story is a work of fiction and nothing more. It was not written to serve as the genesis of a new theology, nor is it meant to present a new slant on Christianity. As far as I know, our Lord and Messiah has never gone by the name of *Ish,* the Hebrew word for *man.* Nor has the world of Noron itself ever existed, other than in the imaginations of Dan Cheney and me. The name is a combination of the Hebrew words *nora(h)* ("terrible, horrifying") and *doron* ("gift"). There is no "plane of existence" that did not know the Flood of Noah and no Egyptian diary that tells how such a place may be reached.

Where this story presents actual Christian doctrine, often through the words of Ish, it accurately does so, according to my own beliefs and those of many respected Christian scholars. The epilogue of the story borrows directly from the book of Revelation, and the theology appearing throughout the remainder of *The Last Guardian* was similarly drawn from the pages of both the Old and New Testaments.

The Last Guardian, however, is not a direct allegory of scriptural events. I was cautious in portraying Earth's end times, making sure never to contradict or add to the biblical account as it is understood within the premillennial framework. The sequence of events in the

Tribulation period will come to pass as prophesied, and there is no room for inventiveness there. On the other hand, the world of Noron provided a fresh canvas upon which I felt free to present biblical doctrines through occurrences and prophecies of a fictitious, allegorical nature. The world of Noron has its own set of Scriptures, its own prophesied chain of last-days events, and its own history. These elements are similar in some ways to those of Revelation but are not intended to match them exactly.

Where Earth and its history are portrayed, I endeavored to be as accurate as possible. Based upon recent studies, it is now believed in many archaeological circles that Amenhotep II was the pharaoh of the Exodus. Astanapha, a wholly fictional character, was placed by me into his court. All of the novel's earthly (and lunar) locales, with the exception of a few of the landmarks said to stand in Ithaca, New York, are real places. The starry sky T. G. sees above the Colorado mountains in chapter 1 is indeed the exact sky an observer would have seen from that position on Earth, on that date, at that time of night. And yes, there really are 161 steps within the Cornell University bell tower.

I suspect this story will prove controversial, and most certainly it will not be everyone's cup of tea. Just as there are many who feel that Christian rock music is inappropriate and does not properly serve our Lord, there are many who feel that extrabiblical fiction of this nature is extraneous and unnecessary. I understand and respect these viewpoints and the faith behind them.

∽◦∾

I wish to emphasize that the character of T. G. Shass is not messianic in nature. Rather, his mission is much like that of the earthly John the Baptist combined with elements derived from the story of the two witnesses in the book of Revelation. These witnesses, like the fictitious T. G., will be invulnerable during most of their service on Earth and will be given control over the forces of nature. Even the death of the Voice in the Dark, as portrayed in this novel, is quite similar to that which will be suffered by these two witnesses of God—their execution will be seen by all the world, their bodies will be left on display as mankind celebrates, and a glorious resurrection will follow three-and-a-half days later. It should at this point be noted that T. G.'s resurrection is akin to that of Lazarus and not the final resurrection of the saints. Lazarus died a second time, and the same would have been true of T. G. had the story not reached its conclusion beforehand.

T. G. is shown to have been a Christian in his childhood, but as the novel opens we see that he has moved far from Christ. He is like many today who are hurt, seriously questioning, or even bitter due to circumstances in their individual lives. *We do not lose our salvation during these times of disbelief, however severe that disbelief may be,* nor can we ever lose it for *any* reason. As stated in 2 Timothy 2:13, "If we are faithless, He remains faithful, for He cannot deny Himself." Each Christian is clearly stated in Scripture to be a part of the body of Christ, not simply a member of a club he or she can quit, or an employee who can be fired. For one to lose one's salvation would be tantamount to the dismemberment of our Lord.

I attempt to convey through T. G.'s language and actions that although he *is* saved, he is not living a Christian life early in the story and has put up a wall between himself and God. He does not want to turn his life or circumstances over to Christ; he wants to be in control himself. He is not receptive to any leading of the Holy Spirit, Who attempts to intervene on T. G.'s behalf (such as when T. G. makes the poor decision to return to Noron via incantation). However, the irresistible redemptive power of God ultimately has its way with him. After realizing that Ish is indeed the Christ, T. G. asks forgiveness for his earlier disbelief, and his life is transformed to better serve our Lord's divine purposes.

T. G. is merely the Voice, not the One Whose word he speaks. In everything, when acting within the Lord's will, T. G. is able to act only because he is empowered by Christ; he does not supplant Him.

∽o∾

The world of Noron, as the reader observes, is morally corrupt beneath the thin veneer of physical beauty that surrounds it. In reality, however, a world that had never seen the Flood of Noah would certainly be a far more hideous place than I have portrayed here. We know that in the days immediately preceding the Deluge the thoughts of mankind were "*only* evil continually" (Genesis 6:5), and this condition, left to itself, could only have worsened. Evil cannot beget good. Assuming man would not have wiped himself out within a mere span of decades, a world such as Noron would by now have become utterly and sickeningly horrifying at *every* level of its existence. However, since it was not my intent to shock or to offend or to make the reader cringe with every page turned, I toned things down.

The world of Noron has one foot in Hell and the other on a banana peel. For this reason, I selectively and deliberately added scenes to this book that some readers will no doubt find quite disturbing. By having the family of the deceased sip from the goblet of blood at the Renewal ceremony, for example, I was able to provide evidence of Noron's moral apostasy as well as portray its unholy communion with the Dark. The Renewal is a religious ceremony, not merely a magical incantation. The practice of drinking blood, while abhorrent, has been common in pagan religious rituals throughout Earth's history.

Nor is the demonic possession presented in *The Last Guardian* pretty. It is not meant to be. We are dealing with an evil the likes of which few have seen face-to-face. Several Christian readers have told me that they believe those scenes that personify the Dark are among the most powerful and vivid in the book and drive home for them the nature of the Enemy. I chose not to water down these scenes, though my written words surely pale when compared to the actual depths of evil within the hearts of Satan and his minions. He and those under him are terrifying—I want my readers to experience that.

Through the deep moral depravity of Noron, I felt it was important to present some measure of commentary on our own culture and the ethical crises facing America today. While Noron is not a true mirror, its dark glass certainly reflects something of ourselves. Similarly, I chose to give Noron a pseudo-Western culture, one with which T. G. (and the reader) could find some measure of common ground.

Despite the darkness it sometimes portrays, this book is about life and salvation, not death and horror. By showing just how wicked the heart of man is, the amazing love and grace of our Lord is by contrast seen more clearly as the infinite wonder it truly is.

∽◦∾

This story, as you have read, takes the creationist point of view. After many years of weighing numerous secular and Christian studies involving the tangible, scientific evidence available to us, I have come to the conclusion that the creationist position provides a far better explanation of the known facts than does the ever-changing evolutionist viewpoint. I would urge my readers likewise to examine the scientific evidence for themselves, reach their own conclusions, and not merely accept the highly questionable theories set forth by many scientists today.

Though it is not widely known, most of the European scientific community has now abandoned the long-held concept of "spontaneous generation," a cornerstone tenet of the theory of evolution. It is both mathematically and scientifically impossible for amino acids to have combined by chance to form rudimentary DNA, and these scholars finally recognize that fact. A void has resulted—how else could life have come into being? To fall back on "panspermia," the theory that microbial life on Earth originally came from outer space via meteorite, would only move the problem one step back—where did *that* life come from?

Even in America today, a drastically modified version of evolutionary theory is touted. Known as "punctuated equilibrium" (the idea that evolution only happens in brief, rapid, and widely separated bursts), it is a desperate attempt to cling to a ramshackle theory that simply cannot explain the known facts. There are too many flaws in its assertions to hold up to any real scrutiny. The entire concept of evolution is a false faith, and that is all it is—*a faith*.

From a biblical standpoint, any noncreationist concept of origins, whether based upon evolution or "theistic evolution," does irreparable violence to the Creation account as presented in Genesis. Either the Bible is true or evolutionary science is; the two *cannot* be harmonized. I have chosen to trust the former. In addition to the solid evidence I have studied, I have seen and learned too much ever to doubt the veracity of the Bible, and it has more than proven itself throughout history. The earth is young, as the Bible states. Most likely its age can be measured in thousands or tens of thousands of years, not the billions demanded by evolutionary preconceptions.

∾

I am also persuaded that the increased occultic phenomena experienced today (UFOs, crop circles, ghost sightings, regression hypnosis, channeling, poltergeist activity, and the like) have come as a result of rising demonic activity as the return of Christ grows nearer. Many reported cases are hoaxes, to be sure, but those that are believed to be authentic have become increasingly numerous. These occurrences share many common traits—surrounding cold areas, secluded sighting locales, isolated power failures, psychic communication, and sensations of dread in the observer, among others. Throughout recorded time, the demonic realm has employed the tactic of discrediting the Bible with what *appears* to be observable, contrary "evidence." For instance, where it is written that the souls of men leave the earth immediately upon death, "ghosts" are manifested. Where it teaches that all men are appointed once to die, "evidence" of past lives is created in the form of implanted, false memory. Where it teaches that the stars were made for the benefit of man for the telling of the times and seasons (an early Earth without physical seasons would need another indicator of when to plant and when to harvest), space beings from other solar systems—who bring with them New Age, specifically anti-Christian philosophies—make themselves known. These "beings" also communicate with us only by psychic means; no one has ever contacted a UFO by radio.

Linking these and other paranormal phenomena to demonic activity is a logical step, for they are ever-changing, self-contradictory puzzles that keep men chasing blind alleys, distracting many from the truth of the Bible and the urgent matter of personal salvation. During this current period of God's grace, I believe this activity is restrained by the indwelling presence of the Holy Spirit—a limitation not shared by the fictitious world of Noron.

We must always weigh the apparent evidences confronting our eyes and ears against the well-established truths of the Bible—not the other way around.

∽∾∾

Much of the doctrinal expression presented in *The Last Guardian* can be found in the exhaustive works of Charles C. Ryrie (of the *Ryrie Study Bible*) and Henry M. Morris, among others. In particular, I would like to recommend Ryrie's *Basic Theology,* Morris' *The Genesis Record* and *The Revelation Record,* and *There's a New World Coming* and *The Liberation of Planet Earth* by Hal Lindsey. These books in particular contain excellent discussions of such doctrinal points as the pre-Flood, demonic effect upon the human bloodline, the existence of a global canopy, the mechanics of the Deluge, the overwhelming evidence for a young Earth, and insights into the doctrines of salvation and the prophecies of Revelation.

The theory of pre-Flood demonic interference in the propagation of man, as touched upon in *The Last Guardian,* is nothing new and indeed finds a basis in Scripture. This theory is not the only interpretation of Genesis 6:1-2, but it is the only one to take into account the revelation of other Scripture and actually presents the least historical and scriptural conflict.

One common interpretation, that which proposes that the term "sons of God" meant the ungodly family line of Cain, fails to explain how mere human procreation could have created the Nephilim, the exceptional giants said to have emerged among men. Also, it fails to explain why the term "daughters of men" should refer only to the female descendants of Seth, as the view holds. The earliest Jewish interpretation of the term "sons of God" was "angels" (see also Job 1:6). Replacing that term in the text, we get, "...angels saw the daughters of men, that they were beautiful, and they took wives for themselves of all whom they chose" (NKJV).

Scripture tells us that angels do not marry or procreate. We also know they do not blaspheme God, or disobey Him, or exist locked away in the Pit, or serve Satan. None of this can be said of *demons,* however. (I'm doubtful that Christ's words in Matthew 22 concerning "the angels of God in heaven" can be used as unequivocally of these unclean spirits.) What can be expected of one should not necessarily be expected of the other. For example, the Bible nowhere mentions an instance of angels indwelling swine. Furthermore, it is possible that the demons locked away in the Pit (Tartarus) as stated in 2 Peter 2:4 and Jude 6 may indeed have been those who (theoretically) took human women for themselves and fathered corrupted children (whether directly or through intense possession of human males).

In *Basic Theology,* Ryrie states, "Though angels do not reproduce after their kind (that is, produce baby angels), they may have been permitted to cohabit with human women on this one occasion to produce human offspring." He goes on to state that such direct demonic cohabitation with women is not necessarily the most likely interpretation of what occurred, but it is certainly possible and may well explain why a certain group of fallen angels is bound in Tartarus, where they remain even now. He states that their confinement "must be punishment for some sin other than the original one, and a unique sin at that."[1]

---

1. Charles C. Ryrie, *Basic Theology* (Wheaton: Victor Books, 1987), 159.

We are told that Noah "found grace in the eyes of the LORD" and was "a just man, perfect in his generations" (Genesis 6:8-9, NKJV). This last unusual phrase may indicate that Noah's family line was the last on Earth to maintain its genetic purity. The original Hebrew supports this interpretation.

The very existence of the Nephilim seems to prove that some measure of supernatural genetic interference did indeed take place on Earth. Why would the normal physical union of men and women suddenly have produced giants, and in such great numbers? Physical corruption in males directly possessed (we are shown repeatedly in the New Testament that demonic possession has a physical effect on the possessed) may well have altered the genetic characteristics of children born to them—likewise, the giantism in these offspring could have resulted from direct supernatural impregnation. We are not talking about some comingling of supposed demon DNA with that of a human—what we are addressing here is a simple, biological corruption of the human bloodline, physical damage done to existing genetic material in order to alter the physicality of man and change what he is.

Genesis 6:4 says that "the Nephilim were on the earth in those days, and also afterward" (NASB). Yet Genesis 7:21 states *clearly* that, in the flood, "*all* flesh died that moved upon the earth" (KJV). Only Noah and his family survived, shielded by God's grace within the ark, so the Nephilim that arose in an obviously minimal fashion *after* the flood could not have been descended from those who were alive beforehand. Any post-Flood "race" of giants would by necessity have come through Noah's lineage, through his sons and their wives. We are not told what their origin was, but it is possible that a second, abortive attempt was made by Satan to repeat his pre-Flood strategy, one stopped—perhaps—by direct divine intervention. The Philistine giant Goliath of Gath, a soldier almost ten feet in height, was apparently among the last of his kind. In any case, a brief re-emergence of such Nephilim does not wipe out any theory of gene pool cleansing, for the desired goal was accomplished—a pure bloodline was indeed preserved, through which Christ was ultimately born.

∽◦∾

Speculations such as these are fascinating, but the main objectives of *The Last Guardian* are to provide an understanding of the workings of personal salvation and a better appreciation for the amazing, unbounded grace of God. The basics of biblical Christianity are wondrous in their simplicity yet complex in the fact that they come from a Mind so utterly above ours that we can understand Him only as our limited perceptions will allow, as He chooses to reveal Himself to us.

And He has. Make no mistake.

It is my hope that this novel has provided answers for those who may be questioning their faith or who simply wish to better understand their Lord's great plan for redeeming fallen man. The absence of such answers caused me to reject Christianity for a time during my teenage years, as I mentioned in the author's note at the beginning of this book.

The good news of Christian salvation is the most important message any of us can share with our fellow brothers and sisters. I encourage my Christian readers to acquaint themselves fully with the tenets of our faith, for this carries great weight in our daily witness. We live in a burning house, my friends, all of us, and those who can smell the smoke and see the flames *must* try to save those who cannot.

As Peter said, "always [be] ready to make a defense to everyone who asks you to give an account for the hope that is in you, yet with gentleness and reverence" (1 Peter 3:15).

Maranatha!

Shane Johnson

Arlington, Texas

July 2000

www.thelastguardian.com

Acknowledgments

This story came to life over a great period of time and was fine-tuned with the help of several kind entities whose input made it a better tale than it otherwise might have been:

Kathy Johnson, my loving and very patient wife, who gave me the encouragement to keep at it during those times when the task appeared too daunting.

Daniel Johnson, my son and the light of my life, who has always inspired me to think of the future.

Shaun Johnson, my brother, who believed in me.

Erin Healy of WaterBrook Press, my editor on this project, whose enthusiasm for and faith in this book were instrumental in getting it published. We spent many long hours editing and refining *The Last Guardian,* and throughout the entire process her concern for maintaining the integrity and flow of the story was matched only by my own.

Ret Martin, creator of *Traveller's Tale,* who spent many hours pre-editing the text, making suggestions, and providing me with hard copies—a cherished friend who helped make this book possible and certainly made it better than it otherwise would have been.

Steve McClellan, who was there when it all began.

Steven 'Doc' Jessup, a good and well-read friend, who has known the blessed light of our Lord as many have not.

Scott Bell, Debbie Dennis, David Holt, John Hopkins, Gene and Maudie Lam, Peter Landrey, Craig Ligon, Barry and Roberta Smith, and Mark Taurog, who took the time to read my phonebook-size manuscript and offered comments and encouragement.

Dr. Carl Baugh of the Creation Evidence Museum, Glen Rose, Texas, whose intriguing theories concerning the harmonious nature of the antediluvian Earth helped to build the basic physical framework for the world of Noron. We cannot yet know the exact nature of the early Earth, but the Creation model proposed by Dr. Baugh helped to make Noron a wondrous place indeed.

Alan Beckner, who thought he would not be mentioned, so there.

The United States Postal Service, which safely delivered Dan's materials to me in 1975 and in so doing gave me the opportunity to finish this work.

And my mother, *Sandra Johnson,* who did not live to see this dream fulfilled.